To Wally ~ Very best wishes!
Glen Paul Scyfield
04/10/02

Lynn Hodgson
9/11

OCT 4/02

SILVER DAGGER

Lynn Philip Hodgson, Alan Paul Longfield

Copyright ©, Blake Books Distribution, 2002
Cover Design and Page Layout
© Peter A. Graziano Limited, 2002

Editors: Barbara Kerr, Michelle Flynn

Distribution by:
Blake Books Distribution
467 Fralicks Beach Road
Port Perry, Ontario
Canada, L9L 1B6
905.985.6434

lynniso@idirect.com

National Library of Canada Cataloguing in Publication Data
Hodgson, Lynn Philip 1946
Camp X - Silver Dagger

Includes bibliographical references and index
ISBN 0-9687062-7-4

1. Great Britain, Special Operations Executive,
    Special Training School 103 (Whitby, Ont.) - Fiction.
2. World War, 1939-1945 - Secret service - Great Britain - Fiction
3. World War, 1939-1945 - Secret service - Canada - Fiction.
4 World War, 1939-1945 - Military intelligence - Canada -Fiction.
I. Longfield, Alan. II. Title.

PS8565.O324C338 2002   C813'.6   C2002-901017-9
PR9199.4.H63C338 2002

Design and Production
Silvio Mattacchione and Co.

Peter A. Graziano Limited
pgraziano@sympatico.ca

Printed and bound in Canada
by Friesens, Manitoba

SILVER DAGGER

4

*Bill "Yorkie" Hardcastle,
as depicted in the Camp X Mural,
Oshawa, Ontario, 2001.*

IN MEMORIAM
WILLIAM "YORKIE" HARDCASTLE
VE3 XRY
22 JUNE 1914 – 2 MAY 2002

"Dictators ride

to and fro upon tigers,

which they dare not

dismount.

And the tigers are

getting hungry."

Sir Winston Churchill
November 11, 1937

TABLE OF CONTENTS

A C K N O W L E D G E M E N T S

The authors wish to express their appreciation to the following people for their contributions to Silver Dagger and the success of the Inside - Camp X series of books:

Leslie Bovie, Ryan Copithorn, Rik Davie, Michelle Flynn, Samantha George, Elizabeth Ginn, Jeff Goodes, Tracy Goose, Chip Gray, Peter Graziano, Bill Hardcastle, Marlene Hodgson, Reverend Elizabeth Hopkins, Elaine Houston, Peter Hvidsten, Terry Johnston, John Kellam, Barbara Kerr, Angela Johnson, Terry Johnstone, John, Judi and Michael Longfield, PC Kelly Mason (OPP # 8769), Jane McDonald, Arthur 'Mac' McDonald, Silvio Mattacchione, Hamish Pelham Burn, Ted Stewart, Robert Stuart, Jennifer Valentyne, and Brian Winter.

Thanks also to these persons whose technical advice in relation to aviation of the era, principally the Halifax bomber, and the Westland Lysander, was invaluable: Colin Blakelock, Roy Cowan, Kaz Nawrot and Peter Snaith.

We owe a special debt of gratitude to you, our readers, who, by purchasing our books, have helped to bring the story of Camp X to light, and honoured the stories and sacrifices of the Canadians who served with British Security Co-ordination and Special Operations Executive. These books are our tribute to all BSC and SOE staff, officials, officers, and most particularly, those men and women whose heroic exploits behind enemy lines have been consigned to 'the shadows' for too many decades.

Lynn Philip Hodgson
Alan Paul Longfield

September 21, 2002

In the tradition of **Camp X The Final Battle**, **Camp X Silver Dagger,** is a story that is woven from documented evidence, informed sources, conjecture and fiction. It is now well known that agencies of the British Intelligence establishment, most notably Special Operations Executive, SOE, had actively considered a variety of possible methods, including poisoning or shooting by a sniper, to bring about the elimination of Adolf Hitler by assassination in 1943-44. Sharp debate about the possible advantages and risks affecting the Allied war strategy as well as the ethical and moral implications of killing the German Führer, eventually led to the abandonment of such tactics. Ultimately, Hitler took his own life in the final days of the war, May 1945.

Camp X Silver Dagger is a fascinating, suspenseful story involving intrigue, espionage, murder, double cross, and romance, realistically exploring the planning and execution of *Mission Shining Oath* to assassinate the Führer.

It involves not only the memorable cast of characters introduced in **The Final Battle**, including Major Hamish Findlay, Major Robert Samson and Major Rebeccah *Jael* Weiss, but as well, a part - Cherokee American cryptanalyst, Major Jack Harris, an Ojibwa Native Canadian signals expert, Burton Johnson, from Port Perry Ontario, and Lieutenant-Colonel Roger Stedman, the new Commandant of Camp X, who, along with a host of supporting players, carry out deeds of valour with incredible courage against near -impossible odds in settings both local and European, from Camp X to Berchtesgaden, Hitler's Bavarian mountain stronghold, to his Berlin bunker and finally, St. Petersburg (Leningrad) today.

CAMP X HOTEL: THE BLUE SWALLOW INN

Unknown to GO commuters and rail travellers, the Oshawa GO/Via Rail station stands on the site of what was until recently, another missing and nearly - forgotten chapter in the Camp X legacy, The Blue Swallow Inn.

The Blue Swallow Inn, a majestic red brick inn of traditional eighteenth century English styling that was built in 1942, was the talk of Camp X. Such was its reputation that everyone of note who visited Camp X wanted to stay at the Blue Swallow. Numbered among its guests were Ian Fleming, General 'Wild Bill' Donovan, chief of the American Office of Strategic Services, and FBI boss, J. Edgar Hoover. What was the attraction of The Blue Swallow Inn? Quite simply, it was an extremely hospitable, luxury-class hotel complete with a pub-style tavern, located within walking distance of Camp X.

The Blue Swallow was situated on the north side of the Canadian National Railway line, and on the west side of Thornton Road, just south of a one-room red brick schoolhouse, which served the south end of Whitby. Bill Hardcastle and his chums from Camp X loved to head up to The Blue Swallow Inn on Saturday nights. Along with the Genosha Hotel in Oshawa, "The Swallow" was the place to go. The grand piano in The Swallow's main hall was the centre of attraction; there was always a line-up of amateur entertainer waiting to play. Bill, and Bernie Sandbrook, his best friend, who was a talented musician, always made sure that they arrived before the rest of the Saturday night crowd, to be assured of seats close to the piano.

At the rear, on the right hand side was the kitchen, which served the Inn's famous hamburgers that were the specialty of the house. Bill enjoyed sitting at the solid oak bar where he could enjoy a draft and a couple of pickled eggs, which, he maintained, were the best anywhere. Situated at the bar with a big grin on his face while listening to his friend Bernie belt out a tune, it was no wonder Bill Hardcastle looked forward eagerly to Saturday night at "The Swallow".

The Blue Swallow Inn viewed from Thornton Road.

RECALLED TO LIFE

"Colonel Stedman ... I need you!"

Despite a throbbing headache, Lieutenant-Colonel Roger Stedman was rather enjoying his first morning on the job as Commanding Officer of Camp X, Special Training School 103 (STS 103). He had arrived at 0700 h, one half-hour before his Secretary, Miss Betty Robertson, was due so that he could take stock of his new headquarters, display his photographs and set out a few pieces of personal bric-a-brac when his office door suddenly burst open, to reveal a diminutive female figure wearing Instructors' fatigues.

"Major Weiss, I assume ...a problem? Please, enter and kindly shut it ... quietly." Setting down his gold and mahogany desk pen set, he wryly noted the rounded cavity that the doorknob had imprinted in the luxurious wood panelling. He sat up, folding his hands on the desk, to wait for the Major's explanation.

Camp-X from Lake Ontario

Upon entering the Oshawa Airport terminal building two days before, Roger Stedman had been greeted cordially by Lieutenant-Colonel Gordon Graham, the outgoing CO, and his driver, Private McDonald, who immediately took possession of Stedman's luggage, and stowed it in the boot of a very large American sedan.

"Smashing machine. One of the perks, Gordon, may I assume?" Stedman inquired.

"Yes, although I'm rarely allowed the privilege of actually driving it myself. Mac has claimed exclusive rights, correct, Private? The Blue Swallow, please." Mac nodded slightly, and smiled as he engaged the Hydramatic transmission. The Buick Roadmaster glided silently over the curb onto Thornton Road.

"Roger, I've arranged to put you up at a pleasant local establishment, called The Blue Swallow Inn. I'll introduce you to Mr. and Mrs. Curtin, the proprietors. You'll find them accommodating, discrete, and very familiar with our requirements ... for absolute privacy. You'll be only minutes from the Camp, which you'll discover tomorrow morning when I take you on the grand tour. I thought you might wish to rest this afternoon, then I'll put you to work after dinner, if you're feeling up for it. Ah, here we are.

"Pull up to the front entrance, Mac, that's a good fellow."

After they had enjoyed a steak dinner, in one of the Blue Swallow's two private dining rooms, and were about to leave, Gordon Graham reached under the table. "This is for you, Roger." Stedman looked down at a black briefcase at his feet. Graham lowered his voice to a whisper.

"I know how exhausted you are after the flight from Halifax, so I'm doing this as a special favour, Roger. Guard it well or we might both end up in the nick. Here are the two keys. It has a double lock. I expect that the contents will make for interesting bedtime reading ... help you put names to faces in the morning. Private McDonald will return here after dropping me back at the Camp with a Sergeant Maloney, to wait in the beverage room, where they are to consume nothing stronger than ginger ale, and keep a watch on the comings and goings. Both men will be carrying side arms in police holsters underneath their civvies. They

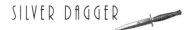

will be directed to patrol the lobby and hallways at irregular intervals.

"Now, at 21:25 precisely, McDonald will be instructed to ring your room twice and come up to knock on your door, two raps, at 21:30 sharp. In the meantime, Maloney will fetch the station wagon and bring it around to the side entrance. When you challenge him, Roger, McDonald will give the password Endeavour, before you open. Make sure that you double lock the case, securely. I have the only other duplicate keys. Oh, yes, for your peace of mind, I've taken the precaution of including a handgun, a US Army Colt .45, M1911A1 pistol. Although I took it out of the wax-paper wrapping, it's new, factory test-fired only. It holds seven rounds, with an additional magazine included. Consider it a welcome gift ... yours to have and to hold."

"That's very, very kind of you, Gordon ..."

"Not at all, old man. Now here's my card with the private number at my ... soon to be your ... residence, should something be amiss. There are two lines in your room; the house phone on the dresser, which connects directly with the desk, lacks a dial. The other one by your bedside, which looks like the black, standard issue model is leak-proof, completely secure. Questions? Well then, breakfast here at ... 0700 shall we say? Then we'll toddle over to the establishment for a look-see followed by lunch in the Officers' Mess. Until tomorrow then, have a pleasant evening, Roger."

Roger Stedman shut his room door, turned the dead bolt, and then switched on the bedside lamp to see his four badly matched pieces of hand baggage were carefully set down in order of size in front of the closet. He set his billfold and the room key on the night table and after placing the leather briefcase at the centre of the bed, walked over to check that the window was locked and pulled the drapes. After rummaging briefly inside his overnight bag, he produced a traveling alarm clock, a zippered leather shaving and toiletries kit, a nightshirt, a flannel dressing gown, and fleece-lined leather slippers. Before hanging his garments in the small closet, he retrieved the briefcase keys from the outer breast pocket of his Harris Tweed jacket, and then proceeded into the bathroom, his shaving and toiletries kit in hand.

After calling the desk to verify the time, he wound and set the travel alarm and reset his wristwatch to 6:55. 'Two and one-half hours should be more than enough' he yawned, sitting down on the side of the bed, the briefcase on his lap. He unlocked the two brass clasps, opened it, and removed two large, plain brown packets. 'What in the devil are these? Ah, look at this, my boy!' Nestled at the bottom of the case on the accordion pleats was The Handgun. He withdrew it, admiring its haft and balance. The blue-black high-carbon steel Parkerized finish was flawless. Verifying that it was loaded and the safety set, he laid it gently on the night table, with the extra ammunition clip. The aroma of new, Moroccan leather, blended with essence of gun oil would make quite an attractive masculine scent, he reflected. With the tip of his room key, he slit open each envelope's gummed flap and removed several legal folders. Without pulling down the bedclothes, he settled back comfortably to begin his 'required reading'. A moment later, he sat up. "Damn, where are my eyeglasses!" he muttered. "It's time to admit that you're close to thirty-five, Stedman." Without bothering to put on his slippers, he trudged over to the closet and fumbled in the inner breast pocket of the tweed sports jacket. "Miraculous, now I can see."

15

The tab on each folder had a white label affixed, displaying a name typed in capital letters in reverse order. 'So, BECK JOHN, MAJOR ... Explosives Instructor ... meet you tomorrow, Beck, John; GREY BLAKE, MAJOR. What's your story Major Grey? Hmm, 2-IC, I see, ha, ha, Second - in – Command; A first-rate fellow it seems ... youngish, twenty-nine, experienced and well qualified! Best watch my back! Next, JONES BRIAN, MAJOR ... A Canadian as Adjutant-Quartermaster and a local worthy at that! Now there's a clever move. I'd imagine he must know where the bodies and the secret caches of goods are buried!'

As he read each profile, he reckoned that he was indeed fortunate to be inheriting command of such an illustrious band of warriors, the crème de la crème of SOE. These reports fairly glow in the dark with superla-tives!' There were two exceptions. GIBSON DANA, CAPTAIN had appar-ently failed to make the cut and had been shipped back to his regiment in England, under a dark cloud. Stedman, unsure why Gordon had included this man's dossier found the reason clipped inside the cover. "Roger: Not one of our shining examples. Thought you would enjoy the read. Regards, G.G. P.S. Destroy this note soonest, SVP." The executive summary was a minor masterpiece of administrative ambiguity; Stedman chuckled as he read aloud. "'In sum, the subject demonstrates a remarkable, native - like fluency in the French language. Possessing extraordinary skills as prescribed in the *Syllabus*, subsection **Burglary**, he would be a most suitable subject for assignment with **F Section**

(France) advanced training unit, when he is better able to clearly and consistently demonstrate differentiated discretion in the selection of suitable targets i.e. objects, locations and persons.'" Stedman smiled, "'...demonstrate differentiated discretion!'" That's damn inventive, old son, if it's you, GG, or whomever. Says nothing and yet says it all." As a former diplomat, Roger Stedman took pride in knowing how to unscramble the code of doublespeak, and get to the real meaning. "This bloke Gibson was badly behaved, a bandit who had either been caught red-handed pilfering from his bunkmates' kits ... or something more scurrilous," he laughed, closing the folder. "Not my problem, thank you, Gordon."

The second file was marked SAMSON ROBERT KENNETH MAJOR. It contained one typed page, with a single-spaced entry. "Robert K. Samson, former Chief Instructor Unarmed Combat, involuntarily re-assigned to duty (detached), British Security Operation (BSO) Toronto, 1941, without alteration in rate of compensation." The authorizing signature was blacked out. The file had been purged of all references to Robert Samson's record of service. Roger Stedman was shocked. Although fifty - some years of age, Robert Samson, 'the quiet Scot' was regarded as the greatest disciple of the Asian arts of unarmed combat in the western hemisphere.

Stedman had been looking forward to meeting the 'Hong Kong Harrier' again at Camp X. He had met Major Samson two years earlier, at a regimental 'dining in', where Robert was the featured guest speaker. The Samson saga: born in Hong Kong, a Royal Marine during the First World War, Constable with the Royal Hong Kong Constabulary and Assistant Superintendent of Police was legend in the dens and corridors of the special ops establishment. Samson was the founder and dean of a school of self-defence, which was enshrined in the SOE *Syllabus* (handbook) under **Close Combat**: "...how to ... fight and kill without firearms." Popularly known as Silent Killing, Samson tried to distance himself from that rubric early on and came to loathe the nicknames: 'Killer', and 'Dangerous Dan' although he was said to tolerate the 'Hong Kong Harrier' moniker. Once, when asked what his middle initial 'K' represented, he allegedly replied, "Kenneth, and if you repeat that old son, I'll have your guts for garters." Hence was born 'K' for 'Killer, not Kenneth', or so the story was told. Roger closed his eyes as he recalled the taciturn Scot's after-dinner address that evening:

"These triads, secret criminal societies, were the unchallenged masters of the streets. Their genius with knives and meat cleavers was only surpassed by their virtuosity in an ancient discipline of bare-knuckled street brawling. We were hopelessly outclassed by the ruffians: our boys, first-rate officers, were demoralized and drifting off into other professions at an alarming rate. Little wonder, as their best efforts usually netted little more than garden-variety thieves, free-lance cutthroats, and common thugs.

"I had three choices: I could stay on to fight a losing fight, resign immediately, or, beat the hoodlums at their own game. I believed that the Asian arts of self-defence could be taught, if broken down into sub - skills. There was the matter of instruction; one of us had to go to school. As none of my colleagues leapt at the opportunity, I elected to be the guinea pig. I shall never forget my first class. It was disaster. Mistakenly, I like to think, I was assigned to an advanced group. As the only non-Asian, barely competent in any but the most fundamental, offensive street Cantonese, with the superior attitude of know-it-all 'white devil' although you might find that hard to credit, I was unprepared for what followed: they made chopsuey of me. One of His Britannic Majesty's coppers and worse, a Scot, presented a choice target for the downtrodden colonials, but I somehow survived, though barely, and kept on getting up from the mat, Lazarus-like. I had no idea how many ways there are to inflict excruciating pain. But I was too proud, stubborn, or dimwitted to concede defeat and eventually, won their grudging respect.

"When I suggested to my Superintendent that I be seconded to set up an experimental training course, he was not overjoyed. "Why not, Samson! You've done bugger all else around here but bitch and grumble about the state of affairs and when you're not bloody complaining, you're making me look like some kind of idler with the higher ups, 'cause it's you gettin' the credit for haulassin' the real villains off the bloody boulevards." I took that to imply, 'Yes'". Super and I did become great mates, however that story will cost you another dinner."

Reputed by his students to be able to dodge bullets, the stern, spare, western gentleman was to become a formidable foe of the Hong Kong underworld. His reputation rapidly spread beyond the Crown Colony and with war on the horizon, he relinquished his post of Assistant Superintendent and set sail for England. His unique methods were so highly valued by Combined Operations Commandos and Special

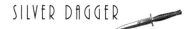

Operations Executive that he was recruited on the spot to set up shop. His invention, the razor-sharp, Samson double-edged dagger, intended for use against German sentries, confirmed his legendary status. He authored the **Close Combat** chapter in the *SOE Syllabus*, training handbook, a.k.a. 'The Bible.' Stedman recalled a phrase from that section which perfectly summed up Samson's philosophy.

"The knife is a silent and deadly weapon that is easily concealed and against which, in the hands of an expert, there is no sure defence, except firearms or running like hell."

Stedman had been informed that Special Training School 103, Camp X, was considered so vital to the success of the Allied effort that Major Samson's appointment there as Unarmed Combat Instructor was awarded over all other SOE training schools.

"Then, why isn't he here? What in blazes could old 'Killer' have pulled to merit the heave-ho?" Stedman queried aloud. "My God, we're scarcely in a position to put outstanding men like Robert Samson out to pasture without bloody good cause!" Roger Stedman made a mental note to make some discrete, 'back door' inquiries.

Stedman glanced at the alarm clock, which indicated 7:45 as he opened the last folder, which bore a cautionary red stamp: MOST URGENT TOP SECRET: YOUR EYES ONLY. The subject line read WEISS REBECCAH, MAJOR. Stedman was well-aware that Weiss was a 'one-off', a rarity, in the exclusive SOE male-dominated command club; Major Weiss, was not only a commissioned officer, and a Chief Instructor, but also a woman, Rebeccah Weiss. The recruitment of females as spies and secret agents for 'ungentlemanly warfare' was standard procedure, yet, Stedman pondered, The Ice Queen, as she was known inside SOE's inner circle, had somehow shattered the gender barrier to take on the position of Chief Instructor, Small Arms at STS 103. 'But how?' he mused, and resumed reading her curriculum vitae with deepening interest.

Weiss' paper qualifications for a position of senior responsibility were flawless, although her route to the top was circuitous. She had been vetted and approved for appointment to the coveted post of Assistant Instructor upon graduation from Beaulieu, the élite SOE 'finishing school'. Beaulieu was the collective name for Special Operation Executive's eleven training centres, scattered in the general vicinity of the village of Beaulieu, Hampshire, southern England. At the epicentre lay Baron Montagu's magnificent ancestral estate, Beaulieu, the 'jewel in the SOE crown'. Rebeccah Weiss, operational name, Silvia, had rejected the offer, for reason or reasons shrouded in official fog. Then, she vanished. Some wag had pencilled in the margin, 'The lady has gone doggo ... to ground ... done a Houdini'. Eventually, she was discovered living in London and approached by Robert Brooks, British Security Operation's (BSO) Deputy Chief. After considerable persuasion, Weiss had agreed to give an interview in a tearoom with none other than The British Prime Minister, code-named *Colonel Warden*, and BSO's Chief, Erik Williamson, *Stalwart*. Together they managed to convince her to undertake an assignment. In return, she demanded conditions that were accepted without reservation.

The recorded details of Operation Tent Peg were sketchily outlined. Under the mission nom de guerre, Jael, she had taken on Adolf Hitler, the Führer himself in London and had very nearly done him in. Then, handily disposing of a Security Service counter-intelligence (SD) officer, one Hauptsturmführer Oster, while on board a high-speed train, she and Captain Hugh Mason, her Mission W/T (wireless) operator, subsequently jumped to safety. As a finale, she and Mason escaped from Nazi custody with the assistance of 'unnamed Allied operatives' and returned to Canada with a Gestapo officer, SS Colonel Waldemar Greilwitz, PoW, in tow.

Weiss's exploits were already the stuff of legend in the short history of the service, where, in recognition of her self-assured, 'cool as a cucumber', personality, she had been unofficially crowned The Ice Queen. As a student, she had excelled in all aspects of the sabotage-special warfare training syllabus at Special Training School 17, (STS 17), Brickendonbury Manor. Her marksmanship with an arsenal of ordnance, particularly special small arms, and rifles was unmatched. She continued on to Beaulieu, where the Chief Instructor's summary in her final fitness assessment stated with uncharacteristic enthusiasm, 'All of the desired and necessary psychological, physical, emotional and intellectual elements for success in the field... are rarely represented in a single individual ... Weiss, is the exception. The subject is superbly prepared and eminently suitable for immediate assignment to the field or training school instructional staff ... possessing excellent judgement, high-intelligence ... combined with immense charm and self-discipline ... in sum, she is extraordinarily dedicated, highly motivated, determined ...

resourceful with all of the attributes of a highly skilled, ruthless, cunning, and lethal adversary.' The folder slipped from Stedman's right hand as he tried to imagine what this extraordinary woman might be like to meet 'in the flesh'. Unfortunately, he reflected, she was nowhere to be seen at the party. The small photograph showed a smiling, dark-haired woman of extraordinary beauty whose eyes communicated an astute intellect combined with a veneer of reserve, which Roger judged, masked an intensely passionate nature.

Robert Stedman was roused when the bedside telephone rang, and then rang again insistently. 'Damn, must have dozed off. 10:25...' He stood up stiffly, placing the Colt pistol in the right pocket of his robe and then after hurriedly stuffing the files back into the envelopes, he inserted the packages in the briefcase. There was a sharp rap on the door. One second later, it was repeated. His wristwatch read 10:30.

"Yes, who's there?"

"Endeavour."

"Very well. One moment." Double locking the bag, he unbolted the door to see Mac, in flannel trousers and a checked jacket, wearing a distressed expression on his face. "Come in, Private." Stedman re-bolted the door. "Something wrong Private? Feeling a bit under the weather are we?"

"Sir, may I please use your facilities? It's ... kind of ... well, Sir, actually it's very urgent! I'll explain, Sir!"

"Facilities? The WC? Yes, yes, of course. In there." He nodded in the direction of the bathroom.

A much-relieved Mac reappeared after five minutes. "Thank you kindly... ready, Sir. Must have poisoned my system, downstairs, in the beverage room."

"How might that have happened, Private? You and Maloney were specifically ordered to consume ginger ale exclusively, weren't you?"

"Yes, Sir. Which we did Sir, Colonel, believe me. But, as the evening wore on, we became a little bit hungry and the pickled eggs and sausages here are famous, very tasty. We ... er, we decided to have a little contest. I might have overdone it slightly."

"A contest, Private ... and you overdid what, exactly?"

"Maloney says that he gave up after I reached twelve."

"Twelve ... eggs? Sausages?"

"Yes, Colonel, twelve pickled eggs and twelve sausages, in eight minutes thirty-five, flat. And here's Maloney's five spot to prove it!"

"Yes, Sir." Weiss saluted and paused, to draw breath. "Please excuse my lack of manners, Colonel Stedman, but I'm afraid there's a bit of a sticky situation, an emergency actually.... at the outdoor firing range."

Stedman's heart sank. The last thing that he could recall from the haze of the previous night, while attempting to creep discreetly upstairs to his room, away from the clamour of the 'Welcome Colonel Stedman' surprise bash at The Blue Swallow Inn, was a hearty clap between the shoulder blades by the out-going CO, Gordon Graham. Graham offered the well-meaning counsel of a well-meaning person well under the influence: "...And whatever else you do, old boy, try ... I mean really do try, to stay clear of 'unfortunate complic ... ations' ... like sud ...suddun ... sudden ... mysterious cas ... casual ... casualties. Had my share, Lord knows. Inquests, police reports, bloody rivers of red tape, mountains of paper, enough to drive you absolutely barmy. Good luck!"

Colonel Stedman shrugged off the mental image as he struggled to refocus on Rebeccah Weiss. "Go on, Major ... and do sit down."

"Thank you, Colonel. Sir, one of the VIP Yanks, a Lieutenant Kepke, has been shot in the head, accidentally, almost certainly a ricochet. Captain Mason and the others are applying first aid to stop the bleeding. We must get the man to hospital immediately."

"Bloody hell. Sorry. How badly hurt is he, Major?"

"Touch and go, Colonel... bleeding heavily from the upper right temple ... fluttery pulse ... dilated pupils ... losing consciousness ... when I ran up."

"Right." He punched his interoffice switch while picking up the telephone receiver. "Miss Robertson, thank God you're there. Yes, good morning. Who is on call for medical emergencies? Dr. Donald Miller? Call Dr. Miller's office. He must come here immediately. A client has been shot ... shot, in the head ... yes, life-threatening ... a training accident. Please have the doctor drive down directly to the open firing range at the lake. Inform the gate to let him through ... unaccompanied ... and no questions. I also want my Buick at the front door, now. Yes, tell Mac to leave it running ... I'll drive ... and hand me that large first aid tin box when I pass your desk. Yes, that's all for now, thank you.

"Are you quite alright, Major Weiss?" he inquired. "Ready, are we?"

"No question, Sir. Shall I bring along this blanket on the couch, then?" she inquired, while she carefully folded the Colonel's woollen throw.

"Yes, yes, of course. I'll pick up the emergency kit. Come along."

"Please, please make way, gentlemen. Captain Mason, escort these men to their barracks. Thank you all for your efforts. Exercises here are cancelled for the remainder of the day. Mason, take that message up to Major Grey's office, right away. Dismissed!"

"Doctor Miller, I'm Colonel Roger Stedman. What do you think? Any hope for this poor fellow?"

"Donald Miller, Colonel. I've staunched the external bleeding as much as possible with compresses, Colonel. It's a large, jagged entry wound. However, it's what's going on inside ... probable massive trauma to brain tissue ... on the border between the temporal and parietal lobes, maybe more extensive... along with bone and metal fragments ... severe cerebral haemorrhage. The chap's vital signs are getting fainter by the minute. Truthfully, Colonel ...Graham... sorry, Stedman ... unless we can get him into neurosurgery within the next twenty or thirty minutes, at the very outside, I would hold out little hope. We'll have to move him gently and drive quickly... in yours or mine?"

"Cars? What about an ambulance?"

"Not possible, Colonel. Regulations forbid civilians on the Camp property, as Colonel Graham and I found out when we dealt with a previous situation. Now, if you two will kindly do exactly as I direct, we can coordinate the lifting while minimizing the ... who's this coming?"

"Excuse me, Colonel Stedman. I heard that one of my men ... Billy Kepke, oh, my God!" the newcomer whispered softly. "What happened? Please, let me help!"

"Doctor Miller, this is Major Harris, the senior American officer on the ground."

"How do you do, Major, I'm Doctor Donald Miller. I didn't realize Americans ... well, as you can see for yourself, your man, Kepke, you said? ... has sustained a serious injury.

23

"Captain Weiss, cover him with that blanket.

"Immediately, Doctor."

"Colonel, we're taking him in your sedan, alright?" My Chev coupe's a bit too cramped in back," Miller ordered.

"Captain Weiss, open the right rear door as wide as possible and then slide into the back seat. We'll load him, toward you, head first. Your job is to keep him immobile on the trip to the General.

"Ready everyone? Gently now. Mind his arm, Major Harris ... slowly ... good. Colonel Stedman, you and Major Weiss follow me. Have your man on the gate call Miss Robertson to tell Dr. Sutton's surgical team to be prepped. Use my name. As quickly as possible, Colonel. We'll wait, but the clock's running out for this man. Jump in with me, Major Harris."

"Thanks for bringing me along, Doctor Miller. Where are we going?" Harris queried.

"Not far ...less than ten minutes ... the Oshawa General Hospital. Glad you were here to help, Major. Are you feeling all right? It must have been quite a shock." He glanced at his muscular young passenger who appeared to be in his early to mid-twenties, with a head of wheat stubble blonde hair.

"Yes, quite a shock ... that's for damn, er, darn... sure, Doctor Miller. Darn shame ... Lieutenant Kepke's a good man, a fine soldier ... and a heck of a radioman. We were both volunteers, joined up with the 501st Parachute Infantry Regiment, Airborne, Fort Benning, Georgia. Well, we got our wings in short order, and in no time at all, our Staff Sergeant told us they were looking for a few guys with college backgrounds in math and science, to train in signals. Since Billy and I both had qualifications, we figured we'd give it a shot and I was accepted. I guess I moved a little faster than Billy, mainly because my degree was in Electrical Engineering and his wasn't. Anyway, as I said, I was selected and found that I really loved COMINT: cryptology, cryptanalysis, encryption, decryption ... that type of hocus – pocus. Next thing I knew, I found myself 'volunteered' for OTC, and by the time I was commissioned, promotions were comin' faster'n bluebottle flies to peach pie, so I was given command of a new, specialized kind of mobile SIGINT unit ..."

"COMINT ... SIGINT, Major?"

"Oh, sorry, communications intelligence and signals intelligence. OTC is the Officer Training Corps. In the army, you get so used to the lingo that..."

"It's as if you're in a kind of secret priesthood, isn't it, whether it's called the army, law, medicine, or the circus, for all I know. It's sort of a professional code, or shorthand, that everyone in the club knows, but to outsiders, it's all mumbo-jumbo. What do you think, Major?" Miller asked.

"Roger, wilco, over, Doctor," Jack chuckled.

"I'm going to drop you at the front entrance up just up ahead and then pull in and park. You said that you and the Lieutenant began as paratroopers? That must have been quite an experience."

"Outstanding! Honest, Doc, do you think Billy 'll pull through?"

"I sincerely hope so, Major. We'll know soon enough. Fort Benning eh? By any chance, are you Georgian?"

"Georgian? Never heard it put quite that way before, but yes, Doctor. Billy Kepke and I both hail from a whistle stop 'bout twenty-five country miles southeast of Macon."

"Really? I know those parts well. Love the red soil, Stone Mountain, sour mash bourbon, and Vidalia onions; pecan pie with whipped cream served with that old southern hospitality and the ladies ... well ... I married one. I did two years of post-graduate surgery at Emory ... Emory Medical School."

"Atlanta? Well, I'll be darned. By any chance are you a football fan?"

"I played a little inter-collegiate ball while I was there ... guard, third string ... have this broken nose as proof. You should have seen the other guy, Mining Engineering, I think. ... A true throwback, a Neanderthal, from Georgia Tech! Speaking of which, there's the stretcher crew. Get out here and help the attendants get him out of the Colonel's car, if they need a hand."

They sat in the cafeteria, hunched over cold coffee in paper cups, the crumbs of half-eaten, muffins scattered like chaff on the tabletop. Kepke had been taken into surgery at ten-fifteen, Dr. Miller said. Major Weiss and Colonel Stedman had begun playing Hearts with a partial deck of dog-eared cards, while Dr. Miller and Major Harris debated the relative merits of American versus Canadian football. At twelve thirty-five, Harris excused himself, rose stiffly from the bench, and stretched, then headed in the direction of a cluster of smokers in a far, dark corner of the room, when a young male wearing a stained surgical gown and cap pushed open the swinging door. "Don, a moment please? Outside."

"He's not smiling, Colonel," Rebeccah remarked under her breath "Not a good sign. And I win!"

Donald Miller followed his colleague into the corridor. Less than a minute later, they re-appeared in the doorway. "Dr. Sutton has some information that he wants you all to hear. Come out here, would you please?" After a brief round of introductions, Dr. Sutton delivered the bad news. "Lieutenant William Joseph Kepke," he stated calmly, "died on the operating table at twelve fifteen pm, despite my team's efforts to resuscitate him. I'm truly sorry. If there's anything further the hospital or I can do, Colonel Stedman, please, let me know. As the attending physicians, Donald and I will look after completing the required documents. Will you be informing the Lieutenant's next - of – kin, Colonel?"

"That's being dealt with by my superiors in Toronto. Thank you very

25

much, Dr. Sutton. Please send your statement of account to the address on this card. I'll be in touch with you shortly about the disposition of the body. Will there be an autopsy, doctor?"

"Routinely, and in this instance, a certainty, given the circumstances of his ... death, Colonel. It will likely be complicated by the fact that he is an American citizen. The body must remain here, pending the coroner's findings and recommendations. It's impossible to second guess the outcome, but until such time, it cannot be released for burial."

26

"I understand. Thank you, Doctor. Can you suggest an undertaking establishment ... discrete ... locally?"

"I'll be more than pleased to make the arrangements, Colonel, when it's time," Donald assured him.

"Very well, then. If there's nothing ..."

"Colonel, I'd like to see him, please?" Harris asked, his eyes starting to swell with tears.

"Is that possible, Doctor Sutton?"

"Of course, Colonel. Give us, say, one half-hour."

Later, while backing out of the parking space, Colonel Stedman stopped the car and looked directly at Rebeccah. "You can be assured that we'll both be called upon to give testimony at the inquest, Major Weiss. Are you prepared for that?"

"Yes, of course, Colonel," she replied crisply, trying not to show her growing resentment towards his apparent lack of confidence in her capabilities. "It did happen on my watch. I take complete responsibility. Has Toronto HQ been notified?"

"Yes, I rang them from the hospital" he replied, engaging first gear. "Erik Williamson will do everything possible to keep it out of the public eye, of course, but he made a point of emphasizing that legalities must not be disregarded; the laws of the land will be obeyed. Moreover, we can't lose sight of the distress and upset that his family will suffer. Mr. Williamson is looking after that. I hope to heaven that we won't have a fully - blown international incident. BSO Toronto is dispatching a team of forensic specialists at first light tomorrow to conduct a thorough investigation, before a Board of Inquiry is convened. The firing range is off-limits, under twenty-four-hour guard, until further notice, by order of HQ. We are to give these chaps our fullest co-operation, of course, although Erik Williamson has directed that our programs must continue, full steam ahead. There is so much to be done in the next fortnight; I shall be calling upon your experience and expertise."

"I would be keen to help out in any way that you require of me, Colonel. Can you foresee any chance down the road that I might see a more ... active level of involvement?" she queried, smiling.

27

"I wouldn't rule out any possibility, Major. It seems rather redundant to be telling you this, Captain Weiss, however, everything you have seen or heard today, of course, is highly classified. I know that I can fully trust both you and Captain Mason in this regard, correct?"

"Correct, Colonel Stedman." 'Ruddy right you can, mate.'

"Thank you. And many thanks for your support today. 'Til mess time then, cheerio!"

"Yes, 'til then, Sir." Closing the car door, she saluted, and began to walk slowly toward the married officers' residence. 'This is not turning out at all as I hoped,' when I agreed to this post. I wonder what Hamish would do? I do miss the Flying Scotsman. He's likely enjoying the wilds of British Columbia, kayaking down raging rivers, hanging upside down from glaciers by his toenails ... photographing exotic fauna ... or rescuing orphaned cougar cubs ... sweet little Delilah.

'And Robert ... dear, brave Robert, Robert Samson, my Beaulieu mentor, consigned to the military dust bin ... a desk job for heaven's sake... to suffer slow death by a thousand paper cuts,' she sighed.

She felt a twinge as she recalled the joy of preparing for Operation Tent Peg, constantly testing and often besting her personal limits. She longed for the physical and mental challenges, the comradeship, even the tears and frustrations at her own ineptness during the gruelling training regime, the thrill of stalking him. When she first viewed him, the make believe Führer, in the optical sight of her rifle, at his cardboard and mirrors, make - believe Berchtesgaden, high in the Canadian Rocky Mountains, she had known that she could take him down without compunction. Then, the bitter let down when she and Hugh were ordered to 'stand down'; after all that, it was only a play-acting prelude to a glorious

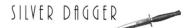

Eagle Day in London ... which as it turned out, it was not: the Führer had survived.

The sudden loss of their unborn child soon after she and Hugh Mason were married in August, took a severe personal toll ... depression ... irritability ... mood swings ... guilt. Fortunately, Colonel Graham had foreseen the possibility of a breakdown, and suggested that she take a leave "... as long as required, to regroup." At Hugh's insistence, and on Betty Robertson's advice, she made an appointment to see Doctor Calder, a General Practitioner in Whitby, the next morning.

On the drive back to Camp, she admitted to Hugh that Dr. Calder had a ... "kind, sympathetic manner, like Grandpa Weiss, actually. He took my history, drained a quart of blood ... did a thorough check-up. I'm booked again for the day after tomorrow, when he expects to have the results of the blood tests ... same time."

When she returned, Dr. Calder shrugged. "All of the tests were negative and apart from your sleeplessness and chronic fatigue, you're as fit as a Stradivarius. Time and the body's capacity for healing itself will take care of it. It's really all in your head, Major Weiss."

Disappointed, Rebeccah looked down, nodding. "Thanks all the same."

Dr. Calder didn't miss the tinge of sarcasm. "Well," he replied, "there is a new specialist in Toronto, a Doctor von Zuben. He's having promising results with a host of experimental therapies. Don't worry; he's accredited, on the up - and - up. It usually takes months to get an appointment, but if I make the referral myself, perhaps he can take you sooner, fit you in if there's a cancellation."

A week later, they arrived at the clinic. The receptionist admitted Rebeccah upon their arrival and indicated to Hugh that it would be advisable to sit down. A large white mass dominated von Zuben's flat-white waiting room. Hugh was undecided whether it was a gargantuan Brussels sprout, a gigantic Spanish onion, or something else. Modern art wasn't Hugh's specialty. Staring at it for half an hour had made him suspect that it was upside down. A magazine would be a nice diversion, he thought.

He rose when Rebeccah came out. Without looking at him, she opened the clinic door and walked down the short hallway, outside to the car, got in, and sat staring silently ahead. By the time they reached Brock Road in Pickering, Hugh finally spoke up.

"So, how did it go?"

She looked out the side window.

"The consultation ... the treatment. How was it?"

After a lengthy interval, she uttered a single word, "Vegetables."

"Vegetables?"

She turned and looked directly into Hugh's eyes. "He said I should eat more vegetables."

"Uh huh. Brussels sprouts?" he volunteered.

"Beets. Do you know how much I hate beets, Hugh?"

"A beet!"

"Are you making fun of me?"

"Forget it. Say, darling, why don't I take you and Sarah to visit your parents for a bit of a holiday?"

The next morning, Hugh drove Rebeccah and his stepdaughter, Sarah, to Toronto. Two weeks later, bored but restored by her mother's homemade cabbage borscht and chicken soup supreme with matzo balls, she presented herself to Colonel Graham. When he asked, she smiled, replying that she knew she was 'fit for duty' when she had finally stopped agonizing over her setbacks at two am every morning and had regained her sense of humour. "You know, yesterday was the first morning that I've slept 'til seven since ... I had a bizarre dream that involved you, Colonel, and Robert Samson, just before I woke."

"Really! Nothing risqué, I hope? And I suppose you're about to tell me about it, Rebeccah?"

"Hitler's a vegetarian, that we know. Well, you and Robert were all dressed up as two poncey actors playing Rhine Maidens and you managed to distract the guards long enough for Robert to slip rat poison, what's it called?"

"Strychnine."

"Yes, strychnine."

"Go on...."

"Where was I ... oh yes, you put strychnine into Adolf's beet borscht."

"Why not cyanide? Just curious."

"Cyanide? Oh, no, that would be far, far too humane, an easy way out. Rat poison ... strychnine has such sinister connotations with very unpleasant effects ... convulsions, seizures, eventually, respiratory shutdown and ... well, enough said."

"I rather suspect that the Führer would rather be found dead than eat Jewish beet borscht! Either way though.... Now, would you mind awfully getting along to your post and doing your ruddy job?" he laughed, shaking his head.

Rebeccah, nearing her quarters, had paused to look at the white-capped lake. 'Colonel Graham's gone as well. Colonel Stedman, his replacement, is ... certainly not in Gordon Graham's league. Oh, well, Rebeccah,' she reflected, 'just be grateful that you had the good luck to have been chosen, once.' She laughed inwardly when she recalled how her Orthodox cantor father, beloved Papa, had winced when she told him of the fiercely cold blizzards up in the Rockies, which had led her to wonder if she was one of the chosen people or the frozen people. 'A once-in-a-lifetime experience, it was, and now it's over and done.'

She suddenly recalled the half-forgotten memory of a gifted teacher, Headmistress Jennifer Wolthorpe, inspiring the girls in Rebeccah's upper class Eng. Lit. Course, with her inspired reading of Tennyson's ode to the restless warrior king, *Ulysses*: "How dull it is to pause, to make an end, to rust unburnished, not to shine in use. As tho' to breathe were life.' "Indeed, Lord Alfred, indeed" she whispered. "Come, my friends" she continued, "'Tis not too late to seek a newer world," etcetera, etcetera ... "Push off, and sitting well in order smite the sounding furrows; for my purpose holds to sail beyond the sunset ... until I die."

She pulled open the screen door.

"Rebeccah love, were you talking to me?" called Hugh.

"Oh ... no, darling, I was ... just having a word with Flying Jenny ..."

"Who?"

"Hello, Sarah darling! Mommy's home."

The Board of Inquiry was convened in the Board Room of Military District 2 HQ on King Street, Toronto. Commanding Officer General C. F. Constantine was Chairman of a six-person panel. For reasons of security, the press and public were barred. Among the observers were Robert Brooks, Deputy Chief of BSO, Major John Harris, and two staff representatives from Washington HQ of the American Bureau of Security and Information Services (ABSIS). General Constantine opened the proceedings by reading from a prepared statement in which it was made clear that the inquiry was not a court of law, nor were he and his colleagues empowered to find fault, nor judge any individual on his or her actions. The purpose of the hearing, he explained, was to hear evidence, under oath, following the rules of evidence as exist under military law, pertaining to, and limited to, the circumstances and conditions which led up to and may have played a role in the death of Lieutenant Kepke.

"It is our role to listen and to hear. It is the responsibility of others to decide whether or not there exist grounds sufficient to merit the issuance of writs of indictment pursuant to the Criminal Code of the Dominion of Canada," he concluded.

Expert witnesses, both military and medical, including Drs. Donald Miller and Douglas Sutton, gave forensic evidence that occupied the first two days. Each was supported by a range of exhibits including ballistics charts, statistical graphs and tables, sketches, photographs and topographic maps of the site of the accident only, at 'the weapon's testing Base', x-ray plates, grisly autopsy photographs, a submachine gun, labelled, Exhibit 1: Thompson, US, 1940, and a deformed bullet, complete with matching fragments, 'Exhibit 2: Calibre .45.'

On the third day, Colonel Stedman was called to the witness stand. His concise, dispassionate account of the incident was probed and queried without success for two hours, and then he was excused. Rebeccah was called next. The Coroner's senior counsel, frustrated at having being unable to create a shred of doubt or pry any admission of liability from Stedman, chose to propose that, as an officer, Rebeccah would surely find the 'accidental' deaths of two trainees in less than a year excessive. She replied that she was unqualified to respond, having had no knowledge of any incident other than the subject of the present hearing, Lieutenant William Kepke, but accepted his accounting, without prejudice, as a statement of fact. Anticipating his next line of questioning, she cited the SOE actuarial tables, which she had memorized, stating that a five percent rate of casualties, while using live ammunition, was statistically acceptable, and within the normal range.

"I have no further questions for this witness at this time, but reserve the right to recall," Coroner's counsel mumbled and returned crestfallen to his chair.

Rebeccah turned toward General Constantine. "With your permission, I wish to make a statement, General. Thank you. I find the death of any good person regrettably tragic and the death of Lieutenant Kepke was that ... the passing of a good person. I do regret it deeply. Lieutenant Kepke was by all accounts a fine officer of excellent character who showed exceptional promise. His family, his comrades, and the country that he loved and served so loyally and so well must mourn his loss deeply. Yet, we must bear in mind this fact: Lieutenant Kepke was a casualty of war, and we should not hesitate to honour him, as we would as if he had fallen in combat. We are at war. We prepare and train our young men and women for the terrible realities war, using the tools of war. Perhaps this young man's death was avoidable, and perhaps it was not. I leave that to the authorities to decide and to a higher authority, my God, to judge me. Thank you.

"Now, if I may be permitted to do the figures in my head, Sir; to the best of my ability, your data in fact produces a training fatality rate of 0.0333 per cent. May I suggest to the court that the annualized rate of loss of lives due to shovelling snow in a city with a population roughly the size of Toronto is twenty-fold more?"

With a final jab at her credibility, the attorney rose to raise the issue of due diligence, which quickly degenerated into an attack on her professional integrity. General Constantine halted the examination and declared a recess, and summoned counsel to his office.

When the hearing reconvened, Dr. Keith M. Padgett, a forensic pathologist from RCMP HQ in Ottawa, took the stand to be examined on his written deposition. Speaking clearly and deliberately, he stated that his conclusions were based on fifteen years in the Dominion crime laboratory, where he served as a licensed pathologist with a special interest and credentials in forensic ballistics. An assistant wheeled in a cart with a slide projector while another brought a portable screen. The equipment was quickly set up and the drapes pulled. Standing beside the screen in the darkened room, and using a wooden yardstick as a pointer, Dr. Padgett proceeded to illustrate, in layman's terms, the characteristic scorings on the surfaces of bullets and fragments, which had been removed from human skulls. He paused as an assistant inserted a new slide.

"It was the unusual striations and deformations on the exhibit bullet, that puzzled me. I had never seen this type of deformity and scoring ... shown here. So, I called on my colleagues for help. Dr. Angus MacLeod, at the University of Edinborough, suggested that he might have an answer, in reference to an incident reported in the British Journal of Forensic Ballistics. I mailed him my photographs." Then, Padgett dropped his bombshell. It was his considered opinion that the lethal projectile had been diverted mid-air, following a one - in- ten million-chance collision with another round, causing it to change trajectory and tumble downward at near-muzzle velocity, penetrating the cranium of the unfortunate Lieutenant Kepke. "This was the only possible cause of the large, jagged entry wound," he asserted. "Even though the probability of such an event approaches zero statistically," he cautioned, "it cannot not be dismissed out-of-hand on those grounds. I have tested my theory in the ballistics laboratory, using two so - called, Tommy guns with identical .45 calibre ammunition. This slide shows the results. As you can see, the test bullets and the specimen from the victim's head are remarkably similar. What I propose in fact is the only logical conclusion to be reached, based upon the body of evidence. In the complete absence of any hint of foul play, may I respectfully suggest, General, that this panel recommend that this be found to be a 'death by misadventure.'" In closing, he referred to the Appendix of his report, where Dr. MacLeod's opinion was reproduced. The room sat in silence. General Constantine declared the hearing adjourned until the following day.

Final arguments began at ten a.m. on day four. At one-thirty, General Constantine rapped his gavel on the oak table, thanked all par-

ties, and declared the hearing indefinitely adjourned.

Rebeccah was making her way through the crowded corridor toward the back exit, where the Colonel's car was waiting to take them back to Camp, when she felt a light tap on her shoulder. She turned to see the American Ranger, Major Harris, offering his hand.

"Well done, Major Weiss. I just want to say how grateful I am for your help when Billy's accident happened and how darn impressed I am with the way you've handled yourself over the last four days. Your speech was wonderful. It really moved me. I wonder if I could have a copy for Billy's folks?"

"Thank you, Major Harris. I hadn't planned to make a speech, at all. It just seemed the thing to do at that moment. Perhaps the stenographer ... No, I tell you what, I'll try to write it out, as much as I can remember, that is and give it to you."

"That would be great. You know, your no-nonsense approach sure cut through the entire load of BS. Say, are you in a rush, Major? I'd just be honoured to buy you a coffee, that is, if you have time."

"Thanks, Major. I appreciate your kind words and your offer, but duty calls. I really must re-introduce myself to my family. Another time, perhaps?"

"Okay, that'd be dandy." He accompanied her to the exit and down the steps when he took her arm. "Major Weiss, before you go, there's something I'd like to ask you. And believe me, this is on a professional level, no tom-foolery."

"Go on, Major..."she looked up at him warily.

"Jack, ma'm."

"Very well, Jack, Rebeccah," she smiled.

"Rebeccah, that's real nice! Well here I go. Ever since I came up here ... to Canada, to the Camp that is, I've been hoping to get more involved ... see some action, if you know what I mean?" he asked, his eyes twinkling.

"What sort of action did you have in mind, Jack?"

"The real thing, Rebeccah. I'm expert in Morse, 25 words per minute, short wave, have cryptanalyst know-how, I can shoot fairly straight on skis, mountain climb, run a mile in ...well ... fast enough and, oh yeah, I'm a pilot ... dually qualified ... on single and twins ... licensed by the American Army Air Corps to prove it. Do you want to see my paper?" he drawled, reaching toward his inside breast pocket.

"Really? No, I'll take your word for it," she laughed. "Well, Jack, that's wonderful! Good for you; that's quite a résumé. I'm not certain why you're telling me this, however, I'm sure that your government will find many uses for your talents. Now, I must be off. The Colonel's already waiting in the car."

35

"Sure, Rebeccah. Hope I haven't been too forward, but my mammy always said that since no else is goin' to blow your horn, darn well better blow it yourself! Thanks for your time. Here, let me get that door for you.

"Afternoon, Colonel Stedman," he saluted, then closed the door as the Buick started to pull away.

"So, what was that all about, Major? Do you like that chap, Harris? I find him an agreeable sort of fellow."

"Yes, I rather think so. It was only a bit of shameless self-promotion, Colonel. He's very anxious to get his feet wet."

"Is he now? Tell me exactly what he said ... but only the self-promotion bits as you call them, please, Major."

Two days later, Dr. Sutton informed Donald Miller that the Coroner's office had authorized William Kepke's release. Doctor Miller immediately contacted Colonel Stedman, and suggested to him that the McIntosh-Anderson Home should be engaged. Miller telephoned Funeral Director John Kellam, and requested that he take charge of all arrangements with "the usual dispatch, discretion, and dignity" ... which, in Miller's opinion, Mr. Kellam had performed admirably under similar circumstances in the recent past.

Lieutenant Kepke's parents flew into Oshawa Airport the following afternoon on a private charter, arranged by Erik Williamson. They were

36

The McIntosh-Anderson Funeral Home, Oshawa, Ontario, 1940.

driven directly by limousine to Parkwood Estate, where the owner, Colonel McLaughlin, Colonel Stedman and Robert Brooks met them.

At seven p.m., Rebeccah and Hugh arrived at McIntosh-Anderson in the Camp station wagon accompanied by Major Blake Grey, the Camp's Second-in-Command, Adjutant Brian Jones and Major Jack Harris. Harris introduced them to Mr. and Mrs. Kepke, who were seated with Colonel Stedman and Robert Brooks. Wreaths and massive floral arrangements on pedestals nearly obscured the two-man honour guard, rifles reversed, and steel helmeted heads bowed, flanking the Stars and Stripes-draped mahogany casket. From her Orthodox Jewish tradition, Rebeccah was relieved that the coffin lid was closed.

By nine p.m., the visitors and soldiers were gone. John appeared with sandwiches and coffee, spoke briefly with Colonel Stedman, and then on his way out, turned down the lights. Rebeccah was trying to listen to Mr. Kepke as he painfully recounted the sunlit pranks that Billy and Jack had played as kids. She glanced at her wristwatch: nine forty. The floral fragrances flooding the room were making her feel queasy. She nudged Hugh. Majors Grey and Jones, at Roger Stedman's suggestion, escorted Billy's parents to a waiting auto. Taking this as her cue, Rebeccah leaned over, "Colonel, Hugh and I should like to be getting back."

"Soon, Major.

"I realize that we're all more than a trifle tired and on edge, however, I'd like everyone to wait a little longer. I promise you that it will be worth the inconvenience. Please, finish up the food and drink and pull your chairs into a circle, if you would."

Feeling like a grammar school student, kept in, 'on report', Rebeccah complied, then began studying the thick burgundy broadloom. The silence in the room was ear shattering. She stifled the urge to snicker at the image of the Colonel rising and bidding them join hands, while he invoked the spirit of the recently departed.

Then, the door slowly opened framing a figure of medium height, male, wearing a dark overcoat and a fedora. 'What's this then, a visitation from beyond?' She glanced at Hugh, who appeared to be napping.

"Good evening. I apologize for keeping you waiting." The soft, deep voice was that of *Stalwart.* John reappeared to take Erik Williamson' coat and hat, while Stedman poured tea. "Please, don't get up," Williamson assured them as he walked around the circle, touching peoples' shoulders, greeting them by name, and then sat down in the chair beside Jack Harris.

'A little touch of Erik in the night,' Rebeccah reflected.

"Thank you Colonel Stedman, but I'd best forego any more tea at this late hour. Doctor's orders," he added wistfully.

"I arranged with Robert and Colonel Stedman to meet with you here tonight for three reasons. I know the circumstances are rather ... unusual, to say the least," he remarked, looking around the room. "However, Mr. John Kellam has dismissed his staff and gave me his assurance me that the room is secure and quite soundproof, which HQ has verified. First, it is my duty to remind you that what I am about to propose is privileged and is not to be disclosed under any conditions or circumstances. Without going overboard on the dramatic aspects, I'm obliged to inform you that the slightest hint of carelessness on the part of

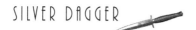
any person will be summarily dealt with by the full range of sanctions provided by the Act. Any person wishing to absent him or herself is invited to do so, now.

"I thought not. Second. Prime Minister Churchill and his senior advisors have determined that we immediately resume where you, Sylvia ... Rebeccah, and Hugh left off. The elimination of Chancellor Hitler is, categorically, back on. In the PM's words, it is of paramount importance that it succeed this time; I must take care to be accurate in reporting the PM's words, quote '...with renewed resolution, fortitude and finality. Let there be no doubt that his continued existence is the greatest threat to the survival of our civilization,' unquote. There's more, but that will give you a sense of his mindset at this time.

"Third," he paused, "you, and others, have been selected to carry out or make preparations for this mission. The PM has assured me that he remains confident that we are up to the task; otherwise, I wouldn't be here, obviously. To clear up any misconceptions, let me be clear, the task is so complex and hazardous that the odds makers have pegged the chances of an agent's survival on the ground ... optimistically ... at less than one in thirty. Again, we can play Ten Little Indians; you may choose to leave ... subject to the restrictions I have stated ... or you may choose to stay. Yes, Major Harris?"

"Sir, I'm in, no question! I'm just wondering ... if the American Army would approve of my involvement in this?"

"I can assure you they would and they have, Major, or else you would have been sent home with the others" he replied, smiling briefly. "You can thank Colonel Stedman for starting the ball rolling, on your behalf. General Constantine has pulled the strings with the Pentagon. Now, I've given Colonel Stedman an outline of the plan, working name *Shining Oath*. Not certain why the PM chose that particularly, but there's a logical reason, we can be sure. It calls for an accelerated schedule of training, which will begin the day after tomorrow's funeral. Robert Brooks and I will be at the Camp then, to give a detailed briefing. I know that you're exhausted but you may want to learn a few more particulars. As the principals in Operation Tent Peg, and because of your first-hand experience, Major Weiss and Captain Mason will form the core of the training team. You will not, I repeat ... will not, be assigned operational responsibilities on Mission Shining Oath, per se. Instead, you will be carrying out critical liaison and support functions. I may add that our old friend Major Hamish Findlay will shortly be joining us." Rebeccah's heart pounded.

"Others will join you as well this week. Colonel Stedman is the de facto leader during the lead up." Rebeccah's heart sank. "Now, I think it's time for us all to get some rest. Thank you for your attention and for holding your burning questions until Wednesday. Good evening."

Rebeccah watched as Erik quietly rose and walked to the bier. He stopped, and then lightly rested the fingertips of his right hand on the casket, his head bowed. Then, taking one step back, he raised his right arm, and saluted. Rebeccah closed her eyes in respect. When she opened them, *Stalwart* was gone.

39

"Major Samson, Mr. Williamson wishes to see you, right away, please … in the blue, sorry, the Small Conference Room."

"Right away? Very good. I'm on my way. Thank you, Miss Ward." Robert Samson set the receiver on the hook. 'Wonder what this could be about? Lord knows a man can only count paperclips for so long before he's ready to … Well, how do we look, Robert? It will have to do … the great man can't be kept waiting.' The door of the Conference Room was open when Robert arrived. Erik Williamson rose and came to the door to greet him.

"Robert, come in, please. Thanks for coming here on very short notice. Rob, you've met Commander Lawson."

"Yes, at Colonel Graham's office. Good to see you again, Commander."

"Rob, please sit there." Williamson pointed to a high back chair as he was shutting the door. "Now, Commander Lawson and I have a proposition to make, Robert, which we think will be of considerable interest to you. We've given this a great deal of thought and frankly, there is no other person with the qualifications and the background of experience. Are you interested yet?"

"Well, yes, Sir, I am interested, particularly if it involves some sort of physical activity. I do miss that aspect very much."

"Major Samson," Lawson interjected, "Mr. Williamson and I are confident that you are the man for the job. Right, Erik?"

"We are indeed. Robert, how would you feel about going back on the active roster immediately, with all previous 'incidents' forgiven and forgotten?"

"A clean slate ... meaning a fresh start, Sir?"

"Wiped out, without a trace," responded Lawson.

"Cast iron promise, we guarantee it," Williamson added.

"And then ... what?"

"You are to report to Camp X tomorrow at 0800; you'll come along with Brooks and me. Briefing at 0900."

"Sir, I'm overwhelmed. Yes, of course! Thank you both very much. May I ask ... why?"

"Let's say we have an old score to settle, Major, and we can use your assistance."

"I am very grateful, gentlemen. It makes me think of a saying that my Mandarin tutor taught me, 'May you live in interesting times.' Thank you again. I won't let you down."

For the first time in many weeks, Robert felt a thrill of anticipation flowing like an electric current through his being, as he strode down the hall to Miss Mary Ward's desk. She looked up at him, smiled, and removed her glasses. Not for the first time did he realize that the guardian of the castle keep, Mary Ward, was what his mother would have called ' a late-blooming blossom.' "And how do you feel now, Major?"

"Do you dance, Miss Ward?"

"Yes, I've taken ballroom dancing lessons on Thursday evenings for four years, Major."

"And do you enjoy ballroom dancing, Miss Ward?"

"Oh, yes, I adore it!" she replied, her eyes twinkling.

"Then you will understand precisely how I feel at this moment."

"On cloud nine?"

"Very close, but more like the old doctor in Dickens' *A Tale of Two Cities.*"

"Yes, I remember. It was Doctor Manette ... He said he had been recalled to life when he was imprisoned unjustly and released after eighteen years, from the Bastille."

"Excellent, I am impressed! Well, that's how I feel, Mary Ward, just like the good doctor, recalled to life, and if I could put two feet straight, I would whisk you from this dreary place down to Rio, where we would tango the night away, under the stars."

41

"Mary, please. Major Samson, you surprise me! ... You do remember your appointment at the Camp at 0800?"

"Tell me this Mary Ward: do you know everything that goes on around here?"

She smiled, "You might say that, Major."

"I just did, my dear... Robert, please. Goodnight, Mary Ward. Or rather, hasta la mañana, senorita."

"I'm off to New York shortly, Robert. Good luck tomorrow!"

"New York! Oh, well...." he replied softly.

"But you can reach me there at HQ," she added brightly.

"Wonderful! I'll come and visit you, that is, if..."

"Just see what happens if you don't!"

THE BLUE SWALLOW INN

Robert Brooks gazed from his eleventh floor office window of the Canadian Imperial Bank of Commerce head office, at 25 King Street West, in Toronto. Watching snowflakes the size of quarters land delicately on the window ledge, he brooded. 'Britain needs agents urgently, where and how in the hell am I going to find them?' Then, it became clear. 'Derek Wainscott ... haven't heard from him in years. Maybe if I call SIS Casa Loma they'll have an idea where he's holed up.' Robert picked up the receiver and dialled the number for Casa Loma: Whitehall 4356.

42

"Hello. Yes, I would like to speak with Commander Lawson, please. Robert Brooks, BSO. Brooks, Robert. Thank you. Yes, I'll hold." 'Commander Lawson' was the pseudonym for Admiral Sir Willson Cunnington, also known as 'G', the head of Great Britain's Secret Intelligence Service, MI-6.

"Lawson here."

"Sir, my name is Robert Brooks. I'm an associate of Erik Williamson in Toronto."

"Are you using the secure line?" Sir Willson inquired edgily.

"Yes, Sir, I am."

"Please, go ahead then."

"Sir, I'm trying to track down an old friend of mine who, last I can recall, worked for your organization."

"What is his name, Robert? First, I must caution you to use his service alias."

"Bill Eaton."

"That's all I will need. Where can you be reached, Robert?"

"BSO HQ in Toronto, Sir."

"I'll have my assistant ring you back with the information first thing in the morning. I hope that will be satisfactory, Robert. And, please say hello to Erik for me next time you see him. Good bye for now."

"Yes, very satisfactory, thanks. I'll await your call tomorrow morning then, many thanks, Commander. Good bye." He prayed that Sir Willson would be able to locate good old, peculiar Derek.

Robert Brooks drove along a lightly snow-dusted Kingston Road to Thornton Road and turned south toward Camp X. Pulling into the old farm laneway, he drove up to the gate and stopped. Private McDonald passed in front of the car to approach the driver's side window.

43

McDonald leaned inside. "Good day, how may I help you?"

"Private, I'm here to see the new Commandant, Lieutenant-Colonel Stedman."

"Yes, Mr. Brooks, who should I say is calling?"

"Robert from BSO, thanks Private," Robert replied. He frequently found Mac's insistence upon 'by the book' procedures vaguely annoying, and sometimes amusing, but never overbearing.

"Sir, just give me one minute please. I'll be right back."

As Private McDonald walked toward the guardhouse, he made a mental note of the license plate number: BSO 1125. 'That's a good start, Mac' he thought to himself as he picked up the telephone. "Colonel Stedman's office, please." A minute later, Mac walked back to the car window. "Colonel Stedman will see you, now, Sir."

"Thanks, Private, and have a pleasant day."

Robert parked and got out of the car in front of the Lecture Hall where Lieutenant-Colonel Stedman was waiting to greet him. "Robert, I'm so pleased to meet you at last," Colonel Stedman remarked warmly as they shook hands.

"And I am delighted to finally meet you, Colonel. I hope that I'm not inconveniencing you."

"Not at all. Just ploughing through the usual mountain of papers ...

you're a welcome excuse to give it a bit of a rest! Come in. Take off your overcoat. Tea, Robert, or something stronger?"

"Tea will be fine thanks, Colonel. That's certainly a brisk wind coming off the lake."

44

The Camp X Lecture Hall

"Indeed! Please, call me Roger. This is my irreplaceable secretary Miss Robertson."

"Yes, we've met. How are you, Miss Robertson? By the way, thank you, for the invitation to Colonel Stedman's welcoming party. I hope it went well ... if previous events are any measure, I'm sure it was memorable. Unfortunately, I was stuck at HQ. I had been scheduled as Duty Officer that evening and couldn't wiggle out of it."

"Very nice to see you again, Mr. Brooks. I would say that it was an unqualified success, wouldn't you agree Colonel? How do you take your tea, Sir?"

"Just milk, please."

"Just pop it in with it when it's ready, Betty, thank you," Stedman stated.

"Come into my office, Robert. Now tell me, what brings you here?"

"Actually, I've been hunting for new clients but I'm running into road blocks ... I have to admit I need some help, Roger. I'm trying to locate an old SIS acquaintance. I know he would be first-rate at recruiting new men. He's a bit of an eccentric renegade, but apart from that, he has everything it takes to get the ball rolling," Robert added apologetically.

45

"Do you need help to find your friend? Is there anyone I can call?" offered Stedman.

"No, not just yet, Roger. I've put in a request to G, at SIS in Toronto. You do know that he's currently stationed at Casa Loma don't you?"

"Yes, I had heard that. Oh, thanks, Miss Robertson."

"Fine gentleman, the Admiral. I met him at a meeting of the London Controlling Committee when I was there making a pitch for a bit of extra staffing at Beaulieu. Well, I'm sure it's all in good hands and that if anyone can find your colleague, Sir Willson Cunnington is your man."

"I do hope you're right Roger. Erik Williamson is expecting results and I'm running out of time. By the way, how is your ... er, payload?" Brooks asked cautiously.

"Fine, just fine. The men are getting quite used to having it around. The room is now temperature controlled. In fact, there's no shortage of volunteers for guard duty during the winter. It's a damn sight warmer than night patrol on the interior fence," he laughed.

"Well, I must be going, Colonel Stedman. I'll keep you posted on my progress," said Brooks. "Thank you for the tea, Miss Robertson. I will make every effort to come here more often!"

'Attractive, bright lady ... wonder if she and Roger...?' Robert noticed that she had flushed slightly when she brought in the tea service.

———

Robert arrived at 0830 to wait for the phone call, which he hoped, would resolve his dilemma. He set down the first section of the *Toronto Globe* to glare at the black telephone on the right hand side of his desk.

"Damn cleaners! Why do they do this? Every morning, I have to move the bloody phone from the right side of my desk to the left. Haven't they caught on by now that I'm left handed?" he muttered testily as he pushed the phone back to the left side. He had just raised the newspaper when the phone rang loudly. He picked it up before it could ring again.

"Hello ... yes, this is Robert. Good morning, Commander Lawson. Good of you to call personally, Sir. I do hope that you have good news for me."

"Yes, Robert I do. Your friend Eaton is in Halifax ... as a matter of fact, he had only just arrived. He was one of the last of our people to get out before the occupation. I let him know that you were searching anxiously for him. You'll be pleased to know that he's about to board a train, heading to Toronto."

"That is terrific news, Sir!" Robert exclaimed.

"He'll call on you as soon as he gets in and settled at the King Edward Hotel. If there is anything else, please, don't hesitate to ring me."

"Thank you, Commander. Oh, there is one more thing. I understand that you aren't able to pass along his file, but I'm very keen to engage him as my head recruiter right away. Might I ask you, Sir, is there any chance of an updated security clearance or personal verification...?"

"Already done, old boy. He checks out."

"Sir, I don't know how I can repay you."

"We'll think of something, Robert," he chuckled. "Cheerio for now."

It seemed to Robert that Sir Willson was pleased to have achieved results so quickly. As for himself, Brooks decided to celebrate this stroke of good luck with an unusually early lunch at Stoodleigh's Restaurant: a heavenly thick, grilled cheese sandwich, with a bowl of their decadently creamy, home made mushroom soup.

'First, call Erik and tell him the good news.' Robert picked up the receiver of the Red Phone, which for some impenetrable reason had never been moved from its proper place on the desk's left side. It rang BSO HQ in New York automatically.

"Good morning, Miss Ward, it's Robert in Toronto; all settled in? How are you? How is the weather in New York?"

"Hello Mr. Brooks, good to hear from you. I'm fine, thanks. It's cloudy and mild, in the fifties."

"In the fifties!" exclaimed Robert. "We had snow up here yesterday."

"Well Sir, you can keep it. That's the only thing I don't miss about Toronto. How can I help you?" she inquired.

"Would Erik be in?"

"He is; I'll patch you through. Stay warm; speak with you later. Go ahead please, Mr. Williamson."

"Robert, how are things in Toronto?" inquired Erik Williamson jovially.

"Excellent Erik, cold, as to be expected."

"You know, as nice as New York is, I do like my flying visits back to Toronto. Anyway, that's not why you called. What do you have for me?" asked Erik.

"I have very good news. Do you remember Derek Wainscott? You met him in London when he was working for me at the Canadian Consulate in '33. He's SIS now ... and more than qualified to take on the recruitment portfolio. He's very bright and..."

"Not offhand, Robert. SIS you say? That sounds promising. Does Sir Willson have any knowledge of him?"

"Well, Erik, as a matter of fact, I took a bit of a gamble and called G personally. He just called back to say that he has located Derek in Halifax. He's on his way to Toronto. SIS ran a security check and he's a choirboy. Wainscott's just the man I need to take on the job of Chief Recruitment Officer and with your permission, I'd like to appoint him at the earliest possible opportunity." Robert crossed his fingers. He was glad that he had not mentioned Derek's somewhat 'peculiar' personal traits.

"If you think he's your man for the task, then permission is granted. I'll leave it to your people up there to look after the transfer protocol. You'll keep me posted on his progress, of course? Thank you for calling Robert ... I'm late for a meeting ... have to run. Nice talking with you, my friend; please give my best to Mabel."

"Roger, wilco, and thank you, Erik. 'Bye for now." Robert set down the receiver. "Damn, I love that man! Robert old boy, I think this calls for a bigger than usual wedge of banana custard cream pie for dessert!"

48

'Charles the 1st', otherwise known as Charles The Younger Waddington, approached the office of Derek Wainscott and knocked gingerly on the partially open door. Wainscott had been temporarily housed in an office, which in Charles Waddington's opinion was more like a large closet than one befitting the prestige of Chief Recruitment Officer, British Security Operation. A 'previously used' oak desk which had hastily been recovered from the scrap pile behind the building dominated the available space, leaving little room for a decrepit credenza, a hand varnished bookcase and a tilting back, wooden desk chair, along with two badly matched visitors' chairs that served as the Chief of Recruitment's unique **Current Action** and **Signature Required** filing system. Upon entering, Waddington almost choked on the acrid cloud of cigarette smoke that enveloped the air.

"Come in Charles ... sit down. No, no, sorry, not there! Now, what do you have for me?" Abstractedly, he thrust a flat metal container of Buckingham Regulars across the desk, retrieving one for himself. "Help yourself. Where's that damn lighter?"

"There, Sir. No, thank you. This file was just delivered by hand. I had to sign in three places, so I thought that you would like to see it directly."

Derek Wainscott looked up quizzically, while the ash of the cigarette which dropped from the right side of his mouth, dangled precariously, "Good, and about bloody time. I've been waiting forever for it. Set it there. Good lad. No calls ... I don't want to be disturbed. And please tell what's his name, Smythe, that I won't be joining him for lunch. Thank you, Charles, now be a good lad and kindly toddle off."

"Yes Sir, call if you need me," Charles Waddington responded and smiled as he exited. His new boss, Mr. Wainscott, was a 'character', but well meaning and 'a clever one', as were most of the 'backroom boys', in Charles' opinion. It was Wainscott who had christened Waddington, Charles I, or Charles The Younger, to distinguish him from Charlie Tripp, Charles II, or Charles The Ancient, the elderly night janitor.

Robert Brooks had not had time to examine the 'Clipper' file before assigning it to Wainscott when he took office. Among his responsibilities, Derek was charged with counter intelligence operations relating to suspected German agents and double agents in Canada. 'Clipper' was the codename for the murder/suicide of an adult male subject at the Blue Swallow Inn, a local watering hole regularly frequented by the Camp X staff. The circumstances surrounding the death were so nebulous, and suspiciously similar to a prior incident at the Genosha Hotel, that the local police, dreading the involvement of yet another person or persons connected with the Camp, willingly handed over the file to the RCMP. RCMP Commissioner Ted Reynolds had contacted Robert Brooks soon after to inform him that the deceased was an illegal, a non – resident alien, perhaps of Dutch or possibly Scandinavian origin, while cautioning that, pending further inquiries, substantive information was thin. Derek had assigned a special investigator, Jim Coward, whose name had been suggested by Robert Brooks. Derek, with little more to offer Coward beyond Reynolds's speculations, nonetheless directed Coward to submit a preliminary report within two weeks. Derek had not expected much to come of it. He put his feet up on his desk, lit a fresh cigarette, leaned back in his chair, and began to read.

49

This report prepared by Special Agent James Coward on this 8th day of November 1941.

On the morning of 14th October 1941, the body of a man was found in an upstairs' bedroom of the Blue Swallow Inn, which is situated just north of SOE STS 103, locally referenced as Camp X. A self-inflicted bullet wound was found above the right ear and death had probably taken place about 24 h before the discovery of the body. A Browning Automatic Revolver, with silencer, marked "Fabrique Nationale de Armes, de guerre, Herstal Belgique," was lying about two feet behind the body and to the side of his right hand.

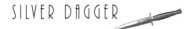
The body was dressed in English clothes, the suit bearing the label of Preston Tailors, Milton Keynes.

Derek paused and closed his eyes. 'Milton Keynes! Jesus! GCHQ! Bletchley Park, the British Government's Communications Headquarters.'

He resumed reading ... and on the body there was found a passport of the Kingdom of the Netherlands number 696873,

Bletchley Park Manor, Buckinghamshire, England.

bearing a photograph of the man and issued in the name of Jan von Braken on the 23rd July, 1940, expiring on the 24th July, 1942. There was also found on the dead body a National Registration Identity Card, bearing the name Jan von Braken and a serial number. This card was a forgery and its authors made the following six gross errors:

The address on the bottom of the left hand inside page was in the same handwriting as the name and serial number at the top of the page;

The name of the street was put after the name of the town;

In the address, the street was given as "Webley Street"; there is no such street in Milton Keynes.

The Christian name was given as Jan and placed before the surname;

The card was machine folded, not hand folded as a genuine card is;

From an examination of von Braken's clothing, it appeared that he had been in The Hague, in Noordwijk in Holland, and in Brussels, though it is not possible to say precisely when he was last in these places.

51

Derek rubbed his chin which was starting to show a premature five o'clock shadow. 'Clumsy bastards! You think that you've covered all the bases and then you discover that you messed up one little detail. In this case, the whole magilla!' Derek continued reading.

A key was found in his left trouser pocket bearing the markings of the Whitby Post Office, number 467. A search of the box showed that the dead man had deposited there on the 14th of July 1941, a suitcase containing clothing and a brown moroccan leather case containing a W/T set similar in all respects to sets brought to this country by enemy agents who had been captured.

From the inquiries that have been made, it has been possible to reconstruct in some detail von Braken's movements in this country. He arrived in Halifax on the 4th day of June 1941 and on that same day obtained through a firm of agents' lodgings, a room in the same house. Von Braken was given a bedroom upstairs at the rear of the house and was supplied with breakfast daily and mid day dinner for the sum of $3.00 per week. He remained at this address until the 30th of June 1941, and during that time, according to the landlady, he never slept a night away. He was out most of the days, usually returning between 9 p.m. and 10 p.m. in the evenings. Von Braken was in the habit of sitting with a bottle of beer when he came back at nights, playing cards and talking, and he informed them that he came from Holland, and that he was connected with

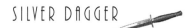
the Free Dutch Forces, and had received permission to visit relatives in Canada while on leave before heading back. On his arrival at the Blue Swallow Inn, he appeared to have only one suitcase but on his departure, the landlady noticed that there was a second case, which was, in fact, the transmitting set.

On the 31st of July 1941, von Braken told his landlady that he had to leave Whitby for Toronto and requested that the landlady get a taxi for him. In fact, Von Braken did not leave the Whitby area but on the same day took a room at the Genosha Hotel in Oshawa where he remained until the 15th of August 1941. According to the desk clerk at the Genosha, von Braken never slept a night away from Oshawa but would spend the whole of the day out and return late in the evening, and on several occasions he told the desk clerk the next day that he was going to Toronto for the day.

Of von Braken's activities in Toronto, little has been established, save that he very often had his lunch at a diner on Yonge Street and that he rented office space from a company at number 12 King Street.

Derek's eyes opened wide as he gulped for a breath of air, 'God, how will I tell Robert? What will I tell him? How much damage did this chap do? He literally set up shop just a few doors down the street from here, BSO HQ! Thank God I wasn't on the job!'

...which he furnished with a kneehole table, davenport, and one wooden armchair and occupied it until the 2nd of October 1941. As far as it can be ascertained, he only visited this office twice and no correspondence was received for him there. He let it be known that he required this office for the purpose of writing a book.

From a number of bus tickets found in von Braken's possessions it is clear that he made the following journeys in this country:

2nd August 1941: from Oshawa to Ajax, Ontario, and return;

5th August 1941:from Oshawa to Barrie, Ontario, and return;

8th August 1941: from Oshawa to Highland Creek, Ontario, (no return ticket);

11th August 1941: from Oshawa to Kingston, Ontario, and return.

On his arrival on 16th August 1941 at the Blue Swallow Inn, von Braken, according to his landlady, had a considerable sum of money. He paid his bill regularly with crisp, $10 bills. On the 20th of September 1941, he requested a fellow lodger, employed at the Canadian Imperial Back of Commerce in Whitby, to cash five $10 U.S. bills. These were cashed and von Braken received approximately $55 in return. On von Braken's body the only money found was one Canadian dollar and there was money owing to his landlady, the bill for the current week.

Von Braken's transmitter set has been examined and the expert opinion is that it had probably been used in an effort to establish contact, but it is impossible to say whether the effort was successful or not.

Von Braken's success in avoiding detection (from the time of his arrival in Whitby until his death on 13 October 1941,) by official contacts, would certainly have brought to light his identity as an enemy agent, is disturbing in the extreme and the following are the relevant details.

Just then, there was a knock at the door. Robert Brooks peeked his head inside.

"Hello Derek, hard at it? What do you say to a bite to eat? I was thinking of walking over to Stoodleigh's ... would you like to join me?"

"Excellent idea, I was getting tired of reading. The detail in Coward's report is overwhelming. Speaking of tired, aren't you getting a little tired of those grilled cheese sandwiches, breakfast and lunch?"

"Never! Did you say, Coward's report on 'Clipper'? Anything of interest?"

"Yes, perhaps more than we want to know. I'll fill you in on the way over." Derek was not very anxious to get into details. As the two men walked up Yonge Street, Derek asked Robert about news from the war front.

"Oh, not much. The Nazis are boasting that it's curtains for the Soviets. It does look grim for Ivan with Heinz Guderian and company soon to be driving their panzers through the gates of Moscow. One small problem: the Russian snows came on like the clappers, the earliest in a century, ... October 6 and it hasn't let up, -40 F., a humdinger, so the meteorological boys say."

"Maybe the Führer should bone up on his Napoleon!" Derek responded dryly.

"Very good, but then you've always managed to outdo me in the pun department, Derek. But, at last, some good news out of Washington! The House of Representatives voted by 212 to 194 to revise the Neutrality Act of 1939 to allow US merchant ships to unload munitions in our ports. You've got to admit that it's a start, Derek," Robert added enthusiastically.

"That is good news!"

"We'll cross here when the light changes. Now, this is very confidential, Derek; MI-5's boys pulled off a real coup. You've heard of the Twenty Committee'?"

"Uh huh. Double cross, for the Roman numerals XX; I believe it became operational last January to feed disinformation to the Germans through their own agents. That's about all I know."

"Right. Basically, captured agents are given two choices: work for us as a spy or be executed. Two German agents were snagged in England last year, 'James', and 'Paul,' to their handlers; anyway, these two chose life over their oath of loyalty to his nibs, and presto, they're double cross wankers, redubbed 'Spring' and 'Fall'. We faked a raid on one of the Spitfire factories in England with minor damage to the rear of one of the buildings. 'James' and 'Paul' reported to their masters that they had carried out a devastating raid, which, according to their report, resulted in a total shut down. No machinery, no parts, equals no Spits, mein Herren!"

"That's a good one."

"Wait ... German air intelligence signalled back that the portly Air Marshall, Hermann Göring himself was so ecstatic that he promised he would personally present each hero with the Iron Cross upon their return. Of course, they'll never collect, poor duffers ... they're needed in England ... so much more war work is required of them. Isn't that the most amusing thing you've ever heard, Derek?"

"As the man said, I wish I had thought of that!"

"Let's rest on this bench for a moment ... change of topic. You mentioned the 'Clipper' report, Derek, what have you learned so far?" asked Robert.

Wainscott lit a cigarette and inhaled deeply before answering. "Well, I haven't finished reading it, Robert, but so far, there's damning evidence that our department has been penetrated by enemy agents. Jim Coward is nothing if not thorough and I would venture to say that it's gospel. Sorry to be the bearer, Robert ... this is a bombshell."

Robert noticed that Derek's nicotine-stained fingers were trembling more than usual. "I assume that you will have a full report for me by tonight, hand written for now. Because of its highly sensitive nature, we wouldn't want Charles 1 to type it, much less read the bloody thing, would we? It will include your recommendations for action, of course?"

Derek had felt the full force of Robert's ire only once in the Consulate. He didn't relish a repeat performance. "Yes, Robert, I will have it on your desk with my recommendations by 8:00 pm tonight." 'Or God help me,' he prayed silently. When Derek returned to his office, he picked up the report, which was turned over on his desk, exactly where he had placed it. The pencil, which he had laid on top, had not moved. He felt confident insofar as he always double locked his office door. One would have to get past Charles I, a feisty Camp X medical reject, and then break down the door to get in, he assured himself.

Derek reread the last sentence in order to refresh his memory ... which would certainly have brought to light his identity as an enemy agent, is disturbing in the extreme and the following are the relevant details which include my personal risk assessment as well as my recommendations for remedial action.

Executive Summary

Von Braken's landlady went and saw the AAO: Assistant
Alien Officer of the local police stationed on Dundas
Street in downtown Whitby shortly after von Braken's
arrival and said that she had a Dutchman staying at the
Blue Swallow. The AAO told her to get hold of a scrapbook
and get the Dutchman to write his name and date of arrival
in it and to obtain as soon as possible, some Alien Forms
and make the Dutchman fill one in. The AAO concluded his
remarks to the landlady by saying, "Don't you worry, the
fellow will be along soon to report himself."

Von Braken, of course, did nothing of the sort and
nothing further was done by the AAO. As mentioned above,
von Braken told his landlady on the 31st of July 1941,
that he was moving to Toronto, whereas, in fact, he merely
moved to Oshawa. A few days after his leaving, the landlady saw Von Braken and her suspicions were raised by this
fact. The landlady went again to the AAO and told him how
von Braken had said that he was leaving for Toronto on the
31st of July 1941, but had been seen by her a few days
later in Oshawa. Unfortunately, the AAO did nothing once
again.

German U-boat off the coast of Halifax photographed by BSC agents.

It is clear that the most cursory examination of von Braken's passport and identity card would have revealed the fact that he had not arrived in this country through recognized travel control and not registered as an alien. In fact, it is well known to us that German agents arrive on the shores of Halifax in a dinghy at night after being released from a 'U' Boat stationed off the coast. The entire process is almost identical to the one used by SOE, Combined Operations and so on.

57

There are strong reasons to believe that von Braken was, in fact, the agent whose dinghy was discovered hidden on the Halifax shoreline on 4 June 1941.

(a) Based upon the evidence that von Braken arrived in Whitby with a ration book which had never been used and which he had apparently not attempted to use before, it may be assumed that he had recently arrived in this country. This conjecture is strengthened by the fact that von Braken immediately bought a new outfit of clothes in Oshawa;

(b) Near the dinghy there was found a paper wrapping from a chocolate bar of Belgian manufacture;

(c) Hurriedly buried near the dinghy was a leather helmet bearing a label on the inside with the size recorded, 6 7/8, the exact size of von Braken's head.

Conclusion

I can only conclude from these facts that Mr. von Braken was a spy/agent of the German Abwehr or SD Ausland Service. One can only guess as to the extent of damage inflicted by him to our side. The fact that he had an office only a few doors from BSO Headquarters in Toronto begs the question as to the depth and range of his knowledge.

In closing, I am obliged to suggest that BSO:

1) Relocate BSO H.Q. to Casa Loma soonest as no one gets within a football field of this location;

U-boat off Halifax coast

2) Increase surveillance of the surrounding area of STS 103 (Camp X), the downtown area of Whitby and Oshawa as well making frequent stops of vehicles along the Kings' Highway # 2;enlist local constabulary but at all costs, prohibit disclosure of true purpose to avoid public panic;

3) Conduct immediate interrogations of all inmates of prisoner of war Camp 30;

4) Conduct forensic interviews with all targeted towns-people, particularly householders who have had, or at present have boarders, as well as landlords and farmers near Camp X. I would suggest Agent Killigan for this job as he has had a lot of experience lately.

Respectfully submitted,

James Coward

Special Agent BSO.

Derek put his finger on the intercom. What he was about to do could end his career almost before it had begun. "Chas. Come in here, please."

"Be right there, Sir."

"Charles, please get in touch with Special Agent James Coward; tell him I would like to meet with him ASAP in order to discuss his recommendations. Tell him this, write it down exactly: it is an excellent report; he has done a noble service ... no, forget that, say, his investigation has exceeded the requirements, etc. Oh, and tell him that I fully support his recommended changes and I wish you and him to implement them, stop. Don't look at me that way, lad, trust me, you'll know what you need to know, when you need to know. I have to have my report ready for Brooks tonight. Gallons of coffee and please run across the street to the drug store for a flat fifty of bucking pigs, and get a gallon of their best butterscotch ripple. There's a tenner in the Players' tobacco tin, top shelf, left side. Understood?"

"Yes, Sir, understood," Charles replied, as he removed the crumpled bill and replaced the lid.

"And get yourself something!" Derek shouted at his departing assistant.

"Thanks, I will." Charles I almost ran from the office. Derek grinned. He knew how much the young man was eager to please and could be trusted to carry out this vital assignment, with Jim Coward as his nursemaid. Robert could be convinced of that also, Derek decided. Charles Waddington had been studying law at The University of Toronto when war broke out. As a first-year member of the Osgoode Moot Court, he had dazzled his professors with the brilliant clarity of his arguments. He was also a fine athlete, a long distance runner with a string of victories from his high school senior track and field team. Recommended for an interview by a BSO talent spotter on the Faculty of Law, he had breezed through the screening and was sent down to Camp X to begin his training. Shortly after, his world literally came crashing down. Hospitalized for a fractured ankle during his first week, it was discovered that he had a congenital heart murmur; 'A dicky mitral valve' was Dr. Miller's unofficial pronouncement. Despite this disappointment, Waddington gamely reported for work at BSO HQ one week later, his right leg in a cast. Derek knew then that if Charles Waddington couldn't be a field agent, he had the makings of an excellent intelligence staff officer, and perhaps more.

Robert picked up the receiver of the red phone. "Hello, Mary, it's me again, Robert."

"Hello, Robert, I'll get him for you. One moment ... Robert, he's on another call ... hold on, he's through." The line clicked, went silent and then Erik answered.

"Good afternoon Robert, what's on?"

"Erik, we've uncovered what I believe is a grave breach of security. Basically, a German agent has been sniffing around the area of Camp X, as well as our office here."

"Good Lord! Well, what does he know? Have you interrogated him yet?" he asked incredulously.

"No, unfortunately, we can't, Erik ..."

"Why can't you?"

"Because he's dead, Erik. Jim Coward and Ted Reynolds think that he was a suicide ... or at least that's what the autopsy report is saying. You never know for sure though, the Germans are good at covering up these things," Robert asserted.

"Where was the body?"

"At The Blue Swallow Inn."

"That's damn close, much too close. One moment, please. Hello, Robert, have you been over there?"

"No, not yet. I've just finished reading Wainscott's summary of Coward's report. I wanted to fill you in first ..."

"Listen, you and Reynolds get over there without further delay. I'm worried that the trail, if there is one, is cooling down with every hour we wait. Try to dig up as much as you can and call me back, any hour of the day or night. Wire me photostats of all the documents today. Thank you for letting me know. Good hunting."

"I'll have them sent right away, Erik. I'm calling Ted now."

The next morning, a gleaming black Buick Road Master pulled into the broad driveway of Robert's house on Elm Road, in Rosedale. Before the plainclothes RCMP driver had rung the doorbell, Robert opened the front door, blinking at the unaccustomed sunshine, and followed the officer to the car. Commissioner Ted Reynolds rolled down the right rear window. "Good morning Robert ... lovely address. You can either squeeze in here with Derek and me, or take the front with Constable Matthews."

They chatted nonchalantly about the welcome change in weather, the possibilities of the Maple Leafs winning the Stanley Cup, and the state of the stock market, as though they were captains of industry on their way downtown to Bay Street for a board meeting.

An hour later, the Buick pulled up at the Blue Swallow Inn. The three men strode up the mulberry bush bracketed walkway to the front door, opened it, and entered the lobby. Reynolds approached the middle-aged woman who was on duty behind the front desk.

"Good morning, madam, my name is Ted Reynolds. Would you by any chance be able to tell us where the manager might be?"

"Good morning, Mr. Reynolds. I'm Wilma Curtin, co-owner and the business manager. What may I do for you?"

He lowered his voice to a conspiratorial whisper. "My colleagues and I are here in regard to a very sensitive matter."

"Oh, dear. You must be from the Liquor License Board," she confided, looking to her left and right. "Mr. Blackburn, the LLBO Inspector never said it would go this high up. He told Wesley, my husband, just to fix it up and that would be as far as it would go. Wes issued strict orders to Wally the beverage room tap man to make sure the clocks are set correctly, every day ... using, you know, that Dominion Observatory time signal on the radio at one o'clock, just before the news? Wes slipped out to the market a ... a half-hour ago. I expect he'll be back by eleven, if you could wait ...

"I'm sure you're right on, to the split second, Mrs. Curtin. Actually, I'm the Commissioner of the RCMP."

Her jaw dropped. "The RCMP! Oh, my ... we had no idea it was that serious an infraction. Wes and I thought it was only a warning. So, you're here to take away our license?" She spoke so rapidly, that Ted was unable to interrupt her tale of woe.

The Blue Swallow Inn viewed from Thornton Road

"Far from it, Mrs. Curtin. That's a matter for the Province. I'm afraid that we're here concerning the death of a former guest, Mr. von Braken. Is there someplace nearby where we could talk privately for a moment?"

A look of relief momentarily crossed her face. "Yes, yes, awful thing that was. I just felt something was wrong right from the get go. You and the gentlemen can come through to the office. Just go around the end of the counter."

After Reynolds introduced her to Derek and Robert, he continued, "Mrs. Curtin, I'd like to say that all of us sincerely appreciate what you tried to do. It was the sort of patriotic act we policemen hope for from all Canadians but encounter very rarely. It's a disgrace that your inquiries were ignored. Here's my card. If in the future, you feel any cause for alarm or suspicion, please, call me directly and I guarantee that I will personally follow up, immediately. Unfortunately, the regulations of the liquor board do not fall under my jurisdiction, but I might have a friendly word with Mr. Blackburn when I return to Toronto," he added.

"Oh, that's okay, Commissioner. Cliff's a good sort, just doing what he's paid for; I'd hate him to be thinking I've been telling tales behind his back. It was more like good advice than an official slap on the wrist. The clock was only three minutes and some slow. Now, how may I help you?"

Robert spoke up. "Mrs. Curtin, has anyone been in his room since Mr. von Braken's body was discovered?"

"No, Sir, the police sealed the room after they removed his body. No one, including the housekeeping staff, or Wes and me has set a foot inside since. To tell the truth, it's starting to hurt our business. Do any of you gentlemen have any idea as to how long it might be before I can open it back up? We'd have to completely redecorate it, first."

"We're going to take a look now," Derek answered.

"I'll have my men come in, package everything up and take it away. I'm making a commitment that you can have the room back by next weekend. You boys are my witnesses. How is that?" asked Reynolds.

"That's fine, Sir ... thank you so much. Wes will be very happy to get inside and get started. I imagine it's going to take some hefty elbow grease. Then there's the matter of fumigatin'." She removed a large metal ring of keys from a cup hook on the wall. If you gentlemen will kindly follow me...."

Wilma walked up the broad staircase with the three men in tow. At the landing, she turned to the right, walked ten steps, and stopped at the padlocked door. Reynolds noted that she had removed the passkey from the ring on the way upstairs as she quickly released the Dominion lock-set. "Here, Mr. Reynolds, for lockin' up. I expect that you have the key for this padlock, eh?"

"I do, thank you," he replied. "There, that should do it. Thank you, Mrs. Curtin, we can take it from here. We promise not to cause you or your guests any further inconvenience."

"If you need anything, Commissioner, just shout."

As they opened the door, a thick bundle of discoloured towels and newspaper rolled across the floor. "What was that for? Whew, there's the matter of fumigatin' for sure!" Robert exclaimed, hacking. "Okay to open the window, Ted?"

"I can't smell anything!" Derek commented.

"Maybe if you didn't smoke fifty a day, your..." Robert began and then stopped, coughing. " How do cops handle this? Beats me!"

"A policeman's lot. Sssh. Okay, open it a notch. If you're going to throw up, Rob, try to make it to the john, first. You can dampen a wash-cloth and hold it over your nose. It's okay to touch things, it's been thoroughly done over for prints. Feel free to poke around ... wherever you like."

"Can I light up, Commish?" Derek queried.

"Commish?" Robert asked incredulously. "No, and no ... you're out-voted two to one," Robert replied firmly.

"Brutal!" Derek commented under his breath as he knelt down to study the chalk outline where the body had lain on the wooden floor. He then carefully surveyed the surrounding area, noting that the desk chair was lying overturned on its side. "Is that the way it was found, Ted? Lying just like this?"

"Yes, exactly like that, as if it's been frozen."

"Okay, thanks. Sorry about the dumb remark, Ted. No disrespect intended." He turned his attention back to a dark amorphous stain of what was likely dried blood on the floor where a head outline had been chalked out. "Von Braken's, right?" he asked to no one in particular.

"Type AB, Rh positive. One hundred percent match with the victim," Ted confirmed.

"Well, I'm thinking that by the size, and spread characteristics of the puddle, see, like there, how it juts out, or there, that it wasn't caused by normal post trauma drainage, it was pumped out, by a living, beating heart."

"Meaning what, Sherlock?" Robert demanded, bristling. Derek knew that he was treading on very thin ice, particularly after the 'Commish' gaffe.

"Meaning that he didn't croak immediately as the autopsy states. He was alive for a bit. Except for the upturned chair, there's no sign of a struggle, none at all. Beyond that, I haven't a clue. But, if you ask me, I'd put my money on suicide. He botched the head shot which is not uncommon in cases of self-inflicted..."

"Tell me, Wainscott, do you have experience in police forensic procedure?" Reynolds asked.

"Oh, no, Sir, I just collect unusual books. You'd be amazed at what treasures you can find buried in some of the rattiest second-hand bookstores on Bloor Street, near the university. I guess I got the habit as a starving undergrad. Couldn't afford to take girls to the movies, so we'd go book slumming instead."

65

"Ted, what do you think?" asked Robert.

"I would tend to agree with Derek. It looks like suicide to me."

"Okay, but why?"

"Well, let's suppose for a moment: he thought that he was about to be picked up. He just panicked and put the gun to his temple and it slipped as he pulled the trigger," Derek suggested, standing up.

"Okay, so why was he found with a single Canadian dollar in his pocket when he was seen with loads of cash on him not long before? It just doesn't add up," Robert stated emphatically.

"I'm not sure what that has to do with it, exactly, Robert," Ted replied.

"Do you fellows mind if I close the window? It's freezing in here," Derek stated. "Hello, what's this?" He bent over to retrieve something that was sticking out from under a loosened strip of floor moulding. "Ted, you'd better have a gander at this."

Reynolds smoothed out a tiny scrap of paper and turned with his back to the window. "Well, well, the boys missed something. It's faded pencil, but it's definitely a phone number: Hyland ... 2, 4, 6, 2. Hyland is a central Toronto exchange," he mused aloud. "Have a look, Robert. It should be interesting to see where this leads. Good work Derek.

"Well gentlemen, if we're finished here and there are no more clues apparently, I'd like to talk with our landlady, Wilma, on the way out. You two go ahead; I'll replace the newspaper and some fresh damp towels against the door while I lock up. It helps to absorb the odour and keep it out of the hallway."

Mr. and Mrs. Curtin were waiting for them at the desk. Wilma introduced Wesley, who asked, "Did you see everything you needed to see, gentlemen?"

"Yes, indeed and many thanks again for your splendid co-operation," Ted replied. "We're all, very, very beholden to you both and want to compensate you for this unfortunate business interruption. Mr. and Mrs. Curtin, I want you to advise me of the total expenses that you've incurred, principally, the total rental income lost because of our investigation. Not the whole hotel mind, just that room," he laughed gently. "Also, kindly let me know the cost to redecorate the room. Receipts will not be required. When you have this information together, send an itemized statement, on your stationery. Mark the envelope "Personal, attn. Commissioner E. Reynolds," to the address on my card, and a certified cheque will be hand delivered to you on the next business day."

"Mr. Reynolds, that's very generous of you. This will certainly help and heaven knows we can use it since the awful affair happened. Thank you kindly, sirs."

"Perhaps you'd like a bite before you leave? We have a wonderful hot roast beef sandwich special today, with gravy, mashed, and fresh green peas.. On the house, of course!" Wesley offered, smiling broadly.

"That sounds very tempting, but thank you, we'd best be getting back. May we take a rain cheque?" asked Robert.

"Anytime. And you won't say anything to Cliff, Commissioner?" Wilma asked.

"My lips are sealed, Mrs. Curtin ... an old Mountie's word of honour."

Ted and Robert walked toward the waiting Road Master sedan, trailed by Derek, puffing furiously on a Buckingham.

"Hurry up, Wainscott, for heaven's sake," Robert stated impatiently.

"Take your time, Sherlock, you've it earned this morning," Ted countered. "As soon as I get to the office I'm going to call this number. Okay, you're finished, Derek? Hop in. Constable Matthews, take our friends to 25 King West, please."

Ted hurried into his office, closed his door, picked up the receiver, and dialled the number on the paper. After two rings, it was picked up.

"Yes, hello, may I speak with Patrick McKenzie please?"

67

"No one here by zis name."

"Are you sure? He gave me this number as his residence," Ted continued.

"Ya, sure." The line went dead.

"Bugger hung up. Try the operator."

"Operator, this is Commissioner Ted Reynolds, RCMP. I require an address for a telephone number. I was wondering if you could help me? Of course, Royal Canadian Mounted Police, I'm the Commissioner, Ted Reynolds: R e y n o l d s. Thanks."

"I'm sorry, Commissioner, but I'll have to ask you to speak to my supervisor. One moment please."

"Hello, Commissioner Reynolds. I'm supervisor Quinn. How may I help you, Sir?" she asked.

"Miss Quinn, I need an address for the following telephone number, it's Hyland - 2462."

"Mrs. Quinn, Sir. One moment, Commissioner ... Sir, that particular listing is for 84 Highvale Crescent in the city of Toronto," she replied.

"Thank you, thank you so much Mrs. Quinn," he replied, jotting on a scratch pad. "Please tell the operator that she was quite correct in referring this query to you," Ted responded graciously. "Good bye."

Ted could barely contain his excitement as he pressed the intercom button and summoned his assistant, Constable John Blair. "John, I want you to draw up an application for a search warrant for the premises at 84 Highvale Crescent. Once I sign it, you'll take it directly to City Hall. Find a Justice of the Peace there to swear out the paper. And check that it's filled out correctly. All of the information that you'll need to show the JP's clerk is in this folder. Have Brian Matthews drive you there. Come straight back with the warrant. I'll be waiting." Ted pressed the intercom button.

"Sergeant Denison, I want six men to execute a search warrant ... a residence. I'll be going with you. When? As soon as Blair comes back with the warrant in his hand. Be ready to move out anytime within the hour," Ted instructed. For the third time he pressed the intercom. "Mildred, get me Howard Shore at police headquarters."

Four unmarked police cars rolled to a stop in front of 84 Highvale Crescent. Reynolds and Sergeant Denison got out of the first car. The six-man squad emptied out of the two other cars. Because of the national security implications of the search, Ted had requested and received verbal clearance from Chief Shore of the Toronto Police Department to serve the warrant. Inside the fourth car was Howard Shore's Deputy Chief.

As the men walked slowly towards the front door of the grey brick, single detached house, Ted Reynolds called over Denison's shoulder, "Be careful Artie, we don't know what to expect. I'll be to the right of the door. Signal the others to spread out and be on the alert for anything."

Denison did as ordered and then rapped on the door. After two seconds, he knocked again. He looked over questioningly at Commissioner Reynolds, who nodded. As Denison was about to knock for the third time, the handle turned. A tall, sandy-haired man, in his early thirties, wearing a white shirt and black slacks, with matching loafers, opened the door. Denison looked straight into his eyes while holding out the document. "Good afternoon, Sir, I am Sergeant Denison of the Royal Canadian Mounted Police. I have here His Majesty's Warrant to search these premises, which I am empowered to execute at this time. Kindly take this and step aside, Sir." Reynolds watched the drama, while holding his breath. He knew his men. 'Arctic Artie' Denison was sharp, completely fearless, calm under fire, and immune to intimidation. Denison watched as the man's eyes glanced down to the folded writ. Suddenly, his right hand dropped to his trouser pocket.

"He's going for a gun ... get down, Commissioner!" A split second later, Denison had pushed the man backward with enough force to smash his head against the partly open, solid oak door. Losing his footing with the violence of the assault, he toppled heavily, to lie splayed out on the terrazzo hallway floor, with the considerable mass of Sergeant Denison straddling his chest. "Don't you move, Fritz, not a muscle, you bastard!"

A terror-stricken 'Fritz' stared up, too stunned to resist as two more Mounties pinned his arms and legs while they ripped at his clothes. "Got it, Sergeant ... a lady's .32!" one of them shouted.

"You two guys turn him over on his belly so I can cuff him!" Denison stated coolly.

"I'll take the gun," Ted commanded. A door slammed. "What the hell? There's more! The rest of you, split up ... go around both sides to the back yard. I'll go to the left. Now!" When Reynolds and his men reached the back yard, they saw the backs of two men disappearing over a six-foot wood fence.

"Two of you follow them over the boards. Go! You, get in the cars and cut them off ... get ahead of them. Maybe the Deputy would care to join in. Hopefully, they'll run smack into you," Ted remarked. He headed back into the house where Denison and his men had the suspect subdued and in handcuffs.

"Stand him up, Denison.

"Sir, can you hear me? Is there anything you want to tell me before we take you to RCMP Headquarters? No?"

"Fine, we'll take him down to HQ and see what he has to say there. Take him out to my car, lock him in and wait there until I'm ready," Ted stated tersely while he walked into the kitchen, picked up a telephone on the kitchen counter, and dialled Robert Brooks.

"Robert, Ted here. You may want to come over to 84 Highvale Crescent. We've just raided a house and made some very interesting discoveries. Yes, 84 Highvale Crescent... that's west off Avenue Road, above St. Clair. Okay, I'll be here, but please, hurry. I have someone you'll love to meet." Ted hung up the receiver and looked around the interior. It was a comfortable, middle-class detached home with a centre hall, living

room on the right, dining room and the kitchen on the left hand side of
the main floor. At the rear, on the same level, were three bedrooms and
a bathroom. Ted opened a door that was situated next to the bathroom
revealing wooden stairs going down to the basement. As he carefully
walked down the stairs, his service pistol drawn, he saw a light switch on
the wall and flicked it on.

He was dumfounded. Six factory-type light fixtures came on, revealing wooden workbenches and stools covered with parts and bits of radio
equipment and other gadgets and things that he didn't recognize lining
the cinder brick basement walls. Each window had been blacked out.
He wondered if it were an unlicensed radio repair shop. He flipped the
switch of one of the radios and was surprised to hear a hissing carrier
wave. That was the extent of Ted's radio technological expertise. 'Come
on, hurry up, Robert! Wait'll he sees this stuff!'

He found a black attaché case under one of the workbenches. It
was locked. 'Surprise!' He reached into his pocket and pulled out a
handy doodad and jimmied the lock. Seconds later the latch popped
open. Inside the case were perhaps twenty brown manila envelopes. He
pulled one of them out and dumped its contents onto the closest unclut-
tered bench top. 'Photographs ... hundreds!' As he examined them, he
thought they looked familiar. "This one, this is DIL, Defence Industries
Limited; and these, Oshawa Airport; a .. ohmygod Camp X!' He sorted
through the next several pictures of Camp X: all were high quality exteri-
or shots taken from different aspects of the Camp. Another envelope
contained nothing but shots of Camp 30 at Bowmanville, and the rail-
road marshalling yards. It was now extremely clear to Commissioner
Reynolds what was going on in an ultra - respectable, upper middle-class
Toronto neighbourhood. Thanks to Derek Wainscott's lucky find, the
scrap of paper, they had stumbled upon a Nazi espionage ring, which,
Ted expected, the dailies would soon be trumpeting as, 'A Nest of Spies
In Our Midst!'

'There has to be a darkroom somewhere. Aha, there beside the fur-
nace.' Ted unlatched the hook and swung the door open, to be met with
the sickly sweet, pungent odours of photo development chemicals. He
switched on the light. In the pale, red glow of the overhead safety light,
he could make out an Agfa timer beside a photo enlarger and a neatly
arranged row of developing trays and tanks on the counter. The room

was criss-crossed with strings on which were suspended negatives and prints, by the score. "Merde!"

Robert called downstairs, "I heard that! Coming down!"

"Watch the stairs!" Ted shouted.

"What do we have here, Ted? A rather well equipped photography lab! This other stuff looks like the radio room at Camp X when Yorkie and Bernie are having a bad day!"

"Rob, you won't believe what we've stumbled on. Here, look, take a look at these," Ted retorted as he passed him the photos.

"Wait a damn minute! Is this some kind of a joke, Ted?" Brooks muttered, flipping through the photographs.

"No, no joke, Rob!"

"What the hell? Did you see this one? Good God, we've been done over, Ted! This is Camp X!" Robert whispered.

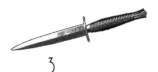

SILVER DAGGER

Robert K. Samson smiled appreciatively as he slowly ran his index finger along the blade of his father's Rolls self-stropping straight razor to remove the few water drops clinging to the stainless steel, before pressing it into its sterling silver case; he then examined the weathered face that was reflected in the steel-framed mirror. 'Cold Sheffield steel, the world's finest,' he mused. 'As for you, old man, no bloody wonder you're still a bachelor at fifty-nine. Ah, well. It was meant to be ... I suppose.' An image of Mary Ellen Ward: light auburn hair upswept to frame her heart-shaped face, the intriguing Cupid's bow mouth, warm hazel eyes, flashed briefly like a Roman candle in Robert's mind, flared briefly and then faded. He had last seen her only two days before, but it seemed like a thousand years.

Robert had made the trip back to Camp alone, without Erik Williamson and Robert Brooks. Brooks had left a telephone message the previous afternoon, stating that an unexpected situation had arisen requiring that the meeting at Camp X be postponed.

Ever since rumours of Robert's return to Camp X had begun to circulate, his colleagues had agreed to be on the watch for any signs of a delayed reaction to the humiliating reversal which he had undergone: summary transfer from the field to a desk. Yet, since his arrival, he had displayed no discernable distress signals. Rebeccah, Hugh, and others of his closest friends noted with delight that Robert Samson was at the top of his form, thriving on the rigours of training men, most of them young enough to be his grandchildren, if he had had any, to make split – second, life and death decisions, in the cold and drafty Sinclair barn. Robert seemed renewed, reinvigorated by the spartan Camp life. "Better by a damn sight, Brian, than perishing of dry rot," he had confided to Major Jones, the Adjutant-Quartermaster. Nevertheless, he had not told anyone of his disappointment that his brother - in - arms from Mission Tent Peg, Hamish Findlay, was no longer at Camp X.

Robert stepped out into the hallway of the east 'H' building and walked quickly toward the mess. He could hear laughter, which was unusual, he thought, as the atmosphere was restrained, as a rule, in the morning. His curiosity aroused, he increased his pace until he reached the door. 'What's this then? It's pandemonium in there. Sir Freddie burned the toast again? Sounds it, or a full-blown bun fight!' He opened the door and peered inside cautiously, prepared to dodge a barrage of flying crockery or food. "What the devil...?" he exclaimed.

The entire mess was standing up, lustily singing, "For he's a jolly good fellow, for he's a jolly good fellow ..."

On the final chorus, the room broke into applause, and foot stamping with shouts of "Happy Sixtieth, Killer," "Glad you're back, Rob!" and "Get plastered ... you bastard!" Robert stared at the chaos, in bewilderment, as Colonel Stedman charged over to shake his hand. "This isn't a training session Robert, so nothing fancy, old man ... Happy birthday!" he exclaimed.

Robert looked about at the grinning faces. Then the penny dropped.

The historic Camp X Officers' Mess.

"Why ... I believe you're right Colonel, so it is ...it's my birthday. I had forgotten, totally," he commented, shyly.

"Well, good thing we didn't, old man and in celebration, our dedicated Cook Frederick stayed up half the night and baked this magnificent cake!

"Roll it out, Freddie!" The kitchen doors swung open on cue as Fred entered, proudly wheeling a cart bearing a mammoth white cake festooned with burning candles.

"And, it's jolly well big enough for the entire Camp to have a slice!" Stedman bellowed above the cheering. "Settle down!"

"Thank you very much, Colonel. I'm truly moved ... at a loss for words, which is quite rare, indeed. Fred, it looks as large as a soccer pitch. And I shan't bother to inquire where or how you managed to round up enough ingredients!" he added, grinning.

"Quiet everyone! Quiet, if you please!" Stedman pleaded again.

"Now, you must do the honours, Robert."

How many candles are on this, Fred, sixty?" Fred nodded.

"Are you up for this, Major Samson? Very good! Ah, ah, first you must make a wish ... you know the drill, eyes closed ... and ... carry on!"

The room erupted in wild hooting and applause as Robert extinguished every candle with one breath.

"Now that's what I would call physically qualified!" Stedman raised his right arm. "Gentlemen, your attention! Gentlemen, quiet down, please ... thank you. I have a presentation that I would like to make to you, Major Samson, on behalf on your fellow instructors and officers. Robert, your fellow mates and I wanted to show you how much we appreciate what you are, and indeed have been doing, since most of us were in nappies. Please! Robert, at a time when you should be casting flies on some bonnie brae far removed from all this, we would like to present you with this token of our admiration ... a Samson dagger, and beyond that, a very special Samson dagger."

"Thank you, Sir, it's ... very handsome."

"And can you make out what is so special about it?"

"I'd say that it's silver plated for starters," Robert replied, turning it over in his hands.

"Almost, but not quite Robert; in fact, it is made of solid, sterling silver ... one of a kind. It was hand crafted by the best silversmith in Toronto. By accepting this, you are initiated as a member of the élite 'Order of the Silver Dagger' and are bestowed all the rights and privileges pertaining thereto."

"Speech! Speech!"

"Colonel, friends, at my advanced age it's difficult to be surprised by much. This is truly a memorable day, made even more special with this remarkable gift. I can't thank you all enough. I shall always cherish it. Thank you Colonel, Fred, your first - rate staff, and everyone else who conspired in this. Do we have to work today, Colonel?" he asked jauntily.

"No rest for the wicked, Robert.

"However, to show Robert how much he's truly appreciated, we'll be continuing this merriment with a gala party in honour of the founding member of the Order, 1800, tonight.

"Oh, for entertainment, I've invited our local maestro, Bernie Sandbrook, to tinkle the ivories, along with Yorkie Hardcastle, and a few other lads from communications. There's a mystery guest as well, whom I know you'll be delighted to welcome. No, sorry to disappoint, chaps, it's a male! Right then, until this evening, carry on."

Colonel Stedman removed Bernie's microphone from its bracket and stood up on the piano bench, as Bernie shifted along to make room, while continuing to play. "Bernie, everyone, may I have your attention for a moment, please? Thanks. Tonight we're not only celebrating Robert's return on his sixtieth, but as promised, we have another lost sheep coming back to the fold. Ladies and gentlemen, please join with me in welcoming another old mate who flew here directly from the wild Canadian west, Major Hamish Findlay! Hamish, a few words, please?"

"It's grand to be back at Camp X ... and Happy birthday, Robert. Missed you all, especially you, Robert, Rebeccah, and Hugh. I'm looking forward you three, to catching up on all the juicy gossip. The bar's not dry yet, and I hear that it's free ... is that so, Colonel? Well then, what's stopping us? Let the party carry on!"

Hamish joined Robert, Rebeccah, and Hugh at their table. After Hugh had brought the second round, Hamish asked to see Robert's dagger.

"Hamish, we're not in the Highlands, for heaven's sake! We don't come armed to social events! However, if you insist." He left the table and returned a few minutes later. "Here, take it ... but don't you dare scratch it."

"Major Findley, Hamish, can you come over here ... a minute please?" Colonel Stedman called.

"Thanks, Robert, it's a real beauty.

"Excuse me for a moment, folks.

"Yes, Colonel?"

"Hamish, old man, tomorrow being Sunday, I would like you to take Robert and yourself in the Jeep, over to the Genosha Hotel, Oshawa, and treat yourselves to their complete roast beef buffet, on me. I apologise that I'm unable to join you, but I've been invited by Colonel Sam McLaughlin to visit him at Parkwood."

"Oh, sorry Sir, I'd love to do that, but Robert's not welcome at the Genosha, unless things have changed considerably in the last while. It's a long story, Sir," Hamish added quietly.

"Is that so? Well, what about The Blue Swallow Inn, then?"

"I haven't had the pleasure, Colonel. It was still not quite completed, when I left for the coast."

"It's a first rate, posh hotel, Hamish. The lads already call it the Camp X annex. And, the dining room's on a par with the Genosha's. I can personally vouch for it! Ready for another Scotch?"

"I left a full one back on the table, thanks though, Colonel. The Blue

Andy: "The best bar keep in Canada."

Swallow sounds A-1! But about my Jeep ... I heard a rumour that it had a tumble over the bluffs."

"True, true, Hamish, it did go over. Unfortunately, when it hit the water it rolled and turned turtle, buried in muck, twenty feet under. The garage tried to put a hook on and wrench it up, but the cable snapped, twice. I'm very sorry."

"I think I'll have that Scotch, neat, if you're still offering, Colonel," Hamish remarked mournfully.

Hurriedly changing the subject, Roger interjected, "Don't forget, Hamish, tomorrow's Sunday, so you don't have to be up with the birds at 0600. Good night."

"Good night, Colonel, believe me, I won't forget ... and many thanks for this grand reunion... and the dinner... in advance!"

The Buick turned off Simcoe Street, passing through the imposing wrought iron and limestone gateway, following the circular driveway, to come to a stop at the main entrance. "So, this is Parkwood Estate, Mac! No small wonder Colonel Graham raved! I hadn't expected anything near this grand." Colonel Sam McLaughlin, Chairman of The Board of

General Motors of Canada, waved in greeting as he and Mrs. McLaughlin approached the car. Mac had told Stedman on the drive over that Colonel Sam had often hosted the previous Commandant, Colonel Gordon Graham, and some of the Camp senior staff.

"This too, Colonel," Mac affirmed.

"This ... what, Private?" he had queried, puzzled.

"This car, it was a donation, personal like, from Colonel McLaughlin

Colonel Sam and General Constantine chat at Parkwood.

to Colonel Graham, Sir," Mac stated with pride.

"Well, then, perhaps we shall be asked to give it back. Don't look so glum, Mac, a cheery smile for our hosts."

Colonel Sam McLaughlin walked around to the passenger side of the car and opened the door for Stedman. "Welcome Colonel Stedman, Sam McLaughlin. I'm so pleased to meet you. This is my wife, Adelaide."

"A pleasure. Roger, please."

"Good, Roger, Sam and Adelaide, it is.

"Mac, nice to see you again, it's been a while. You're still taking good care of black beauty?" Colonel Sam inquired. "No need to ask, eh?" he added as an afterthought.

"I do my best, thanks, Colonel Sam."

"You know where to park at the side. Jennifer and her staff are dying to see you. I expect there's a reception committee already waiting. Enjoy yourself but I'd keep an eye on that new butler, Paul. I lost twenty to him last week at gin rummy. We'll give you a dingle when the Colonel's ready to leave.

79

"Oh, didn't I tell you about that, dear?" Sam chuckled.

"Adelaide, this is simply magnificent," Stedman enthused.

"Come, this way, Roger. So, what do you think of the place?" Colonel McLaughlin asked, expansively.

"I was just saying to Adelaide, it's absolutely marvellous, Sam... like a grand manor house and with such spectacular grounds!"

"We'll have a seat out here on the terrace and Wilfred will bring us some refreshments. Do you have a preference, Roger?"

"On a day like this, Sam, I'd jolly well fancy a well - frosted glass of your Canadian beer."

"Adelaide, my dear?"

"Iced tea, with lemon, Sam."

"Coming right up, make it two beers, Wilfred; what the hell, a change is as good as a rest, eh, Adelaide? After our beer, Roger, I'll take you for a short tour. I think you'll love the smoking parlour and you must try my hand - rolled Havana cigars. After a few games in the pool room, we'll be ready for our Jennifer's world-famous roast beef with Yorkshire pudding."

"Funny thing that; it must be a national tradition here as well, just like over 'ome" Roger joked.

"Ah, thank you Wilfred; cheers, Roger."

*Parkwood, The Terrrace. Here Colonel Sam McLaughlin entertained
the Commandant of Camp X*

"Cheers, Sam and Adelaide, to your very good health."

Sam, please tell me a bit about Parkwood. I'm sure it has a fascinating history."

"Sure Roger; Adelaide and I had it built in 1915. Since it was a once in a lifetime project, I brought in the finest architects and the best craftsmen in the business. Many of the fellows were European, with a lot of experience in stone masonry, fine carpentry and the like. Adelaide made several trips to France and Italy and picked out nearly all of the carpets and furnishings herself, didn't you dear? We really didn't spare any expense on quality. This would be home for us and our daughters, for the rest of our lives."

"Truth to tell, Roger," Adelaide added, "although it might seem extravagant today, at the going rate for things back then, Sam built it for a song, wouldn't you say, dear?"

Sam nodded in agreement. "We pretty well knew exactly what we wanted before we started, and were able to accomplish our dreams, within our means."

"And, how large is the property?"

"This takes up twelve acres here in north Oshawa. It used to be that we felt like country dwellers, although I dare say that it's getting less so now, what with all of these automobiles."

"That's amusing, Sam. 'What ye sow ...' and all that."

"Yes, my father started the McLaughlin Motor Car Company in 1907 and that was the start of what has become a very successful family enterprise."

81

"And, inside Sam?" queried Roger.

"It has fifty-five rooms, including my personal bowling lane, the indoor pool and a first-rate squash court. Adelaide made certain that there'd be a conservatory and many other little touches to make it homey."

"And how many are on staff, if I may ask, Adelaide?"

"Forty-two in all to manage the household, keep the grounds and look after general maintenance and upkeep. That's not counting the chauffeur and people who take care of Sam's automobiles."

"That's amazing; I can't wait to see it all."

"Well, finish your beer and we'll go take a look! Do you like cars, Roger? Good, we'll have a peek in the garage on the way. Then afterwards, a game or two of snooker, shall we? By the way, are you a fishing type of sportsman?"

"Amateur level, but yes, I suppose I am. Don't tell me you have an indoor fishing pond, as well, Sam?"

"No, not yet," he chuckled. "I do have some property just north of here, around Port Perry. The pond, or lake, or whatever you want to call it, is well stocked with fat rainbows. We feed 'em liver. Colonel Graham and Hamish Findley dearly loved to spend the occasional, lazy Sunday fly-fishing and afterwards, we'd have an outdoor fish fry. We must get those expeditions going again. Finished the beer?"

"Yes. You lead, Sam," Roger replied.

The two men walked through the double doors of the grand entrance leading from the terrace to the living room. As they walked up the stairs that led to the main hallway, Sam noted that Roger had a puzzled look on his face.

"What is it, Roger?"

"I was wondering why these rather large wrought iron gates are here, on the inside of the house? And there, there's another one leading off that room as well."

"Yes, that's the study. The idea behind the gates is so that we can lock them at night and even if someone were to break into the living room off the terrace, they wouldn't be able to get into the house proper.

"Ah, that explains it. That is clever!"

"This way to the billiards room. I think it's my favourite hideout." Roger followed Sam into a dark, ornate wood-panelled chamber, which seemed to be dominated by a massive billiards table. There were double French doors at both entrances. The door closed silently behind them. "We won't be bothered now, ... cigar, Roger?" he asked, holding an open humidor for his inspection. I have them shipped up by a chap in Detroit ... he imports them from Cuba, the finest cigars in the world. Go ahead, they're really quite mild. You see? They're delightful. Adelaide's forever trying to get me to quit but I love them so much. Especially with a dram of straight malt scotch whiskey ... or two!" he laughed. Care for a taste? One finger or two? Choose your weapon, Roger," Sam indicated, as he opened a cupboard to display an array of cues. "Your break.

"I heard that the Camp had a small accident with one of the Jeeps," Sam remarked offhandedly, while chalking the felt tip of his cue. "If I recall, it was Hamish's baby. He must have been devastated when he learned of it."

"Oh, yes, he was, poor sod; he was away when it happened. We had a bit of a celebration last night to welcome both him and Robert Samson back. It was Robert's sixtieth, as well. You should have seen Findlay's face when I broke the news. It was as if he had lost his best mate. A little like me at the moment ... drat, that's two games in a row that you've taken from me, Sam."

"Okay Roger, I'm going to give you a break," Sam smiled. "We'll play

The magnificent Billiards Room where Colonel Sam frequently entertained Camp X officers on Sunday afternoons.

for one wager only and then it's off to dinner. We'll each break, the one who sinks the most balls from their single break wins."

"And the wager is ... for Parkwood, Sam?" Roger asked with a wink.

"Not quite, young fellow, not quite. If I win, you pay me $50.00. If you win, you get what's in the envelope on the sideboard. Deal?"

"You've piqued my interest Colonel. Oh what the hell, deal."

"One more little condition..."

"Oh no, here it comes, I'm afraid."

"You have to open the envelope before you play."

"Very well." Calmly, Roger tore open the envelope and silently scanned the contents. He looked up at Colonel Sam, with an inquisitive grin. "Really, Sam? A brand new, aluminium bodied, General Motors Jeep? I say, double deal! Just one small request, Sam: if I botch it, nothing to be said to the lads at the Camp, I beg you."

"Deal, now go ahead Roger, your break."

Bending over the table to take aim at the cue ball, Roger pulled the stick back and forth slightly several times as if to gain momentum. Then with one decisive whack, he fired the cue ball onto the point ball, scattering the rack. First one ... then two ... three ... and then a fourth ball rolled and sank obediently in three pockets. "Will that do, Sam?" Roger asked, surveying his handiwork.

"Well, I'll be ... in my youth, I'd have said I've been snookered, fair and square, my boy. I can see that you have been having me on all along, Roger," Sam guffawed. "You're not in your trade for nothing! Okay, but it's my turn now. How about another drop of Highland dew for good measure, shall we?"

Sam held his cue stick lightly as he took careful aim, and then fired, scattering the balls. He stood back, watching closely as one ... two ... and then three sank in good order. A fourth ball, on its way back to the pocket nearest Sam, stopped abruptly, at the edge of the pocket mouth. With his cue upright on the carpeting, and holding his cigar outright in the other hand like a conductor's baton, he swayed, as though willing the red ball to drop in. It did not.

"Must be a bit of fluff on the cloth, Colonel," Roger commented casually, in as sporting a manner as he could muster. After an appropriate pause, he added, "I say, the chaps at the Camp, and old Hamish in particular, are going to be quite pleased with the CO's accomplishment!" Roger immediately regretted this 'ungentlemanly' display of smugness.

"And so they should! Congratulations Roger, well done! I'll have your new Jeep dropped off to the Camp first thing tomorrow, Monday morning." Sam had determined that he would never tell Roger that it would have been there, win, or lose.

Just then, Paul knocked and entered the room to announce that dinner was being served. "Mrs. McLaughlin is seated, Colonel."

"Then, let's not keep her waiting; shall we Roger?

"How are you treating Private Mac, Paul?"

"I'm afraid to report that he's well on his way to cleaning out the pantry change jar, Sir. A bit of a sharper, Mac is."

Parkwood Estate's Dining Room, where Colonel Sam and Mrs. McLaughlin hosted many famous guests.

"Well, well, you're admitting you've finally met your match, are you Paul? I must say that neither of our guests are slouches in the games of chance department."

Roger followed Colonel Sam and Paul down the hallway while struggling to regain his composure. He silently vowed to curb the urge to gloat.

"Well gentlemen, I hope that you enjoyed your afternoon. How was the game of billiards, Roger?" Adelaide asked graciously while Paul was seating the men.

"We played three, actually. Sam's a fine player. Overall, very ... rewarding, I must admit, Adelaide." As he unfolded his napkin, he thought that he caught an almost imperceptible exchange of smiles between his hosts at either end of the table.

"Good for you, Roger. It's not often that Sam loses, or so he tells me."

After his second flaming Spanish coffee, Colonel Stedman glanced at his wristwatch, rose, thanked Sam and Adelaide for their warm hospitality and after Colonel Sam had directed Wilfred to have Mac drive the car around to the front entrance, repeated his thanks and particularly thanked Sam for the generous wager.

"Roger, you are very welcome. I know Hamish will be pleased. Come back anytime. You and your men are always welcome at Parkwood. Adelaide and I look forward to the next visit. Let me take you to the car."

Holding open the passenger door for Roger, Sam reached out to press something into Roger's right hand. With that, Mac and Colonel Stedman pulled out onto Simcoe Road for the short ride back to the Camp.

"Have a good time, Mac?"

"Top notch. You, Sir?"

"Yes, very fine." He couldn't resist the next question, knowing where it would lead. "Win anything?" he asked offhandedly.

"As a matter of fact, Colonel, I came away forty-nine dollars and seventy-five cents to the good. You, Sir?"

"Turn on the overhead lamp, would you Mac?" He opened his hand. Folded neatly in half was a small, cream-coloured envelope, bearing an embossed Parkwood crest. He opened it and turned toward the roof light to examine the contents ... two crisp, one hundred dollar bills. Clipped to each was a neat, hand-scripted note: "Welcome back, Hamish! Best regards, Adelaide and Sam." "Welcome back and happy 60th, Robert. Sorry we missed your party. Best regards, Adelaide and Sam."

Roger looked up. "Oh, sorry Mac; yes, I did win ...a Jeep, actually."

Upon returning that evening, Roger Stedman was met by his 2-I-C, Major Blake Grey, who reported that he had taken an urgent call from Robert Brooks at HQ. Brooks had asked that Grey inform Colonel Stedman that the meeting which had been scheduled for 0800, was deferred, for the second time. Slightly puzzled, Stedman thanked Major Grey without comment.

By Monday morning, Camp X had returned to situation normal. Neither Samson nor Findlay betrayed any signs of lasting damage from the weekend revelries. At 0700, Major Findlay was addressing a group of three Yugoslav - Canadian client trainees in the Lecture Hall.

"Good morning, gentlemen. My name is Major Findlay. Today you are fortunate to be going on your first overland training scheme. The staging point is Port Perry, marked here, on the map, with the red circle. Your only equipment will be one standard army compass and pocket utility knives. These will be issued when you're dropped off. The objective is quite simple: to arrive back at the Camp within the time allotted! However, to do this, you may not travel the highways, secondary roads, cow paths, or beaver trails. Instead, you will use the natural contours of the land, and travel by stealth, across country, following the rivers and tributaries that wind their way down to Lake Ontario.

"So far, so good, you say. However, I have used the term 'stealth', gentlemen. This means that you will be to all intents and purposes, invisible. You may not speak to anyone for any reason whatsoever, particularly to ask for directions," he paused, to allow the meaning time to sink in, "and you must stay out of sight. You are expected to use your wits, and initiative, and most importantly, your common sense. Feel free to study the map. Questions? Very well. Be ready to leave in one-half hour, at 0745. Oh, and did I mention, chaps, no breakfast today? The next time that you eat will be either of your own choosing during the outing or when you return to Camp."

Dusko, Viktor, and Danijel had listened to the Major very carefully. They didn't need to ask questions. Major Findlay had explained everything very clearly. Besides, they didn't want the Major to think them slow; they intended to excel in all of the tests and assignments at the Camp. Dusko Zekulic was twenty and his brother Viktor, twenty-two. Danijel Bodanic, their best friend, was ten years older than Dusko. The brothers Zekulic, and Danijel Bodanic had met while working as machinists at a General Electric factory in Toronto before the war, turning out electrical motors. The morning after the Prime Minister declared Canada was at war with Nazi Germany, Danijel told the supervisor that he was quitting G.E. to sign up with the Canadian Army. As a relatively young and fit Yugoslavian-born recruit, who was fluent in Slovenian, Military District 2 forwarded Danijel's completed application forms to BSO Recruitment at HQ.

87

For Robert Brooks, it took less than a one half-hour interview to conclude that Danijel was an ideal candidate. He presented as an intelligent, native-born patriot whose politics and national pride were deeply offended by the presence of fascist invaders on his native soil. His closing comment, "We'll bury the Nazis, Sir," had clinched it for Robert. Robert sent on his file to the RCMP for an extensive background check, including forensic interviews with his family. If all were found to be in order, the Camp Adjutant, Major Brian Jones, would re-interview Danijel and in all likelihood, would then sign him on with SOE.

In the case of Dusko and Viktor, who had followed Danijel's urging to volunteer for service, Brooks found it was more difficult to decide whether they were worth interviewing. The report from the army recruiter stated that, although they spoke Yugoslavian, the brothers were otherwise indistinguishable from most Canadian kids, earning good incomes, with cars, chums, and girlfriends, enjoying Toronto life, while living rent-free at home. Unlike Danijel, they didn't really know, much less understand, or particularly care what was going on in the old country. Both boys had been brought to Canada as infants. Dusko and Viktor had signed up to fight for Canada, their country, but in truth, they were also looking for some excitement.

Robert Brooks decided to vet them informally, if possible. His chance came when he was tipped off by MD2 that the Zekulic boys were regulars at the Canadian Sons of Yugoslavia annual picnic in the city's west end, at Christie Pits. When he arrived, Brooks noted approvingly that the Sons were blessed by the presence of a large number of charming 'Sisters'. Chatting amiably with Dusko and Viktor, while consuming homemade sausages with cabbage rolls swimming in rich tomato sauce, washed down with a half-pitcher of beer and one blinding glass of *Sljovica*, Yugoslavian plum brandy, Robert Brooks excused himself after an hour, before the roasted pig was carved. Driving home, he decided to give the two Zekulic boys a chance.

Not surprisingly, the three Yugoslavs had become even closer at Camp X. Client recruits were prohibited from mingling, much less talking with anyone other than members of their immediate group and their instructors. To enforce this, they trained as a unit, took all of their meals together, and shared the same barracks. Staff carefully monitored group cohesiveness.

"Well guys, it sounds like the Major's laying on a real adventure.

Have either of you heard of Port Perry?" asked Danijel.

"Nope, I haven't," Dusko shook his head.

"Yes you have!" Viktor insisted. "Remember Dad's pal, old Kosta, took us ice fishing on Lake Scugog one February, when we were really little. You almost fell in the hole, Dusko!"

"Oh, yeah, now I do! Here, look guys ... it's this small town at the south end of the lake. This ought to be a breeze. It shows the roads leading in and out of Port Perry."

"Okay, genius, but, we can't take the roads. We have to follow the rivers or travel through the woods, remember?" Danijel stated.

"You're right, Danny, this will be interesting. I had forgotten that part," Viktor said.

"Seven forty-five and time, gentlemen!" Hamish announced, re-entering the Lecture Hall. He had been at the garage, trying to convince the chief mechanic, Gus, to loan him the guards' jeep.

"Without papers, not on your bloody life, pardon the English, Major Findlay, Sir. It's the station wagon or nothing, Major!" Gus stated adamantly.

"I hate that bloody thing, Gus! How can you train clients in a wooden bleeding station wagon, tell me that?" Hamish countered.

Gus wiped his ham-sized hands on a greasy red wiping rag and shrugged. "I tried everythin' to haul old Betsey out of the muck, Major. For you, I would have dove personally and hauled her out with my bare hands, but the drop off there's a killer."

Hamish started to laugh at the image. "That I'm sure of, Gus. By the by, who deep-sixed her?"

Gus turned toward his tool chest, muttering, when a horn sounded outside the garage door. "Another happy customer. Hold your horses, mate! I'll be back in a jiff, Major," he remarked, as he tossed the blackened rag into an empty oil drum. "Major Findlay, come out here, right away, Sir!"

SILVER DAGGER

Hamish stared, speechless. Seated at the wheel of an army camouflage green and brown jeep was Colonel Stedman. "Care to go for a spin, Hamish?"

"Where'd that beauty come from, Colonel? It looks...new."

"It is ... straight off the assembly line in Oshawa last Thursday, old boy. It's a present, from your old chum, Colonel Sam."

"For me? Really?"

"Yes, for you. We made a wager over billiards yesterday at Parkwood, and I won it! Come along, hop in; I want to show you how the four-wheel lockup lever works before you head out on a cross-country bash with your clients."

One year before, Hamish had first laid eyes on a battered hulk rusting behind the shop, which Gus had written off as 'Boer War surplus', using it to scavenge for parts. Hamish had fallen in love. He and a fellow car buff, Major Michael Heaviside, the Small Arms Instructor, persuaded Gus to help them put it in running order. For several Sunday afternoons, they tinkered and puttered and eventually restored it to life. Ever since, Hamish had claimed exclusive proprietorship.

"Gentlemen, what you see here is a Jeep ... a prototype at that! Four wheel drive. Have you ever been in a Jeep before?"

"Can't say that I have, Major," Dusko replied. "It looks new!"

"You are correct and we're going to run her in, very carefully!"

"Run her in, Sir?" asked Viktor.

"You know, break her in, like a new car," Danijel asserted.

"I dunno, Pop never had a new one," added Viktor.

"Danijel you're in the front with me. Viktor, Dusko, hop in the back and hang on!" Hamish drove up Thornton Road to Highway # 2, where he turned left. As he accelerated, he looked to the left at Barney's service station, now closed, but with the ever-present Army truck out front. He waved to the guards who waved back. Hamish drove at a moderate speed until he reached Pickering and turned north on Cedar Glen Road. They drove for a couple of miles past farm fields speckled with livestock. "Fellows, see that park on the left just ahead?" Hamish shouted.

"Yes, the sign says Cedar Glen Park," Danijel answered.

Hamish pulled over and stopped. "Bang on ... great spot, what? I found it by accident last year when I was bashing around. It has a small stream meandering through the middle called Duffin's Creek. You couldn't believe the rainbow trout in it. There are deep well-shaded holes where the trout like to lie and wait for a worm to fall in from the bank. Often, that worm was on the end of my fishing line. Up in Scotland, many's the time the gillie tried to show me how to take one by tickling the belly.

"Trout ... tickling, Major?" asked Danijel.

"You see, the gillie's a professional hunting and fishing guide and it's part of the job requirements. When I need to get away from the Camp, I come here and hike upstream to a quiet bend in the river and set up camp: a small tent, a campfire and my frying pan, that's all that I need," Hamish reflected. "I might bring you chaps with me, on a Sunday afternoon, if you'd like," he remarked, engaging low gear.

As they drove on, Dusko turned to Viktor, "Do you have any idea of where we are?"

"Not a clue. I thought that we shoulda turned east at the highway. Instead, we went west. He's lost me now."

"Part of the exercise, gentlemen. All will become clear soon," Hamish proclaimed, with a smile of satisfaction. Once again, he had been able to pull the wool over the eyes of a group of clients.

The Jeep continued on, turning right at what appeared to be a main highway, and then left onto another well-traveled road. They drove up a steep hill and as they came over the ridge, they saw a magnificent view. Beyond a stand of thick of maples and birches lay gently rolling hills dotted with farms. Then, appearing out of nowhere, was a lake nestled in the breast of the hills.

"Now I know where we are!" exclaimed Viktor, excitedly. "That's Lake Scugog, Dusko!"

"Beautiful! Looks like home!" Danijel commented.

"Right you are, lads, Lake Scugog. So, this means that you won't have any trouble finding your way back then?"

"I have a pretty good idea," Viktor stated confidently.

"We'll be okay, Major," Danijel added. "You won't forget you promised us compasses?"

92   "One compass, Danijel, but you each get a pocket knife. We're almost at the drop off point." Three minutes later, Hamish pulled over to the roadside and stopped, just north of Port Perry. The three men jumped out of the Jeep. "Danijel, here's the compass. Take a knife, men. Let's see how well you listened to your instructors. It's 0855. You're due back by supper. Five hours fifty-two minutes is the record. I'm heading into Port Perry to the White Kitchen Restaurant for the best peameal bacon and egg breakfast in Canada. See you at Camp. Cheerio! Good luck!" Hamish called out as he drove away.

"Don't worry about that, it's all part of the psychological training. Well, I know one thing for damn sure. That way is south," Dusko said, pointing in the direction from which they had come.

Danijel held the compass while he took their bearings. "Let's see,

Lake Scugog seen from Simcoe Street, Port Perry.

yes, it's actually southeast, so we'll have to make a small adjustment. Which way do you want to go? Towards the water or take a chance on finding a river west of here? We'll need to head that way sooner or later."

The men walked until they reached the lake and turned due south. It was extremely quiet with only loons and a few fishermen out on Lake Scugog.

"How long do you think it will take us to walk back to the Camp, Danny?"

Well, Viktor, I'd guess that if we keep up a good clip and don't stop for too long we should be back by early afternoon."

"That might be pushing it, Danny. I'd be happy to be back by dinnertime," Dusko replied.

"Are you getting hungry already, Dusko?"

"Now that you mention it. Peameal bacon and eggs ..."

"Wait until we get further south, brother," said Viktor. "I think I saw a river marked on the top map, at the south end of the lake. We'll follow that down, okay?"

The men found the point at which the lake ended, forcing them to cross boggy fields and climb up and over several small hills. At length, they spotted a small creek, which appeared to be fed by a burbling underground artesian spring. They stopped for a drink of the cold water then continued. Soon the creek turned into a stream, and then became a river. They made good time as they walked along the bank, following a path made by fishermen.

"Come on guys, it's okay. He said cow paths or beaver trails," Viktor commented, laughing.

"Ya, how would he know anyway?" added Dusko.

Every half hour they stopped to check their compass.

"So, how're we doing, Danny?"

"Perfect, but we'll have to check more often. This river is starting to wind a lot and could take us way off course. Keep going. But keep quiet. The Major said stealth, remember? There could be someone around."

They continued in silence, enjoying the clean air, birds' songs, and plentiful signs of wildlife.

"Hey," Dusko whispered. "I swear I just saw a deer."

"Ya, sure," Viktor scoffed.

"I saw it, a White Tail buck," Daniejl whispered back. "Sssh!"

"Maybe the Major's gillie guy could have caught it with his bare hands!" Viktor guffawed.

"Shut up, Viktor!" Dusko hissed. They trudged on in silence for five minutes.

"Viktor, what time is it?"

"Twelve forty-five, Dusko. What's the matter, little brother, lose your watch?"

"No, I'm just getting really hungry."

"Well, you know what berries and leaves you can and can't eat. Let's get off the trail, stop for ten minutes and find some food," Danijel suggested.

"I was thinking of something more filling, like maybe a chicken. There was a farm up on the ridge about a quarter of a mile back. Let's go see if there's anything worth eating. It's worth a try. What do you say, Viktor, Danijel?"

"Sure, you two go up to the farm. I'll stay here and start a fire just in case you get lucky," Danijel noted as he knelt down to gather twigs and dry leaves.

"Oh, you mean the farmer's daughter, Danny?" Viktor asked innocently.

"Fat chance! Get going you big lunk and don't get caught. Farms have noisy dogs, geese, turkeys and chickens don't forget... and don't hang around grandstanding. Go!" he whispered softly.

Site of the Yugoslav agents' 'chicken caper.'

Viktor and Dusko started to make their way up the hill toward the barn, assuming their best secret agent techniques, crawling flat on the ground toward the barn, stopping every few seconds to make sure that they weren't being observed. As Dusko reached the barn door, he slowly rose into a crouching position. Looking back slightly toward Viktor, he waited for an all clear. Assuming that the farmer would be in the house having his midday meal, Viktor signalled Dusko to go ahead.

Gingerly, Dusko reached out, unlatched the door, and crept inside the barn. In the shafts of dim light, he could see machinery, implements, horse and cow stalls with straw bales strewn everywhere, but not a sign of chickens. He walked to the end of the barn and cautiously opened the door.

'Ah there it is, the chicken coop! And it's hidden from the house!" Dusko ran back through the barn and opened the barn door slightly.

He gave a low whistle. "Hey, Viktor, the chicken coup is on the other side of the barn, there!" he pointed, for emphasis. "Stay here and watch for the farmer. I'll go get the chickens. Give me five minutes, then head back. As soon as I have them, I'll head straight back to the river. See you there!"

Dusko loped back to the far end of the barn and out the door. Sure that he couldn't be seen, he walked into the chicken coup. "Damn!" he exclaimed, "low ceiling! Ugh, what a stench! Christ, do you have to make so much noise? I guess they're laying, so now what do I do?"

Dusko looked down on the floor and saw a tin pan brimming over with what he presumed to be chicken feed. He scooped up the pan, scattered the seed onto the floor, and walked over slowly to the roost and set down the pan. Gently lifting a large brown and white hen, he was delighted to see three extra large white eggs lying in the straw. He raised her higher, as if searching for the source of his good fortune. She protested, very shrilly. "Shhh, shhh, okay, okay... I'll have to move fast."

Tucking the outraged hen under his left arm, he grabbed the eggs with one hand, set them in the pan, replaced the chicken, and moved on to the next chicken, and then the next. The mounting cacophony of the distressed hens was unnerving Dusko. However, he wasn't finished. Within seconds, he had filled the tin pan with eggs. He figured that eggs were a bonus; he had only promised to bring back a chicken. Two half-filled sacks labelled *Doctor Wilson's Natural Grain Chicken Feed* leaned against the wall. He picked up one sack and poured out its contents. Then he grabbed the other sack and did the same. He carefully placed the eggs in one sack along with the tin pan. Quickly grabbing a fat rooster, he stuffed it into the other sack, hoping that the chicken would make less noise if it couldn't see. He thought he had read that somewhere.

He opened the door and looked around, then dashed across the open field, over the hill and down toward the river, holding the sacks above the ground. Once at the river, he ran along the path until he encountered Viktor and Danijel.

"Mission accomplished boys!" Dusko exclaimed. "Not only a chicken but eight fresh eggs! I even stole a tin pan to fry the eggs!"

"Good work, little brother. I didn't know that we had chicken thieves in the Zekulic family tree! Just joking, let me see them, Dusko! Wow!"

"You're going to make a fine secret agent, Dusko!" Danijel exclaimed, patting him on the arm.

"Nice fire, Danijel. Viktor, you kill the chicken and pluck it and I'll cut some sharp sticks to cook the chicken pieces over the fire. Bring a piece of fat for frying the eggs, too, okay?"

Within ten minutes, the men were enjoying fresh fried eggs while the pieces of chicken slowly roasted over the fire. "Boy, this is amazing," said Dusko. I've always wanted to do this. And to think Major Findlay was worried about whether or not we would know what berries and leaves were good for us to eat and which ones were poisonous."

"Chicken's ready!" Danijel announced. "Dusko, the first piece is yours."

They gorged themselves on the cooked chicken. Danijel broke the silence. "This chicken is so tender, absolutely wonderful. I would have never believed this could be possible."

97

"Yes, you're right. Nothing went to waste and now I'm fit to travel quickly back to the Camp. Are you ready, fellows?" asked Viktor.

"We'll be off as soon as we put out the fire and bury the bones, chicken guts and eggshells," Danijel replied. "Viktor, take the pan and get some water from the river." The three resumed their journey, moving quickly, stopping at ten-minute intervals to check the compass.

"Stop here. It's 1500 hours. I figure that we could only be a few miles from Lake Ontario," Danijel stated. "Did you notice that we're seeing more and more farms, as we get closer to the lake? I think we should split up: one to the left and one to the right. I'll go on straight. Does that make sense? Okay, we should stay at least half a mile apart. Head straight for the lake and then go west. The Camp should be no more than a few miles along."

"See you back at the Camp, Danny," Viktor shouted, waving.

"If you're lucky!"

The White Kitchen Restaurant was bustling. As Hamish looked about for a table, he noted approvingly that nothing had changed, particularly the spotless white décor with an occasional stripe and dash of black trim, for which it had been named. Because all of the tables were occupied, Hamish sat on a black leather counter stool to wait for the waitress to take his order. Although he hadn't eaten here for months, he didn't need a menu to know what he wanted.

"Hi Scottie, where ya been?"

"Hello, Marge, good to see you're still here! Busy, just busy, you know how it is. No rest for the wicked."

"You're tellin' me. Look around this place. What's your pleasure ... the usual? Four slices peameal bacon, two eggs, sunny side up and toast, well done two sides, but not burnt, hold the butter." She scribbled waitress shorthand briefly and then paused, her pencil poised. "With marmalade, right, Hamish?"

"Yes, that's right, marmalade, thanks, Marge," he replied smiling, "and tea, if you please. How are you and Walter keeping?"

"We're well, thanks, Hamish. He's out in the back doing the books. I'll let him know that you're here. Water, serviette, knife, fork, spoon, there you go. Back in two shakes, dear!"

Hamish watched in fascination as the shift boss cook reached up with one hand to examine the procession of order slips suspended on metal clips, while with the other hand, pushed heaping plates of steam-ing food across the white tile ledge and announced the contents in short - order code, which Hamish thought as impenetrable as Assyrian.

The White Kitchen Restaurant, Port Perry, Ontario

"Army?"

"Excuse me?"

"Are you Canadian Army?"

Hamish swivelled slightly to the right to look at his neighbour whom he had not noticed when he had sat down. "Yes, in a way, I am."

"Me too." Signals, Corporal, Kingston. Name's Burton, Burton Johnson. I prefer Burt."

"Hamish. Camp Borden, we're here on manoeuvres, Burt," Hamish replied as they shook hands.

"Uh huh. Just completed a three-dayer myself at Gagetown, N.B last week. You must be here often, eh?"

"Oh, why do you say that?"

"Marge knows her regulars."

"Off and on, not for a few months," Hamish replied offhandedly, impressed with Burton Johnson's mental acuity. "So what are you doing here so far away from Kingston, Burt?"

"Forty-eight hour leave. Celebration, I guess. Completed the training. Visiting my folks for a little bit of business, personal things, ... on the island ... you know the island? ... Scugog?"

"I've been over there ... once, I think. Mainly Mississauga Reserve land, good fishing and camping!"

"Yeah, pretty good. We get by okay, could do better. Are you an officer, Hamish?"

"Afraid so, ... a Major, ... you said, 'we' ... so you're a native?"

"Thought so, Sir. Me? I'm a native, Mississauga. I used to be Council Chief of the Band. That is before I joined the army. It's a long story."

"Really! I'm honoured, Burt. You look too young ... to be a Chief, I mean."

"It's hereditary, so when your time comes, it comes, Major," he replied with a disarming smile. "Better grab it then 'cause if you don't, you're failing your elders and tribal duty and I bet you can guess that's not a good thing."

"Are you two guys going to eat your breakfasts or am I going to have to force feed you?" Marge demanded with mock annoyance, her arms folded.

"Yes, mother," Burt replied with a wink at Hamish. "Got any more ketchup, Margie? I've been slammin' the bottom of this one so hard, my keying hand's like raw hamburger. See?"

She sighed, shaking her head in exasperation with the helplessness of the male species, and called into the kitchen for an immediate shipment of ketchup reserves.

As they ate, and chatted, Hamish was fascinated to learn that many of Burton's Band were in the Royal Canadian Corps of Signals. "That's amazing! Any idea why?"

"Just something we seem to take to, Major. It's a language, so learning Morse was dead easy for me."

"Do you speak any native languages ... other than your own, Burton?"

"Mine's Ojibwa. I can get by in Iroquoian, Algonkian, Cherokee."

"Cherokee? I think I remember reading as a youngster ... aren't the Cherokee in Oklahoma?"

"Scattered like wheat grains on the fall wind. But yes, there's a large population there, Sir."

"May I ask how you learned it, Corporal?"

"Ever work on a wildcat oil drillin' crew, Major? You learn the language damn quick if you want to survive. It's a heck of rough way to earn a living, but the money's fantastic, if you can keep up. Twelve to fifteen hour days and if you get careless and don't pay attention to what the crew boss is yellin', you're likely as not to get your arm torn off, and it's goodbye. You're out in the middle of nowhere, hospital's a hundred miles away, if you're lucky. Oh, I learned Cherokee real quick," he laughed. "Me? I only lost half a finger, see? That's nothing!"

Hamish looked at Burton 's outstretched left hand. It was missing the third joint of the little finger. He looked at his watch. "I am going to buy your breakfast, Corporal and then I must scoot."

"Marge, may I please have one bill for Corporal Johnson and me?"

"Burt, it has been a real pleasure. I'd love to talk with you again. Enjoy your visit at home."

Hamish boarded his Jeep; the engine turned over smartly and started on the first try. 'Now to search out and see how the three musketeers are faring.'

Hamish parked, dismounted from his Jeep, walked up the steps to the veranda, and knocked on the screen door.

"Yes, Sir, can I help you?"

He removed his tartan cap and announced, "Good afternoon, madam. I do hope I'm not disturbing you. My name is Hamish; I'm a Major with the Army. May I come inside?"

"Please do, Major. Excuse my appearance; I was just making bread. Messy thing it is kneading the dough."

"Ah, yes, I was just about to ask what that heavenly aroma was. Madam, is there a man of the house whom I could speak with?" asked Hamish.

"Yes, Wilfred is in the barn if you would care to walk around. Just go right on in. My name is Judith by the way."

"Pleased to meet you, Judith. I can find my way, thanks, I'm sure."

Wilfred was coming out of the barn as Hamish rounded the corner. "Hello there. Can I help you?"

"Hamish, Sir."

"Wilfred Grasby, Hamish. Folks call me Wilf."

"How do you do, Wilf? I was just talking with your good wife..."

"Yes?"

"Wilf, I'm a Major with the Army. Two of my men paid you a visit this afternoon, did you know?"

"No, I don't recall anyone coming around, exactly," replied Wilfred, scratching his arm.

"No, you wouldn't have seen them. I suspect that they might have taken one of your chickens. Could we have a look?" asked Hamish.

"Sure thing, follow me. But what would the Army want with my chickens?"

As the two men walked toward the chicken coup, Wilf suddenly broke into a run and opened the door. "They's been upset by something in the last hour, Hamish. Listen to the rascals. Right skittish they are. Oh, lordy lordy, look at that mess. Feed all over the place! Maybe those dratted raccoons broke in again! Pests! I put up new wire caging, but..."

"Wilf, I assure you these were two-footed vandals. Notice anything else unusual?"

"Well, yes, I see that one of my prize roosters, Billy Boy, is missing from that empty nest and ... wait a minute!" Wilfred lifted some of the hens and noticed that their eggs were missing. "Their feed pan is gone too. What's this all about, Hamish?" asked an increasingly hostile Wilfred.

"Might we go back to the house and I'll explain it?"

Judith was waiting on the veranda with tea, freshly baked bread, and homemade raspberry jam. "So what brings you here, Hamish?" she inquired after serving him.

"Hamish was just telling me that a couple of his men were here earlier and for some reason stole one of our chickens and some eggs," Wilf interjected.

"My heavens! Whatever for? They might have asked. We'd have given them to them."

"Wilfred, Judith, on behalf of the army, my sincere apology. I feel very foolish, however, here's what happened. We're down here from

Camp Borden where these lads are taking basic training. They're being taught how to survive, live off the land, as a part of their soldier's instruction. Thus, they will be able to survive in the wilds in case they find themselves separated from their group. Nevertheless, here's what you want to know: do not worry, they will not be returning. I guarantee that," Hamish stated flatly.

"Oh, I see. And they just happened to pick our farm?"

"That's right Wilfred. Fortunes of war ... again, I apologise deeply and the Army is prepared to set things right. I am authorized to give you one hundred dollars in compensation. Please accept it. I hope that this unfortunate situation could stay between us, if that's alright with you both?" he asked in a confidential manner. "Loose lips etcetera?"

"Oh, certainly Hamish and that's very generous of the Army. My chickens are easily replaced, the eggs too, for that matter ..." Wilf added reassuringly.

"Billy Boy was something special, wasn't he, Wilf? Like a pet; he'd follow Wilf around the yard, strutting and crowing like the king of the ..." She stopped, overcome.

"Judith, I' m so sorry about Billy Boy. What can I do to make up for...?"

"Judith dear, he was getting old and crotchety, you said so yourself. Say, Judith, why don't you go to the pantry and get Hamish a couple dozen eggs? Make them extra large, Jude!"

"That's not necessary, Wilfred. I've enjoyed the tea and refreshments..."

"Nonsense, it's the least that we can do considering your generosity."

She returned, smiling and handed him the containers of eggs. "Excuse me for being such a sentimental old lady. Here, now you take these back to Camp Borden and give your men, our boys, really, a treat on us. Besides, you're doing us a favour ... we can't eat 'em all fast enough. Even after we've had a good day at the farmer's market, we have them six ways from Sunday: omelettes, scrambled, fried, boiled, poached, egg sandwiches, salads, devilled ...

"Not to mention the dozens that goes into Judith's baking! It's a

103

wonder we're not sittin' here, cacklin'!"

"Alright then," Hamish replied, with a grin, "I'll do that and thanks so much for being very understanding. I hope to see you again."

"Hamish, you are welcome anytime. We've enjoyed your company. Come back and drop in on us, anytime."

"I will do that, cheerio." Hamish walked down the veranda steps with three cartons of extra-large, Grade A eggs tucked carefully under his right arm. He honked as he pulled out of the laneway. 'Silly buggers those three... whatever made them think they'd get away with it?"

Danijel trudged along the shoreline, trying not to stumble over the large pebbles that lay in wait to twist his ankles at 0700 every morning. He knew that he was quite close to Camp, as the bluffs were getting higher. As he got to the perimeter of the Camp property, a guard who had been on beach patrol met him.

"Where do you think you're going?" the guard asked.

"25-1-1," Danijel replied.

"Okay, I'll walk you up to the CO's office where you'll have to check in."

Just then, another Guard drove up in a Jeep.

"What's up, Mac?"

"One of the clients, I'm going to take him up to the office for verifyin', Doug."

"Take the Jeep. I'll take over your patrol until you get back. What time are you due off?"

"1800 hours. Thanks, Doug. I shouldn't be long."

Mac drove Danijel up to the Lecture Hall where he and Danijel got out and went inside. Hamish Findlay was reading his new Jeep's service manual, with his chair back tilted against the wall. "Private, a captive?" he inquired, putting down the booklet.

"Major Findlay, I found this client strollin' on the beach."

Camp-X from Corbett Creek

"Very good Private, just leave him with me and thank you. There will be two more coming in shortly," Hamish remarked with a smile.

"I'll watch out for them, Sir," Mac declared firmly as he turned and walked out of the building.

"Danijel, how are you? How did you make out? You're the first one back and in good time, I might add. Stand easy ... here, sit down."

"Thank you, Sir, we split up just north of Oshawa. I came straight down, more or less."

"We'll just wait for the others. I want to conduct the interview with all three of you boys."

Mac drove back down to the beach where Doug was waiting for him.

"The Major says that you should stay with me a while longer, 'cause two more are due sometime. Jump in and we'll take turns watchin' and snoozin'. I go first," Mac sighed happily, as he loosened his shirt collar, then, closing his eyes, he surrendered to the mid-afternoon sun.

"Mac, wake up!"

"What?"

Without replying, Doug vaulted over the side of the Jeep. "Halt!

State your business here!" he demanded, his right hand resting on his holster.

"25-1-1," replied Dusko, followed by Viktor.

"A good start! Okay fellows, jump in the Jeep," a revived Mac ordered. "Doug, do you want to take them up to the Lecture Hall and I'll continue on duty here?"

"Sure, Private," he winked. "See you in the mess later on."

Viktor and Dusko entered the Lecture Hall. "When did you get here, Danijel?"

"'Bout a half an hour ago. You must have been just behind me."

"Gentlemen, I'll bet you're famished. Should we go eat first and then start the debriefing?" asked Hamish.

"Sir, I don't know about the others but I'm not all that hungry right now. The usual mealtime of 1800 hours is fine for me," Dusko answered modestly.

"Same for me!" "And me too!" Danijel and Viktor echoed.

"Very well then gentlemen, let's get started. First, how is it that you're not hungry? Anyone?"

"Well, Sir, we managed to free up a chicken and some eggs," Danijel volunteered.

"From a farm...Sir, Major," Dusko added, shakily.

"I know, I've already paid the farmer for his losses," Hamish stated sternly.

Danijel glanced sideways at Dusko and then stared at the floor. He knew enough not to ask Hamish how he knew about the chicken caper. He hoped that Viktor would know enough to keep quiet, also.

"There isn't a problem is there, Sir?" Viktor queried.

"Should there be? The farmer and his wife seemed very nice people and took it well. I would like to commend you on your ingenuity. And how was the chicken?" Hamish continued.

"Excellent Sir, we ate every bit of it."

"Well, gentlemen, unfortunately your excellent chicken was the Grasby's pet rooster. Not too tough, old Billy Boy? However, I believe that issue has been laid to rest, but I wouldn't advise dropping in on the Grasby's to chitchat for quite a while. Viktor, Dusko, and Danijel, you do lose major points for not realizing that you were being followed. What if that were the Gestapo, lads?"

Dusko spoke up, "Actually Sir, Danny and I were aware of it when we were following the creek. At first, we thought it was a white tail...."

"And you were on the pathway ... but never mind. You've passed the scheme with honours, second-class overall, which means you've done jolly well. And, you'll be happy to know, you shan't have to do it again. Gentlemen, you are dismissed. There's oodles of time for a shower and a nap or whatever takes your fancy. Carry on."

Danijel, getting up to leave, paused and turned to Hamish. "So sorry about Billy Boy, Major, and thanks a million for straightening things out with Grasby's. But Sir, I have to tell you, that was one of the most delicious meals I've had since I got here! No offence meant to Cook Fred, Major."

"He'll never hear it from me. Very well, Danijel, but you boys just wait 'til you try my secret Highland recipe for pan-fried trout! Next Sunday, 1300h: be waiting at the gate."

SHINING OATH

Sunday, 2 August 1942, rest day at STS 103, and a good thing, Erik reflected. It was shaping up to be a typical southern Ontario dog day: an oppressively humid 88 degrees F and rising, at 0830. Erik Williamson never tired of the panorama. From the Commandant's office window in the rear of the Lecture Hall, he could see that the campus was almost deserted, except for Robert Samson, in his faded blue and red Royal Marines shorts, walking off a two-mile run on the gravel pathway. In the distance, two clusters of Yugoslav clients, wearing army-issue khaki shorts, kicked soccer balls, or sprawled on the grass, their exercise shirts flung over their foreheads as makeshift sun shields.

Erik Williamson, *Stalwart*, took immense pride in the existence of Camp X. He and his closest associates, fronted by his Canadian deputy, Robert Brooks, had overcome bureaucratic interference and red tape by personally finagling and financing the land assembly and purchase of the two-hundred seventy-five acres of prime lakefront agricultural property. Employing private architectural and construction firms, 'the farm' was designed and built in record time, without a cent of government support, or, as Erik reminded himself, knowledge. He smiled as he looked in the middle distance where he could see his *Silvia*, Major Rebeccah Weiss, with her husband, Captain Hugh Mason, pushing a young child on a tire swing suspended from the limb of one of several majestic, century - old chestnut trees.

Although his schedule permitted little more than an occasional drop-by, Erik always came away from Camp X with his optimism renewed, by these vigorous, and dedicated young Canadians and Americans. For a moment, he longed for the days when, as idealistic university students, he, and Robert Brooks had actually believed that the world was destined to drift in a perpetual state of peace. That myth was shattered in the year of their graduation, 1914. Today, the world seemed to have tipped over the edge. It was his purpose this morning to begin to redress the balance, but with words.

Betty Robertson, Commandant Stedman's Secretary, who had come in willingly on her day off, was at her desk on the phone speaking calmly with Cook Fred, reinforcing that his kitchen staff deliver the tray of fresh fruit and croissants, as well as thermal containers of fruit juices, ice water, coffee and tea, no later than 0845, as promised. Erik had come to admire Betty's efficiency and was so impressed by and confident of her loyalty and discretion, that he had specifically requested that she be present, to take the minutes. Only one other special assistant in BSO commanded a higher degree of Erik's trust and respect – Miss Mary Ward - but she was now at HQ, New York.

As Erik was about to turn away, he saw a familiar face at the wheel of a jeep, turning onto the gravel roadway leading to the parking area. "Say, Roger, what's that vehicle that Hamish is driving?"

"A jeep, Erik."

"Yes, but it looks new. I thought you told me that his was demolished or some such thing while he was in British Columbia?"

Colonel Stedman joined Erik at the window. "You're quite right, Erik. Michael Heaviside and John Beck lost it over the bluffs. Needless to say, we're keeping mum about the details."

"And this one?"

"Through the kindness of Colonel Sam...."

"Colonel Stedman's much too modest to admit that he won it playing pool at Parkwood, Mr. Williamson," Betty contributed.

"Billiards, actually, Betty," he corrected her gently. "I say, is the food coming? It's nearly 08:55!"

"I'm truly impressed Roger. That's a superb accomplishment, considering that if it were an Olympic event, Sam would be our team captain," he commented, chuckling. "And how are Colonel Sam and Adelaide keeping?"

"Oh, very well. They asked that I pass along their best wishes.

"There's Fred coming to the side door, now, Betty. While you're in there, would you mind checking with Robert Brooks that he's finished setting up the room?" Roger fretted.

"I say, it looks as though Hamish is planning on doing some fishing today, Erik." Four fishing rods stood upright behind the rear seat of the

Jeep, like whip antennae.

"Here come the others now," Erik commented. "Shall we get under-way?"

The meeting, which had been called for 0900, began at 0903 in the Lecture Hall. Despite the stifling heat, Erik wore a conservative, hand tailored, dark blue, three-piece suit. "Major Weiss, gentlemen, good morning. Thank you for being here; I believe you all know Robert Brooks. This is his newly appointed assistant, Mr. Derek Wainscott. Let me begin by assuring you that I am mindful that Sundays are your day off. Robert assured me on the drive here that I could promise you that we will have completed our business by eleven o'clock, correct, Robert? You can see that Mr. Brooks is nodding in agreement. We will hold Mr. Brooks responsible for keeping a vigilant eye on the proceedings.

"Some of you may be wondering why I have called you together. There is a matter of the utmost urgency, which we must address. I apol-ogize for the frequent postponements and last minute delays, but in truth, recent events have added fresh urgency to our agenda. We are about to embark on an undertaking that will have far-reaching implica-tions for each of us, as well as for Camp X, for Canada, our Allies, and indeed for the final outcome of the war itself. You are already aware of Prime Minister Churchill's recent decision to remount a strategy to remove Adolf Hitler as a factor in our prosecution of this war. Colonel Stedman has briefed both Robert Samson and Hamish Findlay, to that effect, thank you. With the close co-operation of Special Operations Executive, British Security Operation will co-ordinate and direct the planning and execution of the enterprise.

"Let me state once more, emphatically: *Mission Tent Peg* was neither a failure nor a dress rehearsal. Rather, it is regarded as a piece of incredible complexity and sophistication, which demonstrated beyond any doubt, our ability to deliver a bold, co-ordinated strike against the heart of the Greater Reich, from within, at a time and place of our choos-ing. It was a remarkable achievement both in the compass and the scope of its daring. The volumes of intelligence and insights which we have gained from that undertaking, have been analyzed, studied, picked apart, re-evaluated, and the relevant strands carefully woven into the fabric of *Mission Shining Oath*. I think you will be pleased to learn that, political considerations aside, which, thankfully, are left to The PM and his advisors, this action has been sanctioned at the highest levels among our Allies, most notably Washington, Major Harris.

"But to get on with it, the planning of *Mission Shining Oath* is now finalized. I'm pleased to call upon Robert and Derek to present the specifics of the Training Phase ...Robert?"

"Thank you, Erik.

"Derek, if you would be good enough to move the chart stand a little closer, we can begin, thanks." *111*

Sixty minutes later, *Shining Oath* had been transformed from theoretical to operational.

"Thank you, Robert. I see that it's 1017. We'll take a brief recess and reconvene at 1030h, please," Erik announced and then joined Hamish, Robert Samson, Rebeccah, Hugh, and Jack Harris at the serving table. "Welcome back Robert, Hamish. Tell me Hamish, how does it feel to be not only Mission Chief, and, the owner of a new Jeep?"

"Unbelievable, Sir. I'm honoured by the first and overjoyed by the second, or perhaps the other way about. My only problem will be to decide in whose hands I can entrust *Billy Boy* ... I mean the Jeep, Sir, when we go over."

"You can trust me, Hamish," Hugh piped up.

"Or me!" Rebeccah offered brightly.

"Thanks you two, but on sober second thought, I think it best if I have Gus garage it, up on wooden blocks. And I'm taking the ignition key along with me to Berchtesgaden! Not that I don't trust you blighters; would you, Mr. Williamson?" Hamish asked, grinning slyly.

"Excuse me," Erik replied, jovially. "At this particular moment, discretion is truly the better part of valour. Derek, could you call the group back together?"

Erik continued, "We will try to answer as many of your questions as possible. But first, I must state the obvious, that given the critical nature of our assignment's timelines as Robert has laid them out, this is but one of countless sessions to follow. I know that I can rely upon each one of you as professionals to be prepared to give Major Findlay and Colonel Stedman your fullest co-operation in all matters, at a moment's notice, and I do mean that to be taken literally. Colonel Stedman, Major Findlay and Robert Brooks will now field your questions."

"Captain Jack Harris, ... my question is for Major Findlay ... Major, I understand and fully accept the risks, as they were described this morning, as well as by Mr. Williamson earlier. Can you offer an opinion or an educated guess, Major, as to what might be the ... the level of expectation, on the part of German Intelligence, that something of this nature might be about to be pulled, that is, attempted, again?"

"Thanks, Captain, a first rate question, but at this point, I'm not yet privy to that information. Perhaps Mr. Brooks or Mr. Wainscott could answer."

"Thanks, Hamish. Derek Wainscott, ... in a word, Captain Harris: yes. We have recently come into very strong evidence to confirm your hypothesis. Does this mean that we're only play-acting, having you on, building you up for the mission that never will be? No. Will that suffice, for now?"

"Captain Hugh Mason, ... given the strict requirements for secrecy, as well as the intensive schedule for training within a relatively short time frame, my question is this: will we be expected to continue with our current assignments at the same time as the project is being geared up?"

"Another short answer: no, Captain," Erik responded "I have made arrangements through our SOE liaison people to bring in backup personnel. These instructors are top calibre, special training school veterans. The learning curve should be almost flat. My expectation is that Colonel Stedman will have these replacements up and running by mid-week."

"Major Rebeccah Weiss, ... Colonel Stedman, I'm not quite clear on the distinction between your role and Major Findlay's. Could you please clarify that, Sir?"

"Yes, Major Findlay is the mission commander with full responsibility for preparation, training and prosecution of the mission. My role is to co-ordinate every aspect of the various support staff functions, as well as liaison with SOE, BSO, ABSIS, and MD2. Robert and Derek will supply intelligence through BSO, SIS, and their usual channels. Although, by seniority, I am the ranking officer, Major Findlay is in fact the supreme operational commander, on the ground. Does this help, Major, or have I served to muddy the waters more?"

"Perfectly clear, thank you, Colonel," Rebeccah answered, thinking otherwise.

"One final question? Yes, Major Samson?" Stedman asked.

"Thanks. Gentlemen, has any thought been given to the concept of a two-pronged, rather than a single thrust approach? My thinking, if you'll bear with me for a moment, is that we might stand a better chance *113* of achieving our objective if we mounted what a boxer like Mr. Williamson would call a feint. By that I mean a diversionary tactic, creating confusion, leading to a false sense of security, and enabling a single individual to slip through the enemy's defences to deliver the knockout blow."

The room was deathly silent until Erik Williamson rose to address the question. "Thank you, Robert, for this thoughtful contribution. As much as I can relate to your analogy, the added layers of difficulty that would be needed to select, prepare, and simultaneously insert a second tactical team, however desirable it may be in theory, is not in the cards at this time.

"Thank you and enjoy the remainder of the day."

Robert Samson walked out of the hall with Hamish to the parking area. As Hamish was climbing into the seat, Robert spoke up. "Listen, Hamish, that wasn't meant to be a personal attack, but we've been there and they haven't."

"I appreciate what you're saying Rob, and I didn't take it at all personally. You know how much I like and respect you, so just bite the damn bullet and give me your word that you'll play on the team."

"You can count on it, Hamish," he smiled giving a 'thumbs up'. "Whenever, whatever, blood, sweat, the sky's the..."

"Oh, knock it off. You've always seen clear through me!"

"Do you think that I have a case, then?" he asked. "I mean it, Hamish. You and I and Andy did what a secondary strike force is expected to do, the flaming saviours of the world, came on like the Seventh Cavalry, but we did it all off the cuff, without any planning or real objectives. I call that happenstance."

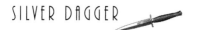
"Happenstance? I'm afraid that you've lost me, Robert," Hamish replied.

"Bloody right, it was a miracle that we were able to get in and pull out our friends. Say what you will, but we hadn't planned, schemed, or in any elementary manner begun to attempt to anticipate the circumstances when we went into England. Oh no, we charged in, six guns blazing and saved the day. I call that sheer cowboy luck. I have spent too many years being told that my concern for planning was due to a lack of fortitude, guts. Well, those people have had to eat their bloody words. Now, because I want you to succeed in pulling this off, I need your assurance that we won't be party to sending you and Major Jack Sprat to a Gestapo torture chamber. Okay?"

"All right old man, now hop up in this seat and I'll take you along with the three Yugoslav musketeers for some world-class worm drowning. And please hold on, Rob, I desperately need you around for the show!"

John Ross 'Jack' Harris had been reared by his mother, Rose, to not only reject, but fight 'tooth and nail' against official prejudice, fuelled by unjust policies propped up by self-serving bureaucrats.

Jack's father, A. H., 'Aces High' Harris, from whom Jack had inherited his charismatic, chiselled features, blonde hair and slim, athletic frame, had borrowed heavily to finance a string of deals at the height of fever-pitch Oklahoma land speculation, then abruptly died in 1923, of 'the alcohol influenza', bequeathing Rose and Jack a mortgage and debt totalling $20,000. The 'fine cut of woman', 'Cherokee' Rose Ross Harris, fended off her suitors and paid off the creditors, more often than not, one and the same, by selling the house along with 'every stick and rag' of furnishings at a public auction, which she herself ran. After settling accounts with Garnet 'Sorrowful' Bede, the undertaker, for A. H.'s modest pine casket and interment, Rose took the slim leftovers and put young Jack and herself on a day coach to Macon, Georgia.

Rose Harris was a direct descendant of 'Little' John Ross, the one-eighth Cherokee Scotsman, who was the first and only elected Chief of the Cherokee Republic, in North Georgia. From his earliest remembrances, Jack had listened while Rose recounted the oral histories of her

American Indian heritage and read to him the history of John Ross' betrayal by friends, topped by the refusal of President Andrew Jackson to honour the Supreme Court decision ruling the 1830 Indian Removal Act unconstitutional. Rose had patiently taught Jack to read the Cherokee alphabet, so that by the age of six, he could recite by heart the sagas chronicling the destruction of the Cherokee Nation, through the terrible 'Trail of Tears' forced march to Oklahoma in the brutal winter of 1838-39. Jack credited his mother's determination to teach him to decode the intricacies of her ancestral language for his remarkable flair for crypt-analysis.

115

To the twenty-five year old Jack Harris, the name *Shining Oath* symbolized the mystic magic embodied by the Cherokee shamans in his mother's stories. He walked alone from the Lecture Hall, eventually ending down at the bluffs, and gazed at the lake's serene calm. He thought how much he wanted to be able to tell Rose and Billy Kepke that he, John Ross Harris, had been chosen to do what Roses' ghosts would expect of her heir: to pierce a vipers' nest of racism, corruption, injustice, appalling tyranny, and slay the reptile. He felt a deep sense of gratitude and obligation to Captain Weiss to whom he had confided his longing.

"Jack! Jack!" He turned to see Rebeccah, running toward him, her long silky black hair flying like a mane. "Hello, Jack, gorgeous view, isn't it?"

Her stunning, smouldering beauty left him at a momentary loss for words. "... Sure ... sure is. What did you think of the meeting, Rebeccah?" There was something about her, actually quite a great deal, that reminded him of Cherokee Rose.

"I thought it went tickety-boo. And you, Jack?"

"Great! I couldn't be happier. It's going to be one heck of a team. I really want to thank you for carrying the ball on my behalf, Rebeccah."

"You're welcome. I don't know how much it helped the cause, but I did whisper in Colonel Stedman's ear," she smiled coyly. Jack felt an almost uncontrollable urge to kiss her full lips.

She shifted topics. "Why don't you come up to our place for the afternoon, Jack? A few glasses of plonk, some laughs, and then an early dinner, say, around five. Sound alright?"

"That sounds terrific. Not a lot for a single guy to do around here on Sundays."

"Besides, you haven't really met my husband, Hugh, or our darling little Sarah. Is it a date then, Jack?"

"I wouldn't miss it!"

"Smashing! On the way, I want to show you the capitol little vegetable patch where I grow the biggest, reddest, and juiciest tomatoes. Yorkie in communications got me started. Come!"

Her scent was intoxicating. 'My God, can this sweetheart really be the deadliest shot in the annals of SOE?' "Beefsteak tomatoes? Haven't had one since I can't remember. Race you!"

"Hugh, the projector please, if you would turn out the lights, Robert," Hamish requested while closing the Lecture Hall's blackout drapes.

To Jack's astonishment, the images which appear on the screen are in vibrant natural colour, perfectly exposed. The *Shining Oath* team watch in fascination as the camera pans to reveal an eerie scene of Adolf Hitler, wearing a grey double breasted jacket and black trousers, over a white shirt, with a black necktie sporting a half Windsor knot; a silver Nazi eagle and swastika medallion is pinned at the dimple below the knot. The Führer is standing on an open balcony against a spectacular alpine backdrop. He pats and fusses with a leaping Alsatian dog, while a slim, pretty, youthful blonde woman in Bavarian mountain dress, who is seated on a ledge watches and laughs, while posing and having an animated conversation with someone off camera. Three security men uniformed in SS dress black survey the proceedings from the left side, clearly ill -at –ease. Visitors arrive and pay homage to the Führer. He struts and preens, occasionally flashing hasty Nazi victory salutes, yet all the while appearing nervous, even uncomfortable. He pays little attention to the attractive woman, to which she seems cheerfully oblivious. The film ends in a stream of white trailer with indecipherable markings flashing past, until Hugh turned off the lamp.

"Lights up, please. Adolf Hitler, his girlfriend Eva Braun, Alsatian dog Blondi, and mid-level officials at the Führer's Berghof retreat atop Kehlstein Mountain, Berchtesgaden, in the Bavarian Alps, circa the present time, approximately. The two SS bruisers on the left, as I'm sure you will recognize, are from the Führer's personal life guard regiment, the Liebstandtarte-SS Adolf Hitler. Their commanding officer Sepp Dietrich, by the by, is the only SS general authorized to report directly to Der Führer. That honour was granted for the regiment's devotion to their leader during that nasty bit of business in '33, the so-called 'Night of the Long Knives'.

"However, they're likely there for the propaganda camera. The Berghof has a security staff, the Reichsicherheitsdienst, or RSD. The commander is a Brigadeführer Rattenhuber, he's the third man, closest to the Führer. Beside him, Hauptsturmführer Müller; both are former Waffen-SS. Rattenhuber is always attached to his Führer like a limpet. The RSD numbers twenty, not including three police dogs. They, the men that is, may sometimes be seen in mufti (civilian dress) or in Waffen-SS uniforms, with distinguishing patches. In wintertime, they are seen wearing Gebirgsjäger-SS mountain troop gear, which seems eminently sensible.

"Unless you think they are semi-superannuated cuckoo clock makers, may I remind you that the majority, almost two-thirds, are former field Waffen-SS while a third were recruited from the Ordnungspolizei, the Reich regular police forces. All are highly trained, physically fit, and tend to be on the ultra - fanatical side in devotion to their Führer. Please study and memorize these detailed sketches on the board in front carefully, noting the distinctive RSD shoulder and lapel badges and denotation of ranks. This will be very important to Jack and me obviously, but we all must share a common base of knowledge. A display of RSD, Gebirgsjäger, and Obersalzburg-SS uniformed mannequins is being readied for our inspection, later in the week.

"Now, comments, queries anyone?" Hamish asked. "Robert?"

"Hamish, I am truly and deeply impressed with the breadth and depth of your knowledge. May I inquire how you found the time to bone up?"

"Thank you, Robert. No secret: briefings, briefings, and more briefings, starting one week before I left British Columbia."

"How did you get it?" asked Jack.

"The briefings or the film? Yes, the film, of course. Erik would prefer I don't say, Jack, except it is one hundred percent authentic. It was shot recently, that much I can tell you."

"What or where is the Berghof's point of entry?" queried Robert Samson.

"Through a marble lined pedestrian tunnel, 124 metres in length, which connects with a brass elevator that rises 124 metres through the rock, interesting symmetry there, to the summit at 1834 metres. Interestingly, Herr Hitler has a morbid fear of heights, explaining perhaps why he doesn't venture from the centre rear of the deck in that footage. That should give you an impressionistic sense of the target zone. There's much, much more detail to come," Hamish asserted.

"However, before we do delve into such things, I have been directed to distribute to each of you your mission nom de guerre. Kindly take your envelope as I pass them around ... Major Harris, Captain Mason, Major Samson, Major Weiss, and Major Findlay. Only two are operations pseudonyms in the customary SOE way of doing business. According to my master list, this is how it plays out: Major Harris is ... Major John Haney, and I am ... Major Hastings Fox, ... Hastings Fox? Really? As director of communications, Captain Mason is to be known as Mercury, the messenger to the gods, Major Samson is Mars, the god of war, very fitting wouldn't you agree? ... Major Weiss is Diana, the huntress ... a goddess especially favoured by Mr. Churchill, so I'm told, and, our Colonel Stedman will be Apollo, god of truth and light, of course. So there you have it, the principal cast, the Olympians, with Haney and Fox, the spear-carriers."

The door opened to admit Colonel Stedman with two visitors. "Ah, greetings, gentlemen!" Hamish announced. "It is my great pleasure to welcome a guest whose knowledge of the topic at hand is unparalleled, Commander Lawson."

Rebeccah glanced at Hugh, searching his face for any hint that he recognized the slight, elegant visitor as Admiral Sir Willson Cunnington, a.k.a. 'G', Chief of Great Britain's Intelligence Service, MI-6, who had 'sat in' during their Tent Peg debriefings with Colonel Graham. During that daylong session, Rebeccah recalled that Commander Lawson had said little, but had written much.

"Good morning," Lawson began cordially, "I am truly honoured and delighted to have been asked by Mr. Williamson to join this exceptional group. I told Erik when he telephoned that our people have been busy pulling together as much information as we have available which may be helpful. This is one of my indispensable right hands, Dr. Leith May, whose role it will be over the next days to keep me on topic and updated with fresh-breaking developments, sometimes, I might add, before they occur, correct, Leith?" The fresh-faced Dr. May, who to Rebeccah looked not much older than herself, smiled and nodded as he continued to erect several large white boards on which diagrams and photographs were neatly arranged and fixed with coloured pins.

119

"I have been cleared by the Prime Minister to let you know that operation *Shining Oath* faced very stiff opposition at the outset, from the same quarters when Tent Peg was first discussed," Lawson stated. "Somewhat surprisingly, this time the ethics question vis-à-vis ungentlemanly warfare did not play a major part in these debates. There is a growing consensus that any means we can employ to weaken the enemy's resolve, should not be rejected out of hand, purely on moral grounds. The resistance was of a more strategic and theoretical nature. The death of Adolf Hitler, some strongly argued, would be less of a setback to the enemy's will to continue, than that of the Propaganda Minister, Dr. Joseph Goebbels, Field Marshall Keitel, Reich Marshall Göring, SS chief Heinrich Himmler, or any of a half-dozen or so political and military figures. One journalist recently made reference to, 'The parade of bonzos,'" he chuckled.

"Nevertheless, events of 27 May this year, namely the assassination of Obergrüppenführer (General)-SS Reinhard Heydrich, in Prague, Czechoslovakia, however deserved and timely, have not produced a noticeable weakening of Nazi determination. Quite to the contrary, the sheer barbarism and brutality of the reprisals taken against the people of Czechoslovakia in general and the village of Lidice, in particular, show no signs of a leadership that is cowed or demoralized. One may ask if his assassination was worth the consequences or cost to the Czech people? I leave it to you to decide.

"Nonetheless, the PM has remained resolute and with the backing of Erik Williamson, me, and others, particularly like-minded chaps within Special Operations, Political Warfare Executive, and so on, and with the enthusiastic backing of our Russian and American counterparts, his view won the day. And with that, you will be pleased to know, we bring to a

close the political awareness tutorial.

"The final selection of *Shining Oath's* personnel was never questioned, as Erik has undoubtedly told you. The daring execution of Tent Peg left no one in doubt of the feasibility of a specialist team's potential and as the German leader, Hitler, has said himself, 'Not a soul could cope with an assassin, who for idealistic reasons ... (is) prepared quite ruthlessly to hazard his own life in the execution of his object. I quite understand why ninety percent of the historic assassinations have been successful,' unquote. Prophetic words, one hopes," Lawson commented dryly.

"In light of this, I do wish to underline again that it is clearly the understanding of BSO and SOE that you have each voluntarily consented to participate in this venture. Is there anyone who has the slightest reservations, qualms, misgivings, second thoughts, or objections, whatsoever?" He paused and looked around the room. "Very well, Leith will sum up our working group's non-preferred approaches to eliminating the subject, Dr. May?"

"Thank you, Commander Lawson. Many options were considered and rejected, including an SAS or Commando attack on his private railway train by sniper fire, or using the British PIAT (Projectile Infantry Anti-Tank), or its American counterpart, the Bazooka, and, sabotage of the rail line on which it travels. The difficulties presented were overwhelming, due to the unpredictability of his travel schedule, the effective range of the PIAT, which, optimistically, I am told, is not more than 100 yards, and the necessity to take him out by sniper fire when exposed, which, our sources say, is rare to non-existent when he is travelling by rail. Several variations of the excellent American rifle-type cross bow were tested," Dr. May continued, citing technical ordnance terms, ending with estimates of its effective range. "Believe me, these weapons can deliver a formidable wallop, although a clear shot within sixty-five yards is necessary to be lethal," he concluded.

"Then, less direct alternatives including the clandestine introduction of an undetectable, slow acting poisonous substance into the train's 540 litre water tank or the placement of a timed bomb device on board by a foreign, i.e. hostile worker, were discussed and ruled out as unreliable. It's interesting that the concentration of poison sufficient to kill Adolf Hitler within one week was calculated by a charming young German émigré, a Dr. Ostermann, to be precisely 768 grams. When we were told, however, of other variables and conditions best understood by boffins such as the good doctor or Lucrezia Borgia, that line of thinking was shelved. Perhaps a break would be in order. Tea anyone?" he asked.

Following a short pause, Sir Will Cunnington thanked Dr. May, and then presented three concise modus operandi, based upon available intelligence relating to Adolf Hitler's habits and movements within the Berghof, and, while approaching and departing the vicinity of the Obersalzberg.

"In summary, Shining Oath, Plan Able, employs two or three snipers, in Gebirgsjäger-SS uniforms, who would either shoot him when he takes the morning air on the balcony or lie in wait for him to take his daily walk to the teahouse where he normally takes breakfast between 1000 and 1100h. Plan Baker entails the ambushing of the motorcade when it is leaving the Berghof, at a tight bend in the road, and Plan Charles entails an SAS parachute troop assault on the RSD in support of Able and or Baker. Following lunch, we'll examine the relative merits of each and come to our decision.

121

"Rebeccah, you have a question?"

"Yes, Commander, I was wondering about anti-aircraft defences. If there are, and I would assume that to be so, do we know their disposition and strength?"

"I understand your interest," he replied, smiling. "Indeed there are six A. A. batteries on the ground, guarding the approaches. The guns are mostly rail-mounted 88's with some 4-barrelled flak types, however there are no searchlights, based on our most recent intelligence. I should mention that all A. A. troops are under the administration of Kommando-SS Obersalzburg. The A.A forces are at battalion strength, between eighty and 100 men.

"Another question, Colonel Stedman?"

"Thank you, Sir. It does seem implausible that twenty or so men, even former crack Waffen-SS and Reich coppers are the sole watchdogs of the stronghold. What do our sources tell us about the drivers, mechanics, maintenance, and other workers such as clerical staff, telephone operators, gardeners, firefighters and the like?"

"A very important question, Colonel. Again, the Kommando-SS

Obersalzburg, which was formed in 1938, provides the majority of the help, but there are other players in the mix. All Kommando troops are required to have seen active service, making them frontline quality Waffen-SS. The place is crawling with patrols and specialists of every stripe and type in the Third Reich. To let us all better understand the complex nature and strength of the fortifications at the Berghof, the tea-house and on the ground, we have prepared an extensive briefing booklet that describes these arrangements in detail. Dr. May will be distributing it tomorrow. Now, lunch ... one half hour, shall we say, Colonel?"

The entire group took their plates and glasses to sit in the sun on the steps of the Lecture Hall. "Well, Major Harris, what do you think of things so far, off the record?" Cunnington asked. "Cigarette? Mind if I do? Old RN habit."

"No thanks, Commander. Honestly? It seems everything's moving along at about the right pace. I've got to admit though that I'm itching to get my hands dirty and begin the next phase of the preparation," Jack answered, "but I respect the need to cover the logistics and basics, beforehand, Sir."

"You won't have to wait much longer, Major. Tell me, again off the record, which plan would be your preference?"

"Baker, by a country mile, but I can live with Able. Charlie, or Charles seems a bit farfetched, Sir."

"I see, and why is that, for interest's sake only, mind, Jack?"

Commander Lawson's natural charm put Jack at ease immediately. He felt like the life-long confidante of a man whom he believed to be one of the top dogs, if not the top dog, in British Intelligence. "Baker seems more do-able, if we can manage to bring in a PIAT or baby bazooka. Charlie, on the other hand, could be a logistical snafu, sorry Sir, dog's breakfast," he flinched inwardly. "There are too many opportunities for communications to go up the spout and to me, Commander, this is all about surprise, which relies upon timing, co-ordinated through flawless communications. As Major Findlay's, I mean Major Fox' communications point man, I'm a bit uneasy about being able to even make Able and Baker fly right, from a radioman's perspective, given the distance and surveillance gear the Germans have at their fingertips."

"'Fly right' ... an interesting choice of words, Jack. I believe you'll find we're already well underway in addressing that aspect. You are absolutely on the mark; it is essential for our success. I do appreciate your forthrightness, Jack, and share your keen interest in the electronics end of it," he affirmed with a warm smile. "Let's keep what we said under the old straw boater, just between you and me, to use the American vernacular," he clarified, his index finger touching his lips. Cunnington stood up, stubbing his cigarette on the railing and brushed the crumbs from his Savile Row navy suit.

"Colonel Stedman, could I suggest we get back and settle this plan business straight away?" he asked. Jack knew from the change in tone that it was not intended to be a suggestion.

In less than twenty minutes, Sir Willson Cunnington officially announced the decision: *Shining Oath* - Plan Baker. The Heydrich job had won over the Able champions. "Thank you, everyone. I don't suppose the PM would mind if I used his phrase, 'This is the end of the beginning.' In the remaining time, Major Fox will take you through the Obersalzberg motor route maps and aerial photographs. Dr. May and I must run." He looked at the Swiss - made chronograph on his wrist. "I make it seven days and eleven hours before the launch of Baker test match. Colonel Stedman and Major Fox have promised to keep you hard at it in the interim. Until tomorrow at 0800 then, carry on! Colonel, Major Fox, a moment please."

Following Cunnington's opening remarks, Colonel Stedman ordered Jack and Hugh to report to Colonel Dr. Philip Truscott, Chief of Hydra, the Camp X communications complex. As they walked to the strange building, it's windows seven feet above ground level, Hugh told Jack what he knew about Colonel Truscott, Chief of Wireless Operations.

"So, he's a full Colonel, and a Professor of Electrical Engineering, a close friend and business associate of Erik Williamson as well as a world leader in wireless encryption technology. Sounds like quite a swell guy, Hugh!"

"He is, Jack. Dr. Phil and his crew, who are top notch, practically built the original 10kW powerhouse from spare parts and bailing wire. Most of those lads were ham radio enthusiasts pre-war. I can understand why BSO recruited only the brightest and the best of them, the

Part of Hydra's main transmitter; note the tuning coil on top of the cabinet at right

crème de la crème of Canada's 'talented amateurs.'"

Bernie, Hughey, and Yorkie, the operations crew with whom Hugh had trained for Tent Peg greeted him enthusiastically. All were anxious to know if he had kept the gold tomato soupcan trophy that they had awarded him for W/T EXCELLENCE. Assuring them that it was not only safe, and residing in a prominent place of honour on his living room bookshelf, he was interrupted by Yorkie asking good- naturedly if he had spent the entire ten-dollar cash award, when Colonel Truscott entered the radio room.

"Well, Captain Mason, a glutton for punishment I see! Welcome back to the inner sanctum. And if I remember anything about that night correctly, thanks to the Captain's exceptional generosity, our cups did run over, and over, am I not right, Yorkie?

Bill Hardcastle hard at the hobby he loved, Morse Code.

"Major Harris I presume, I'm Colonel Phil Truscott. I've been hearing good things about you, Major. Tell me, are they true?"

"Likewise, Colonel Truscott," Jack replied with a tight-lipped smile. Colonel Truscott, he decided, was the sort of officer who earned, rather than demanded, respect.

"Sharp, very sharp, I'm impressed Major!" Truscott replied cordially. "We'll get along swimmingly. I know the boys are keen to show you their newest toys, but I'd first like to introduce an Anzac chap who has been of immense help around here. This way, please, and watch your step, these high voltage cables are not secured, yet."

They followed Truscott to a rear alcove cluttered with radio para-phernalia and ham radio magazines, of indeterminate age. The 'Anzac chap' who was half-buried behind a chaotic desk sprang up, right hand extended. "Frank Briggs, welcome to the war room, mate!" He was a handlebar moustachioed, thirty-ish, utterly unpretentious, and possibly crazy – as –a bag – of –hammers, Section Eight New Zealander, Royal Air Force Squadron Leader, Frank Briggs, transferred from Beaulieu. All of this, Jack learned before he and Hugh sat down. Puzzled to see the nameplate, **Major F. Briggs**, on a Squadron Leader's desk, Jack inquired.

"To placate the mud sloggers, Jacko. They can call me anything includin' a flamin' Kiwi, but these Army Wally's think Squadron Leader's some kind of fairy ballet burke," he responded, bumping his pipe enthusiastically on a tar - blackened shell casing ersatz ashtray. He followed Jack's eyes, "Oh, fifty cal from a Focke-Wulf 190; I smoked the bloke's petrol tank and Jerry had the good sense to hit the silk, good royal luck to him in the drink. I picked up a few of the chunks the next day. The coin's identical," he continued without skipping a beat, "so bloody-hell, I'm His Majesty's bleeding Major! You know how to handle a kite?"

"A kite, like, Benjamin Franklin?" Jack asked, dumbfounded. He was beginning to feel like an anthropologist who had stumbled upon a previously unknown tribe of Trobriand Islanders.

"Good one, Yank, no an air - eo - plane!"

"Oh, yeah, an air - eo - plane. Yes, single, twin, why do you ask, Frank?"

"But can you jump from one of the blighters, Jacko? Hugh's a jumper, aren't you, boyo?"

"501st Airborne, Frank."

"Wizard! A pigeon fancier by any wild chance? Racers, homers, plugs?"

"As a matter of fact, Frank, my chum Billy and I did keep a loft of racing Belgians, in Georgia. I believe the correct term is dove, although pigeon is a collective, if inaccurate name of convenience.

"By God, Sir, you are knowledgeable. Belgians, the royalty of the avian world! Good, then, we're friends for life. You must meet my mate, Silvio Mattachione. There's not a man drawing breath who knows as much about 'em: breeding, raising and racin'. He's just a bit of a stroll up the road in Puerto Perry. He supplies homers to Canadian and American Signals, plus BSO, SOE and heaven knows whom else ... all very hush-hush research. I'm the designated keeper here ... six beauties. Do you want to see them?"

"Sure, but where's Puerto Perry, Frank, Mexico?"

"Port Perry, Ontario, birthplace of D. D. Palmer, 1845, the founder of chiropractic, old lad. Keep talking and I'll show you an interesting new rig. You do know that I'm dying to be your wireless chappy, don't you, Jacko? Then again, likely not. When I got the drift that Hamish was up to something, I volunteered. The Doc, Phil, said he passed it on up the line and what ho! No bloody idea what it's about, but, if Hamish is into it, I'll wager my granny's old straw hat it's a bust up of rare ruddy proportions. Come on, you two!"

As they followed Frank into the repair room, Jack struggled to keep a poker face, at the idea of this oddly engaging joker as a contributing member of Shining Oath's Plan Baker.

"Now take a gander at this little beauty!" Smiling broadly, Frank pointed to a wireless radio set about half the size of a breadbox. "A prototype, X-1, portable, 9 valve double super het sender-receiver, 3 bands, 1.76 to 16 Mc/s, dual: R/T and C/W, battery life max 12 hours, range NFI, hermetically sealed if you have a mind to drown it; a dream, the product of Mr. Williamson's and the Doc's advanced Canadian engineering know how! One of two in the world, but more to come. I'd say you birds are getting the preferential treatment!"

"Jees, what a beaut, eh Jack? I got everything except the model designation or when you mentioned the range, Frank, NF ... something or other?"

"NFI: No effing idea, Hugh. The test specs to date indicate it's on a par or has slightly better performance than the best the Japanese have in their sleek 94-6. Ours is a bleeding prototype as I said, ergo, we call it Model X-1, in honour of the Camp. Now lads, we're going to put X-1 and you through the paces. Let's go into the radio room and get set up. Jacko, bring the X-1, carefully, please!"

With Bernie, Hughie and Yorkie crowding closely around, Frank hooked up the miniature radio to an oscilloscope, and then guided Hugh and Jack step - by - step through a one-hour course in the X-1's technical design and capabilities. At 1130, Colonel Truscott came in. The demonstration over, Hugh and Jack thanked Frank; as they were about to leave, Truscott invited them to stop by his office, which proved to be a shining example of orderliness, organisation, and efficiency, in marked contrast with Frank's cluttered warren.

"So gentlemen, what's your impression? It'll go no further," Truscott stated assuringly, leaning back in his chair, his hands linked behind his head.

"Well, Colonel," Jack began tentatively, "speaking for myself, it's quite a piece of work, really terrific. I'm sure that my government would give its eyeteeth to share the patent rights. Congratulations on achieving so much power and capability in a lightweight and compact design, Sir."

"I agree with Captain Harris one hundred percent, Colonel," Hugh enthused.

"Good. I think it will be the ticket. But I really wanted to hear your read on Frank."

"Eccentric, fascinating, and a brilliant mind, likely verging on severely gifted, if such a thing exists," Jack responded without hesitation, flashing a smile.

"And a certified RAF Ace, flying Hurricanes mostly. Five confirmed kills, and two probables, over Malta. And as a member of your group, Hugh?" Truscott inquired.

"Well, Sir, I can work with him, if that's what you meant."

"Jack?" Phil asked. "I know why you're hesitating. I'm not playing guessing games. I am aware of the Mission. Erik Williamson insisted that I be briefed on the overview, to allow me to co-ordinate the technical parts more or less intelligently, which, in essence, is what Frank and I are doing. X-1 was developed rather hastily, specifically for this task. Moreover, as a first of its kind, X-1 may need some babysitting by its co-inventor. Now that's out of the way, can you work with Frank Briggs, if he were to accompany you for support purposes on Phase Two? His briefing will be strictly 'need to know', it goes without saying, Major."

"The Squadron Leader never mentioned those accomplishments! Yes, Colonel Truscott, I accept him, so long as he speaks English from time to time."

"Good, I'll let Findlay and Stedman know it's a go, ASAP. Well, it's 1205; shall we take our chances on Cook Fred's Tantalising Tuesdays' Macaroni and Cheese Delight? My treat!"

As the intensity of the preparations increased, Jack found himself being drawn into an almost spiritual union with his Shining Oath colleagues, not unlike the sense of pride and 'esprit de corps' he formed at Fort Benning with his fellow airborne troopers. When he reflected further, he realized that he had first experienced a similar sense of camaraderie and co-operation with his college varsity squad teammates as the first string quarterback. His coach had described that as 'esprit de corps'. Yet, at times he was vaguely uneasy in the presence of Rebeccah, and by association, Hugh Mason. Hugh, the ever – reliable inside guard, seemed content to play out the steady – as – a - rock, supporting role. Rebeccah, the all-star pivot, although sidelined due to personal and political circumstances, was his equal, Jack admitted, and more likely his superior in talent, ambition, and brains. Moreover, she was an intriguing and undeniably attractive woman.

He witnessed her drive and cocky self - assurance frequently on the firing range, and during the three practice jumps from Dakotas, but never as dramatically as at the first test firing of their anti-tank weapon of choice, the new American M9A1 Rocket Launcher, Bazooka. It was literally an out – of – the – box demonstration, as the crates had only just been dropped off an army truck when Hamish announced that the display would take place, at the lakefront. The group gathered to watch as Hamish pried open the containers. Rebeccah then removed and wiped the packing grease off the two slender twenty-four inch black metal tubes, then effortlessly slid them together and with a rapid twist, engaged the interlock and snapped on the wooden stock. "The stock has been manufactured in this way especially for use by paratroops," she remarked impassively.

She opened the second carton and reached inside. "Gentlemen, the projectile, a 2.36 calibre shaped charge, an electrically-fired rocket actually, if I'm correct," she announced matter – of – factly. "Yes, the trigger engages a magneto to set it off. One moment please while I load it ... there we go ... back up, Hugh, ... back up more, everyone please, the recoil blast's likely a bit scary. My target is the yellow buoy marker, 100 yards. Hope you don't mind Colonel!" she commented quietly, pulling her hair back, as she knelt, placing the tube on her right shoulder, and sighted it in. "Ready!" Suddenly, a flame erupted from the barrel with a belch of roaring flame and the buoy ceased to exist. "Two degrees more to the right next time," she commented, a smudge of grease on her right cheek accentuating a smile of satisfaction, as she stood upright, with the launcher tipping downward from her shoulder. "Anyone else care for a go? Hamish, then Robert and Jack."

"Were you impressed, Jack?" she asked quietly, looking up inquisitively at supper that evening.

"Damn right I was, Major. Emphatically, yes!"

"Good" she replied enigmatically, then leaning forward, asked, "You won't tell anyone that I fiddled it?"

"You did? How, Rebeccah?" he mumbled, his mouth half-full of apple pie.

"I phoned General Constantine to send me a manual in the next post as soon as we chose Baker! Also, No. 36 M Marks 1 and 2, Frost and Woods, Canadian-made Mills Bombs. What you Yanks call grenades. Do drop by anytime. Buckets of fresh tomatoes ... you might be pleasantly surprised by an English girl's version of your good old boy, down-home country chilli. Must dash. Cheerio."

"Sure thing!" Jack replied. 'I'll bet your chilli's hot'.

"Major Weiss, gentlemen, today, we have completed the preparatory phase of our mission plan. Congratulations. This evening, as you know, we begin the application of your hard - won training," Colonel Stedman announced. "Please be back here, in the Lecture Hall at 1915, with your personal gear in the dunnage bags we provided yesterday. Everything else that you'll require will be provided. Transport to Oshawa airport will leave at 1945 sharp. Our flight will depart at 2025. One more thing: as of this moment, we are in full practice mode. All personnel will adhere to the Mission rules of governance. Thank you. That is all."

"So, where are we going? Does anyone have a clue?" Jack asked, after Stedman's departure.

"The great white Canadian wilderness would be my bet, Major," Hugh confided.

"Makes sense, but where?"

"The western cordillera," Hugh whispered. "But you didn't hear it from me, deal?"

"Really? Okay, deal."

The DC-3/Dakota Mark 111 flight to 15 Wing Base Moose Jaw was uneventful; at 0730, the heavily - laden RCAF twin transport roared heroically off the airstrip headed for the interior of British Columbia.

As the aircraft was levelling out for its approach, Jack leaned across the aisle to Hugh. "So tell me Mercury Mason, where's your armadillo - cordidillo, or whatever you called it?" he shouted.

"Western Cordillera, Major Haney," replied Hugh. "It's the geological term for the western mountains and the continental shelf. That's about the extent of my knowledge," he smiled and shrugged apologetically.

"Well, maybe if your Espãnol were a tad more extensive, Captain, I might have understood you in the first place, deal? It's pronounced Cor-deel-yer-a, not ..." The DC-3's hydraulics whined as the wheels lowered, and locked. A loud thump resonated against the lower fuselage. "Holy Toledo! What the hell was that?" Jack shouted. "Something brushed the belly!"

"Oh, don't worry at all, Major Haney," Hamish replied calmly. Flying Officer Johns is an old friend, ... very experienced at ducking betwixt and between and around through these Rockies. We've flown with him before, haven't we?" Rebeccah and Hugh nodded affirmatively. "Most likely a spot of turbulence," he added unconvincingly, "either that or he kissed the tip of a *pinus strobus*. They can reach upwards of one hundred feet. Could be *Pseudotsuga*. He paused, and continued, "Then again, perhaps Squadron Leader Briggs is having a go. Anyone sighted the mad chap recently? White Pine or Douglas Fir; must inspect the undercarriage," he commented and then resumed reading *The Fly Fishing Enthusiast's Quarterly*.

SILVER DAGGER

When the twin-engined Dakota Mark 111 had come to a complete stop, its engines coughed grey smoke as a parade of two British Army Bren gun carriers, an open transport truck, and a refuelling tanker, proceeded from the edge of the grass runway. Hamish walked up the narrow aisle and turned to face the passengers. "Bring your personal gear and leave the rest. Your kits and assorted belongings will be taken to the Camp by transport. I'd like to hold a short briefing to help orient you before we set out. Follow me, please."

They gathered on the grass in front of a wood hut, which Hamish explained, before he and Flying Officer Johns went inside, served as the flight control communications shack. Hamish emerged with a knapsack and sat down. "Salmon and lettuce sandwiches ... please help yourselves. One map per pair, and if you would please open to this panel, you will see the West Kootenays Region. This was the site of wild gold fever in the 1890's. Now, it's nickel, lead, and zinc, mostly for the war effort of course, and some of the most incredible recreational country in British Columbia. We are here in the Monashee Mountain Range, shown in green. There's the Columbia River. Now, look for Castlegar, and then go due south to Trail and southwest to Rossland. We are almost exactly equal in distance between those two towns. You will notice how close we are to Washington State, at Rossland, less than 11 kilometres, roughly 6.8 miles, Jack. During the boom, it was quite a lively place and American prospectors poured in. As you might assume, Mr. Williamson had many good reasons to select this area for his station. The elevation here, where we are sitting is 2,300 feet, 701 metres above sea level. The Bren carriers will take us in two groups up to base camp, which is situated at 3,398 vertical feet, 1 036 metres, transversely 8.3 miles, 13.3 kilometres on a bearing of 342 degrees 10 minutes. A short distance, however I wager you'll agree that the local term 'switchback' best describes the road. Please distribute yourselves between the two vehicles. I'll take the lead carrier, Robert, the second. They're equipped with radiophones. Questions? Good, off we go, and stay seated!"

"Tally ho!" Frank added lustily.

Forty minutes later, they reached the base, SOE STS 109, known to clients and staff as The Citadel. "I can't believe we made it alive! Must be a sheer drop!" Jack extolled. "There was more than once when I thought we'd had it, one inch to the right and a roll over the edge and splat. But who's complainin'? It's gorgeous! I'd give my eyeteeth to ski Red Mountain!"

Hamish, who had served briefly here as Chief Explosives Instructor before his recall to Camp X, conducted the walkabout upon their arrival. He explained as they watched recruits leaping from the 90 foot high jump tower that it was a fully operational, scaled-down adaptation of Camp X, whose clientele were destined for the Far East Theatre, and in the main, but not entirely, were from East Asia. "Nepalese Ghurkhas, Burmese, Siamese, East Indians, Manchurian Chinese, even Nikkei - Canadian Japanese, although it's officially forbidden by the Canadian Government. If they're fit, bright, and keen to fight, we provide the right tackle. And believe me, these are very, very tough customers, am I right Robert? ...er, Mars?"

Robert Samson agreed and then retold the brief history of The Citadel: constructed in 1936 as a private resort, then purchased in 1939 by Erik Williamson, who expanded it to create an advanced - training station for the Pacific War with Imperial Japan, which he calculated, would start no later than January 1942. And it was more spectacular than the *Tent Peg* Mission team remembered. Rebeccah pointed out the H building, enlarged considerably since her visit, which seemed to float at the edge of an overhang as though suspended by invisible wires.

"I was wondering Major Fox, if there's an airstrip here, why we landed down the flamin' mountain?" Frank queried.

"I will if you tell Haney who landed the flamin' Dakota."

"I did, Major Fox," Briggs replied brightly. "Near run thing it was, you may have noticed!"

"I assure you that we did, Major Briggs, we did. That was a white pine by the way." He reached into his pocket and withdrew a cone. "Here's my evidence," he laughed. "The lower airfield meets RCAF Transport Command regulations. This one is the Camp's training strip," Hamish explained. "Shall we toddle up to Diana's floating palace? I expect that we all have some light housekeeping duties to attend to before supper. I'm anxious to introduce you to The Citadel's Commandant, Lieutenant - Colonel Gerry Quan, who is one of Robert's protégés from Hong Kong days, and, a cordon bleu master chef to boot. If the gods are smiling, Colonel Quan has been overseeing the galley in our honour."

SILVER DAGGER

The dinner was quite unlike anything that Jack or anyone other than Robert Samson and Hamish had ever experienced: a sumptuous, twelve - course Chinese banquet, from traditional Guangdong (Hong Kong), Mandarin, and Shanghainese cuisines, planned, prepared, and described, dish –by – dish, in Cantonese and English, while being served by the amiable, six foot-two Chef, Colonel Quan.

Two hours later, it fell to Robert to thank their host. "Gerry, I remember when we were young Turks, wet - behind - the - ears coppers, a century or two ago, you once confessed me that it was your dream to have your own restaurant by the age of thirty. Your other ambition was to be a soldier of the King. Well, my old friend, you've accomplished both, in spades. Confucius said, 'Eating is the utmost important part of life.' What the wise old sage didn't say was, eating delicious food with dear friends is heavenly; when a comrade at arms prepares it superbly, it is truly sublime. We humbly thank you."

"You are welcome and good luck," Quan replied, bowing slightly. "The Citadel, my staff and I are at your disposal. One moment, please." A technician entered to hand him a yellow paper. "Thank you, Eddy. "

"Major Fox, an OU communication to your attention."

Hamish rose from his chair, taking the document, which he scanned and then turned to address Colonel Quan and spoke to him in Cantonese. "Doh je, M goi," he concluded, bowing.

As the others looked at one another blankly, Robert and Colonel Quan burst out laughing. "Major Fox apologizes that he cannot speak my dialect of Cantonese fluently!" Quan explained. "He said, 'We humbly thank you,' very clearly! Hamish, you have the floor."

"Thank you Colonel Quan," Hamish began. "Unfortunately, we've been ordered to complete the training exercise and return to STS 103 within seventy-two hours. That creates a host of issues. Reason? The situation across the pond has hotted up rather all at once, according to our Intelligence. Therefore, we are to be on fullest alert, on an hour - to - hour footing, for departure to the target zone. We'll assemble at 0630 tomorrow, in the Lecture Hall, to consider the implications. Now, I do believe there's just enough time for a nightcap. Colonel Quan, may we talk privately? Please allow me to buy you a drink."

"Good morning. I'll not candy-coat the seriousness of the situation," Hamish stated. "Plainly put, it is 'condition critical'. For months, SIS has received reliable reports out of Berlin saying that the Führer's personal physicians are convinced that the fellow has become a certified paranoid schizophrenic, 'gone regimental' to use Major Brigg's expression. Our analysts are in accord with the diagnosis. This is not welcome news at all, as it presents a range of wholly unpredictable scenarios for our side in Russia and North Africa, where we are beginning to see some gaping chinks in the armour. His senior commanders are demoralized, intimidated puppets and for good reason. He is clearly out of control and eliminates anyone who disagrees with him in the slightest way. Allied High Command is not prepared to take a 'wait and see' approach and is demanding action soonest by SOE and BSO. That means that we are under the gun, literally. I have consulted with HQ and the decision was taken that the schedule for Shining Oath Plan Baker will permit one run – through, with no chance of a rematch. Haney and I will be taking a practice hop at 1300h this afternoon, after which we will regroup as a team for the final briefing at 1430. Major Briggs and Mercury will take this opportunity to ensure that the radio equipment is functional. Diana, Rebeccah, and Major Samson, Mars, will be responsible for marshalling the supplies, weapons, and any logistics requiring attention. Questions? We'll begin with the aerial photographs, Colonel Quan, if you please?"

135

Jack looked into the full-length mirror, examining the reflected Gebirgsjäger Major. The uniform not only fit him perfectly, but was an exact replica, hand cut and sewn in Montreal by BSO's best Polish Jewish tailors, accurate right down to the buttons and round white edelweiss arm patch signifying Gebirgs, mountain troops. 'The gods of the new Germany will be the SS,' the dopey - looking Reichführer Himmler vowed, didn't he? 'We pledge to you Adolf Hitler, loyalty, and bravery. We swear obedience ... to the death,' and all that. Not bad. Sounds more believable in German. Okay Jack, let's not keep the ladies waiting.'

The Special Duties Westland Mark 111 Lysander was parked facing into the wind on the practice strip. Jack had immediately fallen in love with the strangely - beautiful, single engine, high wing monoplane whose gracefully – tapered fifty foot wingspan resembled a gigantic dragonfly. During the short orientation flight in the afternoon, he had been amazed by the 'Lizzie's' spectacularly short take off and landing capabilities, and was impressed to learn that it was built, assembled actually, Hamish had said, in Toronto. The one-half hour flight took them within viewing distance of the target, which through his binoculars, looked to Jack like a carbon copy of the Berghof.

"Is it fake, Hamish? It sure as heck looks like the real McCoy."

"If it looks real to you, then it is."

Before the flight, the Lysander Pilot Officer whom Hamish had introduced as "P.O. Roy, RCAF," was chatting with Colonel Quan, Fox, Diana, Mars, and Mercury. When Jack approached, P.O. Roy broke into a grin. "Lordy, a Sturmbannführer, and an Obersturmbannführer! What I wouldn't give for a camera right now."

"Yeah, the things you see when you don't have a gun. My mom would sure as hell be thrilled to see me," Jack laughed, performing a half - pirouette. "Is everything aboard, Roy?"

"Yes, it's ready. It's a tight fit, with the equipment. Don't worry, Major. Plenty to spare ... her fighting teeth have been pulled ...no machine guns," he remarked. "Time, Major Fox?"

"2005. We leave in thirteen minutes. Jack and I'll pop inside if you don't mind and give the gear a last once - over. Thanks everyone. See you in the funny papers! Where's Briggs?"

"In the radio room, Major, checking the weather conditions with RCAF Base Comox. There's a strong cold front moving inland from up the coast at about 30 knots," Hugh responded. We're all going up to listen now. Radio on, please, Major Haney."

"Luck!" Rebeccah added brightly.

Just then, Major Briggs appeared at the top of the wooden stairway, waving a flashlight. "I say, chaps, you've forgotten something!" he shouted, holding out a small wooden cage in the other hand.

"Now what?" Hamish called back.

Frank Briggs approached, and smiled as he held out a little bamboo slat pen. "Cleopatra, my Belgian homer queen. Major Haney, I'd appreciate it awfully if you could take her along. You did tell me that you're an experienced handler. Cleo's a rookie bred by my mate, Silvio. It would serve as an important test of our training program. Just release her when the job's done. No fuss, no bother. Her grub and water are in those little aluminium sealed containers. And here's the strap that goes over your shoulder. The metal capsule on her left leg has a slip of paper inside. No need to write anything, but it's there if you need to. Please?"

Jack and Hamish peered inside at the beautiful silver grey and black creature. She peered back, her bright eyes flashing red and white as she blinked. "Well, Haney?" Hamish queried. "It's your choice."

"She's gorgeous, Jack. I'd take her, if I had the choice. You never know!" Rebeccah enthused.

137

"Oh, all right. Hand the cage here, Frank."

Frank beamed, "Thank you. Grazie mille ... Signor Silvio will be tickled. Come home to Papa, Cleo!"

Jack carried the small cage up the short stepladder, following Roy and turned to wave before hoisting himself and Cleo into the glass enclosed cabin. He caught a glimpse of Rebeccah as she walked up the wooden stairs. She paused on the top step and made the 'V for Victory' sign. He returned her gesture with a 'thumbs up', but she had vanished into the dusk. Clambering over the passenger seat, Jack set down Cleo amidst their equipment and leaned against the bulkhead in the cramped cargo area, then reached into the carrying pack, switched on his X-1 radio and put on the headset. A moment later he raised his right headphone. "Is this causing interference for your set, or your instruments Roy?" he shouted to be heard over the lusty growl of the nine – cylinder radial Bristol Mercury engine.

"Negative. Take - off in one minute, twenty ... the leading edge of the disturbance..." he remarked, indicating with his gloved right hand the rain droplets glistening on the glass canopy. Are you sure you want to do this, Major Fox?"

"Hobson's choice. Are you, Roy?"

"Buckle up!" Roy directed grimly.

Hamish looked back. "Are you and Cleo secured, Major?"

Jack nodded affirmatively as Roy gunned the engine and slipped the brake lever. The Lysander lurched forward, its airframe straining momentarily at the sudden surge of power under full throttle, as it began rolling along the grass. Silently Jack counted off the seconds until it was airborne. '...Seven Mississippi ...eight Mississippi ... nine Miss ... son of a gun! We're in the air, Cleo!'

Fifteen minutes after lift-off, rain and hail were dancing noisily on the canopy forcing Jack to lean forward to hear Roy as he turned to speak to Hamish. "Rain mixed with ice pellets. Winds are west south-west at 38 knots ..."

138

"We're going to be flying in gale force winds!"

"Can't fly through it, Major, so Comox control advises we climb above it to four thousand, five hundred.

"Comox this is Charley Fox Oboe. Wilco. Over." Roy adjusted the rim, advanced the throttle, and pulled back on the control stick. "Her rate of climb is less than 1000 feet per minute, so this won't be a holiday," he cautioned.

"What's our airspeed?" Jack shouted, bracing himself as the equipment shifted with the sudden change in the aircraft's attitude. He looked in the cage. Cleo seemed unperturbed.

"One hundred fifty nine knots," Roy replied loudly. Strong updrafts were flexing and battering the huge wings as the Lysander struggled to pierce the sullen cumulo-nimbus storm clouds.

Hamish turned around to Jack, "Are you two alright?"

"I've flown open cockpit Stearman crop dusters in hailstorms over Illinois cornfields. Yeah, we're fine, thanks, Major. Cleo looks like she's asleep," he smiled. How are you doin'?" A sudden brilliant iridescent flash illuminated the cockpit. The lights on the instrument panel dimmed then flickered on momentarily before they were extinguished. Roy pounded the face of the altimeter in frustration. Jack knew immediately that it was a near hit lightning strike. The aircraft heaved drunkenly then recovered, shaking laterally like a large, drenched dog after a swim.

"Goddammit boys, we've been hit!" Roy exclaimed. "This ruddy radio's been knocked for a loop and the instruments are goin' screwy! Call Base Comox, Jack, tell 'em my last compass bearing was North 20

West magnetic. Azimuth 340°. Do you read that, Major?"

"I read it, I'm copying it now, with an SOS. Hold on to your shirt, Roy!" Jack countered calmly. He used the X-1's high-speed 'bug' key to transmit their location, followed by *dididi dahdahdah dididit*, the International Distress Call. He repeated the groups and waited for an acknowledgement. A second later, he received the reply *didahdit* "Mercury says received and understood!"

The nose of the Lizzie pitched down suddenly and violently. "What the hell's happening?" Hamish yelled.

"I've lost the hydraulics."

"Meaning?" Hamish demanded.

"Meaning the hydraulic assists for the tail section and the wings are screwed, Hamish!" Jack shouted into Hamish's ear. "And we've just lost power! The static discharge from the lightning bolt took out all the electrics ... no ignition. We're going down, unless he can get his nose up!"

"Jesus H! The circuits must have been designed by the Prince of Darkness!" Hamish intoned.

"Who?"

Hamish shook his head, "Only an English sports car driver would understand."

"Ever do a dead stick in this bird, Roy?" Jack yelled, as he wiped the haze from the side glass.

"In flight school. What about you?"

"Yep, but this baby should sail in like a glider. How many hours you got logged? Want me to take over?" Jack shouted.

"Enough. Nah, I can handle it," he countered, as the aircraft yawed violently from port to starboard, buffeted by intense crosswinds.

"Well I sure as hell hope so. Take a good look out your window, buddy, cause that's a heap of prime Canadian mountain real estate coming at us! You've lost a hell of a lot of sky, Roy! Pull back on the stick for crissakes! Glide attitude, Roy! Hamish, help him yank the nose up and get ready ... Brace yourselves! I'm sending another distress..."

The Lysander ploughed to a rest, tail upright, its four propeller blades, and most of the nose section buried firmly in the soggy blanket of a Canadian muskeg swamp.

Jack drifted in and out of a state of unconsciousness, hearing strange voices and seeing eerie visions of soaring eagles and sacred fires. He awoke to the softly comforting sounds of his racing pigeons cooing in their backyard loft. He struggled to control his body's violent shivering. The ice water had seeped in through the shattered windscreen glass, filling his boots. With an effort, he managed to wrench himself to sit up. "Hamish? Roy?" "Hamish? Roy?" Both men were bent forward, facing downward, motionless. Jack tore off his gloves and reached forward, groping, trying to locate each man's throat, to feel for a pulse. His fingers were numb. He could feel nothing. The cooing grew louder. Then the realization dawned on him that it was Cleo. "Hello baby! Are you okay? Where are you?" His hands trembled, as he poked around blindly for the cage. It was floating right side up, the door open, the water and feed containers drifting in the brackish swamp water, but Cleo appeared to be unhurt. He scooped her into his hands and stroked her to calm her fluttering, then gently tucked her inside his Gebirgsjäger down-lined jacket. "Ssh ...stay there, baby stay there. We have to help Hamish and Roy. We have to help Hamish and Roy... have to help Hamish and Roy. My radio. Where's my goddam radio? Here's my goddam radio." He fished in the darkness until he located it the deepening pool of black swamp water and pushed the toggle switch to 'on.' "Damn, I thought Franko said it was hermet... hermetic ...you know, Jack, goddamm waterproof! Hamish? Roy?" He was answered by a muffled groan, followed by another. "Who was that? Hamish?"

"Jack, is that you, old man?" Hamish called weakly.

"Yes, it's me, Hamish. Jack, I'm behind you. Can you move?"

"Hold on old man, I'm trying. Yes, I think so. My left hand feels numb, but everything else seems to be working. My watch is buggered all to hell. What time do you have?"

"Five forty – one. Now, try to reach over and see if you can rouse Roy."

"I'm trying. Oh, God, there's a lot of blood on his forehead and in his ears. He's concussed. Where's the first aid kit?"

After ten minutes of struggling, they had managed to extricate themselves from the wreckage without attempting to move Roy who sat sprawled, sagging forward, his rag doll arms dangling downward, with his head lolling sideways on the top of the control stick. The fury of the rain and wind now exhausted, it had settled down to a west coast drizzle, with the promise of a glorious sunrise in twenty minutes. "He's in a deep coma or dead, Jack. I can't locate a ghost of pulse," Hamish declared softly. "He may have spinal injury. Bundle him up with the emergency blankets just in case and we'll get some help. Take off his boots, they're waterlogged, and wrap up his feet and legs. Let's head over there, to the point of land, it seems the shortest distance. We'll set up camp and then come back for him."

Hamish and Jack slogged and slid their way twenty-five miserable feet through the muck until they reached the bank, and lay down on their backs, exhausted. "Give me your compass. Is the radio working, man?"

"Negative, Hamish. Screwed, blued and tattooed. But I have an ace in the hole," he smiled, while reached inside his soaking jacket to produce Cleopatra. Remember Rebeccah's last words, 'You never know?'"

"I'm sure you'd remember. Excellent! Is there paper in the capsule? I have a pencil. We're damn lucky we hit the swamp. While I'm going back to the plane, you scrounge up some sphagnum peat moss and wood for a fire. I need some supplies, like waterproof matches, a protractor, and a stick of some kind. We'll use the spare petrol jerry can in the rear of the plane to get it started, and then we'll build some ground beacons with a hell of a lot of smoke. Damp moss will be perfect for that."

Jack set about to gather dry moss for kindling and firewood and then waited for Hamish to return. "Victory!" Findlay shouted excitedly as he scrambled up the bank, "I've found everything a boy scout could hope for, Jack!"

"How's Roy doing?"

"Not well, but we'll have to risk it and move him here promptly. There's a collapsible stretcher on the port side, halfway back. All right old chap, here's the petrol and dry matches. Do your damndest ... and loan me your watch!"

A pair of whiskey jays screamed in protest at this intrusion into their territory, while Jack tended the blazing fire and watched Hamish improvise a sextant using a yardstick, a length of string weighted with a spare sparkplug, a navigator's protractor and compass and proceeded to carry out his observations. Hamish sat on a rock while doing the calculations. "Jack, we're fortunate that the sun is out. Now, as closely as I can reckon, this is our location," Hamish announced, pointing his left index finger to the Government of British Columbia Geologic Survey map. "Damn it, that's tender! The storm played ruddy havoc with the Lizzie's navigation instruments. We're just a south of Nelson. It's all jotted down here on the paper, with a note about Roy's condition. Take it."

"Okay. Hamish, that looks like a real bad sprain or it could be broken. I can splint it as soon as Cleo's bag is packed." Jack inserted the rolled scroll into the capsule and replaced the cap carefully, while Cleo raised her leg as if to assist him. "There we are. Okay, darlin', it's been one hell of a night, sorry. I can't even offer you breakfast ... now off you go straight to Frankie!" he whispered, stroking her head and then he gently wafted her upward from his outstretched hand. Without hesitation, she launched herself upward, spreading her wings, and was in her element, the air. She rose fifty feet into the cloudless, sunlit sky, circling once to get her bearings, and then took off, to the southeast.

"Magnificent!" Jack and Hamish stared up in awe as their little envoy swiftly disappeared behind a stand of Ponderosa Pines.

"Go you beauty, go, go!" Hamish shouted. "And God keep her safe from falcons and hawks!" he added under his breath, wiping his eyes with his sleeve.

"There is a Cherokee saying, U-le-nu e-me-nv e-qua a-wa-hi-li ... amen; it translates... and the talons of the great eagle!" Jack intoned quietly. "Let's get Roy out of that tin Lizzie and then I'll tend to that finger, old buddy!"

PLAN BAKER

"He did, Hamish, he definitely squeezed my hand!" Jack affirmed. "You try it! I'd swear that he blinked, too!"

"Gentlemen, please! I'm afraid you're overdoing it! Pilot Officer Brewer requires a great deal of rest after his ordeal."

Hamish apologized to the middle-aged RCAF surgeon, on whose nametag was embossed Flight Lt. Dr. Paul Jeffs, MD. "Yes, we understand, sorry, Flight Lieutenant Jeffs." As they walked together along the hallway, Hamish asked quietly, "Do you think he'll make a full recovery, eventually, or ever, Flight Lieutenant?"

"The Chief of Surgery, Wing Commander Thomas, is cautiously optimistic, Major Fox. When he's satisfied that P.O. Brewer can be moved, we're sending him off to Vancouver for more extensive neurological workups. Fortunately, there's no sign of spinal cord damage, except for extensive bruising, but the brain tissue sustained a moderately severe insult to the motor area of the cortex, when his head collided repeatedly against the controls. Of course, a patient with youth and excellent physical markers going in will have a much better chance of pulling through, if, and I repeat, if, he has the support and the inner strength to make it. Nevertheless, it won't be a piece of cake."

"Sorry, Doctor, but what exactly do you mean by a 'moderately severe insult to the motor area of the cortex'? Will he ever walk again?" Jack inquired.

"Excuse the medical jargon, Major Haney. The white matter, which controls muscle movement, here ...has been ...bruised, by repeatedly bumping against the inside of the brain case ... his skull, in other words," he explained, indicating an imaginary ear-to-ear arch on top of Jack's head.

"Okay, but even so, he's not necessarily paralysed for life?"

"Not necessarily. Recovery is possible and if all goes well, after he's mobile again, he'll have to give up any prospect of flying, until the specialists see how things are working out with his motor functions: balance, co-ordination, vision could be a major concern, and such. Rehabilitation could take a month, or a year, but frankly, if it weren't for you two, we wouldn't be discussing any such possibilities. Congratulations!"

"We four actually, Doctor ... including a brave little lady named Cleo and a gutsy, ace of a pilot, a New Zealander, named Frank!" Jack responded.

"A Squadron Leader Frank Briggs, who told us he plans to settle here after the war and start up a bush pilot service for hunters and fishermen," Hamish explained. "I can see him making a go of it, too."

"Yes, I've heard all about your friends. Young Roy Brewer has one other factor in his favour ... he's a Newfoundlander and from my experience, they're about as feisty and determined a people as any in this or any other service. And as for that finger, Major Fox, are you remembering to apply the liniment, as I directed?"

"Faithfully, he says," Jack answered, smiling. "Well, we'll be off, Flight Lieutenant. Thanks again for your excellent care."

"Three times daily!" Hamish commented wryly. "By the way, when do you expect Roy's parents to arrive from St. John's?" he queried.

"Late tonight. Take care, gentlemen," he added, saluting.

"Goodbye." Hamish and Jack walked outside and sat down on a bench in front of the medical wing. "Poor kid. Thank God, there's a glimmer of hope," Jack remarked.

"'Moderately severe insult' ... that's pulling your punches wouldn't you say?" Hamish mused aloud. "Then again, I don't blame the medicos. Tricky business neurology! So, it's back to Camp X for us to find out if the operation's still on or it's kyboshed. How's your knee, all right?"

"Fair to middlin' thanks. We're a pair of lucky hombres, Hamish, when I think how often I've been beaten up black and blue during a friendly team scrimmage!"

"Try British rugby, Association Rules, for a lark, Jack. They eat their dead. What's the blinkin' time? The flight's at 1330."

"*1145;* do you think they'll wash us out as a couple of invalid has - beens?"

"I'd think not, but it's a slim possibility, Jack. Any one of the team could easily step in as replacements, Robert, Hugh, in particular, Rebeccah, of course, in a pinch."

Jack smiled briefly, and then looked away, self-consciously.

"You're about as subtle as cello. Listen to some advice, old man, from a contented bachelor. Leave it alone, Jack. The woman is happily married with a child and has come through some terribly rough sailing since Tent Peg. She's a tower of strength, but she needs calm, order, and a semblance of stability now, not your raging hormones and emotional topsy-turvy land. She would have been going out on this one, if it weren't for her recent troubles. I mean, she saw the father of her child shot dead by Hugh, there were the horrors of imprisonment and humiliation at the hands of a Gestapo clown, name of Colonel Greilwitz, and that's just the half of it. Erik Williamson and the PM honestly believe she walks on water, and with damn good cause."

145

"Okay, I hear you. Cello? What the heck is 'cello'?" Jack asked, as a diversionary tactic.

"The crinkly clear wrappers on sweets. I would suppose that Colonel Stedman would send us to MD2 straightaway for physicals and then leave it up to HQ to make the call. There's no time for lollygagging about. A decision will have to be made immediately, or drop Baker like a hot potato, a non - starter."

"My gut tells me we'll be okay."

"And mine tells me it's lunchtime. I just wish we could arrange a quick stopover at The Citadel; guaranteed that Jerry Quan could whip up an herbal brew for our aches and sprains; that'd be a sight better than that goop the Doc fobbed off on me ... as useless as Shinola for shampoo and it reeks like turpentine."

To their immense relief, Colonel Stedman had arranged with Doctor Donald Miller to conduct their medicals at the Camp. He signed off their fitness reports, without reservations. That evening, the Colonel held a quiet gathering of the mission team in his sitting room, to reveal that Plan Baker was on hold, indefinitely. As the team members filed dejectedly into the hallway, the secure telephone rang in the Commandant's study. Colonel Stedman excused himself, went inside, and then emerged moments later. "Come in here, quickly, all of you! Listen, sssh!" He placed the receiver on a metal amplifying device and spoke out loudly. "We're all here, Sir."

"Hello and good evening, this is Colonel Warden with my good friend, Stalwart." Jack immediately knew by the slight tinniness of the speaker's voice that it was a short - wave - radio - to - telephone hook up. "I know you're enjoying a bit of a party, and shan't keep you from it, but I did want to offer my deepest appreciation and very best wishes in your endeavours. We're grateful to each of you for the excellent job you are doing and know that you will carry on splendidly. Stalwart?"

"Thank you, I just want to echo Colonel Warden's sentiments and add my warmest regards to you all ... good luck and may God bless."

"Good luck. God speed." With a muffled click, the line disconnected.

"Mr. Williamson and Mr. Churchill?" Jack asked, in awe.

"Mr. Churchill and Mr. Williamson," Rebeccah replied, nodding.

"Good news," Stedman announced enthusiastically, "that's what we wanted to hear, '...Enjoying a bit of a party, and shan't keep you from it... very best wishes in your endeavours...carry on.' We're back on track, departure in less than forty-eight hours. Now, who'd like a nip? I have gin, rum, scotch, and rye whiskey, help yourselves, and Kaintucky sour mash bourbon especially for you, Jack, if you wouldn't mind coming to the kitchen to pour it yourself. Hamish, join us, please?"

"Cheers!" Stedman toasted Jack and Hamish. "Now, there's a wrinkle that HQ has tacked, well, not precisely, tacked on ...however," he paused.

Hamish looked at Jack, and slowly set down his drink on the countertop. "Yes, Colonel?"

"It concerns communications. You might recall telling me about the Ojibwa Canadian Signals man you met at the restaurant, Hamish?"

"Yes, I do, Colonel, Burton Johnson."

"Yes. I found what you told me about him fascinating and decided to do some probing. The short version is this; he has joined the team, here, not on the ground."

"To do what, exactly, Colonel?" Hamish inquired, his voice rising. "Excuse me, Sir, but where's the wisdom of adding another person at the eleventh hour?"

"I know you're upset about not being consulted, Hamish, but it's a vital safeguard and has been blessed all the way up the line. Let me explain, please."

147

"Very well..."

"While you and Jack were on training at 109, it occurred to me that communications is our weakest link, so I called upon Colonel Truscott."

"How so, Sir?" Jack pressed.

"Please, let me finish. The plan we've agreed upon is to maintain a radio blackout, correct? Yet, realistically, we must have a means of making contact, otherwise there's no sense in pretending to have a communications protocol. We know from the Tent Peg de-briefing transcripts and our information from RAF listening posts that Rebeccah and Hugh were under SD electronic surveillance. Now, Dr. Phil tells me that X-1 is capable of sending transmissions at ultra high-speed, in bursts of code groups, which might be undetectable. I say, might. Now, imagine those code groups wrapped in a cipher that is unbreakable, if detected. Another drink?"

"Yes, please. You have my attention, Colonel," Jack stated. "An unbreakable cipher is mathematically and theoretically possible, but realistically, we're not there yet. We can make them near – infallible, almost impossible to decipher by using the classic methods of encryption: transposition, substitution, vowel – consonant shifts, random functions, and fancy it up with machines that have moveable rotors, but there are always inherent mechanical, human and structural weaknesses, not the least of which are codebooks that fall into enemy hands, operator laziness and lapses, designer carelessness or downright asinine stupidity ... the list goes on. It's all about looking for patterns and once the root of the pattern is unlocked, the dominos eventually fall into place and the game's up. Still, we continue to pursue the improbable dream."

"Agreed, and you are the cryptography expert, but just suppose the language itself is incomprehensible to any listeners, except the operator and controller?"

"Non-European, non-Asian then, are you saying?" Hamish suggested.

"Right you are, Hamish."

"I get it, and they 'talk' if you will, using Morse, in this language, which is encrypted and ... Sir, you said this native fellow, Burton Johnson is Ojibwa ... by any chance is he a Cherokee speaker?" Jack inquired excitedly.

"Yes, fluent!"

"Wow, do you see the advantage, Hamish? This is pure genius! Is there enough time to pull it together? When can I meet Burton?"

"This way to Hydra, gentlemen. Dr. Phil has put everything else aside," Colonel Stedman explained while they walked across the damp grass to the communications building. "He, Hugh, Frank and the encryption group here have been slaving at ironing out the problems, as I hope you'll agree." He knocked on Frank's office door.

The Communications Building as seen from the entrance to Camp X

"Burton, meet Major Fox, and Major Haney."

"Whew, that's a helluvan aircraft. All just for us?" exclaimed Jack, in appreciation of the four engine, twin tail RCAF Halifax Mark 11 heavy bomber lumbering to a halt outside the heavily – guarded Oshawa Airport terminal building.

Frank smiled. "She's as reliable as rain, right up there with the Lancs for popularity with the crews, Jacko. New Rolls - Royce Merlin supercharged engines, well - armed, good body armour, decent top speed, long range fuel tanks, with no bad habits of which to speak, now that they've put right the tail section flaw in the Mark 1's."

149

"Right, let's be going, Jack!" Hamish urged impatiently. "Thanks, Briggsy. We'll be in touch!" he quietly commented as he and Jack walked down the line of outstretched hands.

"Thanks, thanks for everything," Jack repeated to each member of the Shining Oath Team.

Speaking softly, Rebeccah pressed a small object into his palm, "Something to take with you for luck, Jack. It's my charm and has kept me from harm," she whispered. "I sewed it inside the lining of my jacket."

"Thank you, Major." He grinned shyly, hoping that he might hold onto her hand for even a second longer.

"Major Haney!"

"Okay, Hamish, I'm coming!" he shouted, fastening the zipper of his sheepskin flight jacket and hurrying to the exit door.

Together he and Hamish trudged out of the terminal toward the waiting bomber, whose twin bomb bay doors were gaping open, waiting to swallow them.

Saluting briskly, the young man on the ground stated, "Sergeant Brisco, Midsection Gunner. May I help you up, gentlemen?"

"Thank you, Sergeant Brisco, we'll be fine," Hamish replied, reaching up for handholds and then slowly drawing himself up and inside. Jack followed suit. Inside the confining belly of the Halifax, Sergeant Thomas,

Bomb Aimer greeted and then escorted them forward, introducing each crewmember, on the way.

"That's my station!" he remarked with pride, indicating a short, narrow indentation in the floor.

"Not exactly spacious, eh, Sergeant?" Jack remarked, noting the large piece of complex equipment, which bore a striking similarity to the top – secret American Norden bombsight/auto pilot.

"No, it's not Sir," he replied, smiling briefly, "but I didn't enlist for comfort. This is our Skipper, Flying Officer Andrews," he shouted over the start-up whine of the superchargers, which became a ground-shaking bellow as each of four Merlin 1,280 horsepower engines caught.

"Welcome aboard G V for George Victor, gentlemen. I'm F.O. Archie Andrews and this is our Navigator, Warrant Officer Billy Bauer. Try to make yourselves comfortable. Wireless Op Givens has patched in the headsets in your helmets so you can listen in, or chat, if you feel like it, until we depart Gander. Put on the masks, please. Oxygen will switch on automatically when it's needed, but if you start to feel woozy, use the thumb switch for manual flow control. We're cleared for takeoff, so sit back, relax, and we'll have some juice and a sandwich in about a half an hour. Flying time to Gander is... Excuse me..." He readjusted his right earphone as he resumed communications with the tower.

Hamish and Jack pulled on the leather flying helmets and adjusted the oxygen masks, then making themselves as comfortable as possible, leaned against the cylindrical aluminium cargo canisters as the aircraft ascended until Archie levelled off.

"17,000 feet, cruising altitude," Bauer reported. "How are you gentlemen doing?"

"Just fine, WO!" Hamish responded. "Where are we?"

"Over Dorval, north of Montréal, and heading north, north east, Sir. Bologna sandwich and apple juice?"

Afterwards, when Jack was quite certain that Hamish had dozed off, he slipped off his right glove and reached into the slash pocket of his flight jacket to retrieve Rebeccah's keepsake. He switched off his microphone, and raised his goggles, then holding the object between his thumb and forefinger, tilted it forward and back, to catch the light. He was able to recognise that it was a silver coin, about the size of an American quarter, bearing the imprint of a monarch.

"Very nice! Silver sixpence, George V, or perhaps Edward V11, either way, becoming rarer by the minute ... quite valuable actually; I should think she does like you, Jack. Let me have a peek?" Hamish requested, matter – of - factly. "George five, in excellent condition ... worth a few bob. Here, keep it well out of sight, old man. We don't want Jerry finding that if we're picked up."

151

"I thought you were asleep, dammit!"

"Don't worry, lad. Your secret's safe with Hamish Findlay," he murmured, closing his eyes. "Wake me when we're landing."

George Victor took off for an undisclosed destination in Northern Scotland via Rejavik, Iceland, from RCAF Base Gander, Newfoundland, in a light drizzle at 0600 the following morning.

"So tell me this, Hamish, you've a Scottish name, but you haven't much of a Scottish accent. Why's that?"

"True, I am a Scot, or Scottish, but never say 'Scotch' mind, by birthright, and proud of it, Jack. Some non – Scots boast that they're 'Scotch by absorption,'" he added. "However, as a lad, I was sent south to be educated in English public schools, what you'd call in America, boarding schools. I was a stranger in a strange land at a time when Scots, particularly Highlanders, were still regarded with dark suspicion, although I didn't really pay much attention to the rebellion of 1776 until I got to university. I suppose over the years, I absorbed, no joke intended, or was absorbed into what you'd call the dominant culture in which I grew up."

"How does that make you feel?"

"We're probably the planet's most successful colonizers, Jack; Scots fit in and make a contribution wherever we settle. Why? Qualities such as ambition certainly, ability, adaptability, canniness, steely intestinal fortitude, are typified by our heroes, like William Wallace, and Robert the Bruce. Americans love the rags – to - riches success stories like that of the fabulously - wealthy steel tycoon, Andrew Carnegie, from Dumferline, or Civil War Generals Robert E. Lee, George McClellan, and likely,

Ulysses S. Grant, who became President, as you know, while Canada's first Prime Minister, John A. MacDonald was a Glaswegian. The list is enormously long and I haven't mentioned England, Australia, and New Zealand. Oh, we've produced our share of scallywags and scoundrels, too. But I think Robbie Burns said it best for Scots no matter where, 'Farewell to the Highlands, farewell to the North, The birthplace of valour, the country of worth! Wherever I wander, wherever I roam, the hills of the Highlands forever I love ... my heart's in the Highlands, wherever I go!'"

"That's beautiful; it reminds me that my mother's roots are Cherokee and Scots."

"See, there you are, lad. We're also noted for being trustworthy and secretive, cagey, and canny, enterprising you might say, as the disproportionate number of Scots in the Allied intelligence services proves. Now let's get some kip. I don't know about you, but I found those bunk beds deplorably soft," Hamish commented, fastening his oxygen mask.

Lulled by the droning hum of the engines, Jack zipped up his flight jacket and settled back, to fall asleep. He wakened with a start, looking up at Flying Officer 'Pinky' Booth, Flight Engineer, holding a waxed paper - wrapped sandwich and a thermal container.

"Chef's day off, Major," Booth remarked with a crooked grin, "do mystery meat treat and warm tea sound alright for breakfast?"

"Sure sounds good to me, thanks Flying Officer," Jack answered, yawning. "Say, where'd my partner get to?" he inquired, biting into the sandwich. "Whew, that's a lot of mustard!"

"Yes Sir, it helps kill the taste. Major Fox? He's been forward for two hours. I'll pour if you'd hold the cup," he responded, his legs apart, steadying himself.

"What's he doing up there?"

"Playing pilot."

"Hmm. I need to use the head..."

"We call it the P tube, Sir. Just you, a funnel, and a rubber hose leadin' to God's great out - of - doors. It's over there," Booth indicated, nodding, "and watch your head, Major. I'd suggest that you batten down the hatches when you finish. Skipper says we're within fifteen minutes of touchdown in Iceland and warns that things might get exciting ... holy Nelly!" The aircraft suddenly banked sharply to starboard, and then levelled off, causing Jack to spill the entire contents of the metal cup onto Booth's flight boots.

"Damn it, sorry."

"Not a problem, Major. Here, take the container. On second thought, no," he smiled. "Well, I'd best be getting back to my post. Cheerio for now, Major."

153

"The P tube, trust me, Pinky," Jack shouted, crossing his heart. "While you're at it, send back Major Fox before he does us all in!"

"Were you at the stick just now, Hamish?"

"Yes, why?"

"Just curious."

"It had been on autopilot, so I asked the Skipper's permission to go on manual. Just a slight trim adjustment, old man, nothing to wet your pants about," Hamish declared nonchalantly. "We're coming into Keflavik Airport, Iceland. I've been following the development of this airfield since the American military constructed it. Four runways, fully illuminated, excellent communications ... could have done it ... piece of cake."

The aircraft landed, taxiing smoothly to a stop. Jack and Hamish deplaned quickly to take advantage of the sixty-five minute refuelling stop, intending to stretch their legs while enjoying the refreshing 500 F air, in spite of pelting rain and occasional gusts of chilled Arctic blasts beneath the moody grey Icelandic sky. Instead, on the urging of Skipper Archie and the crew, they lounged for twenty minutes in the sauna. After a hot shower, they shaved, dressed, and then walked a short distance to the USAF canteen. Inside, an exuberant Royal Australian Air Force crew were debating loudly how best to abduct and smuggle Carole - Ann, the pretty, petite, brunette waitress onto their new B-25 bomber, under the nose of their skipper who, it appeared, was temporarily absent from the table. Following the example of their VG mates, Jack and Hamish ordered T-bone steaks with peas and mashed potatoes, followed by fresh apple pie à la mode, and brewed coffee with dairy cream.

Abandoning the raucous Australians to self-service status, Carole - Ann had immediately homed in on Jack's All-American quarterback looks. Captivated by his 'soft -as – fresh peaches Georgia drawl,' she took it upon herself to bolster the charming airman's morale addressing him as 'Sugar.'

Chatting and ribbing 'Sugar' good -naturedly, the men sauntered back and climbed back on board V G. Ten minutes later, the Halifax was airborne, on a heading described by Billy Bauer as 'the bleeding backside of beyond,' somewhere in the Shetland Islands.

"Tell me once more, Admiral. You've just stated that the Abwehr Ausland (Foreign Intelligence Service) cannot perform Operation Diamond because you lack the necessary tools? I find that very hard to countenance, frankly," he remarked dryly, drumming the fingers of his left hand on the desktop. "As you are aware, Admiral, my late predecessor, Obergruppenführer Heydrich, always held you in the highest regard. Yes, you were like a father, a mentor to him, as he remarked more than once. So naturally, should I not expect the same level of shall we say, inter-service collegiality and co-operation?" Ernst Kaltenbrunner inquired coldly, while rubbing his jaw.

The 'little Admiral' despised almost as much as he feared this fanatical Austrian Nazi, a one – time lawyer and Party hack, Ernst Kaltenbrunner, Doctor of Laws, his deadliest opponent in the labyrinthine corridors of power in the Nazi hierarchy and his equal in ambition. Kaltenbrunner, the blunt, brutal, unscrupulous and vicious anti-Semite, now wielded absolute control over the Gestapo and the numerous civil and military Nazi police agencies as Chief of the SD, the SS Reich Security Service. Upon their first meeting, the Admiral had noted that Kaltenbrunner's character was matched physically by a host of remarkably unappealing features. The too long, protruding jaw was exaggerated by a deep scar, which zigzagged from the left side of his mouth to his nose. A wrestler's bull neck emphasized his overbearing presence, which, combined with his enormous height, and ungainly physique, permitted him to intimidate his victims and bully his peers with equal ease.

Feeling his palms sweating profusely, the Admiral shrugged and continued calmly. "It's not my intention to resist or subvert SD policies, Dr. Kaltenbrunner, far from it. But, I have neither the qualified personnel nor the available means at my disposal. Furthermore, our information clearly indicates that the target is extremely well guarded, perhaps impossible to get to, Obergruppenführer. What do you suggest?"

"One might be led to suspect that your heart really isn't in the game, Admiral. May I offer in evidence this rather interesting, ah, dossier? There are photographs of a certain silver-haired Abwehr Chief in Ibiza, Madrid, even Lisbon, Portugal of all places, all perfectly innocent, or extremely incriminating depending upon one's point of view, no? However, I would hate to see these fall into the wrong hands, wouldn't you?" he inquired, his reedy voice rising with attempted subtlety.

155

The Admiral froze. Kaltenbrunner was holding out a thick brown file folder, which meant that the Gestapo had either gathered substantive proof of his devious attempts to deal directly with the Allies through sympathetic channels in Spain and Portugal, or God forbid, his arms - length but damning connections with anti – Führer elements within the German High Command. For a moment, the Admiral considered just how much worse the hands could be than those of this Neanderthal. "What could be so interesting about an old spymaster on a junket in Spain, Obergruppenführer?" he asked with feigned innocence.

Kaltenbrunner carefully set down the file on his green desktop blotter and steepled his fingertips. "Plenty, Wilhelm, plenty. Let's not play games," he suddenly shouted, rising partway from his chair, while pounding the desk with his left fist. "Admiral, I am warning you and it will go no further, yet..." he continued coolly, "but a water - tight case could be easily made that you refuse to avenge the attempted assassination of the Führer by the British Secret Service because it is your own wish to see our leader done away with!"

"That is patently unfair and untrue! I am a good German, an honourable soldier and I say categorically, that I am not a traitor!" he retorted loudly, his voice quavering.

"Then prove it, prove it, my Admiral. We'll supply the means, something lethal, subtle, and undetectable. You provide the people and the plan. If Mr. Erik Williamson can't be dealt with in New York City, choose an alternate, someone very, very close to the heart of his gangster empire, like his bootlicker Brooks or that crazed thug, Samson at Camp X. Weiss, the Jew woman, is off her head and not worth the bother. Cunnington's a tempting possibility, but for later. I want to send an unequivocal message to these BSO bastards; the mischief their Tent Peg cowboy misadventure caused for Reich Protector Speer, the Security Service and most particularly for our Führer has not been forgotten. Do you understand, yes? Good, you have one week. You won't fail me, will you, Wilhelm?"

"No, understood, Ernst."

"Oh, one other thing, Admiral..." Kaltenbrunner purred.

"Yes?" Wilhelm stopped at the door, and turned slowly around, bracing for another outburst.

"Do you think they would be so foolhardy as to try again?"

"Do you mean the Camp X ... hooligans?"

"Another futile assassination ploy devised by BSO at STS 103, along with perhaps SIS, SOE...? One or all three?"

"Definitely; yes, all three, with their damn British Commandos and the SAS probably thrown in for insurance. And this time, Ernst, the Americans will be in it up to their chins."

"Then, where would they attempt to strike him, in your professional opinion, confidentially, off the record, of course. There are no hidden microphones, Wilhelm! So, you can tell me honestly what you think," he stated expansively.

Recognizing Kaltenbrunner's patronizing tone and use of the familiar 'du' as a typically clumsy overture, Wilhelm debated whether to withhold or divulge his guilty knowledge. 'Now,' he decided. If not, it would be ultimately be extracted by the Gestapo through far more persuasive and unpleasant methods. "No question of it, Obergruppenführer," he declared.

"Well for God's sake, where?"

Wilhelm paused for effect, savouring the moment, then softly uttered, "The Berghof."

"Scheiss!" Kaltenbrunner swore. "Natürlich!" He stopped pacing and glared at the Admiral, whom he judged the silver fox of German espionage, the Führer's grand master of deception, intrigue, and the double-cross. For a moment, Obergruppenführer Kaltenbrunner felt the urge to stride over and strangle this aristocratic, condescending little Chief of Military Intelligence, who had never lowered himself to become a card - carrying Nazi. In truth, Kaltenbrunner was the ultimate pragmatist who paid lip service to, but cared little for the well being of this or any future Führer, so long as the Nazi Party and the Third Reich survived to ensure his personal advancement and as protection for his hard won, newfound career. The Admiral's dalliances with suspected pro-Allied, anti-Nazi plotters made him a threat to Kaltenbrunner's continued existence. Making a mental note to order his organization to dig more deeply, Kaltenbrunner continued, "Admiral, are you merely guessing or do you know this as hard fact?"

157

"Let's just say, Ernst, trust an old spy's intuition."

"Yes, yes, but when, Wilhelm?"

"Sooner, rather than later. You know the reasoning as well as I," he confided, tapping his right index finger against his temple. "And they're anything but stupid. Good day, Obergruppenführer."

As Hamish and Jack were vaulting onto the ground from the underside of the Halifax, they were greeted with a shout, "Hamish, you old bandit! About bloody time! Who's your mate?" Hamish introduced Major Jack Haney to Lieutenant - Colonel Jacob 'Jack' Blackmore, Special Air Service. "Lord love a duck, another 'Jack,'" the fatigues – clad paratrooper roared. "I expect you're knackered, ravenous, and horny, am I right? We can help with the first two! Step into my Bentley," he grinned, leading them to a battered jeep. "This is Chief Warrant Officer Ronny West, same unit."

"What about the crew and our supplies, Colonel?" Jack asked. "Oh, I see." Their two canisters had been placed on the ground. A fuelling lorry was pulled up beside Victor George.

"Archie's been ordered to return to base soonest; after they've replenished their petrol we'll load them up with some grub and it's fare thee well. They never stay for a layover unless they're socked in by the weather."

"Grand bunch of lads!" Hamish remarked. "Last time I was here, Jack, this place looked like something left over from the siege of

Omdurman: a few rag tag tents, a hut, temporary this and that and that ruddy cave like the hall of the mountain king. Now you've actual barracks and a hangar ...all very civilised. Tell me, does that Jerry aircraft, Charley Four, still fly over to keep an eye on you chaps?" Hamish queried.

"Charley? No, not anymore," Blackmore responded shaking his head. "He was one of many casualties in the Luftwaffe's demise here in the isles."

"You Brits! Who the hell is Charley Four?" Jack asked impatiently. "And what was the siege of Omdurman?"

"Charley Four was a German observer plane serial C 4, that used to stooge around once - a – day, a Henschel-123 biplane ... a sweet little ship it was. I hated to have to bring it down in bits. We managed to salvage the engine ... a jewel: BMW, nine cylinder, radial, 880 horses. I'm looking forward to designing a racecar around it. Imagine lapping Brooklands in that beast! We have the pilot with us here. The blighter's name's Karl Kaiser, so naturally, we named him 'the emperor'; he's a clarinettist, if your tastes run to Mozart's Concerto and the German Dances at bedtime, but he is a wizard carpenter as well ... and happy as a clam to be out of the action, as you might imagine. Right then, hop out here lads and I'll show you around our new and improved digs!" Blackmore exclaimed.

"Omdurman, Jack," Blackmore explained as they walked the campsite grounds, "was a city in the Sudan, North Africa. We were beaten, actually severely thrashed both there and at the capitol, Khartoum in 1884 by the Mahdi, a charismatic, spiritual leader of the Sudanese; the Mahdi beheaded our very popular General 'Chinese' Gordon. You can picture the public outrage and cries for retaliation at home! We returned, up the Nile in '95, heavily armed, and reinforced with Egyptian troops, Maxim guns, long-range artillery, the works, and in '98, we crushed the Dervishes, the holy warriors of Islam. Fine soldiers they were ... but hoodwinked by their leaders into believing themselves immortal; it turned out a pitiful blood bath."

"A young cavalryman with the 21st Lancers who was also filing reports for the *Morning Post*, by-line: Winston Churchill, saw action there. Did you know, in 1899, he wrote a national best seller documenting the horrors of the Sudanese campaigns, called *The River War?*" Hamish asked.

"And required reading for any officer," Blackmore responded. "Now, as you lads are off at twilight tomorrow evening, I'd like to propose that we have a bit of a wing ding to wish you luck tonight and then spend the day recovering," Blackmore announced. He stopped at a massive rock overhanging the entrance of what Jack took to be an underground cavern. "Come inside," Colonel Blackmore urged, "this is our ops centre and living space. It's fully electrified and a damn sight improved since you were here, Hamish. Some sections are off - limits for security, but I'll show you around what's not."

During dinner, Colonel Blackmore and his officers regaled Hamish and Jack with stories of their missions including some near - misses and mishaps which they had encountered on their lightning forays into England. One incident which Hamish and Jack found particularly amusing involved the 'snatching' of Reich Protector Speer's Chief of Homeland Security, Gruppenführer Hugo Haas, while he was walking his dog in Mayfair.

"Hugo had been appointed to replace Gruppenführer Walther Richard Lange, whom you might recall, they executed for botching the capture of you and your cronies. It turned out that old Hugo was actually a 'plant', a double agent of British SIS and the dog belonged to his mistress, a secretary in the same office. He was more than a little put out until we verified his claim with G."

It struck Jack that the feat which required that they 'reinsert' Haas with his dog, onto a sidewalk in one of London's most elegant districts, complete with a contrived cover story, under the nose of his family and staff, while leaving no evidence of his abduction or his return, and the existence of his paramour, was a classic example of the Special Air Service' legendary ability to carry out the most demanding clandestine operations with apparent ease.

"But, hold on, weren't you informed about his status before the operation, Colonel?" Jack inquired.

"My general orders, Jack, were to undermine the enemy's confidence, morale, etcetera, by disrupting his decision – making abilities at the command level, by any means at my disposal. I didn't ask and no one informed me that Haas was one of ours! C'est la guerre! Now, one more before we turn in? By the by, how's the lovely lady Sylvia? Is she well? Survived her trials and tribulations has she? Did she have the baby?"

Jack glanced at Hamish. "No, sadly, that didn't work out, but she's fully recovered now and back on the active roster. She and Hugh were married shortly after their return ... and she's as charming, bright and attractive a lass as ever, right Jack?"

"Uhmm. Right."

"Capitol. Please give them both my best regards. Well, a big day tomorrow so it's good night then. Warrant Officer West will show you to your quarters."

Undressing quickly, Jack and Hamish lay on their cots. "How's your head?" Jack whispered.

"Spinning. Yours?"

"Yeah, mine too, but it's nearly stopped. Try putting your outside foot on the floor."

"You must be joking, man!"

"No, I'm not. Just try it."

"Damn, that's cold. Okay, there. Now what?"

"Keep it there. Just lie quietly and try to relax," Jack answered soothingly. "It's working for me."

"If you say so..." Hamish responded uneasily. "I should have remembered that this lot blend their five star brandy with aviation petrol!"

"Son of a bitch! What's that, bagpipes?" Jack suddenly shouted, sitting up. A piercing wail drifted along the corridor.

"Bagpipes? And you say you have Scot's blood? Really! It's a clarinet, playing Mozart, old man!" Hamish replied.

"It's the German, Klaus Keister, or whatever the hell his name is."

"Karl Kaiser. He's quite good, listen to how smoothly he handles the triplets," Hamish responded, humming softly. The music reached a crescendo and then gradually receded. "There, he's gone past."

"This is bizarre!" Jack declared. "She'll never believe it! A German PoW who makes furniture by day and wanders around a top – secret base at night, playing the licorice stick."

"They'd break his neck in a tick if he set a foot wrong," Hamish stated flatly, then paused and continued. "Who won't believe it?"

"Never mind. Good night."

Bleary – eyed, Jack awoke at 0615 to see Hamish, in undershorts, seated on the bare concrete floor, vigorously doing sit ups.

"You'll get piles from sitting on that cold cement! Did you sleep at all? ... Are you worried?" Jack asked, yawning.

"Yes to both, you?" Hamish puffed. "And that's an old wive's tale."

"Whatever... I had this dream about being captured, thrown into a squalid, rat - infested prison, and being forced to listen to Hitler and Eva Braun play the bagpipes."

"Exquisite torture that," Hamish commented with a grimace. "Forty-nine ... fifty. Your turn while I take over the shower. What time is your radio check with Corporal Johnson?"

"I'll add fifty finger-tip push-ups to that!" Jack grinned.

"Good on you mate! Throw me that towel like a good fellow?"

"Thirteen fifteen, GMT here, which is 0915 there, adjusted for daylight saving. Leave some hot water, okay?" he shouted at Hamish's retreating backside.

Following breakfast, Colonel Blackmore beckoned Hamish and Jack to follow him through the underground passageways to a small, windowless room tucked behind the Ops Centre. After placing a guard outside, he left. First, they removed, unrolled, and laid out their Gebirgsjäger uniforms, then spread out and examined their maps, and then unpacked, checked, rechecked and finally, after Jack verified that the X-1's battery packs were fully charged, he carefully repacked their two supplies canisters. Satisfied, they locked the door and headed out doors to look for something to keep them occupied until lunchtime.

They each made a walking stick and hiked slowly, taking in the scenery, until Jack halted on a rock outcropping, which provided a spectacular vista of the mountains and the North Sea. "Unbelievably beautiful ... what are you thinking, Hamish?"

"Oh, mainly about our chances of pulling it off, and returning, I suppose. I'd love to come back to Scotland some day..." he responded, shading his eyes as he gazed.

"What's your estimate ... of either?"

"To be truthful, I would never knowingly take an assignment voluntarily if I thought it had less than a fifty - fifty chance of succeeding, Jack. Beyond that? It's in the laps of the gods, no pun intended. As to whether or not we'll survive? Yes, I think so. One question, and pardon me for being personal, but where's the lass' sixpence?"

"Safely hidden inside my jacket lining, with the Reichsmarks."

"I'd be a great deal happier if you'd leave it behind, but I've long since resigned myself that you'll do as you will, lad," he sighed. "Let's get back."

By 1305h, they were in the radio room, standing behind Sergeant Terry Smythe the W/T operator, awaiting a signal from Camp X. At 1310, Smythe handed Jack an extra set of earphone as he sat down. Hamish watched the electric clock and waited. At 131503, Jack held up his left thumb briefly as he rapidly tapped out his user identification and secret code word, and then began jotting symbols on a yellow pad. Seconds later, he swung around in the chair. "That's my man! Everything's set, pickup at 2120 tonight. But get this, Major, Colonel Stedman has asked if we intend to continue. Is that usual? I have to reply within thirty seconds."

"Send 'affirmative!'" Hamish answered tersely. "Standard procedure, in case an agent develops cold feet," he explained, looking over Jack's shoulder at the message pad. "I assume that's written in Cherokee?"

"Yessir," Jack nodded affirmatively, "Tsalagi."

"Tsalagi?"

"Our word for Cherokee."

"Ripping..."

"Would you two enjoy a bit of recreational rock climbing? Of course you would, Hamish, I know, for sure! Jack? Jolly good. Ronny West has the jeep loaded up, waiting. Can't afford to have you sittin' around, rustin' away, what?"

Happy to be distracted, they followed Colonel Blackmore outside.

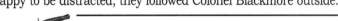

163

They looked up in fascination trying to pinpoint the source of a buzzing drone overhead which quickly revealed itself, becoming the distinct outline of a Lysander, emerging from a low cloudbank like a wraith, then gliding down eerily in the moonless sky, landing delicately, and after taxiing three-hundred yards, coming to a halt, its motor idling. Jack and Hamish noted that it was painted black. "Move it, Ronny, damn it!" Blackmore shouted to Warrant Officer West, who responded by over revving the jeep's engine, and crashing low gear, causing Hamish to flinch involuntarily, as the jeep lunged the short distance across the field toward the single engine airplane.. "Let's go!" Blackmore ordered. West jammed on the brakes. Following the Colonel and Ronny, they leapt out of the vehicle and rushed to take hold of the Lysander's tubular wing struts, and pushed, in attempting to help the pilot face the plane's nose into the wind. Ducking the strong propeller wash, while covering their ears, Hamish and Jack scrambled, stooping, to reach and clamber up a short ladder, which was fixed to the Lizzie's side. Three minutes later, they and their cargo containers were aloft, bound for Bavaria.

"Kaz, I don't believe it! Talk about luck!" Hamish shouted excitedly, reaching forward to briefly clasp the pilot's free hand. "Jack, we're going to be fine! This is champion! Meet Kaz, the ace of Lysander pilots! Kaz, this is Jack."

Aware of their recent setback with Pilot Officer Brewer, who, Kaz remarked, was recovering much more quickly than expected, he reassured them that the odds of coming to grief this time were fewer, as the weather reports promised overcast conditions, free of major disturbances all the way to southern Germany, via France. Also, the likelihood of running out of gasoline was unlikely, he explained, as this aircraft had been fitted with the newest, large - capacity auxiliary fuel tanks and all armaments had been removed in order to reduce its weight. As Jack was about to inquire, Kaz acknowledged that being caught in German radar and shot down by Luftwaffe fighters, or hit by ground ack-ack, anti-aircraft fire, were possible, despite the intricate flight plan which had been set out.

"Intricate ... did you say we're going into France? When was that decided?" Hamish asked.

"I don't really know, but have a look at the map." Kaz handed a clipboard to Hamish. Leaning forward, Jack could see a blue-pencil line marking their route into Central France. "Valencay," Kaz announced, jabbing the map with his index finger. "It's an SOE and French Resistance stronghold. I have to deliver a package, and at the same time top off the fuel, then we'll be off." He looked at Hamish. "Less than ten minutes on the ground, I swear to God!" he remarked, making the sign of the cross on his chest. The voices trailed off. Jack sat back as Hamish and Kaz relived their flight in an overloaded Mosquito fighter-bomber to the SAS base, Scotland. Able to overhear fragments of the conversation, he was on the verge of commenting when Kaz referred to an agent, Silvia; then thinking better of saying anything, Jack closed his eyes.

A drop in pitch of the aircraft's engine wakened him. "What's up?"

"The Loire Valley," Hamish answered. "There's the Loire River, curving like a bow over there. Ever visited here? Magnifique!"

Jack shook his head. "I should have, right?"

"Only if your tastes run to magnificent chateaus, medieval castles, superb wines from the hundreds of local vineyards, great hotels, comfortable hostels and more history than you can possibly soak up in a month, definitely. Pity it's dark. There's a ground beacon. Is that the correct pattern, Kaz?"

As soon as Kaz brought the aircraft to a stop, two figures carrying Sten guns, wearing black pea jackets and woollen caps materialized out of the darkness and approached Hamish's side of the cockpit.

"What's the password, Kaz?"

"Les gens français sont formidables," Kaz replied, with something approaching a French pronunciation. "Have your pistol ready!"

"That's a mouthful! Right, here goes," Hamish announced, placing his German issue Walther PPK on his lap and then pushing open his side window. As he started to speak, the two figures raised their weapons, taking careful aim at Hamish's head. "Bloody hell, the uniform! They think I'm German!

"Je suis Anglais! SOE, Anglais, SOE! Suis pas Allemand, English, not bloody German!" he shouted.

Jack's pulse raced as he released the safety lock on his Luger. He was unable to understand any of the rapid exchange except 'anglais, americain, français and formidable'. A minute later, Kaz, apparently having defused the situation and satisfied with the guerrillas' own bona fides, asked Jack to reach behind his seat and locate a small rectangular metal box. Jack retrieved it, passing it forward to Hamish, who was conversing fluently with the two Maquisards when a horse - drawn farm wagon appeared from the edge of the field.

"What's that?" Jack asked anxiously, straining to see into the darkness. "Shouldn't we be getting the hell out of here about now? We've been on the ground eight minutes, Kaz!"

"L'essence, petrol, the gasoline," Hamish explained as the cart's driver having alighted, was scampering across the field, toting two large jerry cans, the contents of which he proceeded to pour one after the other into the Lysander's fuel tank. "He's hurrying. Henri said they spotted an armoured German patrol on the main road, three kilometres south, coming..." He was cut short by two loud taps on the fuselage and a shout from the two Resistance persons.

With an 'Au revoir, bonne chance, vive la France!' accompanied by a 'V for victory' sign, Hamish closed the hatch window just as Kaz began manoeuvring the aircraft's nose into the prevailing wind.

"The 'bloody' convinced them, you know, Hamish," Kaz remarked with a grin. "Hold on, we're taking off!"

"What a stupid blunder!" Hamish commented, shaking his head in disbelief. "That was a wrinkle we obviously overlooked, right, Jack?"

"I won't put it in my report, promise, if you don't. Besides, I owe you one, buddy."

"Can I ask what was in the container, Kaz?" Jack asked at length.

Kaz shrugged. "Sure, coins, gold Napoleons. It's the only safe currency. How much or how many, I don't know. They needed it to bribe the German jail guards in Tours. The Gestapo rounded up one of their leaders recently, last Friday, apparently."

"Where is he being held?" Jack inquired.

"She ... for now, Tours. If she's transported to that Gestapo hellhole, Hotel Terminus, in Lyon, it'll be too late."

"She'll be tortured unmercifully by the SS butcher of Lyon, Klaus Barbie, until she's forced to give up their network ... or dead. If she talks, she'll be hanged anyway, at Buchenwald. Nobody gets out of that devil's clutches alive," Hamish commented sombrely.

"Put on those headphones, Hamish," Kaz exclaimed, excitedly.

"Here Jack, take mine. Listen... Could you get that fragment of chatter? That's the United States Army Air Force ... I'd guess B-25's with P-51 Mustang escorts, flying at the bombers' maximum, around 25,000 feet. It's unusual, because the Americans carry out daylight raids, mostly. German air defences are going to be throwing up everything but the kitchen sink in their path and then some."

"That could be good news for us," Jack commented, "if they're kept busy elsewhere."

"We'll see, my friends," Kaz replied. "We'll see. Care to take over for a while, Major Haney?"

"No thanks," Jack responded. "You're doin' just fine, skip. A-1!"

"Thanks, just as well, it's going to get dicey when we cross into the Fatherland in a few minutes. We've been skirting the northernmost Alps but as you can see on the map, we have to head south to reach the target and we'll get our share of mountain dodging in Bavaria ...oh, there it is now, look down, on your right."

"The mighty Rhine River, Jack! That's really a breathtaking sight, isn't it? Hamish observed.

"By the way, Kaz, precisely where do you intend to head after you drop us?"

"The Special Operations bases at either Bari, or Brindisi, Italy, rest, relax and wait to be called back," Kaz explained jauntily. "The Swiss are neutral, but might not be that welcoming, frankly. I could be impounded there for the duration. Besides, I like my days sun-drenched and my vino full bodied, like the women in Italia! Care for a sandwich and some chicory coffee?"

"Yes, anything, thanks. Here, Jack. Good Lord man! Bari or Brinsidi? Either one, that's a long way down the Italian boot!" Hamish acknowledged. "Where do you call home?"

167

Kaz didn't reply for several seconds, carefully weighing his response. "Oshawa. Ever heard of it? Oh, it'll be nip and tuck, but I'll make it, God willing. The extra fuel we took on in France was, I guess you'd say, my insurance. I'm still okay. Take the map, would you please, Hamish? Here's where we are and there's the target. The length of each leg in nautical miles is shown in red. Our airspeed is 180 knots, helped by a steady tailwind of 23 knots; the altimeter reads... 5,300 feet. Can you calculate our remaining flying time?"

"Fifty-four minutes," Jack shot back immediately.

"Good show, Major!" Hamish responded. "Is he correct?"

"He's spot on the money, Hamish," Kaz affirmed.

"It's no big deal you know, guys," Jack replied casually; privately, he was pleased that he had managed to impress his mission commander. "It's a simple stunt I learned from a Marine pilot instructor at Fort Benning, Georgia." He looked at his chronometer wristwatch; then his tone became serious. "I figure we have just over an hour before sunrise, so we'd best get ready ... Hard to believe that nothing's come up at us!"

"I didn't tell you back there that we're equipped with the latest top-secret RAF black box, an anti - radar detection device; in theory, it should makes us invisible to ground radar stations," Kaz stated. "It was rushed out of the factory, not fully tested, so it's not proven that it works at all, particularly aircraft to aircraft. It's so hush-hush that I had to take an oath, swearing to destroy it if we're shot down. It was fitted expressly for your mission. That's quite a tribute."

"Huh, exactly like the drill with our Norden bombsite," Jack replied. Our bombardiers swear to protect it with their lives. Oh, oh, where'd they come from? We have company ... three bandits, Messerschmidtt 109's, stooging around at 4,000 feet, two o'clock. We may be in luck; they're swinging to the north. Do you eyeball them, Hamish?" he asked, pointing.

"Roger," Hamish responded.

"Roger, I see them too," Kaz replied tersely. We might pass ourselves off as a Luftwaffe Fieseler Storch F-153 if they're not paying close attention. What's a Fieseler Storch, you're asking yourselves? I'm going into the clouds at 5,000 and staying there until we're on the mark." After fifteen minutes, he broke silence, reading out his flight data. "Flying time, please Jack?"

"Eleven minutes, Skip ... eight minutes ... four..."

"Too bad you're missing the sights of beautiful Bavaria, but you'll get your chance. Okay, Jack, see these coordinates here? That's where I'm going to bring it down. I could use you both right this instant to guide me in visually. I have one crack at it. If I overshoot, and miss the sweet spot, well... Wait until I descend out of this cloudbank.

"The Fieseler Storch is a short take-off, short landing, low speed, German reconnaissance aircraft. Apart from those features, it also bears more than a passing physical resemblance to the Lysander. Can you make out the landing area, yet?"

"There she blows, dead ahead!" Jack affirmed. He reflected on Kaz' warning and agreed that the rugged, mountainous terrain beneath them, provided an unforgiving, forbidding prospect if they failed to land precisely where planned. 'We're canned meat if we smash into that cliff face,' he reflected wryly. He looked on, feeling a mixture of dread and anticipation, as Kaz manoeuvred the little plane, despite strong headwinds, which at times appeared to be suspending it motionless, to touch the aircraft down lightly, with breath-taking accuracy. The first rays of morning sun were chasing away the shadows in the valley, as he threw on the brakes and throttled back.

A rush of frigid air invaded the interior of the cockpit when Hamish swung open his hatch window. "Throw the canisters out, Jack, now!" Hamish ordered. "Thanks for everything, Kaz, good luck. We'll be calling on you soon, we hope. In the meantime, enjoy Italy old man. Ciao!"

"Ciao! Happy hunting!"

Jack and Hamish waved farewell and then, holding their breath, watched as the Lysander, at full throttle, its wheels skidding, causing the tail end to swing out wildly and veer dangerously close to the cliff edge, finally lifted off sideways, like a wounded dragonfly, then climbed until it became a speck in the rising sun.

"That's one gutsy son of a gun!" Jack observed.

"That he is. Let me get our bearings then make tracks to our staging location to bury the canisters. I reckon it's five kilometres, in that direction, as the eagle flies," he added, holding his compass level for Jack. "Agreed?"

169

"Or a pigeon! Agreed. Let me take the heavier container, Hamish."

With Hamish leading they set out, avoiding clearings, and staying close to the fringes whenever possible in exposed areas, knowing they and the canisters in particular would be readily visible to the naked eye. To conserve energy in the thinner mountain air, they had agreed to speak only when needed. As they walked in silence across the alpine meadows, Jack felt a growing sense of wonder at the sheer grandeur and stunning beauty of the geography. They came upon a lake, encircled by deciduous and evergreen trees, its crystal-blue water with barely a ripple, perfectly reflecting a majestic mountainous backdrop. They halted and sat on a large rock.

"Könisgsee, the King's Lake, magnificent and it's huge!" Hamish remarked quietly. "Water?" he asked holding up his flask.

"Thanks, I'll use mine."

"This was once the private pond of the Bavarian royal family and their close friends. Common folks had to apply for a special pass."

"I guess that's one way to keep out the riff-raff. How much further?"

"Psssssst! Get down!" Jack stared in the direction in which Hamish was pointing ... was it a deer or a German patrol? Something had caused a loud crackling sound in the brush behind and to their right. Not waiting to find out, Jack grabbed the leather strap of his canister and lunged forward to fall face down beside Hamish, his aluminum container thudding against the rock on which, a moment before, they had been enjoying the lakeside's tranquil calm.

They lay motionless, time and their breathing suspended. Something was prodding Jack in the middle of his back. As he was reaching down very slowly to draw his dagger from its scabbard, a voice demanded in German, "Why are you angels lying on your faces in the mud?"

"Why are you angels lying on your faces in the mud?" the voice repeated. "Come, please get up. I won't hurt you. It's only an old stick anyway."

Jack's meagre German was sufficient to parse her meaning. He turned slightly, to look at their captor and was startled to see Hamish already sitting up and engaged in a conversation with an angelic child.

"It's alright, Jack. I was expecting someone, using der Engel, the Angel."

"Oh really! And where the hell was I when *that little detail* was decided?" Jack demanded, angrily.

"Sssh! Look, I'm sorry, old man, but I was sworn not to divulge it, even to you. It's all on the up - and – up, strictly legitimate. I wasn't told any details. Honestly.

"Who sent you, Greta?" Hamish asked the girl in German. Greta was a blonde, blue-eyed female child who, Jack estimated to be some-what younger than a teenager but older than her years.

"Mein Papa, Herr Franck," she replied matter-of-factly, idly poking her stick at some moss.

"Her father..." Hamish translated for Jack. "Franck. That's the cor-rect name."

"I got that much. And where is Herr Franck, ask her."

"We're to follow her, the Angel, Greta, that is. Hold on.

"What did you say, dear?" Hamish asked.

"She says we're to hide the containers over there in that notch, cover them with brush and then she'll go ahead of us, fifty paces, to be the lookout. If she holds up her walking stick, hit the ground."

"Are you sure? It sounds damn iffy..."

"Positive. C'mon, give me a hand hauling these things. Ready?"

"Aye, lead on McDuff. Just one question, stupid as it may sound, why a kid?" Jack queried when the canisters had been concealed.

171

"Stalwart's brainwave. His theory is that no one pays attention to a child doing whatever it is a child does. Think of it. When was the last time you noticed, I mean really noticed so that it registered, what children are doing beyond perhaps 'playing', 'running', 'skipping,' right? I think it's rare genius. They can slip in and out, spy ... No doubt you remember Oliver Twist's Fagan and his den of street urchins ... the Artful Dodger? Not so fast, fifty giant steps!"

They followed Greta at the specified distance, trudging down a grassed slope covered with alpen wildflowers, toward a thatched - roof cottage that had a small barn behind it. "Not to be sacrilegious, Hamish, but do you know where this comes from: 'And a little child shall lead them?'"

"Isaiah 11. Stop there. She's paused to speak with someone at the gate. No danger signal. Freeze, 'til I give the word. She's opening the gate, turning, and motioning us to come up. Walk... quickly, but do not run."

As they approached the gate, they could see that the cottage door was ajar. "It could be a trap!" Jack hissed. "Go carefully, I'll cover you."

Hamish nodded, opening the gate slowly, and crept forward, his Walther revolver drawn. Jack moved toward the fence, and knelt, watching, listening, his Luger at the ready.

After a pause, which to Jack seemed an eternity, Hamish softly called out "Hallo!"

"Hallo!" a voice replied from inside.

"Wer das? Who's there?" Hamish replied.

SILVER DAGGER

"Freunde, die Engel!"

"Show yourself, friendly angels!"

"Willkommen." A young woman in a blue and white flowered apron appeared, smiling, in the doorway. Greta was standing behind her. "Herein, schnell!" the woman uttered, as Greta motioned them to come forward. A memory from his childhood of a terrifying illustration in Hansel and Gretel flashed into Jack's mind.

"Jack, inside, on the double!' Hamish ordered.

"Schnell!" she repeated. Half crouching, Jack made a dash for the cottage; the door slammed behind him as he entered.

The interior of native granite and white pine, looked to Jack like a movie set for *Heidi* or *Frankenstein*. Two men in shirtsleeves, one middle-aged and the other somewhat younger, were seated on wooden chairs at a huge wooden kitchen table at the centre of which sat a bottle of liquor. An elaborately decorated long barrelled shotgun rested on the lap of the younger male, who was wearing a black tie, loosened at his starched collar. He spoke first, with a distinctively Oxfordian accent, "Hello chaps, I'm Russell. Awfully glad you're here, Hamish, Jack. Allow me to introduce our hosts, Herr Otto and Frau Hilde Franck. They haven't much English. You've already met their lovely Greta. Please sit down. You must be hungry. Schnapps, first?"

"A small one, yes, thanks," Hamish answered. "Jack?"

Frau Franck served a Bavarian breakfast of eggs, and sausage links, with fried potatoes and home - baked rolls. Jack and Hamish ate ravenously and listened as Russell talked. He told them that he was a German citizen, educated in England, and had been a lecturer in applied mathematics at a technical university in Munich. Alarmed at the racist excesses of the Bavarian Nazi party, he joined an underground anti - Hitler movement at the school. In 1938, he was introduced by the faculty chairman to an English gentleman, a Commander Lawson, who had no difficulty in recruiting him into SIS. In '39, the school was taken over by the Ministry of Armaments as a centre for weapons development. I requested a service transfer."

"What do you do now? I can't help but notice the tie and trousers that you're wearing," asked Jack.

"I'm a technical supervisor with the Bavarian office of the Reichsbahn, Railway."

"And the Francks, Russell? What is their connection with this?"

"I'd best let them speak for themselves, Hamish," he stated and translated the question.

With some assistance from Russell and Hamish, Jack was able to follow Mr. Franck's explanation that he and his wife, devout Roman Catholics and intensely nationalistic Bavarians, had been dismayed and disgusted at the growth of paganism under the Nazi seal of approval in their homeland, the most Catholic region in Germany. Through their parish priest, they had become members of a small but vital chapter of the southern Bavarian resistance movement.

173

"You are all taking terrible risks. We, both Jack and I, are deeply grateful to you. Thank you and a special thanks to you, Greta. You are a clever and very brave girl," Hamish announced as Hilde was clearing away the dishes.

"Thank you, but you must realize that it is our duty, as Christians and as Germans. Now, you gentlemen rest," Otto replied as Hamish translated for Jack.

"Thanks, but before we do, we must get the containers," Jack asserted.

"Otto and I will take the hay wagon and pick them up at twilight," Russell confirmed. "Did you bury them exactly where Greta showed? Good, leave it to us then. I do suggest that you take Otto's suggestion seriously. We're on the job tomorrow at first light. The Führer is in residence at the Berghof, but only until tomorrow, we believe. He's leaving on his private train from Salzburg for his so-called wolf's lair in Rastenberg, East Prussia. It helps to be a trainman to know these things. Sleep until it's suppertime, and then afterwards, I can perhaps assist you in reviewing your action plan."

Hilde led Jack and Hamish down a pine log - lined hallway to a small corner bedroom, well furnished with a dresser, night table, and bunk bed. Bidding them a pleasant rest, she closed the door. Jack looked out the window, admiring the view of the mountain upon which was perched the Berghof, and comparing the vista with that of The

Citadel while he undressed. Hamish picked up a book resting on the bedside table and lay down on the lower bunk, leafing through the pages. "Listen to this: '*The Berghof. Three thousand two hundred and eighty one feet above Berchtesgaden,*'... funny, you'd think they'd be able to get that right... '*a lawyer named Winter from Hamburg built the Bavarian - style chalet which he called Haus Wachenfeld, his wife's maiden name. Winter rented the house to the Führer in 1928 for 100 marks a month. The tearoom, das Kehlsteinhaus, was a present from the Party faithful. When Herr Hitler finally bought the property*' ... from his royalties on Mein Kampf ... '*he had it substantially enlarged. It was known as the little cottage of the People's Chancellor.*' How charming."

"The People's Chancellor,' gees, what a pal. Let me climb up there and grab some shuteye." He drifted off, wistfully thinking of he and Rebeccah making love in front of a fireplace in an Alpine ski chalet.

"The motorcade will depart at 1300 sharp. You understand that you must be in position here, on the roadway, where it takes a hard hairpin right turn," he emphasized, pointing to Hamish' sketch map. We know that his SS chauffeur, Kempka, always slows down there to precisely 10 kilometres an hour to avoid a reprimand and a mess in the back seat. The Führer is not a good passenger under the best of circumstances. He easily becomes violently carsick, unless he's well doped - up beforehand. Anyway...."

"Russell, this we know already, thanks," Hamish interjected, barely masking his impatience. "What we don't know is this. Which vehicle will he actually be riding in?"

Russell paused, looking crestfallen. "I apologize for prattling on. In truth, we can never be sure."

"In other words, you don't know!" Jack retorted. "Sorry, but it's rather important, Russell."

"I can go with you, as a bird dog, your spotter," he offered apologetically.

"Wait just a damn minute," Jack interrupted, "this is news to me! What about it, Hamish, is this another of your secret arrangements?"

Hamish shook his head. "It's not in the plan book, Russell. No offence, but it's just Jack and me. You've been a real trooper, a great help, and we certainly might have to rely upon you and the Francks after the event, but that's it, full stop. As mission commander, I can't go off willy nilly, taking on unauthorized personnel. They'd have my head at HQ."

"Very well, I understand. I wasn't trying to horn in. Just a thought."

"And appreciated. Can you please excuse us? Jack and I need to have a short conference."

"Of course. I'll be heading home in a few minutes to freshen up, and then I'm off to work. I'm on nights this week."

They waited until they heard the basement door close. "Get on the radio now and find out who the hell this blighter Russell is!" Hamish whispered. "Something about that gentleman smells fishy!"

"I'm on it, right away. Hope to hell I can raise Burt!" Seated on the earthen basement floor, Jack quickly unpacked the X-1 and keyed a preliminary code grouping. His fingertips drummed on the case impatiently as he waited; then he looked up at Hamish. "It's him, thank God. At least, no one else would recognize the signature. Okay, sending now, Major."

"Well, anything?" Hamish asked after a minute.

"Acknowledged that's all ... Lord, I can't stay on air much longer. This is way too dicey, Hamish. Hold on, here's the reply ... oh, boy, we've been set up! SIS never heard of the guy!"

"Tell HQ to have a plane sent to our pickup location and then shut down. Now listen, here's what we... Bloody hell, my weapons are upstairs. Where are yours?"

They froze as the door at the top of the wooden staircase opened. "Hallo! Are you there? It's Russell. Just want to say ta ta, good luck, and all that tripe!"

"Bag that radio and get under the staircase; you know what to do ... hurry!

"We're here. Finished our chit chat and packing up. Come to say goodbye, have you?"

"Yes." He slipped on the steps and stumbled, falling headfirst as Jack darted out from beneath the open staircase, took hold of the barrel of the shotgun, twisting it from his grasp. "God damn it   let go ... what the hell do you two idiots think you're doing?" he gasped, as he lay on the ground, Hamish' hands pressing on his throat. Jack held the shotgun at his left temple.

"Search him, Jack, and keep the gun on him, if you can."

"Nothing ... wait a minute. Where's his billfold. Here it is. Hold on." Jack cradled the shotgun as he sorted the wallet's contents. It appears that our friend Russell is an employee of the Reichsbann. Here's his ID, along with a few hundred Reichmarks, a photo, black and white, naughty boy, hmm, she's rather delectable, a driver's license in the name of Rutger Essen and that's it.

"You have ten seconds before I put your lights out, Rutger Essen. Who are you working for, and don't give me that railway supervisor nonsense," Hamish demanded softy. "Ten, nine, eight ... tell me, or I swear..."

"Back off and I'll tell you, alright? I can't bloody breathe! That's better. Can I sit up?"

"Hands behind your back; lock your thumbs."

"Go behind. Watch him, Jack. Over there, a ball of bailing twine. Get it, and tie his wrists.

"We're listening," Hamish stated flatly.

He winced, "Damn it, that's tight! Alright, does the term 'freebooter' mean anything to you?"

"Such as pirate, buccaneer?" Hamish suggested.

"I prefer entrepreneur," he smiled weakly. "You see, I am first and foremost a survivor and secondly, a businessman. I sell my services to the highest bidder."

"Meaning, you work both sides of the street," Jack asserted. "Sounds to me like a traitor, plain and simple."

"I'm not surprised that you would draw that conclusion, Major...Haney, is it?"

"And who's your paymaster this month?" Jack queried.

"Well, dear boy," he shrugged, "it may not surprise you that I'm free-lancing at the moment."

"Christ, Hamish, I've heard enough. Let's do him!"

"No, no, dear boy, you need me!" he stated.

177

"Need you, for what?"

"To get you out of this mess you lads have gotten yourselves into. I know that His Majesty's Agents are well supplied with, shall I say, coin of the realm?"

"Stop the crap," Hamish barked. "What are you saying, in plain English?"

"They know that you're coming and have set up an ambush... and quite a clever one, too. Must hand it to the Admiral, he's a corker!"

"Ambush? The Admiral?"

"Yes, Admiral Canaris, Chief of the Abwehr. He had to do it, other-wise..."

"And you know all this. How?"

"It's my business to know. If you don't believe me, there's proof. In my shirt pocket."

Hamish reached in and pulled out a folded paper. "What's this?" He opened it and read silently. "It's a directive from Abwehr HQ, Berlin, signed by Wilhelm Canaris, authorizing Operation Canned Meat. Dated six weeks ago," Hamish reflected. "It's not genuine, Jack, see?"

"It's a forgery," Jack asserted, "a fake."

"No, my friends, it is not, although I copied it verbatim from the orig-inal wire. It was sent here to the Obersalzberg commandant by military telegraph, which is my job to oversee."

"What's Operation Canned Meat?" Hamish demanded.

"All in good time. Either of you chaps know a gentleman, Derek Wainscott?"

"Why?" Hamish demanded.

"He was my department head in SIS, but the bastard reported me for carrying on, to put it delicately, a dalliance with that lovely lady in the photo. Turned out she was a ringer and I was cashiered. Worse, she was also the mistress of one of the top dogs in Whitehall tsk, tsk. He didn't miss a beat. The old school wall of silence closed in. I took the fall and that was most unfair, wouldn't you say?"

"What name were you going by at the time?" Hamish asked.

"Wallace. William Wallace. Russell's just a name of convenience."

"The Francks? Are they a part of this sordid story?" Jack asked.

"Oh, no, not at all, dear boy. They're true patriots, anti-Nazi, pure as the driven snow."

"So, given the chance, you'd turn them in for your thirty pieces of silver," Hamish declared.

"No, they're small game. So idealistic, so naïve." His voice trailed off. "Still, sometimes Hilde gets on my nerves. Too many questions. Little Greta's a wonder, quite remarkably charming, invaluable to me. She runs my errands ... no idea why or what, of course.... and so innocent, you'd think. You were taken in, by those eyes, the little..."

"She's a baby! You are disgusting!" Hamish spat out. "Back to the so-called ambush."

"I was well trained by my masters in SIS," he replied harshly. "The ambush, ah yes, well, for starters, he's not here!"

"Hitler's not at the Berghof?"

"No, no. He's in his bunker in Prussia near the Eastern Front. Must be barking mad. It'll be overrun by the Soviet hordes at any moment. The plan is, to lure you to the place, and then, using some poor Polish bastard who bears a striking resemblance, they found him in a concentration camp, employ him as a decoy, and do you over. There are four hundred additional security men eagerly awaiting the word. The operation's called 'Canned Meat' an allusion, I would think, to the invasion of Poland in 1939 which was code-named..."

"Canned Goods," Hamish commented flatly. "Go on."

"Very good, Hamish! Yes, you both, as well as the unfortunate Pole are to end up in the same place, eventually, Dachau, hanging by piano wire until you rot on meat hooks. Do you fancy that? All very neat and tidy. How Germanic you might say!" he added chuckling.

179

"Now that I've given you the facts, do you two SOE supermen really think you can just toddle on out of here on your own? I mean, if you believe that..."

"What do you want, Essen?" Hamish demanded.

"Five thousand in cash, apiece, and passage to Blighty. I'd love to bring along my little angel!"

"The kid? Jesus, this pervert is really pissing me off! What's Blighty?"

"Over 'ome, Haney my boy, England's green and pleasant land. I do miss it. She'd love it too, I know. I'd rather do a sentence there, hardscrabble, thank you. I could afford to set her up, the best prep schools, she could wait for me, in luxury..." he hummed.

"You'll be hanged, you piece of garbage," Hamish stated flatly. "I'll see to it! What good is your money to you then?"

"I'd take my chances, dear boy. Ever heard of a Swiss bank account? Souls of discretion, they are, the gnomes of Zurich. Now listen, there are roughly six hours before your Plan Baker is to be played out. This is your last chance to get out, alive. Trust me, I do know every detail of the Abwehr's counter measures. That's my business. Now, I could just as easily sell you both to the SD for a lark or..."

"And this is my business... dear boy!" Jack responded emphatically, then reaching forward, with one quick sideways motion, snapped Essen's neck. His head drooped, his tongue lolling, and he slowly collapsed in a heap. "I told you, you were pissing me off," he stated firmly.

"Well, well. I do believe you. We have to dispose of him, or the Francks are for it! There's no way out except up these stairs and through the house. Have a look upstairs and see if they're in bed."

"You've got it, back in a jif!" Jack responded. Seconds later, he called down, "Hamish, come up here, now!"

Hamish bounded up the steps. Upon reaching the landing and seeing Jack's face, he sensed what to expect. He followed Jack down the hallway to the master bedroom; the door was open wide. Otto and Hilde lay on the bed, side-by-side, motionless. Blood was everywhere. A bloody carving knife was set with care between the bodies. "The sick, psychopathic bastard! He slit their throats! It must have been quick. No signs at all of a struggle, poor beggars."

"Yep, and there's no sign of Greta in here, so she must have made it out the window, thank God," Jack observed quietly. They were greeted by a blast of frigid air when he swung open the door, to reveal a child's bedroom, with fairy tale characters on patterned wallpaper, and miniature pine furniture, the bed with neatly arranged clusters of small, stuffed animals on either side of the pillow. The window was open halfway. Underneath the window sill, was a small, wooden framed wicker chair that had been hastily pushed against the wall. "We have to find her, Hamish. Hamish?"

"He tipped them off, Jack. Look, out there. I see an armoured column making tracks this way. I'll get the weapons from our room and you get the radio, leave the rest. Meet me at the lake. If we're in luck, that's where Greta's gone to ground. We'll scoop her and take her with us to the landing place. Well man, what are you waiting for?"

POISON DART

Miss Mary Ward hesitated, and then pressed the intercom button firmly. "Mr. Williamson, may I see you for a moment? It's personal, Sir."

"Of course, Mary, come in now. Would it be an imposition to order a fresh carafe of coffee? It's three-fifteen; time for a break, wouldn't you say?"

"I would, Mr. Williamson. Something sweet to go with it, Sir?"

"I'm in your hands, Mary. Whatever you wish."

Mary phoned the manager of the Lobby Coffee Shop; after placing the order she walked around her desk to the door of Erik Williamson's corner office suite. She knocked, at the same time closing her eyes for a moment to prepare for the sudden burst of brilliant daylight and the accompanying giddiness, brought on by sudden exposure to the spectacular vista of Lower Manhattan from his thirty-sixth floor windows, in combination with the musty aroma of cigar fumes.

"Sit down please, Mary. How's everything going? Did you call Wainscott? Good, thanks," he nodded, acknowledging her responses as he carefully tamped the end of a large Havana hand-rolled cigar in an oversized stainless steel ashtray. "I'm quitting, soon, Mary, really!"

She smiled non-committally. "The order will be here in less than ten minutes." She paused, and then continued, "Mr. Williamson, my mother is not well. I wonder if you might be able to spare me for a few days so that I can go to Toronto?"

"I'm sorry to hear that. I hope she's going to be all right, Mary. What's wrong?"

"I hope so too. We're not sure. She's in the Toronto General undergoing some tests. That's why I really hope to go now, so that I can be with her as well as look after her cat and take care of the house. My brother, Rodney, lives at home with her but works days. Mom's only going to be in for a few days," she said.

"Well of course you may go. And please, use my account with the railway when you book your ticket. Just make arrangements with Helen Stapleton to fill in and wish your mother and Rodney well for me."

"I will Mr. Williamson, and thank you very much."

As she rose to leave, there was soft rap on the door.

"That must be the restaurant delivery. I'll get it, Sir."

She opened the door to a white - jacketed busboy who for a split second seemed taken aback. "Your...your order, M' am. Where shall I set it?" he asked uneasily, indicating with a dip of his head the sterling silver serving tray on his shoulder. "Please sign here, Miss Ward," he remarked, after placing the tray on the coffee table, proffering a black leather folder, with a gold - tipped fountain pen. "Thanks kindly," he smiled, pocketing the pen and folder inside his jacket, saluted, and exited.

Mary poured coffee for Erik and herself in the fine china cups that had been provided. As she was setting Erik's on his desk, she remarked, "I hope you won't object if I take mine back to my desk, Sir. I'd best get things in order for Helen ... that's curious, Mr. Williamson..."

"What's curious?"

"The busboy. He knew my name."

"Did you give it to the person downstairs when you ordered?"

"You know, Sir, I don't remember now. I never do, just our office number ... I was a bit nervous about coming in to ask a favour so I might have. Of course, it's on the nameplate on my desk! I really think I'm being a little silly. It must be because of Mom's situation. Sorry, Sir."

"Not at all, Mary. Do pop in before you leave to say goodbye."

"I will. Thank you again, Mr. Williamson. You've always been so kind and generous, Sir. My sister is eternally grateful for aiding her family when you were in England before the occupation..."

He smiled self-consciously, shrugging, "Glad to help out. Now, take a cinnamon roll or two and off you go to get ready, Mary!"

Mary returned to her desk, opened the top right drawer, and studied her list of frequently called numbers, then picked up the receiver and dialled Grand Central Station, on Park Avenue.

"Good afternoon, Grand Central switchboard. Information; how may I help you?"

"I would like to purchase a return ticket to Toronto for tomorrow morning, please."

"You'll wanna speak with a ticket agent. One moment ... while I connect ... you ... thank you." Mary reflected that a switchboard operator should never chew gum on the job.

183

Five minutes later, she had made a reservation, round trip, Coach class, return date open, departing at nine o'clock the following morning, billed to British American Overseas Importing Ltd. The ticket would be waiting at a kiosk she was told. She gulped the hot coffee, and nibbled on the sweet roll, as she hastily cleared and arranged her desktop, and then walked over to Helen Stapleton's desk to announce her sudden, but temporary promotion. That finished, but before visiting the Ladies' Room, she went to Erik's door, and knocked.

"Mary?" he called.

"Yes, Sir. Just stopping by as you asked." She briefly told him the details of her travel arrangements as well as Helen's enthusiastic acceptance.

"Do be careful, Mary," Erik declared earnestly, standing up to take her hand. "I wouldn't tell any of the others here about your business. I'll speak with Helen now and caution her. When it's all over will be time enough. You do have my unlisted home number? Good." Upon bidding one another goodbye, she closed his door and walked quickly past the twelve secretarial desks and into the powder room.

The usual wait for the down elevator was under two minutes, as Mary was leaving an hour before the peak rush by the thousands of employees in the Manhattan office tower. As she rode down, she thought about how much she was looking forward to her trip home to Toronto to take care of her mother. As much as she loved the glamour, rhythm, and excitement of New York City, Mary's heart was still in her hometown.

Her career with British Security Operation had begun when she answered a Help Wanted advertisement in the Toronto Telegram, one of Canada's largest dailies. Robert Brooks, the Director of BSO operations in Canada, had placed the one ad, from which over seven hundred Canadian women were recruited. Of these, Mary had advanced the most rapidly, when Brooks, already impressed with her résumé, was entranced with her exceptional potential and personal qualities during her interviews, and had sent her directly to BSO Headquarters in Manhattan, to be inducted and groomed under Erik's senior staffers.

There, she immediately demonstrated the skills, mental agility, ironclad loyalty, impeccable judgement, subtle intelligence, and discretion, as well as a phenomenal memory for detail combined with a quiet personal charm that Erik had been seeking at the front desk, and within a year, she had become his Special Assistant. Robert had never forgotten an after - dinner conversation at Erik's Rosedale Toronto home, with Mary present, when Erik had remarked that if he and Robert were to pass on, BSO could continue to operate, on the strength of Mary's intimate knowledge of the who, where, how and what, and how much, of his far-flung, clandestine network of operations.

Mary awoke as usual, at six-fifteen a.m., and opened her night drapes to the familiar, ever - changing view of the east midtown Manhattan skyline. She had shopped for an few personal items on the way home from the office, and had packed one small bag in the evening, so that she could be ready to leave early for Grand Central to enjoy a leisurely breakfast while waiting for the train. At seven, she called her usual service, PLAZA CAB to request a seven thirty a.m. pick up.

At seven twenty-three, she took the elevator down to the swank, Italian marble - tiled lobby, walked to the main entrance, and pushed through the turnabout onto Park Avenue.

"Good morning ... a little late today Miss Ward?" inquired the portly, red – faced morning doorman.

"Yes, Eldred, you know the insurance business. Claims, and more claims, here and everywhere. Follow the money," she explained, smiling sweetly.

"Well, you have a safe journey Miss Ward, and I'll look forward to seeing you when you get back. Here's your cab now, Miss," Eldred announced, taking her bag while holding the rear door open.

Mary got into the cab, retrieved her bag, and thanked Eldred, then travelled the short distance to the terminal building. After paying the fare and tipping the driver, she walked into the immense, noisy and already - packed station then immediately picked out the CNR agent's booth. After signing for her ticket, she strolled to the likeliest restaurant, Les Dejeuners Toujours. 'Breakfasts forever,' she laughed to herself, 'that sounds perfect.'

At eight-forty, she asked for the check, and then placed the waiter's tray with a one-dollar bill on top of the neatly folded morning paper. When she emerged onto the concourse, the large overhead clock said it was eight forty-six, leaving her just enough time to find the track and board her train. She had taken the ticket from her purse and checked it while inside the restaurant and knew which track number she wanted. She stopped at a newsstand to buy her favourite magazine, The New Yorker, and then walked at a brisk pace, to Track Six. With a friendly greeting from the rather elderly conductor who held her bag as he assisted her up onto the low metal step stool, she was about to step inside her car, and paused, to adjust her heel, and casually glanced to her right. Standing on the platform, against a steel pillar, she noticed an oddly – familiar man in a light coloured trench coat, reading a newspaper.

Then, it clicked. The man had been in a booth across from her at Breakfasts Forever. At that time, she had thought that he vaguely resembled the bug – eyed busboy, but it was difficult to say exactly. Yesterday's man was wearing a server's jacket and peaked hat; today's, a rumpled trench coat and a grey fedora. She noted that he was carrying a briefcase. She shrugged mentally, 'People in train station restaurants often do go on trains, some even go to work, and for daytrips, Mary,' making a note to see if he did in fact get on board. As she walked along the aisle to her seat, she bent her head to be able to look out the windows and saw him folding his paper as he strode quickly towards her train. The conductor had just scooped up his step stool when the man leapt up, grabbing the hand railing and swinging inside, almost knocking the conductor onto the platform. He turned to the right and went through the connecting door into the Lounge Car.

The trip to Canada was without incident. Half way across the Niagara Gorge, Mary looked up from her New Yorker to see the 'Welcome to Canada' sign, knowing that within an hour and a half, the conductor would be ambling through the car proclaiming in the singsong, nasal tone and cadence peculiar to railway conductors, "Toronto Union Station, Toronto Union!"

She retrieved her bag from the overhead storage bin and walked out of the terminal onto Front Street, where the drivers of a line of black and orange taxicabs were jostling for the attention of her fellow travellers. Choosing one who was wearing a fresh white shirt and tie, she held onto her small suitcase despite his politely persistent efforts to detach it from her grasp, and glanced about for good measure as she got into the back seat. 'Stop being a worrywart, Mary! Must be my imagination,' she chided herself.

The driver turned left illegally onto Yonge Street northbound; at the Queen Street intersection, on a red signal light, he honked impatiently and edged right, then blasted his way through a gaggle of irate pedestrians, and headed east. It served as a reminder to Mary that Toronto's taxi drivers shared a number of qualities with their more famous New York counterparts. Following a near miss with a Lake Simcoe Ice and Fuel wagon, she leaned forward to suggest that he might slow down. He shrugged but complied, pouting. She sighed, and sat back, able at last to savour the sight of the city's famous 'Red Rocket' trolley cars, and the old shops that she remembered, including Bernie's Smoked Meats. 'Oh, what sandwiches they made, hot, piled this high! Wonder if they still do?'

When they were approaching the Woodbine Racetrack, her driver decided to end his vow of silence, introducing himself as 'Tommy'. Discovering that they shared east end Toronto childhood memories, Mary and Tommy reminisced about darting across Queen Street, dodging traffic, and crawling under the enclosure to watch the jockeys running their horses. She directed Tommy, the now reformed cabbie, to turn left onto Rainsford Road and stop at number six.

"Thank you, Tommy. Here's a little extra towards the down payment on your Queen's Plate champion." He grinned, and thanked her effusively.

Mary's younger brother Rodney ran out to greet her as she stepped onto the curb. "Mary, how are you? You look wonderful!" he exclaimed. "Here, give me your luggage."

"Thanks, I'm just fine, Rodney!" she replied, bestowing a sisterly kiss on his cheek. "And you look well. How's Mother?" she inquired when they reached the veranda's wooden steps.

"Resting comfortably, thank goodness. But you must be worn out. It's ten o'clock and you've been traveling since early morning, I'd imagine."

"Yes, I am a little weary," she remarked quietly. "A cup of tea would be very nice, Rodney."

"Come inside Mary. I'll fix you a cup; you can relax and head off to your bed whenever you feel like it. It's made up; fresh sheets, by yours truly, if you can believe that? Tomorrow's Saturday, we'll go see Mom first thing in the morning, okay, Sis?"

The next day Rodney and Mary drove to Toronto General Hospital to visit their Mother. Rodney waited in the hallway, observing the posted visitation rules, while Mary tiptoed into the ward. Her Mother's bed was closest to the door. Gathering all of her self-control, Mary beamed as she bent down to kiss her and whispered. "Mother, it's Mary. How are you?"

Her eyelids fluttered open. "Oh, Mary, you're here," she responded wanly. "I've been lying here hoping that you would come through that door any minute... and you did, bless you, Mary." Mrs. Ward partially raised herself on her elbows. "My hair is such a mess...but I'm fine dear; your brother has been taking good care of me. The nurses and doctors here are wonderful!" she added, her face brightening.

"Lie back, Mom. There. Have they given you the results of the tests yet?"

"No, they said on Friday they'll tell me tomorrow, no Monday. Now, tell me about New York. What's it like? It must be busy and noisy."

"It's great, Mom, fabulous restaurants, snazzy shops, the theatres are fantastic, and my apartment is quite classy, very comfortable, fairly quiet actually and close to everything."

"Where do you work again, Dear?"

"Mom, you know I can't say. I work for the war office, that's all. You wouldn't want to be visiting me in jail, now would you?" she jested, patting her Mother's folded hands.

"Oh yes, I remember you telling me. It's a secret. Okay, we'll leave it at that," she sighed.

On the way home, Rodney insisted upon taking Mary Ward to Simpson's Arcadian Court for brunch. Unknown to her brother, this elegant restaurant held a special cachet for Mary, as the setting, some two and one-half years before, of a delightful luncheon meeting with a darkly-handsome, ever – so –charming and witty, 'Mr. Brooker', a.k.a. Robert Brooks. When reporting the outcome to Erik Williamson, Robert confided that Mary Ward, B.A. English and History, Hon., had sealed her recruitment with BSO within the first three minutes of their conversation.

She ordered Eggs Benedict, and waited until Rodney had made his selection, and then opened the topic of Mrs. Mary Ward's condition, as tactfully as possible.

"Rodney, dear, I am concerned about Mom; but you're with her all the time, tell me, honestly, what's your opinion?"

"She's as strong as ever and looks at things positively, as always. I'm sure she's going to be fine, Mary; but I've been thinking. What we don't need is you in New York working on important war matters, and not being able to concentrate because of the situation at home. So, I promise to keep you posted if anything, anything, at all happens and I'll call you once a week, regardless, into the bargain. Does that make you feel better, kiddo?"

"Yes, it does," Mary conceded, brightly, "but I can call you weekly at my agency's expense. They won't bat an eyelash. Bargain?"

"If you think so, that's great; it's a bargain!"

The next morning when Mary came downstairs Rodney was making breakfast.

"Well, how did you sleep?"

"Wonderful Rodney, no ambulances and fire trucks in the middle of the night. It was so peaceful."

"I'm making you Dad's specialty, a good old - fashioned English breakfast, just like he used to make it for us on Sunday morning after church: home fries, peameal bacon, black pudding and eggs. What do you think about that?"

"Goodness, you're going to spoil me but it sounds delicious. Rodney, I'm going to take the streetcar to the hospital today. I want you to take the day off and do whatever it is that you normally do; I'll take your shift at the hospital today. Besides, I want to spend as much time with Mom as I can."

"Are you sure, Sis? I don't mind driving you."

"Nonsense, besides I need the exercise. I don't get enough in New York... taxi here, taxi there. I'll be off right after breakfast."

After helping Rodney tidy up and dry the dishes, Mary finished dressing, kissed him goodbye, then putting on her best white gloves, set out at a moderate pace down to Queen Street to catch the westbound Queen streetcar. The wait for a car was long, as the schedule was reduced on Sundays. As she was stepping down from the trolley at Queen and University Avenue, she thanked the conductor and proceeded to cross Queen on the green light. It occurred to her to pray that Sunday was Tommy's day of rest. Mary set off on the trek up University Avenue to the Toronto General Hospital. The weather was enjoyably warm and sunny with a light breeze. As she passed The Royal Canadian Military Institute's twin bronze Crimean War cannons guarding the front entrance like sentinels, she contemplated dropping in for a courtesy visit, but knew that they would understand the circumstances if she didn't. Her father, Charles, Adjutant General of the Canadian Militia, had been a lifetime member before his death, five years before.

Crossing Dundas, she was reminded of her undergraduate days at the University of Toronto's Victoria College, particularly her one stint as an actor playing the slightly dotty and deaf Dean of Ladies' Residence in 'Campus Capers' and made a mental note to pay her overdue alumnus fee. Her mind wandered back to her last discussion with Robert Samson in Toronto; she wondered if he would be offended if she were to telephone him at the Camp. She dismissed the idea as 'bold and pushy', two qualities she downright despised in women. 'Not only that,' she thought, 'just imagine the fuss that would create in the Camp about her, or him? He'd had enough problems,' she concluded. 'But I do hope he remembers his promise!'

SILVER DAGGER

Mary drew near the hospital entrance, reflecting on the contrast between the frenetic twenty-four hour, seven - day - a - week pace in New York City and the relative peace of a Toronto Sunday morning, when she felt a sudden, sharp, stinging pain in her right calf. She stumbled slightly, as she reacted, bending sideways to clutch her leg, then collapsed onto the sidewalk. A male pedestrian stepped over her body and kept walking quickly north. Moments later, a second man rushed up and knelt beside her. "My God, Mary, what happened?" he shouted.

"Edmond, Eddy Wuerth, is that you?" she mumbled, "What on earth are you doing here?" Her eyes fluttered closed, and then opened.

Taking her hand, Special Agent Edmond Wuerth explained that he had been assigned by Mr. Williamson to follow her from New York.

"Was that you in ... in the Breakfazz For...rezz ... tauran, Ed...dy?" she slurred weakly. Flecks of saliva were forming on her lips.

He answered her question calmly with nods. "...And the train station, with the help of a B-movie fedora, private-eye raincoat and crummy makeup. Don't talk now, Mary, let me help you lie down on the grass. Here, we'll use my jacket under your head." He raised her shoulders and pulled her gently onto a tiny patch of grass. Edmond then stood up, striding halfway up and down the block, searching vainly in all directions. Her attacker had simply walked away, vanishing into the landscape. 'Damn.' He ran back to Mary who was now unconscious. Edmond got up and raced out onto University Avenue, flailing his arms in a desperate effort to attract a passing motorist. A southbound police cruiser that had just pulled out from Gerrard Street screeched to a halt.

"Please help us, officer. Something's happened to my friend, there, on the grass. She just kinda collapsed."

"Well, luckily, here's the hospital. I'll pull into Emerg and have them send a stretcher. Stay with her, Sir." His siren on, the policeman made an abrupt, tire –squealing u-turn, then the cruiser veered left and disappeared into the Toronto General's Admissions driveway.

Two minutes later, a stretcher team arrived, strapped her onto the gurney, and pushed Mary along the sidewalk, through the Emergency entrance directly into Emergency Surgery. Edmond gave the Admission nurse her name and address. The nurse looked at him quizzically. "Did you say the patient's name is Mary Ward, Sir?"

"Yes, that's right, M a r y W a r d, 6 Rainsford Road. Is there a problem, Nurse?"

"Well, Sir, that's the second Mary Ward of that particular address listed as a patient here. Are you certain?"

"Oh, that'd be Mary Ward senior, her mother. She's in for some cardiac testing."

"I see. Tsk, not a good week for the Mary Wards of Rainsford, it seems," she commented, shaking her head sympathetically. "I'll need your full name, address, etcetera. Kindly take this clipboard and fill out the form fully in pen, please. You can sit on the bench, over there. Bring it back to this counter when it's completed."

The police officer, having spotted Edmond, walked over and sat down heavily beside him. "Constable McManus, Sir," he sighed. "I have to ask you some questions." He put on steel-rimmed glasses and set to work. " Now, how would you say you came to find her, Sir?" he inquired, thumbing through a small notepad and wetting the end of pencil stub.

"Edmond Wuerth, Constable. Actually, I work for a private security outfit and was keeping an eye on her for her boss ... and not very successfully it appears."

"Can you spell Wuerth?"

W u e r t h."

"Is that German?" McManus asked while examining the name he had printed.

"Yes, originally; but my family's from Kitchener, second generation. Dad never got around to changing the spelling to Worth before he went overseas in '15. He was killed in the line of, Ypres, April 9, 1917."

"Sorry, Mr. Wuerth. Now, this security outfit you mentioned, what can you tell me about it?"

"Confidentially, it's classified, Constable, under the Department of National Defence," he whispered. But I do have a business card here, inside my billfold. Have your precinct commander call this number for further information from the RCMP."

"'Precinct', hmm, you must be American!" he reflected, tapping the pencil eraser against his lower lip. "The RCMP you say? Okay, I'll call it in to the station from the desk there and request some assistance. You say you have no idea of what happened? She just collapsed unconscious like?"

"Yes, positively. May I call her brother, Constable?"

"Sure, go ahead, but keep it as brief as possible, please. I need to use the phone. I could go to the car and radio in, but I think I'll wait right here, with you."

Reluctantly, the duty nurse pushed the telephone across the counter to within Edmond's reach. "One minute, Sir. No more," she cautioned gravely. The Ward's telephone rang three times.

"Hello?"

"Hello, Mr. Rodney Ward, please?"

"Yes, speaking."

"Sir, my name is Edmond Wuerth. I'm a friend of Mary's."

"Yes..." Rodney said hesitantly.

"Sir, I'm afraid I have some bad news."

"Is it mother? What's happened?"

"No, I'm afraid that it's your sister, Mary. There's been an ... she's been injured ... no, she wasn't struck by a car, Sir, she collapsed, on the street ... the sidewalk, on University, almost in front of the Toronto General Hospital. The doctors are working on her right now. Unfortunately, no, I don't know her condition. Yes, in fact, I'm with the police at Emergency. I suggest that you come to the Toronto General right away ... the Toronto General, the Emergency Entrance. Yes, we'll be waiting. Goodbye." He thanked the nurse and then moved aside to allow Constable McManus access to the telephone.

Edmond then walked to the far end of the hall to an isolated pay telephone booth. He entered, closed the cantilevered glass and wooden door, and upon inserting a nickel, dialled the number of BSO HQ Toronto, Casa Loma. It was answered on the first ring. "25-1-1. Edmond."

192

"One moment, please," the female voice responded.

Derek Wainscott came on. "How is the weather?" he commented flatly. "Anything new?"

Edmond hesitated, realizing that Wainscott's non-questions were standard ploys, a game, playing for time to permit the Casa Loma backroom men and women to place a trace on the location of Edmond's payphone. "It was quite pleasant earlier, thanks," he stated tersely, "however, there's been an unexpected storm, quite severe."

Following a five second pause, Wainscott replied, "Thanks very much for calling, use your umbrella, stay dry. Goodbye."

Eighteen minutes later, a distraught Rodney Ward pushed the Emergency door crash bar, and burst into the lobby. "Where is she? Where's my sister?"

Edmond and McManus looked up. Reaching him before McManus stirred himself, Edmond led Rodney to the bench. "Easy, easy. Sit down here. I'm Edmond. This is Constable McManus."

"Hello ... what's going on?" Rodney pleaded.

"We don't know, Mr. Ward; we're still waiting for the doctor to come out of surgery," Edmond offered.

"This is all too much. I, I... don't understand what's happening. You said she wasn't run over? Did she have a seizure or something? Can't have ... she's not diabetic or epilil ... God, why did I let her take the streetcar? It's my fault." At this, he began weeping, and shaking uncontrollably.

"No, not at all, Mr. Ward..."

"Rodney..."

"Rodney..."

"Excuse me, Mr. ah, Wuerth? This is Sergeant of Detectives Thomas, from Police Headquarters," McManus announced ponderously. "Sergeant Thomas, Edmond Wuerth. And this is Miss Ward's brother, Rodney."

"How do you do," Detective Thomas stated softly. "That's all for now, Constable, you can carry on with your regular duties, thank you. I'll expect your notebook on my desk at the conclusion of your shift."

"Yes, Detective. You'll have it. I hope your sister's fine, Sir." He arose and with a sigh of relief, flipped closed the notepad cover as he ambled to the exit.

"Mr. Wuerth, may I see you privately for a moment?" Wuerth was forced to listen closely, as the detective had a tendency to speak almost inaudibly. "As you would expect, Sir, I'm under a certain amount, correction, a great amount of pressure. My superiors are rightly concerned about this unfortunate affair. Broad daylight, Sunday morning, subject, an attractive single woman ... suddenly collapses, unknown cause ... very sensational in the wrong hands, if you get my meaning, Sir?" he asked conspiratorially. "You can imagine Monday's headlines: **Angry Mayor Orders Police Chief: "Calm City's Fears!"** Or, **Are Toronto Sabbaths Safe?** ...that sort of nonsense. They'll have nazi spies running loose on the rampage. Fortunately, we rarely see reporters around this place on Sunday mornings. Inquiries are being carried out, but in the meantime, I'm asking for your complete co-operation and absolute discretion."

"You have it."

"Of course, good," he smiled. "I need to take your statement, for the record, Mr. Wuerth."

"Is it okay if Mr. Ward listens in? He's waiting anxiously to find out what happened to his sister."

"Not at this time. Let's step into the Consultation Room over there, shall we?" He caught the eye of the duty nurse and motioned toward the door. She nodded in tacit consent. "Go inside, please. I'll speak with Mr. Ward."

"Now, Mr. Wuerth, tell me exactly what happened. From the beginning, please."

".... And that's when I flagged down Constable McManus."

"Thank you. We're following up on that 25-1-1 business with the RCMP," he smiled reassuringly. He turned the page. "Now, you said you suspect the man of doing something to her?"

"Yes, yes, I do."

"Please describe him."

"About five feet eight, medium build, fair skin. He had on a dark suit, a matching bowler hat, and he had an umbrella in his left hand. That struck me as peculiar."

195

"Peculiar, Mr. Wuerth?"

"It's sunny and promises to continue nice all day. Maybe he was a bit of a dandy. He was using it as a walking stick."

"Good. Anything else? His gait? Colour of his...?"

There was a rap and the door opened. "Hello, Doctor McPhee, any news?" the detective inquired.

"Hello, Detective Thomas. Is this gentleman Miss Ward's next of kin?"

"No, I am. I'm her brother, Rodney Ward," he asserted, entering into the room. "How is she?" he demanded. The doctor shook his head. Rodney's face fell. "Oh, no!" he whispered, "how bad is she?"

"I'm very sorry, but your sister passed away three minutes ago. She never regained consciousness," Doctor McPhee stated. "We attempted to resuscitate her, but her heart had stopped beating, and ... I'm sorry."

"Oh my God, no, this isn't happening. This is some kind of terrible joke!" he cried, and staggered backwards. Detective Thomas took his arm and gently lowered him into a chair, where he sat, twitching, and sobbing.

Doctor McPhee pressed a button on the wall beneath the light switch. A red light flashed on. "Nurse, Dr. Allan McPhee, ... a sedative, with orange juice, and a blanket. Stat!"

"Immediately Doctor." They moved to the opposite side of the room as the nurse carried out her duties as ordered.

"Doctor McPhee, anything you can tell me in regard to a probable cause of death?" Detective Thomas whispered, while glancing sideways at the grieving brother.

McPhee shrugged. "Sorry, nothing official. You know that's the coroner's bailiwick, Detective Thomas," he admonished.

"Yes, but a hint ... anything, Doctor?" Thomas pleaded.

"Yes, please?" Edmond echoed.

"As long as it doesn't go in your preliminary reports. I'd deny it, if you did," he confided. "I am not a Toxicologist. Off the record, it might have been caused by a nerve toxin: she exhibited all the classic indicators: convulsions, seizures, paralysis, cardiac arrest..."

"So, in layman's terms, do you mean ... a poison?" Edmond asked.

"Poison? What do you mean, poison?" Rodney shouted, struggling to free himself from the hospital blanket in which he had been tightly wrapped.

Doctor McPhee glared at Edmond, and then turning toward Rodney, replied "I'm sorry, Mr. Ward, we won't know anything until the coroner's autopsy report is completed."

"Autopsy? Suffering Jesus, I can't believe this is happening. What am I going to tell Mother?" he asked plaintively, continuing to flail weakly in an effort to untangle himself.

"Okay, I'm treating this as a murder," Thomas snapped under his breath. "Doctor McPhee, contact the coroner's office. And take her to the morgue directly. I don't want anyone other than the Provincial Forensics people, and that includes hospital personnel, examining the body. Evidence gets easily contaminated by amateurish fiddling..."

Dr. McPhee bristled.

"Sorry, Allan, I don't mean you. I was referring to that Lovatt murder trial four years back in Hamilton, where the intern botched the examination so crudely that the Crown had its case thrown out by the judge."

"And the investigating officers were reprimanded in court and consequently demoted to bicycle patrol, Jocko?"

"The very same," Thomas replied grimly. "In the meantime, I'll have a description of the suspect circulated to all stations and units.

"Can you estimate his age, Mr. Wuerth?"

"Mmm, I'd guess somewhere between twenty-five and thirty. Oh, yes, I do recall from the little that I could see of it, his hair was light, sandy brown."

"Excellent, that's extremely helpful, Mr. Wuerth. I'll be in touch later this afternoon, Allan. Will he be okay?" tilting his head, indicating Rodney, who was sitting, head down, muttering groggily, "I don't understand."

197

"The sedative seems to be having an effect. I can keep him here..."

"I'll take care of him, Doctor," Edmond volunteered.

"I want to make sure that he's fit to travel. Wait another fifteen minutes, if you wouldn't mind, Mr. Wuerth."

"Sure, whatever you think best, Doctor McPhee."

"I'll be over this evening to ask him a few questions. Well, I'm off," Thomas announced and walked to the door. "Just routine," he paused, "the questioning, that is. I may bring a warrant," he warned before exiting.

A recent model, black Buick sedan pulled up to the curb in front of the Toronto General. From the rear emerged a tall, middle-aged man of military bearing. Looking south on University Avenue, he could see two Toronto policemen blocking the passage of pedestrians on the sidewalk about 150 feet away. RCMP Commissioner Ted Reynolds hurried inside the hospital's front entrance to be met by Edmond Wuerth.

"Edmond, good to see you," he stated briskly. "Where can we talk?"

"Hello, Commissioner, I wish it were under better circumstances," replied Edmond. "Here, in the Consultation Room. That's Mary Ward's brother, Rodney."

"Looks as if he's been hit by a sledge hammer."

"He's sedated; the shock was overwhelming for the poor fellow."

"I can imagine. Bring me up - to - date. Derek was able to give only the scantiest of details."

"...And that's about all I know except Detective Thomas is treating the death as a murder, Commissioner."

"And this male person is the primary suspect, I assume?"

"It's about all we have to go on, yes, Commissioner."

Doctor McPhee entered. Edmond introduced them. McPhee summarized his findings and intuition. Reynolds listened intently, and then thanked the doctor who walked over to examine Rodney.

"This is going to be a tricky one, Edmond," Reynolds sighed. "These jurisdictional battles often get political and blown out of proportion, downright nasty business. I must get in touch immediately with the Detective ... what's his name and division again? Is there a private telephone I can use?"

"At the nursing station or the pay phone down the hall."

Commissioner Reynolds returned, looking relieved. "He says he'll cooperate with us, thank God. I'll speak to the Chief to make certain that all the ducks are in a row. Your organization wants the autopsy carried out by their people. Very well, shall we go out and take a look?"

Edmond and Ted Reynolds walked down University toward the two policemen. Edmond noted that both men were sweating profusely. He wondered if it was because of the heat or the protests of passing pedestrians, annoyed at being forced to step off the sidewalk, at the crime scene.

"A scorcher, eh? I'm RCMP Commissioner Ted Reynolds, and this is Edmond Wuerth," he announced affably, holding up his identification. "You've done a great job of protecting the site, thank you officers. I've spoken with Detective Sergeant Thomas and have his permission to look around. You can take a break. Here's a dollar; get yourselves a cold drink in the cafeteria. Mr. Wuerth and I'll be nosing around here for ten or twenty minutes if you'd like to come back then."

They searched for evidence on the sidewalk. There was none. The only sign of the incident that remained was a slight discolouration and depression in the rain – starved grass marking the location where Mary's body had been brought to rest. Ted leaned over and removed a few blades. "I want this area combed thoroughly by my forensic team," he stated, as he placed the samples inside a white envelope, which he sealed and put in his suit jacket pocket. As he stood up, a battered sedan car pulled up beside them. "It's a crime reporter, Harry Blyth. He has a column in the *National Liberty* magazine and does a popular radio spot at noon on CFGB. It's not bad, actually. Let me handle this!"

The driver called out the window. "As I live and breathe, Commissioner Reynolds! What's up?"

"Good morning, Harry!"

"Too hot on the golf course, Commissioner?"

"Something like that, Harry," he smiled. "You?"

"My wife sold my clubs, I'm sure of it. I'm damned if I can find them! Who's your friend?"

"An associate."

"May I ask what you and your associate are doin' here in the heart of Hog Town on a sunny Sunday morning?"

Reynolds stepped over to the window. "Your east coast bias is showing, Harry, and the short answer is, no."

"Gees, Commissioner. Won't you give a working boy a break? My editor's been in a rotten mood lately."

An unmarked Toronto Police car pulled up to nudge the rear bumper of Harry's Ford coupe. The Commissioner's Buick pulled in front, and backed up. A plainclothes officer exited from each vehicle. "Problems, Sir?" the Mountie asked.

"One minute, constable. Harry...!" Reynolds walked around to the passenger's door and entered the reporter's car. After a minute he got out, smiled, and closed the door.

"This vehicle is stopped in a restricted hospital zone, Harry," the

Toronto police officer interjected. "Move it or lose it!"

"Mr. Blyth was just leaving, weren't you Harry?" He smiled sardonically.

"Okay, Commissioner, I got the picture. You didn't have to bring in the cavalry already," Harry grumbled. "Right, I'm leavin', if you'll move your patrol car! But I'll be back."

"He won't after he talks to his publisher's lawyers," Reynolds confided to Edmond after Harry had pulled away in a cloud of blue exhaust.

"Why?"

"I suggested that he might not want to spend the next fifty years in Kingston Penitentiary. Somewhat reluctantly, he saw the light."

"Ah, the Official Secrets Act trick."

"No trick, Edmond," he retorted. "I suspect we have something very extraordinary on our hands. One moment.

"Now, constable, I want this area from here, to there, sealed off. You are to co-operate with the Toronto boys. Second, I want the Forensic squad down here within thirty minutes to comb it thoroughly. Get on the radio, now.

"Here's Robert Brooks. Excellent!" Reynolds remarked to Edmond as the Deputy Chief of British Security approached them. After a brief discussion with Edmond, Reynolds and Brooks excused themselves and set out on a walk together. Edmond returned to the hospital to find Rodney, alert and composed, chatting quietly with a female member of the Salvation Army. She rose and assured Edmond that a volunteer would drive Rodney to his home.

"How's Erik ... taking the news?" Ted inquired. "It must have been a terrible blow."

"Not well. He's very upset, as you would expect," Robert replied grimly. "He's coming in from New York tonight."

Minutes later, Ted and Robert had decided upon a course of action, which required the aid of a trusted partner. In the privacy of Dr.

McPhee's office, Robert waited while Reynolds dialled the number on a business card, which he had fished from his wallet.

"McIntosh – Anderson Funeral Home. John Kellam, Director, how may I help you?"

"John, good Sunday morning! Ted Reynolds here."

"Commissioner Reynolds, always good to hear from you. How are you? How's the golf?

"Underwhelming, to say the least. I've been out maybe six times since May 24. We must get a foursome together for another round at my club before summer's over, John."

"I'd love to, Ted! And hopefully, this time I can break par. What have you got for me?"

"You knew I wouldn't just be calling out of the blue about a golf invitation, didn't you John? Robert Brooks and I have an urgent situation at the Toronto General on University Avenue. We need you to transport a body to your establishment today, and have Doctor Miller arrange for an autopsy as soon as the body arrives."

"No problem, Ted."

"Excellent. Again, we're at the Toronto General Hospital, Emergency. The attending physician is Doctor Allan McPhee. Robert and I will wait for you here in his office."

"We'll be there in a flash. Are you going to call Doc Miller or should I?"

"On second thought, Robert'll call him, you take care of the body."

"Okey doke. Got his home number? I've got it, here ... I'll see you there soon, 'bye Ted."

Robert took the receiver and dialled Doctor Miller's residence in Oshawa.

"Doc, Robert Brooks here. Sorry to disturb you at home. Fine thanks. I need you to meet me at John Kellam's funeral home in say two and a half, three hours. John's picking up a woman's body at T. G. H.

and taking her back. She's one of ours. Is there a pathologist at the hospital who you can get hold of on short notice?"

"Reg Sutton's our man; if you remember, he handled Lieutenant Kepke."

"Yes, first-rate job."

"I'll ring him. See you there, Robert."

At three o'clock that afternoon, Ted Reynolds, Robert Brooks, and Edmond Wuerth, were gathered in a cool anteroom in the basement as Doctors Miller and Sutton conducted the preliminary examination in the preparation room next door.

At three fifty p.m., Doctor Miller came out, wearing a white surgical gown and rubber gloves. "We're finished with the prelim workup. Dr. Sutton's taking body fluid samples for analysis. Is everyone going to be okay with this? Sure? Come inside, please."

The air was laden with the cloying reek of formaldehyde. For a moment, Robert thought his heart would stop. He had seen death many, many times as a veteran of the Royal Flying Corps. Nonetheless, he was not ready. It was not the scent of embalming fluid, but the realization that this colourless, lifeless cadaver was all that remained of Miss Mary Ward, the all - knowing, charming guardian angel of BSO. Could this be his ingénue, Mary Ward - vibrant, witty - the vivacious, young graduate student whom he had hired over lunch that afternoon at the Arcadian Court? Doc Miller's voice interrupted his reverie.

"Edmond, you told the detective that Miss Ward grabbed her right calf, is that correct?" Doc Miller asked over his shoulder.

"Yes, Doctor, that's correct."

"Swing the magnifier light a little more this way, please, Doctor Miller," Sutton requested quietly. He slowly moved the device from her heel upward as he scanned the leg. "Yes, there is a tiny puncture mid-calf," he murmured. "Run your finger across there, Doctor. Can you feel something?"

"Uh huh, seems hard, like a piece of metal, shrapnel, is buried just below the epidermis," Miller affirmed.

"Let's see if you're right, Donald," Sutton said, choosing a scalpel from a selection arranged on a white cloth towel.

Doctor Sutton made a vertical incision mid-centre along the calf. "Forceps." Doctor Miller complied. "Here it is," he declared. It made a pinging sound as he let the object drop into a small, kidney-shaped stainless steel basin. "Take a look." Under the light magnifier, they saw a miniature dart. "No doubt fired in some fashion, perhaps from the umbrella which the man in the bowler was carrying." He set down the metal bowl, and as he dried his hands, turned toward the group. "I need a complete toxicology analysis done on this object, and the blood and tissue samples," he stated, looking at his wristwatch, "within six hours. Whatever was used, it's highly likely that it's designed to deteriorate rapidly, become unstable, and then break down completely, making it all but impossible to identify. Our lab is closed on Sunday afternoon. Any ideas?"

"I'll set it up," Ted stated and walked quickly out of the room. Five minutes elapsed. "Done," he announced. "The chief and his assistant are willing to come in."

"That's excellent, Ted!" Robert exclaimed. "I'm prepared to drive it into Toronto..."

"I have an idea, Rob," Ted interjected. "I know Peter Snell the manager of the airport. Let me run back to John's office and call him."

Within thirty minutes, Ted had made the arrangements. John Kellam, accompanied by a City of Oshawa police motorcycle escort, would rush the samples, now packed in dry ice, inside sealed containers, to Oshawa airport. From there, the containers would be flown by Mr. Snell to the Toronto Island Airport where they would be transferred to an RCMP car for delivery to the forensic lab at headquarters. "Estimated time from McIntosh–Anderson to the Toronto lab, sixty-five to seventy-five minutes," Ted declared. "I know we can do this!"

Edmond and Robert Brooks followed Doctors Miller and Sutton upstairs to the rear entrance and outside to the parking lot. "In the back, John?" Doc Miller asked, indicating the two boxes.

"I'll take them, Donald," John volunteered. He loaded the two small aluminum containers, then closed and locked the rear door of the silver 1933 vintage McLaughlin Buick hearse and signalled to the officer. Lead by the motorcycle, they hurtled up the short driveway to Bond Street. The motorbike's siren suddenly cut in, as they swung left onto Bond, and continued to wail intermittently, and then faded as the procession raced northbound on Simcoe Street.

"Four-fifteen," Ted commented. "How long do you think it might take to run the tests, Doctor?"

"That depends on the state of the facilities, the quality of the equipment," Doctor Sutton responded. "Assuming those are up–to-snap, and with top-notch technicians, I'd estimate, oh, between eight to ten hours. Normally, it would require two days, plus or minus. What do you think, Doctor Miller?"

"Midnight, if we're lucky. I think we'd be smart to find a decent restaurant to start..."

"Gentlemen, I have the solution: The Blue Swallow Inn," Robert announced. "I'll phone Roger Stedman to make reservations for five o'clock. Perhaps he can arrange to have Erik brought there when his flight arrives. All in favour?"

"I think I'll head home, thanks anyway," Doctor Sutton replied. "Sunday dinner at the aged mother-in–law's, a not-to-be-missed monthly event!" he laughed. "Actually, she's a gem and at eighty-three, an avid connoisseur of ridiculously rare and outrageously expensive Bordeaux, of which she seems to have an inexhaustible supply. Cheers, then. I'd appreciate knowing the outcome."

"You certainly will. Thank you so much for everything, Reg, am I right?" Robert asked.

"Yes, Reg."

"Robert, Rob. Don Miller'll call you first thing in the morning, all right Doc? Send your account to my personal attention, Reg. Here's my card."

"This one's gratis, Robert. Consider it my contribution to the war effort. Carry on."

At nine-thirty p.m., Mr. Wesley Curtin, the proprietor of The Blue Swallow came to the doorway of the dark and nearly empty cocktail lounge to announce, "Mr. Reynolds? Sorry to disturb you Sir, but there's a long distance call from Toronto, extremely urgent. In my office, Sir."

"Thanks, Wesley. This could be it, gentlemen," he commented as he arose from the table and followed Curtin out.

"Wish I could have served you gentlemen something after dinner, Sir, but the rules are the rules," Wesley stated solemnly as they walked together.

"Yes, Sunday in good old dry Ontario. Say, I noticed that your clock is running slow," Ted commented, and then paused, noting the response on Wesley's face. "Just kidding, Wesley. Would you mind closing the door? Thank you."

Ted shut the office door. "Reynolds here, what have you got so far, Glenn?" As he listened, he scribbled notes on a small pad of hotel stationery. "Okay, Glenn, let me read back to you what I have..."

The men at the cocktail table were sipping their third and fourth cups of coffee, waiting expectantly when Ted came back inside. He sat down, and proceeded to reread his notes. Finally, he looked up. "Sorry, I wanted to make sure of this. Doc, what do you know, if anything, about toxic frogs ... their venoms?"

He shrugged, "Well, South American natives in the Amazon Basin have used the venom on their blow guns. The toxin is produced on the frogs' skin, as their natural defence mechanism. These compounds rank among the deadliest known natural chemicals on earth. Apart from that, not much, Ted."

"That's a hell of a lot! ... Very helpful, thanks. Help me out here; is this correct, Phyllobates terriblis?" Ted asked, passing the pad to Miller.

"Yes, that's a particular frog's biological name, Genus: *Phyllobates*, Species *terriblis*," he responded, returning the notepad.

"Well, according to my toxicology man Glenn, this little fellow, Phyllobates terriblis, commonly called Poison Dart ranks among the deadliest. Listen to the symptoms: rapid breathing, muscle contractions, heart arryth..."

"Arrhythmia...the heart beats wildly; it goes out of control, basically," Doctor Miller clarified.

"Thanks, arrhythmia and ... let me see if I can figure out what I've scrawled, yes, cardiac failure, and then, death. Glenn said the paper he referred to states, 'fatal within a minute in average – size laboratory mice,' and that's with a dose so small, that I can't pronounce the word."

"Jesus!" Robert exclaimed, letting out his breath abruptly, "death by toxic frog venom injected with a poison dart. We're dealing with either a very sophisticated or a very sick mind."

"Or both," Edmond commented.

"It might have been a random act, but let's stop kidding ourselves. This was a premeditated attack. But why Mary?" Robert mused aloud.

"There's Roger with Erik," Doc Miller announced. "Oh, my God, even in this light, he looks terrible. Let me break the news, Robert."

"Sure, thanks, Doc. We're going to find her killer or ..." He stopped, unable to finish.

"Erik, so good to see you. Here, have a seat ..." Doc Miller stated cordially, rising to shake Williamson's hand.

...IT TOLLS FOR THEE

Roger Stedman rubbed his eyes again and blinked, and then, in frustration, threw down the document that he was reading. He pressed the intercom button on the side of his desk, picked up the receiver and paused, counting to three, "Good morning Miss Robertson. Could you do me a rather large personal favour?"

"Good morning. Yes, of course, Colonel Stedman!" she responded as light-heartedly as a Commandant's private secretary might be allowed. It had been a very, very pleasant evening, she reflected, and then shunted the recollection to a mental siding.

"Would you please make an appointment with Doctor Johnson, Betty? My eyes are bloody killing me; I think that I might need bi-focals, or a white cane."

"Sure, yes Sir. Any particular preference, day, time?" He heard pages being turned. "I'm looking at your appointment calendar," she continued, "Mr. Williamson at Casa Loma tomorrow, Tuesday, all day. Wednesday's clear so far ... Thursday after three, Mary Ward's funeral at 11:00; Friday, not good ..."

"Mary Ward's funeral ... Try to make it for Wednesday morning. Lunch today?"

"Not possible. I'm swamped," she responded.

"Dinner then?"

"Not possible again, sorry, Roger, I really am. Mother is hosting a baby shower this evening for my little sister. Now let me call Doctor Ted, before you go blind, thank you." She switched off her intercom; using the eraser end of her pencil, she dialled Dr. Johnson's office.

"Hello, may I speak with Doctor Johnson please?"

"I'm his secretary, may I help you?"

"No, I need to speak with him ... in person, thank you."

"One minute. Whom may I say is calling?"

"Elizabeth Robertson," she replied and transferred the receiver to her left hand. She picked up her Royal Doulton teacup and was taking a sip when a cheerful male voice came on the line.

"Miss Elizabeth Robertson, Ted Johnson! Betty my dear, what's a lovely girl like you still doing single?"

"Always the optimist, eh, Doctor? You know I'm destined to be just a poor but honest working girl," she laughed.

"Honest, but I sincerely doubt the rest. What can I do for you, Betty?" he inquired.

"I have a special patient in desperate need of an examination. When could you take him?"

"Desperate? Okay, Wednesday morning at 9:00 is fine, if that's acceptable with him."

"That's perfect, thanks, bye."

Betty buzzed Stedman. "Doctor Ted, Wednesday at 9:00 am."

"Thank you so much! Busy? Can you spare a moment?"

"Mmm, so - so, why?"

"I'll come out there then. A second later, he was bending over, kissing her lightly on her cheek. "You do look smashing this morning," he whispered. "Anything interesting in the mailbag?"

"Thanks, you don't look so bad yourself, Colonel. The mail? You can't read anyway," she chided him playfully.

"You're right, I think I need to give up on this report until Ted fits me out. So kindly take it from my faltering hands, lock it up and remind me to finish it?"

"With pleasure. There's something else on your mind, Roger, is it Mary?"

"No, I didn't actually meet her more than once, perhaps twice. But it is depressing as hell, don't you think?"

"We were acquainted by telephone only, but yes, it is a tragedy."

"The truth? It's the gold, Betty. I can't get to sleep knowing what's buried there. I think I'd be better off if I were to move my bed to the Great Room."

She turned from the filing drawer to look at him directly. "Roger Stedman, that is a noble, gallant and utterly futile idea. I hate to disillusion you, Sir, but the cache is perfectly safe, whether you personally are on guard twenty-four hours or not. Besides, I can think of greater rooms and more interesting company with whom to spend the night, than Mac or Doug, nice as they are," she responded gently, sitting down at her desk. "Why don't you take a stroll and see how well - managed things are down there? I'm quite sure you'll feel reassured."

209

"You're right, thanks. Hold the fort?"

"As always," she replied nonchalantly.

Wilma and Wesley Curtin sat at their breakfast table. "I can't eat another thing, Wesley, dear. Every Sunday morning I say, 'not so much today, Wesley', but you always just go ahead merrily and fix, fix anyway. It's a good thing that we have Jack as cook for the guests or we'd be flat bony broke."

"Stony broke, my love. Jack's all right, I suppose, for an amateur. I'm a cook, always have been a cook; you knew that when you married me. I learned the habit from Dad when I was a kid. Every Sunday morning he'd make us boys a grand old English breakfast, fried potatoes, pea meal bacon, fried tomatoes, eggs and blood pudding. Makes my mouth water just thinking about it!" Wesley replied with conviction.

"Well, I don't imagine how it could possibly be watering now. You've just put away enough for ten stevedores. Just remember, I don't eat as much as you do. A piece of toast, with some of your lovely fruit preserves, a soft boiled egg and a cup of tea would suffice quite nicely," she added as gently as she could muster.

"Yes dear, I'll try to remember that in the future," he offered meekly.

"Right, I'm off to chapel now. I'll see you when I get back. The Reverend Renshaw is going to be speaking about an inspiring new book this morning, all about friendship. I have some questions to ask him, private like, before the gross majority of the congregation gets there. For that reason I'm going to get there bright and early for a chat."

SILVER DAGGER

How many Sunday mornings had he heard the same old story, 'bright and early for a chat'? 'Poor duffer, probably just wants to have it off with the wife!' Wesley thought it highly presumptuous of Wilma to expect that the Rector, The Reverend Stuart Renshaw should spend time with her before eleven o'clock service every week. "Have a good time Wilma dear," he called out as she retreated down the walkway. 'I'll do the dishes and mind the shop while you and Saint Paul are busy slaying the Philistines, with Christian goodness,' he added mutely.

'Saint Paul', Paul Eccles, the Blue Swallow Inn's handyman/chauffeur was waiting patiently, as usual, at 10:00 a.m. in the Curtin's immaculate cream and brown 1938 Packard. Wilma depended upon Paul, her jack-of-all-trades, for many reasons. As she often said, 'He had come as part of the property deed, a fixture, like the furniture, but much more useful, in his entirety.' His age, like the furniture, was the subject of some speculation. Wesley, she had long accepted, was a cook, born and bred, but quite hopeless when it came to doing repairs requiring the simple ability to drive a nail straight or replace a roofing tile without endangering life and limb, his and other's.

Paul's only Sunday duty was to take Wilma to church in Whitby. He never attended with her, despite Wesley's suspicion that the two were kindred religious zealots. In reality, while Wilma was attending the service, Paul cruised into Whitby to meet his good friend, Yvonne Fleurie, a stunningly voluptuous red-haired manicurist formerly of Longueuil, Quebec. They always had cinnamon buns with coffee before driving down to park for an hour on a secluded stretch of the lakefront, following which he drove Yvonne back into town, returning to pick up Wilma promptly at 12:00. In two years, he was never late, nor early. Wilma admired a man who could be punctual and so 'useful' with never a complaint, a curse word, nor a day of illness.

Paul drove west along Highway 2, at his customary rate, slightly below the speed limit to Brock Street and turned south toward Lake Ontario. At Victoria Street, he went left and turned sharply left again to enter the parking lot driveway of St. John's Anglican Church where he stopped, pulled on the parking brake, jumped out, and opened Wilma's door.

"I'll see you at 12:00 then, Mrs. Curtin?"

"Yes, Paul. Have a lovely breakfast and a safe drive, Paul," she declared as she reached out to take his hand for support, pressing two carefully folded dollar bills into his palm.

"Thank you, Mrs. Curtin. Indeed I will."

Wilma glanced at her wristwatch as she slowly negotiated the low stone steps of the church and with some difficulty pulled open the heavy front door, which had not been hooked open as was usual at this time of the year, to permit some ventilation between services. She looked up at the multi-hued stained glass depiction of the Last Supper, which filled the three windows directly over the immense, plain wooden crucifix.

St. John's Anglican Church, Whitby, Ontario

Halting briefly, she bowed her head, and then continued walking on the maroon carpeting to the front row of pews. She backed carefully onto the oak seat, slid tight to the aisle, and pulled down the prayer bench kneeling rest. She dutifully knelt and offered a prayer for her Wesley, a truly kind and good man, whose ungenerous remarks about 'Saint Paul' and cynical jibes about her faith she had attributed to his mother's lack of a strong moral fibre, rather than a deficit in Wesley's makeup.

She opened her eyes to look towards the altar for her spiritual mentor, The Reverend Stuart Renshaw. The irises, day lilies and black – eyed Susans that she had ordered on Friday, anonymously of course, were a long-overdue touch of splendour on the altar, she decided approvingly. But there was no sign of Rector Renshaw to enjoy them. 'Unusual,' she muttered and looked at her silver and diamond wristwatch again. The Reverend Renshaw was always to be seen there with his Assistant, between ten - twenty and ten – thirty, fussing, or as he preferred to say, 'making preparations'. Afterwards, he would spend five or perhaps seven - minutes with Wilma, in the Vestry office, patiently answering one, or two of her religious studies questions, while he slipped his vestments over his suit.

"Sorry madam, the service doesn't start until 11:00. You're here early!" a male voice declared. She turned to see a clergyman in the aisle, wearing a white surplice and black trousers, standing closely enough to rest his left hand on the back of her pew. 'Rather tall, slim, well-brushed black hair, debonair, distinguished even, like that English actor the young women rave on about, Ronald Colbert ... or some such, but this one needs a good, close shave, and a good deodorant," she concluded.

"Oh, dear, I'm sorry, Reverend. I'm a regular, Wilma Curtin, can you tell me where Rector Stuart Renshaw might be?"

"Pleasure, Mrs. Vilma. Reverend Schmidt," he enunciated slowly. "Yes, unfortunately, Mr. Renshaw's been taken away, to a family matter in United States. He asked me quite late to speak the service."

"Oh, and I was so looking forward to his sermon this morning on A Friend For Life."

"A friend for life?" He looked at her intently. "Ah, friend, for life, that's the point of it, naturally."

"Yes. It's an inspirational, wonderful book, the collected sermons of a clergyman; I'll just sit here and wait for the service."

"That is good."

"Thank you, Reverend." She gathered her courage. "I hope this won't sound rude, but are you visiting our parish from someplace, far away?"

"Quite a lot farther, Vilma. Suid-Afrikaans, South African."

"Oh, how interesting! The author of my book, well it's Rector Renshaw's book really, is from there. Bishop Jan Pietersen. You've heard of him, perhaps?"

"No, sorry, Suid - Afrika, it's a very big country. Please excuse me, Mrs. Curtin, I must get ready." He smiled gracefully, turned away, and walked quickly up the steps toward the altar. Wilma, ever a stickler for detail, noticed that his trouser cuffs rode up at least one half inch too high above his heels to be fashionable. The heels ... the man was wearing Wellingtons, or riding boots, definitely not Sunday Oxford shoes, with a trace of mud on the edges of the soles. That's odd, possibly he's been out horseback riding, we are in the country and why shouldn't he? I wouldn't be at all surprised if it's quite common in South Africa. So few roads, I'd imagine...'

Throughout the service, Wilma was unable to stop thinking about the handsome South African clergyman's footwear. It fascinated and distracted her; she tried hard not to be seen trying to catch another glimpse. The service was disjointed, and seemed rushed; the scripture readings and prayers inaudible, the sermon was flat, humdrum, and uninspiring, and very difficult to follow. It was as though he was inventing it as he went along, she thought. The small congregation soon became restless; their coughing and foot – shuffling nearly drowning out his words several times, which Wilma thought very inappropriate, although his frequent mixing of Afrikaans and English together made understanding him a challenge.

Wilma persevered, and managed to work out that his message was vaguely related to the notion of friendship, although the content bore no similarity to the book. That was understandable, as Schmidt had not read it, of course. As the organist was on vacation, the choir was not present. Nor was the Assistant Rector. When it was finally concluded,

Wilma walked quickly out into the bright sunlight. There was no sign of Paul. She looked at her wristwatch. The service had lasted barely forty minutes. 'That's a blessing, but there's still twenty minutes to wait for Paul,' she fretted. She walked down two steps to the landing where several younger women who were clearly enthralled surrounded The Reverend Schmidt. While shaking his hand, she found to her embarrassment that her eyes were drawn inexorably to the boots. 'Very peculiar for a man of the cloth, on Sunday.'

A small group of senior parishioners were holding a post mortem a short distance away on the sidewalk. It was Wilma's sense that it was intentional so that their comments would be overheard by the visiting cleric. It was obvious from the chitchat, that to a person, they had missed the gist of his sermon and most else. Miss McEvoy, the forthright President of the Ladies Auxiliary was holding forth, insisting that each one write a strong letter of complaint to the Diocese office in Toronto. Wilma broke in, suggesting that the hapless Reverend Schmidt was rather more like an occasional teacher, thrust into a classroom at the last moment without time to prepare any lessons.

Mr. Thompson, the semi - retired criminal lawyer, and thrice –failed candidate for political office was holding court. He took exception to Wilma's explanation, pointing the finger of blame as well as his silver - tipped cane vaguely in the direction of the Dominion government in Ottawa, criticizing its typically lax immigration policies, for allowing 'anyone with an accent and enough money or influence to buy his way into the country these days.' Offended and embarrassed by the barrister's remarks, Wilma decided to leave and get out of the dazzling noontime sunlight as well. She walked over to the picturesque little churchyard, which was blessed with mature horse chestnuts and sat down on a wooden bench to read her church calendar while waiting for Paul. A voice from behind startled her.

"How was it you found the service today, Mrs. Vilma?"

It was the booted minister. "You gave me a start! You do have a way of coming up on people suddenly, Reverend!" she replied irritably. Feeling uncharitable, she immediately regained her composure. "Oh, it was interesting…" she smiled gamely. "Where did you say your home parish is located?

"Kaapstad."

"Pardon me?"

"Kaapstad. Cape Town.

"That reminds me, Bishop Pietersen is from Cape Town. Oh, how forgetful of me, I mentioned that earlier." 'You're from Cape Town and you've never heard of an Anglican Bishop there? Curious...' she reflected. "For six months of the year, he's away with the native people in Botswanaland, a missionary, you know. Have you ever done mission work?"

"No, I regret, I haven't. Are you waiting to be driven away, Vilma?" He had now sat down on the bench.

"Yes, as a matter of fact, my driver should be here at any moment," she replied, peering anxiously over the picket fence onto Victoria Street, just as her Packard pulled up in front of the churchyard. "There he is now!"

"Mrs. Curtin! I've been looking everywhere for you. Are you alright?" Paul called.

"Paul, yes, I'm fine!" She waved, getting up hurriedly, and feeling a twinge of guilt as though Paul, her knight, had come to her rescue. "Good-bye, Reverend Schmidt. Give my best to Rector Renshaw!"

"So, was that a new minister, Mrs. Curtin?"

"It was a very unusual service, Paul. Rector Renshaw wasn't there and there was something peculiar about the clergyman, Schmidt, who filled in for him."

"What was peculiar about him, Mrs. Curtin?"

"It seemed that he was trying too hard to be a minister, but he was missing some of the basics. He also wore riding boots, and they were muddy. I'll think about it. Paul?"

"Yes, Mrs. Curtin?"

"Let's stop for an ice cream cone, do you mind?"

"No, indeed Mrs. Curtin, double scoop? My treat!"

Roger Stedman walked from his office in the Lecture Hall to the lake in less than five minutes. When he was within fifty feet of the concrete and steel entrance, the guard snapped to attention. "Good morning, Private," Stedman called as he approached. "All's well, I take it?" he inquired glancing around casually.

"Good morning, Colonel. Yes, Sir, all's well. Fine weather, isn't it Sir? Does the Colonel wish to go in this morning?"

"That's why I'm here, Private. Who's down today?"

"Private Mac, Sir."

"You may proceed, Private," Stedman ordered.

He watched Private Doug reach under his tunic to remove a chain from around his neck.

"Key number one, Sir; proceeding to open exterior padlock," he announced, holding out for inspection one of the two keys fastened to the chain; then kneeling, he inserted it with deliberation into a sturdy chromium steel padlock.

"Just get on with it, Doug!" Stedman commented impatiently, "before the war's over."

"Sorry, Sir." Upon removing the padlock, using both hands, Doug raised a hinged steel plate, which was inset into a six-inch thick reinforced concrete pad. Roger watched as he swung the cover back to its rest position, and reached inside. Doug worked silently, methodically opening one, and then a second combination lock on the top of a strong box. When he had opened that, there was a smaller box inside. He dialled the combination, and then opened the container to finally reveal a keyed lock. He then inserted the second key, and turned it to the left. Ten feet away, twin steel doors, which were set into a one foot high reinforced steel and concrete enclosure on the ground responded immediately, sliding open soundlessly.

"Never ceases to amaze ... well done, Doug."

"Chinese puzzle box, that's for sure. Just give me a dingle when you're coming up, Sir. Oh, Sir, if you wouldn't mind," he remarked, offering Stedman a metal clipboard.

"Of course." Roger printed his name and signed the Access Control Record Form, also noting his 'In Time', and then handed it back to Doug.

Private Mac McDonald had been seated on a chair in the corridor outside the temperature-controlled environment of the Great Room. He relished guard duty here, especially on sticky and hot summer days. As the doors at the top of the stairway started opening, Mac leapt up, at attention.

"Hello Private McDonald. All's well I see?"

"Yes, Sir, everything's hunky – dory," he replied with pride.

"Tell me, Mac, what's it like, down here, all by yourself, surrounded by this incredible store of wealth?"

"Well, Sir, first of all, it's cool and fairly dry, not at all damp, and it's quiet. It's no worse than sitting down in the guardhouse at Thornton Road by your lonesome. Second, it's a little like working as a bank teller, like my cousin Merv says, I suppose. Merv says you just get used to it, handing all that money day in, day out, but you don't really think about it after a while, on account of it's not yours. It's like it's not real, Merv says. It's the same thing here."

"Very astute of you, and Merv. Tell me, Mac, are you prepared if something were to happen, say, a bomb blast blew off the doors, or attackers got past the barriers and forced Doug, or whoever out there, to open up?

"Yes sir. All hell would break loose. The second set of safety doors would close by themselves like, if he were to turn the key to the right, instead of the left, and that would trigger the silent alarm system, which would notify you of a break - in on the panel behind Miss Robertson's desk. I might be done for of course by then, and after that, it's up to you and your men to repel the invaders, Sir."

"Yes, very good, Mac," Roger replied, well pleased and impressed by Mac's enthusiasm. "I think I'll take the short tour." As Roger hurried along the passageway to the entrance of the Great Room, his heart pounded. He was the chief custodian and minder of Great Britain's rich-

es; the gold ingots, neatly arranged in stacks like gleaming loaves of bread, filled the entire cavern. Roger found the sight surreal: magnificent, extraordinary, and unsettling. In 1922, a nine- year –old Roger Stedman had become, like millions of others, an overnight Egyptology buff when photographs of the spectacular treasures found in the tomb of the boy Pharaoh Tutankhamen were revealed to the outside world. Then, as a student of eighteen, Roger had volunteered for a dig in the Valley of the Kings at Thebes, eager for fame and adventure. Instead, he reaped twelve-hour days of backbreaking labour, punctuated by the misery of dysentery, bouts of heat exhaustion, acute homesickness, and an agonizing black scorpion's sting, which had hospitalized him for nearly a fortnight. But never a glimpse of the golden hoard. Now, at thirty-one, he was the overseer of riches undreamt of even by Howard Carter, of King Tut renown, or the Emperors of Cathay, Genghis Khan and Montezuma.

He walked back to Mac's station, feeling reassured as Betty had predicted. "Well Mac, I'll be off now, if you could buzz Doug."

"Yes, Colonel. Everything satisfactory?"

"You're doing a tip - top job, Private McDonald. The King's gold is in safe hands," he stated, then walked toward the steep concrete stairs.

"Thank you, Colonel. Drop by anytime!" Mac called out.

Roger surfaced, and couldn't help noting the dramatic sea change in temperature and humidity, reflected that the underground storehouse would indeed make ideal sleeping quarters, for the time being. Upon completing Doug's time sheet, Roger surveyed the shoreline, noting approvingly the rolls of barbed wire and the four heavily armed sentries patrolling the pebble – strewn beach. Taking Private Doug's field glasses, he could make out the silhouette of a Royal Canadian Navy corvette on picket duty. When he entered his office, Betty addressed him without looking up from her typewriter, "Did you have nice walk, Colonel?"

"Very, thanks. Any calls?"

"Robert Brooks; he said it wasn't pressing."

"Pressing, Betty?" he chuckled. "Was that his choice or yours?"

"Unless you want a full-scale mutiny by the troops on Thursday, I'd strongly suggest you let me finish this pay sheet, thank you Colonel."

"Oh, very well. Wonder what he wants? With Robert, nothing and everything's urgent. I'd best call."

"Yes, it might be pressing!" she responded with mock seriousness.

"Paul ... Paul, could you please drive me into town?"

Paul set down his paintbrush on the sheets of newspaper covering the top of the old garden table and wiped his hands. He had just finished laying down the final coat of lacquer on the wings of his latest creation, a 1/10 scale model Tiger Moth, when Wilma summoned him from the kitchen. "Okay Mrs. Curtin, where'd you want to go exactly?" he shouted back.

"Back to St. John's Church, Paul."

"The Church, Mrs. Curtin? At two o'clock on Sunday afternoon?"

"Yes Paul, I did say St. John's Church. And I want to leave now, please."

"Let me slip out of these overalls." 'What is that woman up to now? Ever since the Nazi spy did himself in here at the Swallow, she's been a bit peculiar. Oh well, face it, Paul, this is the greatest job in the world.' "Ready, Mrs. Curtin!"

He stopped in front of the Church, opened Wilma's door, and then offered to help her out, which she declined. She then instructed him to wait in the Packard, as that was the only way to avoid receiving a ticket. Wilma marched up the steps of the old church and opened the door. Without hesitation, she strode to the base of the altar and cast her eyes around. "Hello, is anyone here?" There was a slight echo, then silence. "Hello, hello, is anyone here?" she repeated loudly.

The Vestry door on her right opened. Schmidt emerged, and seeing her, seemed momentarily taken aback. "Mrs. Vilma? ... Good to see you. You perhaps forget something? Is that why you are back?"

"Well, Reverend Schmidt, I was just passing by and thought I'd return Rector Renshaw's book and while I'm here, pick out another one from his library. Here it is," she announced, withdrawing a slim volume from her purse."

"That is good." He looked back over his shoulder, and then continued. "Another book, you said?"

"Yes, please. I'm sure he wouldn't mind. I always sign them out. The library is in the Rector's Study, beside the kitchen. I'm sure you know ... down the back stairs." Wilma paused, noting a growing look of concern on the face of The Reverend Schmidt of Kaapstad.

He cleared his throat. "I..."

She pressed on. "I was just wondering when Reverend Renshaw would be returning?"

"He said only a short time, two, maybe three days. You could wait that long for the book, no?"

"No, I can't, and to be frank, I find the whole situation strange as he always announces to the parishioners if he's going to be away." As she held out *A Friend for Life* in both hands, she glanced down at Schmidt's feet. 'Ugly dirty boots, with no class at all.'

"Yes, yes, Vilma, I understand," he responded with a trace of irritation. "This was a surprise...no warning. The telephone...please, sit, rest, I'll return." Schmidt turned away abruptly, and entered the Vestry office, closed the door, and in three steps was at the Vestry's back entrance. He went out the door and ran down a half flight of metal stairs to the concrete block walled basement, walked along the hallway past the serving kitchen to a door labelled in gold and black gothic lettering, **Private-Rector's Study**. He entered, slamming the door. "Verdomp!"

A brown haired man looked up from the Rector's desk, and asked in German, "Hallo...what's wrong with you, Lieutenant?"

"A problem Max, we've got a woman upstairs asking questions!" Kurt exclaimed in Afrikaans.

"Speak real German, dammit. You know I barely understand that bastard language!"

"Sorry, Colonel, I forget sometimes," he exclaimed, and then quickly lowered his voice. "I said there's a woman in the church asking questions."

"Thank you, that's better. So, answer them and then she'll go away!" Max responded flippantly. "I'm not surprised," he added, "you made a complete mishmash of the service!"

Kurt bristled. He was sensitive to criticism that his mother, who was of Dutch Boer and English stock had taught him to speak passable English but with an indelible Afrikaans' accent. "Your English is far worse than mine. We agreed I'd do it, so don't go playing your, 'I was born in the Fatherland', superiority games. If you remember, I was the first to enlist ten recruits in the Party's youth division in all of Cape Town."

221

"You were actually quite good, Reverend Schmidt," he answered, smiling.

"I really think she's on to us, Max, at least, that's the impression she gives!"

"Highly unlikely, Kurt, but if it's causing you so damn much worry, we'll fix it, straightaway!" Max responded dryly. "Bring her down."

"Another problem, Max; she has a male driver, waiting outside. From what I could see of him this morning, he's an Englander, older, but a beefy, healthy 'strength through joy' type."

"I know you'll persuade him to co-operate. Bring him down too, what's another abduction more or less?"

"Güt, give me my pistol, please? I'll have them both in here straightaway."

Max opened the Rector's desk drawer and handed Kurt a Luger pistol, grip-end first. Checking that it was loaded and the safety off, Kurt placed it between the covers of a large hymnbook. He hurried upstairs, and out of the Vestry into the church to the front pew where Wilma was sitting. "Vilma, sorry I was so long. Thank you for waiting. Come, if you would, please, follow me downstairs to the Study; we'll get you a new book."

Wilma had waited patiently for five minutes, and was starting to feel slighted until Schmidt reappeared and apologized for the delay.

Clutching her purse, she followed him without hesitation into the Vestry, and downstairs to the door of the Study. He knocked once, opened the Hymnal, turned, and pointed an ugly black pistol directly at her chest.

"Oh, my gracious!"

"Vilma, take off the hat and give me your purse."

"I most certainly will not. This is a church; in Canada we..."

"And this is a loaded pistol. The purse. And now, the hat, take it off ... take it off, I said! ... Hands high, on top of your head. Like this!" he ordered, forcing her to clasp her fingertips. "Now, go in. Not a sound." The door opened from inside. Schmidt pushed her ahead gently with one hand on her shoulder while prodding her in the small of her back with the barrel of the Luger. As Wilma entered, she hesitated; Max took hold of her upraised left arm and spun her face first into the bookshelf. Seconds later, he had fastened a length of cloth behind her head, which bit into her mouth painfully, making her moan.

"Not that tight! The old lady can't breathe," Kurt urged.

"She'll survive. Here, take this and tie her hands. I'll lead!" Max commanded and walked across the Study to the wooden door marked Washroom.

Kurt quickly trussed Wilma's hands with a short length of rope and then led her to the washroom. Inside, Max was on his knees, prying at the wooden floor with a screwdriver. "Got it!" With a heave, he raised and removed a large square of planking and leaned it against the porcelain base of the wash sink. "After me!" he ordered then stepped into a hole where the flooring had been removed.

Kurt took Wilma's arm and directed her to the top of a stairway. When she balked, he encouraged her with a push, causing her to stumble. Max turned quickly, took her by the shoulders, and caught her mid – fall, then guided her slowly down the remaining steps.

Terrified, Wilma nonetheless looked around at what appeared to be a sub – basement. It was earthen floored with pieces of timber, stone and brick lying scattered everywhere. The walls were bare fieldstone. It smelled dank, and musty, as though it hadn't been exposed to fresh air for a century. In the near-darkness, a single low – wattage light bulb that was suspended in a socket on two wires from an overhead joist, provided enough light to dimly illuminate the figure of a man, seated at an awkward angle in a chair, with his back to her. "Who's that?" she mumbled.

"Come, see!" Max answered and guided her to the corner. "Reverend, your good friend Vilma's here, to visit you!"

The man raised his head and stared at her, uncomprehendingly. His face was discoloured with purple welts and his mouth badly swollen.

223

"Reverend Renshaw!" she gasped through the gag.

"Colonel, you forgot the extra chairs. I have to get the man from the car before he takes off."

"They can sit on that big wooden timber ... see it? I'll drag it over here by myself, while you bring him in. Hurry, Lieutenant, go now."

Kurt rushed up the stairs into the Vestry and quickly tucked the pistol into his trouser belt then threw the Rector's frock over his clothes, and walked outside to the top step at the door of the church. "Mister, please come! Mrs. Curtin fainted!" he called. "Mrs. Curtin fainted!" he repeated loudly.

Paul looked up, startled. "What?" he replied, cupping his ear.

"Come, please. Mrs. Curtin fainted," Kurt shouted again. 'Stupid deaf English bastard.'

"Coming!" Paul jumped out of the car and ran up the steps. "Where is she?"

"Inside ...I don't know what happened, she dropped to the floor, like that! Please, follow after me."

Paul walked along the aisle, closely behind Schmidt. "Where did you say she is?"

"Here!" Kurt turned and delivered a blow with the pistol butt to Paul's forehead, felling him instantly. Kurt lugged the body to the front, up the altar steps, bypassing the Vestry and around the side to the stairwell. By the time he had dragged Paul down the stairs and along the hallway to the Study, Kurt was exhausted. With a mighty effort, he pulled Paul's unconscious body across the floor of the Study to the top of the stairwell, then called down, "Hallo, Max! Help me! This one's heavy!"

Ten minutes later, they rested to survey their handiwork: Renshaw, tied and gagged in the chair, Wilma, the same, on the timber and Paul lying inert on the ground in front of her.

"That's it, all three are secure. Mein Gott, he hasn't moved yet. How hard did you hit him?"

"Hard enough," Schmidt shrugged. "I thought that he was going to get the jump on me. There is blood from the Altar steps all the way to down here. I'll clean it up in case someone else comes along. That reminds me Max, I wonder where the caretaker is?"

"Where what is?"

"The man who cleans and..."

"On holidays, sick, who the hell cares? If he shows his face, we'll add him to the party. Listen to me, Kurt, we don't have any time to lose. After you clean up the floor, take this big brute's car out into the country and get rid of it. Then get back here as soon as possible."

"Why Max? I can park it a few hundred metres away and then it's ready, when we need it, nein?" Kurt protested.

"Nein, just do as I tell you! And take off that goddamn skirt. It makes you look like a fancy boy. And do not hitch a ride back, understood?" Max demanded.

Kurt dug into each of Paul's pockets searching vainly for the keys. "Not there. He must have left them in the car!" he shouted and then vaulted up the stairs. Finding them on the front seat, he drove the Packard up Brock Street. When he approached Highway 2, the northbound traffic signal turned red. Kurt waited for the light to change. A black and white car drove up behind him. 'Scheiss, polizei! Ontario Provincial Police.' Kurt stared straight-ahead at the traffic light, in an attempt to avoid eye contact with the driver in the rear view mirror. When the light changed, the police car pulled out and around, stopping alongside Kurt. The young constable called over "Nice car!" Kurt looked over and smiled, nodding in agreement. With that, the policeman accelerated, leaving Kurt still searching for first gear. 'Christ that was close!

225

Whitby's 'Four Corners', Dundas and Brock Streets

Where's he going so damn fast?' Two miles north of Highway 2, Kurt turned left onto a dirt road, drove three kilometres, and after carefully checking for cars in the rear view mirror, pulled onto the shoulder. He got out, wound up the windows, and after locking the door, threw the Packard's keys as far as he could into a cornfield.

'There, it shouldn't take that long for me to walk back, maybe two hours.' He set out toward Brock Street. His boots crunched and slipped on the roadside gravel as he walked, while reflecting on their mission's success. He hoped that Max wouldn't order him to kill Vilma; she was nosey, but nice, and she was harmless. He would try to convince Max that she might prove to be useful as a hostage. As for the other two, he knew Max would have no qualms about shooting them.

As the late Sunday afternoon sightseeing traffic had picked up, Kurt purposely tried to stay far to the right on the shoulder, in the hope of attracting as little attention as possible. He realized that Max's warning to avoid contact was an order, and not a suggestion. About one kilometre from Brock Street, he suddenly heard the sickening sound of gravel being thrown up at the underside of a car, which was quickly bearing down on him from behind. 'Kalm! Kalm, Kurt!' He kept walking while the car pulled up very close, before coming to a slow stop. There was silence. Kurt had no choice. He turned around.

"Hey there, need help?"

"Oh, hallo! No thanks, my car has a break up so I'm just valking down to the gas station on Brock, at the bottom hill. I'll get tow truck to take me back, officer."

"Nonsense, it's way too hot for that. Hop in; I'll take you back and have a look at it. I was a mechanic before I joined the Force," he offered pleasantly. "Come on, get in!"

Kurt tried to appear pleased as he trudged back to the cruiser and opened the passenger side. He got inside and gingerly closed the door.

"Give it a good slam, it's not closed. The doors are heavy in these Chevy's. Constable Delaney's my name. What's yours?"

"Kurt, Constable, Sir" he replied. The Luger, which he had jammed in the back of his trouser waistband, was feeling as large as a cannon. 'Thank god I wore a jacket!' he thought.

"Kurt, Constable will do and pleased to meet you. I always enjoy picking up folks in distress. It sure beats the bejeebers out of my usual job. Okay, I saw the car back there, not very far." Delaney pulled a left u-turn onto the highway and headed back west on Rossland Road.

"Kurt, you Dutch? I only asked 'cause there's a lot of Dutch folks settled around these parts of Ontario County."

"Yes, Sir. Constable, your car drives so fast," Kurt remarked.

"You can say that again, Kurt!"

"Constable, your car drives so fast!"

"No, sorry, I didn't mean, 'say it again', I meant... never mind. Yes, she is fast, 2-barrel carb, 216 cubic inch, straight six. She's two years old, but in great shape and goes like the wind. The Department bought 45 of these Chevy Coups back in '41. Yep, she's a beauty, fastest thing on the road as far as I'm concerned, at least nothing has been able to outrun me yet." He pulled in behind Wilma's Packard. "There she is! Sure a pretty thing! Okay, open her up and get in. I'll lift the hood and you try it when I say go. What's the matter? Can't you open it, Kurt?" Delaney inquired with sarcasm.

"I ... I don't have the key, Officer."

"You lost them, did you, Kurt? That's very careless of you."

"Ya, I guess so," he smiled weakly.

"Show me your licence, son."

227

"Just a minute. I know it's in here..." Kurt responded nervously, digging inside his inner breast pocket. "Not there, maybe in the auto," he replied feebly, as sweat began to roll down his forehead.

"Maybe not. Face the car. Put your hands on the back of your head, now!" Constable Delaney unclipped his .38 Colt revolver and proceeded to search Kurt with his right hand. "Well, well, what do we have here?" he exclaimed, withdrawing the Luger from Kurt's waistband. "Nasty - looking article, 9 mm Parabellum Luger PO8, Wehrmacht issue. Not overly common here," he reflected, mockingly.

"I'm a collector, Officer Delaney, I swear it!" Kurt protested.

"And I'm the man on the moon!" Delaney muttered, as he placed the pistol under his Sam Browne belt and then released his handcuffs from their clip. "Give me your right arm, lower it, slowly, slowly."

Schmidt, taking advantage of Delaney's momentary distraction, pivoted swiftly on his toes, swinging his outstretched arm to land a sharp blow on Delaney's right temple. Delaney, wincing with shock and pain, managed to grab his adversary's clenched fist and spun him leftward, his shoulder smashing against the car's windshield pillar.

"My God, maklik, maklik, easy!" he screamed.

"Maklik yourself. Now are you going to behave?" Delaney muttered as he increased the upward force on Schmidt's arm socket.

"Ja, ja, yes, Englishman, damn it, sweer!" Schmidt protested, slamming his left hand against the car in agony.

"Good boy ... just take it real slow." Quickly, Delaney fastened a cuff on Kurt's right wrist. "That's it and now the left, slowly, slow, back here. While he was fastening the second restraint on Kurt's wrist, he recited a litany of charges, concluding, "Well Mr. Kurt, I'd say you're heading to the pen for life or the gallows!"

"Gallows? Why, I get hanged defending myself or for the car?"

"No, not me or the Curtin's car, Kurt. We're at war with Germany, in case you're not aware and I don't know of a judge or jury in Canada that would believe you're not a German spy, carrying around that hardware, concealed at that. The list goes on, my friend. And by the way, my wife and her family are Dutch. That accent of yours is not Dutch, South African ... Afrikaans, with some German I'd be willing to bet, buster. Don't move. Keep the legs far apart, that's a boy."

Delaney radioed in for a paddy wagon. As they waited, Delaney continued, "Do you really think I'm stupid? Like I said, I was a mechanic in Town for many years and I've been on the Provincial Force here in Whitby for seven years. So, you'd expect that I know everybody in town and what kind of car they drive. And, mister, everyone knows that this car belongs to the Curtin's from the Blue Swallow. I just hope for your sake you haven't done anything to harm Wilma and Wesley!"

The police wagon arrived. "Take him straight to the Station, Chuck, no coffee stops with this one; I'll be right on your tail to make sure!" Delaney ordered, as he got into his black and white Chevrolet Coupe and picked up the microphone. "Staff Sergeant Shea, Delaney again, over. Can you have Duff's dispatch a tow truck for the Curtin's Packard? I think you'll want to have a thorough going over ... Oh you have. Do they know they'll have to use a jimmy? Good, thanks, Staff. We're on our way, out."

Staff Sergeant Shea appraised the handcuffed suspect hunched over on the bench and the Luger lying on the desktop, then motioned Delaney to approach. He leaned forward and whispered "This is a big fish, too big for us, Dell. I'm calling in the reinforcements. Is your face okay?"

"Tingles a bit, he got me a good one. Nothing I haven't had on defence with the OPP Old Timers'. I'll put some ice on it. You said, reinforcements, Staff Sergeant?"

"Mounties, I've dealt with their top man, Reynolds. He's an okay fellow. It's a string of federal offences we're lookin' at, maybe treason, espionage, god knows what else, not counting the car theft and assaulting a peace officer. So, it's going on up the chain of command to our Commissioner Swan, and then Swannee can take it up the river to Commissioner Reynolds." He chuckled at his cleverness. "Always cover your backside, lad. Remember Shea's golden rule: When in doubt, pass it up to the brass castle. Those boys earn the big bucks for something!"

"Yes, Staff."

"You've done a great job, Dell. I'll finish bookin' him, and then we'll stick him downstairs in the holdin' cells, pending orders. I've assigned Patrick to guard the bugger all night," he grinned. "Now, go and have a coffee before you start your end of the paperwork. But keep the particulars to yourself for now, even Sue, okay, lad?

"Thanks, Staff, I promise. But don't you think someone should be checking to make certain that Wilma and Wes are okay ... and to let them know we have their car? I'll gladly do it, if no one else's available."

"Good thinkin', I'll call The Swallow right away."

Delaney went down the corridor and entered the staff lounge. "Whew, who's been smokin' cigars in here? Oh, it's you, Patrick. I shoulda known," he remarked while pouring a coffee. "Any fresh milk? Oh, ya, I see it. Pew, it's off! Forget it, I'll have it black," he muttered, pouring the bottle's thick, yellowish contents into the sink. "Anyone ever hear of a fridge? Miracle invention. So, what's new, Will?"

"Not much, Del, same old routine. That little delinquent Tommy Rankin rode through old Mrs. Calvert's backyard on his bicycle. Hooked all her freshly - hung undies on his hockey stick and took off like a cat with its tail on fire draggin' 'em through the mud."

"I can imagine that old bat's language!" Derek Patrick chimed in.

"I thought she'd peel the paint off the side of the garage!" Will asserted, with a laugh.

"Wow, sounds like you've had an exciting day, Will," Delaney replied, stirring in the third spoon of sugar. "Everything work out okay?"

"Settled it in the usual way, took the culprit home to momma," Will remarked. "I doubt he'll be riding that bike again anytime soon. What about you, Dell? Get hit with a puck again buddy? That eye's going to be a beaut!"

"Yeah, I had some excitement. I caught a guy stealing the Curtin's Packard, west on Rossland, a couple of miles. He put up a bit of a struggle," he explained as he wrapped an ice cube in paper hand towel and held it to the edge of his swollen right eye.

"Jesus, I saw the Packard on Brock at the Four Corners around four-fifteen!" Will Penny exclaimed. "It must have been him!"

"Well, he's outside being booked right now with Staff, if you want to check."

"I'm sure you got the same guy ... good looking in a kind of European - type movie star way, slicked back, dark hair?"

"Uh, huh."

"Good for you for getting the pinch, Dell. Teaches me a lesson," Will observed.

"And I drew extra duty to baby-sit the bugger tonight! Gees Louise!"

The Whitby Jail

Derek Patrick always complained bitterly about any extra assignment that got in the way of his regular Sunday night poker game with the Mayor and his cronies. "What's the big deal with this guy? He's just a two – bit run – of - the – mill car thief, or did he run off with some bigwig's wife, into the bargain?"

Derek Patrick's voice grated on Delaney at the best of times. He bit his tongue, "Beats me, Derek," Delaney replied. "Paperwork calls. See you, boys!" Coffee in hand, Constable Dell Delaney had reached the lounge door when it flew open to reveal an extremely agitated Staff Sergeant Shea. "My coffee, Staff!" Delaney exclaimed, as the contents spattered on the wall and linoleum floor.

"Come out here and shut the door, Del," Shea hissed, then continued under his breath, "Wilma's not been seen since two p.m., and the Swallow's handyman, that big galoot, Paul Eccles, you know, with the red-haired Frenchie girlfriend, is missing too. Wes is beside himself; hey, you can imagine what he's thinkin'! I have to doubt it myself. You've seen the lovely Yvonne, Dell? 'Nough said. Anyway, I called Commissioner Swan so he's coming out from Toronto with the Mountie Commissioner Reynolds, pdq. They're bringin' Forensics, too. Hell's a poppin'! Commissioner Swan wants this Kurt Schmidt character locked up in solitary in the Whitby Jail, so of course, that's what I'm gonna do when I'm finished printing him. They're going to put the thumbscrews to this boyo. Just so you know, Dell, a damn fine job bringin' this guy in. If he's a German spy, you're going to be a hero, my boy! And by the way, I owe you a coffee."

"Thanks, Staff, I'm on my way to The Swallow. I'll take Will Penny ... and give us two shotguns, please Staff!" As he and Constable Penny ran across the OPP station parking lot to the black and white Chevy 'Holstein', Delaney hoped that Shea would typically forget to tell Patrick about the change in plan for at least two hours, to royally piss him off.

An hour later, Delaney and Penny re-entered the OPP Station's lot to find their parking space occupied by a glistening black Buick Road Master sedan. "Commissioner Swan's" Delaney remarked unhappily, as he pulled around to the building's rear entrance, where a black and white OPP Chevrolet station wagon was parked. "Forensics Unit." He tried the rear door. "Damn, locked," he muttered, "we'll have to hoof it around to the front, Will."

Carrying their shotguns, Delaney and Penny trudged around the corner of the red brick police station and up the main steps. Delaney had agreed to inform Staff Sergeant Shea that their search of the Blue Swallow and grounds had turned up nothing unusual, except a model airplane sitting on an outside table, which, a distraught Wesley Curtin was able to confirm, was the property of Paul Eccles. All indications pointed to a sudden departure, but no other clues were visible in the limited twilight, they had agreed. Penny followed Delaney to the gun cabinet, where Staff Sergeant Shea intercepted them, with two men in suits.

"Commissioner Swan, Commissioner Reynolds, meet two of my best, Constables First Class Dell Delaney and Will Penny!" Shea declared, beaming. "Delaney's the one who nabbed Schmidt," he continued proudly, as Swan and Reynolds shook hands with both officers.

"You've done a great service for the Province of Ontario, son. I'll see to it that there's a Commendation forthcoming from the Lieutenant - Governor, Officer Delaney," Commissioner Swan announced. "How's your eye?"

"Thank you, Commissioner, it's fine. It was a routine arrest, Sir. It was really only afterwards..."

"I think you might have to change your mind. Look at this photograph, Constable. May I call you Dell?" Ted Reynolds picked up a black and white photo from Shea' s desk and handed it to Delaney.

"Sure, Sir. Look at this, Will. That sure looks like Kurt Schmidt. What the... what's he wearing?" Delaney asked excitedly.

"We think it's him, Dell," Reynolds commented. "He's wearing the uniform of a German Naval Lieutenant here, but in reality, we don't think he's navy; he's actually an agent of the Abwehr, German military intelligence, born and raised in South Africa, and a fanatical Nazi. He escaped from the Bowmanville prisoner of war camp more than two years ago and has eluded us ever since. A crafty and dangerous operator! He may have been involved in a spy ring in Toronto. So, how do you feel about your 'routine arrest' now?"

Delaney stared at the photo silently. "I knew his accent wasn't Dutch."

"Afrikaans," Reynolds added.

"Yes Sir, but it was only a hunch on my part, until he started cursing. You see, Sue, my wife, has an uncle from Bloemfontein. Met Oncle Pieter just once, when he came to our wedding. Quite a character!"

"Some guess, Dell!" Swan commented. "It appears from what Ted said that you've single-handedly caught an – honest – to - god German spy. I am deeply impressed by your outstanding police work, and very, very, grateful."

"You might be thinking about a new career in federal law enforcement," Ted remarked with a smile. "Just joking Terry," he assured Swan.

233

"Thanks, Commissioner Reynolds. Where's Schmidt now, Staff?" Delaney inquired.

"Whitby Jail, solitary," Shea commented. "Guarded like the Bank of England. Can Dell and Will go home gentlemen, or do you need them down there?"

"By all means, go home and get some rest! Ted and I'll head down in a few minutes. Staff Sergeant Shea will phone you tomorrow, if you're needed early. Oh, one other thing. Don't talk to any reporters and keep mum with your wife, Sue, you said, for the time being. Ted and I will make sure that you have a proper sit down with all the local and national news boys, photos, autographs, a hero's parade, you name it, but all in good time. Will, you're on the hook, as well."

"Yes, Commissioner," Delaney and Penny replied and saluted. "It's normally our day off, but you can call anytime, right, Will? By the way, Staff, did Patrick get to his appointment with His Worship on time?"

"Sad to say, no. By the time I released Schmidt for transport to the jail, it was too late. Martha Patrick has a curfew for the poor lad on Sunday night, home sober and promptly by 10:30 sharp. Pity, eh?" he added, with a wink.

"Real shame, Staff, that's for sure," he replied jokingly. "I sure hope Wilma and Paul turn up safely," Delaney added quietly. "You'll let me know?"

"We're on it, Dell, rest assured," Commissioner Terry Swan replied. "Forensics is already at work. I have ten extra units on their way from

Toronto; with Ted's contributions, along with some specialists' help with interrogation, we'll find them," he commented grimly. "Now, home, you two, and that's an order!"

"Colonel Stedman, Commissioner Reynolds!"

"Thanks, Betty. Put him through."

"Ted, how are you?"

234

"Roger, we have quite a situation. Terry Swan of the OPP and I think that a Whitby - based Provincial caught one of the spies who got away from us when we raided that house in Toronto. We're waiting for fingerprint analysis for confirmation."

"Good show!"

"Wait. It's more complicated, Roger. Wilma Curtin and the handy-man from the Blue Swallow are missing and we're beginning to suspect foul play. There's more, but I can't go into it on the phone. We need to question the prisoner as soon as possible but we don't have anyone here in Toronto with the language capability or the expertise. Our top linguists were transferred en masse to Ottawa. Anyway, I was wondering if you could help us out?"

"His language?"

"Languages: Primary, Afrikaans, secondary German, with enough English to navigate on the loose here for two years ... from Camp 30. Take your pick." Reynolds paused. "What do you think?"

"German, I'm better than adequate. I picked up a smattering of Afrikaans from a South African lady archaeologist when I spent an otherwise disastrous summer in Egypt, believe it or not."

"That's great, Roger. I believe you. What was her name?" Ted inquired mischievously.

"Erika, Erika DeJong, Doctor DeJong, actually. She's now one of us, with SIS. I believe that the good doctor and Derek Wainscott were quite chummy for a bit. Should I bring Hamish Findlay along? His German is as good or better than mine and he's a superbly skilled interrogator. He uses quite unique methods."

"Yes, do that. But you won't have to go anywhere, Roger, that is, if you agree. I'd like to bring him to you."

"Absolutely, tell your driver to come directly to the Lecture Hall, Ted. I'll have Hamish there. We'll improvise, would you mind?"

"No, do whatever you think might work. Thanks Roger, I know we'll crack this nut. I owe you another one."

Max looked at his wristwatch and swore. Kurt had been gone for three hours. 'How far had he taken the automobile ... Bowmanville?' he reflected irritably. The damp and cold and stale odour of the underground cellar as well as the moans and grunts of the three captives were wearing on his nerves. He found the driver the most annoying, slumped against the wood beam; his shifty eyes following Max everywhere, like a wolf, waiting for a sign of weakness, ready to pounce. 'Impossible, he's tied up like the fat swine that he is.' Max wished that Kurt had finished him off. 'I'll give Schmidt one hour more, until sundown, and then I'll decide whether or not I leave ... and what I'll do with these simpering, spineless morons.'

A nondescript Chevrolet sedan turned south off Highway 2 and sped down Thornton Road. Two men were in the back seat, although the dark – tinted windows made them invisible to the occupants of passing vehicles. One wore handcuffs, leg shackles, and a blindfold. At the sound of an approaching vehicle, his companion insisted on forcing him to bend forward for no apparent reason, aggravating Kurt's inflamed shoulder. The guard was expecting them; after a quick verification of their credentials, he directed them to the Lecture Hall. Kurt's companion rooted him out of the back seat and frogmarched him into an empty room where he was deposited without ceremony on a bench, still bound, and blindfolded.

Outside the door, Ted Reynolds briefed Stedman and Findlay on what they needed to know.

"Not to worry, we've been through this a dozen times and with far tougher villains than this one, Ted. Wait here. Hamish, after you?"

Ted Reynolds paced and sat, and then walked outside for some fresh air. When he returned he stopped and listened. The only sounds filtering through the door were an occasional cough and indistinct muttering. A low buzzing sound filtered out. It lasted for six minutes. After that, he thought he recognized Hamish' voice, but it might have been Roger's. A bone-chilling scream punctured the silence, followed by the distinct sound of furniture being smashed, then another, louder scream, and then babbling in German.

Five minutes later, Roger and Hamish stepped out of the Lecture Hall. Hamish was rubbing his right hand.

236

"You can take him back to the nick Commissioner. We've got everything you wanted," Roger announced calmly.

"And?" asked Ted.

"He's not working alone. His senior, a Colonel named Maximilian Schneider, is holed up in the sub-basement of St. John's Church in Whitby, where he's holding the church's Rector, Mr. Renshaw, Mrs. Curtin and the Swallow's handyman, Paul Eccles. This one, Schmidt, claims he doesn't know what the mission is all about, and that Maximilian Schneider, won't say. I tend to believe him as this is typical of how German Intelligence operates," Roger stated. "Anything I missed, Hamish?"

"No, I think that sums it up perfectly, Colonel," he shrugged.

"Well done! May I ask how you managed to get this bird to spill his guts so readily?" Reynolds inquired. "I mean, are we carrying him back in a bushel basket?"

"Quite the contrary, Ted," Hamish replied nonchalantly. "Have a look."

"Hmmm. Yes, quite so. How did you do it? I mean he's obviously cowed, blubbering, a complete emotional train wreck, but he seems to be intact, more or less, physically."

"Ah, the power of suggestion on the impressionable and befuddled mind. I ran one of Robert Samson's old police training films describing and demonstrating the niceties of knife fighting. Do you know the one? Very grainy, no sound, primitive colour, shaky camera, shot on location, in Hong Kong, with a gang of six real criminals receiving their just rewards from the master, in graphic close-ups. So, when I produced the genuine article after, Samson's prized silver dagger, he wet his pants, fell off the bench, and grovelled, pleading for mercy. It helped loosen his tongue wonderfully when Roger rang up Killer on the intercom to come in and join us."

"Ted, just one thing, do you mind if a few of us tag along on this one? This gentleman is extremely dangerous and we've had more experience dealing with the Abwehr and their ilk."

"Not at all Roger, pleased to have you. Do you have a plan?"

237

"I think I so, but I need to pay a visit to the church. Let's go have a look Hamish, shall we?"

"Very well. We'll take Schmidt back and then Swan and I should make a flying visit to see Wesley and reassure him that we're on the job. No details, but enough to give the poor fellow some hope. I'll see you at St. John's ASAP."

The blacked - out car crept to a stop two hundred yards from the church. Roger Stedman, Hamish Findlay, and Robert Samson exited, closing their doors silently. Minutes later, Ted Reynolds pulled up behind Colonel Stedman's Buick. He got out, leaving his door partly ajar, and stood stock-still to get his bearings in the near darkness and then set out toward the churchyard. He stopped at the fence. The moon cast a pale, eerie radiance on the stone faces of the grave markers. Ted flinched when a field mouse shrieked suddenly as a nighthawk's talons carried it aloft. A figure stepped out slowly from under a chestnut tree.

"Ted?"

"Here, Roger," he whispered. "Have you had a chance to look around?"

"Yes, Samson and Findlay have come up with a scheme. It's chancy, but with stealth and the element of surprise, it should be the ticket and frankly, we have no other options, short of mounting a full frontal assault. That requires experienced storm troops, minimum platoon strength, which is entirely out of the question."

"Agreed. So...?"

"I'm going to let Robert describe it." Stedman whistled and Robert

Samson materialized from the shadows. He was wearing combat fatigues and boots. His face was smeared with camouflage paint. "Tell the Commissioner, Rob."

"Sir, we know that he's holding them in the sub – basement, and that is only accessible via a trapdoor in the rector's study, which is in the basement. We also know that he's armed and will use his weapon. The plan is, essentially, to create a scenario, which will draw his attention and allow us to infiltrate the area and take him down."

"I'm no military strategist, Robert, but what about the hostages? How do we know that he won't shoot them at the first opportunity? He must be getting fairly edgy by now."

"We don't, Sir. It's called a calculated risk."

"A scenario, Robert?"

"Call it a two-legged Trojan horse. It occurred to me as a possibility after Hamish and the Colonel told me about their session with Herr Schmidt. Anything else, Sir?"

"We're running short of time. Where the devil are Swan and Andy?" Stedman muttered.

"What does Terry have to do with this, Roger?" Ted asked sceptically.

"Oh, logistical support largely, Ted. Andy's one of our newest staff men. Up through the ranks. Hamish and Robert took him overseas recently and were quite impressed. Aha! Here we are!" An unmarked OPP car cruised past slowly, flashed its lights, then turned and parked behind Stedman. Swan and Delaney exited from either side of the rear of the vehicle as Andy got out from the passenger's side. Andy and Hamish walked away a few paces and conferred, as they applied camou-flage paint to one another's face.

"Okay, Robert. He's yours ...but five minutes. If you sense it won't wash, I want to know instantly," Stedman stated firmly.

"Right, Colonel," replied Robert. "Five minutes." He set off toward the parked cruiser, entered the rear door curbside, and closed it.

Robert and Hamish briefed Andy and Commissioner Swan while

Roger Stedman paced anxiously, consulting his watch repeatedly and with difficulty in the darkness. He turned abruptly toward the OPP cruiser and held up his hand, fingers wide apart. No one spoke, as all eyes focussed on the darkened squad car. Stedman waved his hand in the air, for emphasis. The curbside rear door opened, Robert exited, and then bent over, reached inside, and extracted Kurt Schmidt.

"What in the hell's going on, Roger? Have you lost your mind? Do you really think that playing at Commando tactics will save these people?" Ted protested as Robert marched a downcast and visibly shaken Kurt Schmidt along the sidewalk.

239

"With respect, Sir, I'm taking full responsibility for this operation, Commissioner," Roger stated, his speech clipped. "Please, stand aside and let Major Samson pass. We have a task to carry out and if we don't act immediately, our hostages could be dead. If you attempt to interfere, Sir..."

"It will be on your head, Colonel Stedman. Be forewarned."

"Oh, indeed, Commissioner Reynolds," Roger responded frostily.

"Commissioner Swan, for the record, I am taking prisoner Kurt Schmidt into my protective custody, under the provisions of British Military Code, in full knowledge of the consequences for myself. Clear, Sir?"

"Understood, Colonel. Here's the church key. I dispatched an officer on foot to lock the front door earlier, just as a precaution. Hope you don't mind."

"Good work, thanks Commissioner. Very well, Major Samson, proceed with the prisoner," Stedman stated calmly. "Hamish, wait for it, then follow me." "Andy, eight minutes, mark, now!" Andy took off at a loping run toward the side of the church and melted into the shadows.

Ted Reynolds reluctantly yielded passage to Schmidt, dishevelled and bare-foot, without handcuffs or leg restraints, closely tailed by Robert Samson, whose only visible weapon was a knife sheath fastened to his belt. Reynolds shook his head in disapproval as the pair mounted the front steps. After a brief delay while Robert inserted the key, they went inside, and closed the door.

Lieutenant - Colonel Stedman peered closely at his watch, raised his left arm; and then lowered it swiftly, signalling Hamish who fell in behind. In single file, side arms drawn, they quickly mounted the steps, and entered the building.

In the semi-gloom of the church, Robert ordered a halt. On his command, Schmidt turned around to look down at Robert's right hand, and backed away one step. The object flashed briefly, Schmidt nodded, faced forward, and continued walking, slowly, nervously, two steps in front of Samson. They approached the altar where Schmidt inclined his head leftward and led Robert around to a stairway. Samson tapped Schmidt on the right shoulder and they halted.

Samson whispered a command and they proceeded to go down the metal steps, cautiously, noiselessly. At the bottom, Samson signalled a halt, to permit their eyes to adjust to the pitch-black basement hallway. Schmidt pointed down the corridor, and held up two fingers. Robert nodded and they proceeded stealthily to the first door and paused. The odour of stale coffee grounds assured Robert that they were indeed by the kitchen. He tapped Schmidt's left shoulder and they resumed creeping forward, hugging the wall.

A sudden, metallic clatter split the silence. Robert pushed Kurt's face firmly against the wall, causing him to cry out. "Sorry! ... Quiet!" While holding Schmidt immobile with his left arm, Robert crouched and extended his right hand to investigate the surroundings. "Coffee urn lid! ... Continue," he whispered, his teeth clenched as he stood up, releasing Schmidt.

After six paces, Schmidt stopped and whispered "Office." Robert stepped in front, took hold of the door handle, and tried it gently. The sturdy oak door opened without a sound, one quarter, then half way. Robert offered a silent prayer of thanks to the unknown church custodian and beckoned Kurt to follow him inside the Rector's Study. They halted on the carpet. The only sound Robert could detect was Schmidt's short, shallow breathing. Surveying the layout in the dim light, Robert could make out the dark form of the washroom door across the room.

With the agility and grace of a cat, he glided stealthily across the carpeting, signalling Schmidt to follow. Kurt hesitated, then stiffened, immobilized. Glancing back, Robert repeated the gesture. Kurt shook his head determinedly. Calculating that the man was as terrified of his companion in the cellar as of him, Robert edged his way over and addressed him softly in German. "Kurt, I swear I won't let him hurt you! In another second or two, you'll be free of him. Now, follow me ... please." Trembling, Schmidt slowly raised his head and searched Robert's face, and smiled slightly, then proceeded into the large wash-room. Roger and Hamish silently watched the drama play out from the Study entrance. Roger exhaled in relief, knowing that he had witnessed the renowned 'Samson Effect'.

The trap door yawned open. Kurt stood at the opening, facing down the stairs. Samson glanced sideways into the Study to ensure that Roger and Hamish were in position. He nodded to Kurt.

241

"Hallo, hallo, Max? Max! Kurt here!" he called down.

"About goddam time! Nearly five hours you've been away!" he shouted back, irritably. "I'm damn hungry and need a litre of beer. Come down here, Schmidt, on the double and I mean, on the double, and explain yourself!"

"I've been shot ... but, but I have escaped. I'm bleeding pretty badly, Max. Hilf mir, bitte!"

"Alright, alright, coming. Christ, you really know how to screw things up! I should have left you to rot in that solitary rat hole in the prison camp!"

Robert withdrew backward into the darkness on the far wall. On cue, Kurt glanced quickly at Robert who motioned him to draw back from the opening, as the sound of Max's footsteps grew louder on the wooden steps. Max's head emerged; he glared with disgust at this snivelling, incompetent weakling, a pathetic excuse for an Abwehr agent. "So, where are you bleeding?"

Farther down the corridor, a window imploded, loudly.

"What the hell was that?" Max crouched and executed a sharp one-quarter turn in the general direction of the sound, firing four rapid shots with his Mauser HSc pistol through the washroom entranceway. As if on cue, Kurt dropped, face - first. For a split second, Max stared down in disbelief at his collaborator lying prone, "Schweinhund! You set me up!" he shouted and bent down, pressing the snub – nosed automatic's barrel against the crown of Kurt's head.

Before he could squeeze off a shot, the silver missile had been launched from Robert's fingertips. It rotated on its axis, generating an eerie supernatural wind song, arcing end - over - end, until it arched downward, its blade embedded half-way up to the hilt in Max's rib cage, precisely left of centre, shattering ribs and shredding cartilage, to penetrate the pulsating left ventricle of his heart. Max screamed in shocked agony and disbelief. As his body convulsed, the Mauser flew from his right hand, skittering directly at Hamish. Roger fired his Colt revolver twice. The hollow - point slugs bracketed Max's right ear, removing the left side of his skull as they exited.

Hamish, having managed to trap the Mauser mid-air, simultaneously fired off two rounds, which impacted the Nazi mid - back, driving him sideways, staggering, to topple awkwardly into the hole. His body thumped on each step as he slid down where the shattered remains of his head struck the earth floor.

"That's for Mary. You bastard. Heil Hitler!" Robert muttered and then turned to Kurt. "Very courageously done, young fellow. Your timing was outstanding. Thank you." He took the surprised young South African's hand and shook it warmly. I'd suggest though that you give up any thought of joining the ministry.

"Colonel Stedman, where is our heroic Herr Schmidt to report?" Samson queried.

"He can stay here with us for the moment; apart from that, I really have no idea. Reynolds or Swan can decide that."

"Nice work, guys!" Andy enthused. "How did I do?"

"A smashing success, Andy!" Roger replied jovially. "Pop out and give Commissioners Reynolds and Swan the all clear. Tell Mr. Swan I want ambulance attendants with stretchers in there immediately ... for the hostages lad, now run!"

"Yes, Sir!"

"Hamish, Robert, let's see how they've fared down there. You two had best go ahead. I'll use the phone in the study to call John Kellam for a pickup. I should have the number memorized by now," he murmured, "but I haven't."

"Hello Miss Robertson, Colonel Stedman here. Please call John Kellam, and tell him there's a package to be picked up at St. John's Anglican, Whitby. Rush delivery, please. Yes, it worked quite satisfactorily, thank you. Pardon? Yes, I'd fancy that. Two hours then. Cheerio, and, bring my glasses, please. I can never decipher the menu by candlelight in those ritzy grottoes. Goodbye!"

As the attendants were closing the ambulance's rear doors, Ted Reynolds and Commissioner Swan leaned inside to speak with Wilma Curtin. "Mrs. Curtin, I thought we had agreed the last time that you would call me at the first sign of anything suspicious?" Ted queried.

243

"Oh, Commissioner," she answered quietly, "I just didn't want to bother you on a Sunday afternoon. But we got our man in the end, didn't we? Has someone told Wesley that I'm all right?"

"That we did, Wilma, and we're all very proud of you, very proud of you all!" Ted responded, smiling. "Wesley's fine now and looking forward eagerly to seeing you.

"And thank you Rector Renshaw. I apologize for your mistreatment, Sir. Commissioner Swan and I will be in touch with your wife immediately."

"Is there someone we can contact for you, Paul?" Terry Swan asked.

Eccles raised himself from the stretcher and looked over at Wilma, before responding. "Yes, yes there is, Sir. Yvonne Fleurie, at Fine Fingertips, on Brock Street."

Wilma stared at him with astonishment. "Why Paul, you rascal, I never knew! Yvonne does my nails every Tuesday morning! She's absolutely delightful, and so French in her ways!"

"Yes she is, thanks, Mrs. Curtin," he replied with a self - conscious grin. "I've been thinking lately that she and I should be joining your congregation, Mr. Renshaw ... you know, to belong, in case..."

"Time soon enough to chat about that when the Rector's feeling better. We'll make darn certain they all visit with you tomorrow. God bless you!" Ted stated. "Anytime, driver...!"

"Take good care of these heroes!" Swan called out as the ambulance pulled away.

"Well gentlemen, overall, I think we came out of this thing rather well, fortunately. Would you agree?" Colonel Stedman asked expectantly.

"Absolutely, Roger, it could have been a disaster. My apologies for doubting your methods," Reynolds replied quietly.

"You did what you had to, Ted. I understand totally, no harm done and that's the end of it."

"Thanks, Colonel. Well, Terry, shall we call it a night?"

"Just before you go, I'd like to invite you to join us for a meeting to discuss these events at the Camp tomorrow morning, if you can possibly make it. We'd be remiss if we don't include Robert Brooks, agreed? Breakfast at 0900h, my residence?" asked Roger.

"Agreed, yes, of course!" Ted replied.

"I'll be there," Swan confirmed.

"Perhaps you'd rather stay over to avoid the early morning drive back? You and your drivers are more than welcome to bunk in at the Blue Swallow Inn. Wes and Wilma always keep a room or two available for our visiting VIP's," Roger offered.

"Thanks very much, Roger, but I hardly think Terry and I rank with some of your 'very special guests!'" Ted joked.

"Of course you do. It's there at your disposal; so if you do decide to stay, please don't hesitate. Well, I must be getting on my way. Till tomorrow morning then."

Wearing a starched, white serving jacket and his chef's hat, Cook Fred served breakfast, after which Roger invited his guests to bring their coffee into the Commandant's parlour. Betty Robertson had rearranged the sofas and chairs to accommodate the party of ten, and then she excused herself to fetch some pencils and a stenographer's pad. Roger had told her over their late evening Italian dinner that he thought it would be quite appropriate if she were to sit in and record the highlights of the discussion, which she agreed to do.

Roger began the meeting with a briefing for Robert Brooks. Commissioner Swan summarized the contribution of his officer,

Camp X, aerial view, 1943

Constable Delaney, which was followed by an outline of the operational plan and its execution by Majors Samson and Findlay and Colonel Stedman. Robert Samson paid tribute to Andy, whose role, he affirmed, was anything but inconsequential.

"Everything hinged on split second timing. If you had been one fraction early or late, Kurt would be dead and the operation would have turned into a bloodbath. I fully expect that Max would have executed the hostages, just for spite."

"Thanks Major Samson. That's very kind of you, Sir."

"Well, Robert, what do you think?" Ted asked.

"Un-bloody-believable! I only wish I could have been there to see you gentleman in action. Truly. Now, are you at all interested in knowing what you have accomplished?" Brooks inquired.

Hamish and Andy looked at Roger. Robert Samson answered on their behalf. "Accomplished? We know that the dead man, Max Schneider was Mary Ward's assassin. Kurt Schmidt was his junior. So if there's more, please tell us."

"Very well," he responded coyly. "Let me read you this brief:

Dear Colonel Stedman:

It is with my deepest gratitude and admiration that I personally commend you and your outstanding team of specialists for the decisive outcome that you have achieved. The success of your bold and daring approach is a tribute to the exceptional calibre of the men and officers at STS 103.

We now know that these two men were operatives of German military Intelligence, the Abwehr. Each had been given the identity of a Kriegsmarine naval officer and their capture by Royal Canadian naval forces was engineered, without our knowledge, by their masters in Berlin to ensure that they would be taken to a Canadian PoW internment camp, where they were to remain neutral until required for special action. However, they escaped from Camp 30, Bowmanville Ontario in September 1942 without authorization from their superiors. With a third man, they quickly set up a flourishing clandestine operational base in Toronto, engaging in common criminal activities to support their covert operations which included surveillance and acts of sabotage at such locations as, but not limited to, General Motors, Defence Industries Limited, General Electric and STS 103, Camp X. Future actions that were being prepared included sabotage of the Commonwealth Air Training Program at Oshawa, kidnappings, and infiltration of Camp X, which had been accomplished earlier but subsequently exposed and terminated. Following a raid on their safe house, during which their colleague was captured, these two individuals were forced to live by their wits, successfully eluding our security services for several months. When the German chiefs of Intelligence were ordered by Adolf Hitler to act in retaliation for Operation Tent Peg, these men were contacted through as yet unknown channels and ordered to assassinate a high-level member of our organization. Unfortunately, the person targeted was Executive Assistant Miss Mary Ward.

Maximilian Schneider, a German citizen holding the rank of Lieutenant - Colonel with the Abwehr, perpetrated the murder of Miss Ward. His accomplice, Lieutenant Kurt Schmidt, a South African, may have been the unwilling conduit for the toxin, which we know now, was imported from sources in South America.

In summary, you, Sir, and your Camp X colleagues are responsible for the destruction of an extremely treacherous, destructive, and elusive network of hostile foreign agents on our soil.

247

With my congratulations and gratitude to you Colonel Roger Stedman, Major Robert Samson, Major Hamish Findlay, and Lance Corporal Andrew McGregor, I remain,

Yours very truly,

Erik Williamson, BSO.'"

The room was still. At length, Roger Stedman broke the silence. "I say, Robert, when did the man write this?"

"Sometime yesterday apparently. It was on my desk when I dropped by the office at seven this morning. And I have a personalized, signed version for each of you in my briefcase."

"So, let me get this straight. Mr. Williamson wrote this, even before the operation had taken place, and he is in New York City. How is that possible?" inquired Commissioner Swan.

"The Lord and Stalwart work in mysterious ways, Commissioner," Brooks replied in a serious tone. "I've known him longer than anyone here and I have to confess, I simply do not know how he knows what he knows when he knows it."

Stedman walked his guests out. When he returned, Betty Robertson took his hand and placed it under her blouse, on her left breast. "Can you feel that?" she asked, with a seductive smile.

"Well, yes, of course. It's quite ... delightfully soft ... succulent, would describe it."

"No, no silly man. Beneath that."

"Beneath it?"

"Yes, feel it, my love, it's my heart pounding just as it was throughout the meeting."

"Really, why, pray tell?"

"If I have to explain it ... come over here, on the couch. I've locked the doors."

"You're wicked. This is Government property and we're on duty."

"Good," she whispered as she drew him down onto her. "In your case, a man shouldn't let duty interfere with the pursuit of his just rewards."

"Mmm, trés juste they are, too."

VENGEANCE IS MINE...

Berlin Friday 20 April 1945

At eight o'clock in the morning on Adolf Hitler's 56th birthday, there is no reason to rejoice. There will be no state celebrations, no grand speeches, no galas at the Chancellery, and no parades. Four days before, on April 16, the Russians launched their great offensive against Berlin, the capitol of Frederick the Great. Joseph Stalin, the Soviet dictator, has vowed that Berlin, the heart of the Führer's One Thousand Year Reich will be turned into a wasteland of smoking rubble.

Inside the Führer's thirty-room concrete bunker, buried beneath the Chancellery building, the mood is reserved, even gloomy. The Führer appears, and begins shuffling down the line of his assembled staff, to receive their murmured greetings. Vacantly, he offers a limp handshake to each one and then returns to his study, where he and his mistress Eva Braun sip tea. Exhausted and depressed, he goes to bed. Minutes later, just after nine a.m., General Burgdorf, one of the few commanders whom he still trusts, wakens Hitler to report that Russian forces have smashed through another line of the German defences. Soviet forces are advancing so rapidly, warns Burgdorf, that within two days, they will be at the city gates.

Berlin Sunday 22 April 1945

The military vehicle - recovery truck backs up and stops beside a low, makeshift wooden platform, where a thirteen-year-old boy waits quietly, wearing a much too – large, mud – spattered and ragged uniform of a private soldier in the Wehrmacht. His armband, which has been partially torn away, identifies his unit as the Hitler Youth *Werwolf* partisan brigade. His cloth cap has been removed, revealing tousled, medium brown hair. Although he is trembling, Jürgen stands erect; his wrists are tightly trussed with rubber tubing, criss — crossed, in front. His ankles are tied. One week before, Jürgen and two school chums, his guards, had been conscripted for the defence of the Third Reich, at rifle point.

The guards step aside, watching nervously as the winch at the vehicle's rear whines while the driver attempts to manoeuvre the crane and windlass to suspend a wire loop over the young soldier's head. An SS Field Police sergeant, wearing the chain and breastplate of his regiment, stands on the running board, shouting commands into the cab. When it is in place, the sergeant steps down and leaps onto the platform, seizes the noose with his gloved hands and tries to place it over Jürgen's head: it dangles, scarcely reaching the young man's eyes. The sergeant curses and bangs the back of the cab until sufficient slack is played out. The slim line is slipped over the condemned soldier's head; seconds later, his executioner professionally snugs the steel hangman's knot at an angle behind his right ear. Then, at a signal, the winch rewinds, slowly raising the toes of the boy's boots only inches above the stand. It suddenly jerks to a stop, instantly separating his spinal cord, then pauses momentarily, and changes direction to drop Jürgen's lifeless body onto the gallows. The sergeant hastily removes the noose and bindings, and jumps into the truck. With a diesel snarl, the truck pulls away in a billow of bluish - white exhaust. The two guards head back to their post.

It has taken fewer than thirty minutes, from Jürgen's arrest, to his dishonourable death. Minutes later, after the tow - truck leaves, a band of Werwolf militia carrying ladders and printed signs enthusiastically hoist Jürgen's corpse and suspend it from a lamppost. Around his neck, the troop leader, a teen-aged girl, affixes a placard: **I died because I did not have faith in my Führer**. She reaches over from her perch on the ladder to replace Jürgen's cap, sideways.

Jürgen's capital crime was to ask his *Werwolf* brigade leader for per-mission to dash three blocks and back to see if his father and mother had survived several direct hits on their apartment by a squad of Soviet T-34 tanks. His Captain, having refused the request, declared Jürgen guilty of cowardice and desertion, and then ordered his summary execu-tion, as an example to others. In this northeastern sector of the sub-urbs, a similar scene is repeated seven times before midnight. All those executed have betrayed their Führer's will by word or act. Among the recent harvest are blackening corpses in various stages of decay, includ-ing eighteen regular Wehrmacht field troops, a dozen Volkssturm, 'peoples' battalion home guard senior volunteers, six *Werwolves*, and ten non –combatant civilians, including four women and two infants under ten.

Their Führer will join them in eleven days. The 'official' cause of death, based upon post - mortems conducted on the charred remains by Russian forensic specialists: suicide by cyanide - poisoning and a self-administered coup de grâce, a pistol bullet to the right temple, or perhaps the mouth. Scores of historians, respected and otherwise, have reservations. Eyewitness accounts by staff present in the Führerbunker are at odds, often wildly inconsistent, to contradict the Soviet verdict. Some say he was forced to swallow a cyanide capsule by his butler, strangled, and then shot. Another claims that an SS bodyguard shot his Führer with Hitler's personal Walther 7.65 mm pistol then placed it on the sofa, beside his body, which lay sprawled beside Eva Braun's.

Berlin Monday 23 April 1945

"Wo ist Wenck? Wo ist Steiner?" To his stunned audience in the briefing room, the Führer's tirade had seemed to last for hours. Relieved to be dismissed at last, all but General Burgdorf and two other commanders filed out in silence. Many of them have secretly arranged to leave the doomed city. Distraught, Adolf Hitler sinks slowly into his armchair, muttering then sobbing, "the war is lost." It is finally clear to him that he has been betrayed, mislead, fed false information by the army, and now, lied to by his SS. The armies of Generals Wenck and Steiner are paper tigers; there will be no counter- offensive because they do not exist. Shocked and alarmed at this, his first admission of defeat, and his rapidly deteriorating condition, Burgdorf, and the others stare at one another in stony silence.

At length, Adolf Hitler composes himself, rises from the chair, and trudges out of the briefing room, leaving the door open. As Hitler walks toward the staircase, the captain of the Führer's élite SS bodyguard detachment salutes and inquires if he can be of help, but is waved away. Grasping the railing for support, Hitler slowly climbs to the main floor and steps into the Chancellery garden where a dozen *Werwolf* and Volksturm 'volunteers' have been standing at attention for an hour. Despite the thunderous, earth-shaking rumblings of the approaching Russian artillery, Hitler presents each man with a medal, shaking each man's hand and pausing briefly to have a word. He salutes them, turns haltingly, and then withdraws into his underground fortress to await a phone call of acceptance from his chosen successor, Grand Admiral Karl Dönitz.

Setting down the receiver, he beams with elation, "it is not over, yet." Summoning Burgdorf, they begin to flesh out the details of a master plan that has been taking shape in the Führer's mind. He will not leave Berlin to take refuge in the Berghof, as many of his associates have urged and his Chief of the Luftwaffe, Hermann Göring, among others have done without his knowledge or permission; rather, he will remain at his command post, to personally direct a combined Volksturm/*Werwolf* counterthrust, which will halt Stalin's murderous Bolshevik ambitions.

Mid-afternoon, he receives Albert Speer, formerly Deputy Protector of the British Territorial Reich and Reich Minister of Armaments. The meeting is brief and relatively convivial, despite Speer's bold defiance of Hitler's decree ordering the destruction of Germany's vital Ruhr Valley industries. At four o'clock, an SS adjutant delivers a telegram. Hitler looks up at the man but doesn't recognize him. The soldier explains that SS troops are being cycled in and out of the bunker more frequently for logistical reasons. Hitler shrugs and opens the envelope. It begins, 'From Berchtesgaden   Mein Führer! In view of your decision to remain in the fortress of Berlin, do you agree that I take over at once the total leadership of the Reich, with full freedom of action at home and abroad as your deputy, in accordance with your decree of June 29, 1941?' It closes with 'May God protect you, and speed you quickly here in spite of all.

Your loyal

Hermann Göring'

Hitler's face contorts with rage. His arms tremble and his right hand shakes violently when he seizes the telephone receiver to demand a direct connection with Nazi Party Secretary Bormann. Göring's life will be spared, they agree, if he gives up all posturing and pretensions of office.

Hitler issues a proclamation that stuns the staff. In it, he gives permission for all personnel in the bunker who wish to leave, to do so. Many do so.

Camp X Tuesday 17 April 1945

Betty Robertson flinched as Colonel Stedman's voice boomed angrily through the plywood wall. She knew that he had dreaded this meeting, ever since Major Samson had come in to ask for an appointment, as soon as possible. Roger had not told her anything about the agenda and uncharacteristically, had ordered that she allow no interruptions, saying, "Stay outside and keep your ears covered. There might be blood on the floor before this is done...mine!"

"Really, Robert, you've more than wiped the slate with the operation at the church for starters. Tell me, why in heaven's name would you want to do this? No, please, don't tell me. Is it personal? At any rate, the answer is categorically, and finally, no!"

"Colonel, Roger, please listen ..." Robert Samson pleaded. "We have nothing to lose..."

"...And nothing to gain, Major! Why risk it? He's downright batty, a doddering madman, a toothless tiger who's about as capable of mounting a counter assault as ... Stilton cheese."

253

"That's what the Americans thought, Roger. Remember the Ardennes, the Battle of the Bulge... the invasion of Great Britain? Or, let's take D Day, Normandy itself, not what you'd call cakewalks."

"That was then, for God's sake, Robert! This is now, 1945! Things ... conditions, situations are vastly different."

"How, Roger?"

"Right. One: He has no bloody armies to speak of, anymore! Two through ten: he has no generals left capable of leading what remains of his armies. Eleven through twenty: The Soviets have three brilliant generals who together command a combined force of one and a third million men, with ten times the German strength in tanks, and fifteen times in artillery, bearing down like the clappers of hell on Berlin..."

"Colonel, you're quite right." Robert interjected.

"Excuse me?" Roger stared at Robert in disbelief.

"You were quite correct, Roger, a moment ago," he paused. "This is a personal matter."

"Really? How so?"

"I have a score to settle."

"You do? So do we all, Rob, that's what this bloody awful war is about..."

"Beyond that, I do."

"Very well, I'm listening."

"It's Mary...Mary Ward. I... I had a great affection for her," he stated gently. "She was ... special. Do you understand, Roger?"

"I think I do. Do you want something, Robert? Coffee? Tea? A nip? Alright, please, go on."

"I haven't many close friends, Roger, and most of them would probably tell you that I'm a one-dimensional, obsessive bore, and completely absorbed by my so - called craft, all likely true. But, the truth is, I am all that and yet, in my heart of hearts, I always wanted to be a family man. Yes, truly, but I never seemed to cultivate the knack for getting on with women, not really. Perhaps I come across as distant, reserved, and disinterested in the day –to - day 'jolly what ho's' of the chattering classes, but how I wished and prayed I could just relax and drop my inhibitions.... A 'Ere's our good old mate, Bob!' instead of...well, you know the story. Am I boring you, yet, Roger?"

"Good God no! A nip, whether you want it or not ... there ... now, please continue."

"Mary, may God rest her Celtic heart, could somehow pierce the exterior shell right into the soul of the other Robert Samson and she valued that part of me as no other person ever has." Robert stopped, his eyes overflowing with tears. "I'm sorry," he smiled wiping his face with a handkerchief, and then drank his scotch in one gulp. "Ah, nectar, thanks. Where was I? The amazing part of all is that we had spoken no more than four or five times over all these years, that is, until I was transferred to the Castle in Toronto. But I knew from the first sight of the lass, that she and I were soul mates ... destiny? I don't know about that, I'm a Celt too, and so are you, you told me once, on your mother's side ... powerful that is, but I'm not too big on the mystical end of things: third eye, and all that tomfoolery, except I know in my being that we were intended to be together. He took away that possibility, brutally, unbearably painfully, and most of all, in such a way as to humiliate her, in public; her ... death was dreadfully ... cruel. I know this sounds sappy, Roger, but poor Mary is to me a symbol of the millions of innocents who have been slaughtered by this butcher, for no other reason than they existed and he decided they were a nuisance, superfluous, or beneath contempt, sub-human. His archenemy Joseph Stalin in the Kremlin is no better; he may actually be his equal, in terms of the enormity of the slaughter of the innocents. Do you know what this all proves, Roger? Forgive me; those drinks went straight to my head."

"What does it prove, Rob?" Roger invited quietly.

"The sorry history of the human animal makes it clear that it is us; we are the architects of our own destruction. Right now, it's the Nazi death machine, or Stalin's purges and the starvation of an entire nation, the Ukraine, but it's not that the German or Russian people inherently bear some fatal flaw. We all share the capacity for evil and God help the world when no one is willing to step up to the wicket to confront it and stuff the evil genie back into the bottle, for a time. I'm rambling, sorry..."

"You want to punish him, for her death..."

255

"Yes, I do. 'Vengeance is Mine, and recompense, against the time when their foot shall slip; for the day of their calamity is at hand, and the things that are to come upon them shall make haste.' And I will do whatever you require to keep you clear and free of any 'complications', Roger."

"Deuteronomy 32: 35 or 36. You realize HQ will never give its approval."

"Deuteronomy 32:35; I know that and I've thought it out," Robert responded brightly. "Do you want to hear it?"

"And if I refuse, or report you to HQ for desertion?"

"You won't do either one. Besides, it's all over for us lot here. This place will be mothballed within the month, I reckon. Let me tell you how I plan to carry this out," Robert stated confidently. "First, I wouldn't be mindin' another of dose, tanks, Colonel, Sir," he wisecracked.

"You've fooled me all along, Rob; here, I thought you were a Scot," Robert replied with a chuckle as he poured their drinks.

"'Tis the seventeenth, St. Patty's Day, or was that last month? Whichever, it's close enough!"

Camp X Wednesday 18 April 1945

Robert Brooks had signed Samson's application immediately when the Discretionary Leave of Absence form arrived via the morning courier bag on the eighteenth, at Toronto HQ on King Street. He had long suspected that Robert Samson and Mary Ward were 'keeping company after school' during Major Samson's 'exile' at Casa Loma. He assumed that the Request for Leave was associated with Robert's distress at her death. Moreover, Brooks felt that Samson's outstanding performance in dealing with the Schneider and Schmidt business merited some special form of recognition on behalf of Erik Williamson and the organization. And according to the unwritten rules of unconventional warfare, medals, citations, and town hall banquets were few to none.

Camp X Thursday 19 April 1945

"Well, old man, it went through. Congratulations. I suppose now you'll be lurking on the runways at the airport to grab yourself a lift to Germany. Good bloody British luck!" Roger joked.

"It's done."

"Really? Who do you know in the Air Ministry or whatever in blazes it's called here?"

"Never you mind, Colonel," Samson replied with a sly grin. "I've used up all of my chits on this go 'round."

"You have the uniform.... money.... papers too?"

Nodding affirmatively, Samson then executed the Nazi salute. "Jawohl, Oberst! Over the course of my long career I have cultivated many ... you don't really care... except, yes, Roger, I have made all the arrangements."

"God, I pity those poor bastards!" Stedman commented. "When do you leave?"

"In three hours."

"Does Hamish have any idea what's going on?"

"Most likely, but in typical Hamish fashion, he's being discrete and dutifully letting on that he hasn't a clue."

"You're certain you want to do this?"

"I am, but thank you for asking. Here's something I'd like you to have, Roger, in appreciation for...helping me get back on my feet. Both you and Colonel Graham have put up with me, and I thank you both." Robert reached inside his jacket and withdrew a black felt sack fastened with a white drawstring, which he presented to Roger.

"What's this then?"

"Open it, man!"

Roger withdrew a ten and three quarter inch Samson dagger, with a six-inch stainless steel partially serrated blade and lead weighted, black composite handle in a dark brown kid leather sheath.

"My God, Robert, it's beautiful!" Roger pronounced. May I touch it?"

"Of course, but be careful ... It's the second of three prototypes. Here, on the blade, see the engraving? That's the hallmark and serial designation; this envelope contains the Sheffield craftsman's signed certificate of authenticity and date of manufacture. Models one and three are safely squirreled away with my legal firm, in Edinburgh."

"Thank you, but I can't accept this, Robert," Roger stated emotionally.

"Please, you must. If you should decide later not to keep it, please pass it on to a public trust or museum that will preserve it for ... not a private collector. Take it."

"I don't know what to say, Rob. It's extremely difficult ... no, impossible to thank you, in words. I promise to honour your wish."

"Good, then that's done! Oh, a few more details. That envelope also contains a letter of explanation for Mr. Williamson and legal information to be forwarded to my solicitors; you'll see that he gets it ...at the appropriate time of course? There are some items in my personal effects that I'd like Hamish to have, including my sterling silver Rolls Razor. They'll be in my top right bureau drawer in my quarters. Now, I'm going back there to finish my preparations."

"Can I accompany you to the airport, at the least?"

"I'll find my own way, but thanks. Good bye, Roger, and keep the aspidistra flying!" Robert saluted and then they shook hands warmly.

"I'll miss you too, Killer! Adieu, Major. Godspeed!" Roger replied saluting his comrade. "You'll be back!"

"I think not. 'Morituri te salutamus,' the gladiators used to say,

Colonel," Robert stated.

'We who are about to die, salute you!' Roger whispered as Robert went out of his office to bid farewell to Betty Robertson. 'I do not think we shall see his like again.'

Betty interrupted his musings. "Excuse me, Colonel, where's Major Samson going?"

"The Coliseum..."

"In Rome?"

"Berlin..."

```
Berlin Wednesday 25 April 1945
```

At dawn, Hermann Göring is taken into custody by the SS detachment at Berchtesgaden. Above the Führerbunker, Russian artillery is 'ranging in' on the Chancellery building although no direct hits are scored.

```
Berlin Thursday 26 April 1945
```

Soviet tank and artillery gunners commence shelling the Chancellery building and grounds. The bunker resonates with the shockwaves. Clerical and military personnel calmly carry out their tasks, despite the constant explosions. By early afternoon, the atmosphere has become extremely stressful. Supervisors are forced to take over the duties of several workers who have been sent to the infirmary to be treated for fatigue and shock.

At seven p.m., Adolf Hitler has dinner with Eva Braun to which he has invited two of his most senior secretaries. Despite Eva's dislike for vegetarian food, she and the other women nibble at their bland, meagre portions. The clerks report that the conversation was pleasant and non –political.

By nine p.m., the Russian guns are almost stilled, except for an occasional salvo. At nine fifteen, Hitler receives a call on the study intercom. He leaves Eva, who is lounging on the carpet, at work on a very large jigsaw picture puzzle of the Alps, and walks along the brightly lit corridor to the briefing room doorway. The huge SS guard salutes and steps aside to let him go in. A blonde, attractive woman wearing flying gear jumps to her feet as he enters. She is Hana Greiff, test pilot extraordinaire, who, next to his mother, Eva Braun, and his deceased niece Geli, is Hitler's highest ideal of Aryan womanhood. Her male companion remains seated, and salutes, awkwardly. His right foot is bandaged with a bloody rag.

"My Führer, thank God, you're safe!" she exclaims.

"Hana! Hana Greiff! How good of you to come! You've brought von Tripps! Excellent! Thank you both! Are you injured, Wolff?"

259

Wolff von Tripps nods in affirmation. He has come at the Führer's insistence to accept command of the non-existent Luftwaffe, as Hermann Göring's replacement, after his arrest for 'high treason'. "Oh, some Mongolian sharpshooter likely took a pot shot at us when Hana was coming in to land and it came through the cabin floor, my Führer. It's nothing, my Führer," he responds, modestly.

"Nonsense, I'll have it attended to immediately." Hitler strides to the door and gives a command to the guard. Moments later, two medical orderlies arrive and carefully assist von Tripps onto a gurney. Hitler bends over to speak with him, takes von Tripps' right hand in his, squeezes it, and then backs away to allow the gurney to be pushed out of the room.

"He accepts!" Hitler announces enthusiastically to Hana. "Now, tell me about your flight! Where did you land?"

Hana briefly recounts their flight in the same Fieseler Storch short take –off and landing aircraft that she piloted to bring the Führer to London for his Eagle Day victory celebration, 20 April, 1941, almost exactly four years before. "Do you remember how we touched down on the Westminster Bridge, my Führer? Well, this time, I brought in The Eagle on a quiet street, near the Brandenburg Gate, as far away from the invaders as I could manage," she stated quietly; her eyes were blazing with pride. "Wolff and I picked up an extra passenger, an SS Sturmbannführer, name, Todt, he said. I didn't have time to ask his first."

"Tea? Interesting name. And why was Major Todt coming here, did he say?"

"Yes, thanks. His left arm was bandaged; apparently, he was slightly wounded in a skirmish but rather than go to a hospital, he asked to be transferred here, to be of whatever assistance he can."

"Sweetener? ... It's artificial, unfortunately. I must meet the Sturmbannführer and commend him for his heroism. Now, tell me, Hana, what's it like out there, honestly? Everyone else lies and fabricates fairy tales."

Berlin Friday 27 April 1945

260 People are falling apart under the strain of the incessant artillery bombardment. Despite severe penalties imposed by Hitler for the possession of alcohol, several cases of brandy and champagne have found their way into the bunker. This evening, at the height of the onslaught on the Chancellery complex overhead, many staff who are still capable of performing their duties retreat to their rooms for a furtive glass, or more.

With a cursory examination of his papers, the harried captain of the guard assigns Sturmbannführer Todt to sentry detail outside the Führer's briefing room. The door is locked on the inside, where Adolf Hitler and his secretary, Trudi, frantically sort through reams of his personal papers, choosing which will be burnt and which will be preserved so that future generations may read and understand his struggles. Todt is relieved at four a.m.; Hitler has not emerged on his watch.

Berlin Saturday 28 April 1945

A late breakfast with Eva, the Goebbels: Joseph, his wife Magda and their six children, is interrupted when a message is delivered from Dr. Goebbel's Ministry of Propaganda offices in the bunker. Hitler reads it aloud, in disbelief. "British Broadcasting has reported that Reichsführer of the SS, Heinrich Himmler, has made overtures to representatives of the American and British military powers, in an attempt to negotiate his surrender.

"That treacherous little bastard!" he screams. Alarmed at their Uncle Adi's sudden outburst, the children look at their parents, who continue eating. "Listen to this: it says he even has had the gall to offer Eisenhower our armies in the west on a platter! Our true believer, Heinrich, leaves us to face these Asiatic sub-humans while he runs off to save his skinny ass in the arms of the degenerate Americans ... I'll rip out his throat!

"Their President, Harry, what's his name, will have him for lunch, the fool..." Goebbels sets down his knife and fork. "Magda, my dear, please take the children back," he requests calmly. The pounding of artillery bursts above ground rattles the chinaware.

"Uncle has had some bad news, children. Papa and he must discuss it as grownups." Magda pauses and looks up as a particularly loud explosion creates a shower of mortar dust. "Come, Mommy will take you back to our big room and read a story. Hansi gets to choose this time. Don't pout Freya, it was your turn yesterday, dear."

The Führer pushes back his chair in a fury and begins pacing, screaming insults, and vulgarities. His fists clenched, he beats his temples, while cursing Himmler, the model Nazi bureaucrat, the Reich's coldly - calculating merchant of mass-murder, founder and supreme leader of the 'black order' the SS. Dr. Joseph Goebbels, who since 1924 has worshipped the man he has compared favourably to 'Christ or St. John', is shocked into silence by his hero's childish display of wrath, and slips away unnoticed, leaving the door slightly ajar. Civilian staff members are immobilized with astonishment and dread at the intensity of the Führer's ravings, which echo up and down the hallways. Even Burgdorf, who has been present at most of the Führer's monumental outbursts of pique in the past two years is flabbergasted by the sheer ferocity of this rant. It is otherworldly, operatic Sturm und Drang, 'Götterdämmerung, Twilight of the Gods,' he reflects, as the Führer's stream of invective is punctuated by earth - rattling reverberations fifty- feet overhead.

Stuttering and foaming at the mouth, Hitler rushes into the corridor where two Liebstandarte-SS men have just taken up duty. "Who ... who are you? I...identify yourselves!" he rages, like a madman.

"Keppler, my Führer, Warrant-Officer, Liebstandarte Regiment ... at your command."

"Todt, my Führer, Major, Life Guard Regiment." They salute the leader simultaneously.

Hitler eyes Todt, and asks him civilly, "You're new here, Sturmbannführer, no?"

"Yes, my Führer!"

"How's your arm, better? Good! Fetch Lieutenant-General Fegelein here!"

"Sir?"

"Get him! Bring your commander here, understood?" Hitler bellows as flecks of foam fly in Todt's face.

Todt turns on his heels and runs down the corridor, his Mauser semi automatic rifle thumping against his chest. Having no idea who or where Fegelein is or might be, he stops at each doorway to inquire.

"Not here, further down!" "Officer's Lounge, that way!" "Try the can!" "Damned if I know, Major. Shut the bloody door. His bellowing is ruining our card game!" "Who, that slut Braun's brother-in law? What's he getting this time, another Iron Cross for pimping?" "Shut your mouth, you fool. Sorry about this loudmouthed boor, Major, the General's digs are two doors down."

Todt locates Lieutenant-General Fegelein's room and knocks softly.

"Yes?"

"Your presence is requested by the Führer, General."

"A moment." The door opens to reveal a dark-haired man wearing cavalry breeches with black riding boots and an undershirt. He holds a cigarette in his right hand while he looks Todt up and down tentatively. "He sent you, a Sturmbannführer, for me, did he? Just who the hell are you, soldier?" he queries. "I've never laid eyes on you!"

As Todt is about to react, two chain and breast plated SS Military Police non-coms materialize. "We'll take it from here, thank you Major."

"General Fegelein, by order of the Führer, I am authorized to place you under arrest! Your pistol, please, General. Unload it. Thank you. Come with us, please."

"May I put on my tunic first, Sergeant-Major?"

"No, forbidden. You must come, immediately."

Todt walks behind the two 'chain dogs' and the General. At the briefing room doorway, they prod the General and proceed into the room. The door is slammed shut. Keppler glances at Todt. They both shrug.

Hitler's muffled words carry through the door. Keppler whispers, "He's crow bait!" and snaps to attention when the door opens. General Fegelein walks out between the 'chain dogs' along the corridor to the Chancellery garden stairs. Todt and Keppler listen until their footsteps fade. Ten minutes later, they hear the clatter of hobnailed boots on the metal steps and the Field Policemen reappear, shouldering their arms.

"What happened, Sergeant?" Keppler calls over softly.

"What do you think? He's kaput!"

"Why?"

"How the hell would we know? We were following orders."

"He was making deals with the enemy, like that snake Himmler. Not very smart around this goddam tomb!" replies the other.

"Even if he was as pure as the driven snow, someone had to pay for it. Talk about bad luck! He was Himmler's personal representative in this hell-hole, and he was handy!" the Sergeant explains, then adds, "too bad, he was a true war hero." Together the 'chain dogs' saunter away.

Keppler and Todt resume their posts on either side of the entrance. Five minutes later, a large man in civilian clothes arrives carrying a black satchel. Impatiently, he holds up his identification card to Keppler. "Enter, Doktor." The man bustles into the room officiously and closes the door.

"Who's that?" Todt inquires.

"His personal physician, Dr. Stief. It's time for the Führer's morning medication. Actually, he's a touch early ... probably Dr. Goebbels sent for him."

"What medication, do you know?"

"Christ, you're curious, Todt! Are you writing a book about this? He gives him injections, for his nerves. Haven't you noticed how badly he shakes, even when he's calm?"

Stifling a yawn, Todt replies, "Just filling in the time, Warrant – Officer, filling in the time. Is ....was the General actually married to Miss Braun's sister?"

"Uh huh. And we thought mothers - in - law were deadly," Keppler remarks jovially. They're not hitched yet, but the word around here is, they'll be tying the knot tonight. God knows why."

Camp X Saturday 28 April 1945

As predicted by Robert Samson, STS 103 is in the process of being 'decommed', decommissioned, before being turned over to the Royal Canadian Corps of Signals to serve as a key military short wave radio installation, at the end of May. Of the more than two hundred civilian and support staff on the payroll during the height of hostilities, few remain, the majority of who are the Hydra operators, including Yorkie, Hughie and Bernie. Private Mac has elected to stay and tend to plumbing and heating maintenance.

The remaining instructors are to be transferred to the Citadel as well as STS 106 at Lake Okanagan, British Columbia, where Chinese - Canadians are being trained for the Pacific theatre showdown.

SOE London and BSO Toronto have directed Colonel Stedman, Robert Brooks, and Betty Robertson to sort through the Camp's classified records and destroy any and all files which might prove 'damaging or embarrassing' for the Canadian, British and American governments in the emergent post-war era. Over sixty percent are consigned to the Camp's incinerator, although Brooks is authorized to keep letters and official documents that Erik Williamson wishes to retain as a private history of British Security Operation. There is virtually no official photographic archive, although scores of illegal snapshots are hidden in the private collections of former clerks, and instructional staffers. What remains of the record of Camp X, the operation that never was, will lie undisturbed for thirty years, buried in official amnesia under the National Archives file number, S25-1-1.

Berlin Sunday 29 April 1945

Adolf Hitler and Trudi, his senior secretary, have laboured most of the previous night to produce the Führer's Last Will and a two-part Political Testament. As expected, the testaments amount to nothing more than a long-winded justification of his virulent anti-Semitism and paranoia and praise for the essential nobility of the Nazi 'mission'. Burgdorf, who with Bormann and Goebbels signs as a witness, notes

CHAPTER 8 - VENGEANCE IS MINE...

that the Führer has spent three paragraphs spewing contempt for
Göring, Himmler and others he accuses of treason '...by illegally attempting to seize power in the State for themselves...'

Martin Bormann, Admiral Dönitz, Joseph Goebbels and family, on
the other hand, are lauded for their intense loyalty and directed to lead
Germany into a new age, 'that of continuing the building of a National
Socialist (Nazi) ... State... Let them be hard but never unjust ... and set
the honour of the nation above everything in the world'.

Near midnight, witnessed by Party Secretary Bormann, along with
Dr. Joseph and Magda Goebbels, Adolf Hitler and Eva Braun are married
in a brief Nazi civil ceremony, following which a celebration is held in his
study. Keppler and Todt are invited to a spontaneous gathering in the
central bunker where the few remaining workers, who have broken open
an illicit case of magnums of expensive French champagne, are smoking
and dancing to schmaltzy ballads being played on a wind - up gramo-
phone. The bombardment overhead is unbearably loud, almost drowning out the music. Todt and Keppler watch the activities from the side-
lines, sipping their drinks sparingly. Todt is asked to dance by a slightly
inebriated, striking thirty-year old brunette technician. He declines
gracefully, but she insists. Keppler pushes him forward. He accepts and
she whirls him around the room while drinking from her glass, which is
spilling on his right shoulder. He steers her toward a chair and deposits
her as gently as possible. She looks up forlornly and protests, saying
that she wants to make the most of the evening, before the curtain rings
down. She tugs on his right arm to make him sit down on her lap,
which he does, very carefully.

"So, what's your name, handsome?" she asks, lightly stroking his
hair.

"Todt, what's yours?"

"Todt? Really? That's fitting around here, sweetheart ... Major
Death!" she replies, with a shrug. "What happened to your arm? I...
am... Li...sa, little Lisa." She is slurring but making an effort to enunci-
ate clearly.

"A pleasure, Lisa ... just a scratch. What do you do here?"

"I work in... there!" She points in the direction of the communications room.

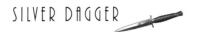

"And what do you do in there, Lisa?"

"I'm not telling you SS man, you might be a se...se...secret agent. It's a great big fat state secret," she giggles. "But you're kind of cute, so, if you get me a full glass of this fancy French stuff, I'll take you in and show you. Hurry back, Todt!"

He returns with a partial bottle held under his sling and two fresh glasses. He glances around while he pours. Keppler is nowhere to be seen. The music is now very slow, and the four or five couples that haven't disappeared into dark corners are swaying, embracing, oblivious to everything else. "Let's go, Lisa! No one's paying any attention!"

Together they tiptoe around the perimeter of the makeshift dance floor, and then Lisa takes him by the hand. "Down there," she whispers. She leads him to a large room, which is partially darkened. He can make out scores of vacuum tubes glowing in the shadows. "It's okay, there's no one else here, Todt. They're all drunk or getting laid ... now kiss me and then maybe I'll show you my ... secret." She sets down her fluted champagne glass but it topples over and shatters on the concrete floor. "Oh well, easy come, easy go! Come here, Todt!" The passion and intensity of her kiss takes Todt by surprise. Their mouths separate and she looks up at him. "Whew, who was your teacher!" she softly exclaims. "You passed the first test, Todt ... are you sure you don't have a vorname (first name)? Oh, who cares? Look, there it is on that far bench. Come!"

Todt sees a typewriter. "It's a typewriter ... that's your secret, Lisa?"

"Todt, my dear boy, you are looking at the war's best kept secret, that is until now, I suppose. It's called Enigma," she confides. "Have you got a cigarette for Little Lisa, darling?"

"I'm sorry, Lisa, no, I don't."

"That's okay, I can't smoke in here anyway. God, what am I saying? We'd both be shot if anyone knew ... Any more champers?"

"Why's Enigma so special ... a typewriter?" he persists.

"It's a cipher machine, this one is the standard Enigma M3, used by the Luftwaffe, Wehrmacht, and diplomatic corps. It enciphers and deciphers; I mean it encodes and decodes our commanders' communications ...orders, and battle plans, anything we want to keep secure, top secret!

The mathematical functions are complex, but see those three spindle wheel things with the numerals on them?" she asks, while she pauses to kiss his cheek. "They're called rotors; they're set and reset at intervals by the operator, me, and no one else except the operator who's receiving the message knows the right combination of settings. I type the message in plain text on the keyboard, the rotors scramble it, the lights glow, and then if the rotor settings are correct at the receiving end, it's deciphered in plain text. The permutations and combinations of the rotor settings are nearly in..fin..ite. Amazing eh, Liebchen? The concept behind it is straightforward, yet it's completely, and utterly unbreachable, unless someone steals the settings manuals, but new ones are issued randomly. Major Todt, my dear, Germany and Japan are the only two countries in the world that have it! Where's the champers, darling? I am becoming much too sober with all this serious technical hoo ha."

"So you, the operator, simply type and the Enigma does the magic! Good thing we have it and not the bad guys!" he remarks sarcastically. "But, it didn't really help a hell of a lot, did it?"

"What do you mean? Sure it did!"

"To judge from what I'm seeing and hearing around here lately, I'd say we came in second. Can I try it?"

"Nein!" she replies softly while nuzzling his ear.

"Just one sentence...?"

"Don't be a bore, darling. Now be a good Sturmbannführer and come with Lisa!" While they were examining the Enigma machine, she has unbuttoned her tunic as well as the top three buttons of her blouse.

"Where, Lisa?"

"To my room. I'm alone ... no roomy who'll want to share you... Kiss me again ... these, my darling, are for you!"

Her breasts are thrusting upward; Todt responds awkwardly, eagerly caressing, and kissing her as she reaches out and begins fumbling with his shirt buttons. "Don't you think that we should be getting back?" he mumbles earnestly, although he is becoming aroused. "Keppler's likely looking for me and someone's liable to come..."

"And waste that? Are you an SS-Mann or a monk?" she taunts,

smiling lasciviously, and then her mood shifts; suddenly she has become serious. "The world as we know it will end in less than twenty-four hours, Todt. I don't know or really care if you have a wife and six mistresses, a girl friend or if you're a homosexual. The latter I seriously doubt and the others won't matter when you're still in a Soviet labour camp at seventy-five, that is, if you're lucky. So, I say, what the hell, 'gather we rosebuds while we may'. Are you coming, or do I have to take you by force?"

"Well, yes, no, I'm coming."

"Sehr Gut! Kommen ... and please take off that arm sling."

"I can't."

"Well, we'll see about that, won't we?"

Lying on his left side next to her on the narrow cot, Todt absent-mindedly stroked her hair. She quivered playfully, turned and kissed his mouth, then sighed and curled up against his belly. He was utterly drained, physically and emotionally.

Minutes passed, then she opened her eyes. "Todt, what's going to happen to us, you and me? We're going to die ... I think the Russians will burst in and rape and torture the women, then machinegun us. Tell me the truth, please, darling."

"Not necessarily, Lisa. Tell me, why did you choose to stay? You could have left here a week ago with so many of the others."

"Maybe I should tell you why I'm here in the first place."

"I'm interested."

She confessed that at the outset of war in 1939, she was a nineteenth century romantic idealist, in love with and engaged to the epitome of German heroism, a Luftwaffe fighter pilot officer. When it was reported to her that his aircraft was missing, and last seen by his wingman careening down into the English Channel on 15 September 1940, she refused to believe the telegram. When his death was confirmed, she threw herself into her work as a cipher clerk with the Air Ministry, seeking and receiving promotions to the rank of Technical Specialist, at Luftwaffe HQ, Cipher Communications. On the night of July 25, 1943, the city of Hamburg was devastated by an RAF 800 bomber raid in which more than 50,000 civilians were killed, including her entire family. It was a disaster, and a major personal defeat for Göring the Air Marshall who had boasted often and loudly about the superiority of German technology and air defence capabilities. It was at about that time, she recounted, that she realized the war was lost, and that Germany's leaders from the Führer and Air Marshall Göring downward were thoroughly incompetent, corrupt liars, interested only in saving their own hides at the expense of German people such as her family, her beloved Hans and herself.

"May I have a tumbler of water, lover? There's a pitcher on the dresser."

Todt brought a glass to her. "Go on, please."

"I tried everything I could think of to wriggle out of my duties, and even considered desertion, but, I wasn't strong enough. In 1944, I was transferred here and that's about all there is to tell, except, your question, why didn't I leave? Even though I know that the Führer is a truly evil despot who's taken Germany down the road to ruin? I have no one out there, nowhere to go..." she sobbed. "You'll kill me now, won't you? You should for what I've said. But there was something in your eyes, a kindness ... warmth, understanding, compassion, and a deep sadness too. You've suffered as I have, a loss, and I knew instinctively I could trust you. That's why I asked you to dance with me."

"You saw all that ..." he asked, in astonishment, "in my eyes?"

"Uh huh ... surprised?"

He didn't answer, and held her close for a moment. "Lisa, I must go. It's three in the morning. Keppler's likely reported me missing to the detail commander. Tell me something: do you want to get out of here, with me?" he asked, buttoning his tunic.

"Y... yes, I do now...how?"

"Good. Is there a back entrance or exit to Hitler's quarters?"

"Yes, of course."

"Where?"

"Why?"

"It's essential that I know, if we're going to make it out."

"It's in the north stairwell. Do you know the one I mean?"

"Yes, thanks, that's first rate. Be here in this room at 1500. I'll come for you. Change into something plain and warm ... nothing military, all right?"

"Right. I'll be waiting. Kiss before you go...?

He bent over the bed and brushed her forehead and eyes gently with his lips. "I'll be back for you."

"Be careful, Todt, or whoever you are. Your friend Keppler's a dangerous man... most of us are convinced that he's a Gestapo die-hard who'll shoot anyone that attempts to escape. Fanatical to the end!"

"Thanks, I'll bear that in mind... Sweet dreams, liebchen."

Berlin Monday 30 April 1945 0335h

"Where the hell did you get to, or need I ask?" Keppler demands with an ill - concealed sneer when Todt enters their bedroom. He is sitting at the desk, wearing a burgundy housecoat. "Do you know that you missed the Führer's reception an hour ago? Not good form!"

"God, must you smoke that pipe in here, Keppler?"

"The Soviets are closing in ... less than a kilometre away. Hitler came out to say farewell and distributed cyanide capsules to each of the female staff and then apologized profusely for not having something more ...upbeat to give them. There's Lisa's on the dresser. It was extremely moving, Todt, touching even. Made me proud to be a witness to this historic moment in the Reich's rebirth of a new, and revitalized National Socialist world order. We can only be stronger... because of how we manage this transition.

"Benito Mussolini, Il Duce, is dead. Marxist partisans shot him and his mistress, then their bodies were hanged upside down in the centre of Milan, to be spat upon and violated by the mob... disgusting! Our Führer will go out with dignity, not a disembowelled chicken. How was Lisa, by the way? She looked hot enough to melt asphalt in Siberia!" he remarked snidely.

"None of your damn business. Put that out and go to bed, please?"

"I'm on the second to last page... five more minutes..."

Todt stands behind Keppler's chair while he loosens his tie. "What are you reading that's so interesting at three in the morning?" he inquires casually. He can see the glint of a pistol barrel, which has been partially covered - over on Keppler's lap.

"An English murder mystery. God, what bloody-minded people they are!"

"That's God's own truth, isn't it?" The tie arcs over Keppler's head and under his chin, flinging his pipe into the air. As it tightens, his body arches off the chair, his heels drumming the rung. A lightning – swift chop to his neck crushes the right carotid artery, and he collapses soundlessly. Warrant – officer Keppler's Walther .765 pistol slips out of the folds of the dressing gown and skitters onto the floor. "Bad idea, mate; I'm sure you planned to survive the glorious transition, God forbid," Robert Samson mutters. "It's the wardrobe closet for you!"

Berlin Monday 30 April 1945 1245h

"Where's Keppler, Todt?" demands the SS captain. The nervous tic in his right eye is flickering at about five cycles per second, Robert notices. "Not too well at the moment, Captain. He overdid it last night and has a splitting migraine. I'm fine on my own ... just letting him sleep a touch longer...if that's all right?"

"Very well, for the time being. Be vigilant Todt, the Führer is conducting private state business inside, no entry ...carry on! Heil Hitler!" He salutes decisively and stalks away, head down, feet splayed outward, swagger stick tucked under his left armpit, with his right arm behind his back as though searching for coins on the floor or preparing to take the final bow, Robert reflects wryly.

"Heil Hitler!" 'Carry on, mate.'

Berlin Monday 30 April 1945 1510h

The door to the Führer's private quarters opens. Robert stands aside, saluting, as Dr. Joseph Goebbels, Generals Burgdorf and Krebs, and Martin Bormann, all in full dress uniforms, except Bormann, who was wearing his usual rumpled, dark grey jacket and black trousers, and carrying a black briefcase, file out. They turn to face the entranceway where Hitler stands; they stiffen to attention, salute smartly, and solemnly utter in unison, "Heil, mein Führer." There is no response to this courtesy from their leader, who silently closes the door and turns the lock. After the Nazi potentates have departed, Robert listens at the entrance. He can faintly overhear a woman's murmurings, then Hitler's voice, more strident, followed by a low, indistinct exchange, and then at length, dead silence.

272

Berlin Monday 30 April 1945 1520h

Quickly checking up and down the corridor, Robert removes his arm sling and extracts a small metal probe from beneath the elasticized bandage. He silently inserts the burglar's 'jimmy' into the keyhole, jiggles, and then twists it, snapping the pin and tumbler mechanism inside the housing.

Praying that there is no deadbolt, he cautiously pushes down on the brass door lever. It opens soundlessly on well-oiled hinges. Momentarily, Robert's mind flashes back to the Rector's Study door in Whitby. 'Twice lucky!'

Hitler is bent over a prostrate female's body on the sofa, with his back toward Robert. The air is heavy with the odour of bitter almonds. 'Potassium cyanide ...he poisoned Eva Braun.'

The bunker resonates deafeningly with a violent overhead explosion. Hitler looks up, and catches sight of the SS Sturmbannführer. "How the hell did you get in here?" he demands, his voice trembling. "You're the new one, Todt, aren't you?" he queries, peering through red-rimmed eyes. In his right hand, he holds a Walther .765 mm pistol, pointing impotently at the floor.

"No, actually you are 'todt', sir, if you don't hand me the pistol. I am arresting you, Sir, and we're going on a journey. Give me that pistol," he repeats menacingly.

Hitler backs up against the couch. "No, no journey, with you. Who are you? Who sent you? Where are you from?" he demands as he reaches up with his left hand to brush his hair from his forehead.

"Robert Samson, British Intelligence Service, SOE. Actually, I'm here on my own hook, Herr Schickelgruber."

"Schickelgruber, how amusing! What name did you say?"

"Robert Samson."

"What? The Robert Samson? Samson, the Beaulieu gangster, the Camp X strangler?" he gasped in astonishment.

"The same. Now hand me the gun, butt first."

"No. You don't understand do you, Robert Samson? I am leaving here in, five minutes. Bormann has made the arrangements." He speaks rapidly, his eyes darting wildly. "An SS armoured vehicle, Russian paint, is coming for us..."

"You're snookered, Bormann's gone, stuffed it, pulled the pin, gone over the hill, without you!"

"Bormann would not leave me!" he screams. "He is faithful, until death."

"Wrong, little Corporal, he has scarpered, just like your 'true Heinrich' Himmler and fat Hermann Göring. I can assure you. Wait and see."

"You lying British schwein!"

"You murdered her!" Robert growled accusatorially, indicating Eva's corpse. "You married her yesterday and now you've poisoned her?"

"The cyanide was her choice. Eva was a child, a tiresome, inconvenient, self-absorbed peasant princess; we only wed because she wanted it, to be a respectable woman, she whined. I could have cared less. I am above such moronic matters. Your time is running out, Samson."

"You murdered my woman, as well... foully..."

"Really, did I?"

"Mr. Erik Williamson's personal assistant, Mary Ward. She died horribly, for no reason, like millions of others."

"Pity, but most of these so-called victims were useless, sub

–humans, cannon-fodder. I have no regrets when I reflect how I purified the German, indeed the European racial stock in preparation for the next National Socialist millennium. Let me think, Ward, yes, that was a set up by the SD and Abwehr, in revenge, a warning to your thug Stalwart, for his agent, Jael, taking that shot at me in London, the bitch. My chest still pains me, there, at night. You have one minute, Samson, before four truly loyal SS troopers arrive."

"And I suppose you think you can sneak through the Russian lines? The Russky comrades will nab you and Stalin will exhibit your pathetic remains in a cage in Red Square until your worthless carcass rots. But first, your old ally Stalin's up to his elbows in the blood of his own people, like you, but don't think he won't take extreme pleasure in getting even for every last one of his Russian peasants whom your roving bands of SS Einsaztgruppen torturers burned alive, mutilated, raped, crucified and murdered."

"You have a vivid imagination, Samson. The Russians? Of course not, we're not that stupid. We're flying directly out of here. Now, get the bloody hell out of my way!" he warns, his pistol hand trembling.

"No, you're coming with me as my prisoner of war. I can get through to the British High Command. You'll have a fair trial in England before they hang you by your balls."

"England!" he spat derisively. "Napoleon Bonaparte was right, a despicable, in - bred herd of mental defectives, aristocratic nincompoops and bourgeois shop-keepers, not worth my trouble. Time is up, Major. Move, or I will shoot you. I've never killed a person you know? Maybe in the 1914-18 debacle, you can't ever be sure." He raises the Walther to point the polished barrel directly at Robert's chest.

Robert's right hand flashes under his bandage and flings the silver dagger in a flat trajectory. "From the herd." Hitler stares down in astonishment as the weapon homes in and thuds into his belly precisely at centre above the skull and crossbones insignia on his silver SS belt buckle. The Walther tumbles out of his hand, as he gropes frantically for the hilt, twisting it more deeply, and then his knees slowly buckle. A revolver shot rings out. His head jerks violently to the left; he collapses heavily on his knees, his forehead on the rug, and then topples over, bleeding heavily from both entry points, his mouth agape, fishlike.

Robert turns halfway to see Lisa holding a Luger, its barrel still smoking. "This way. The goons are coming!" she shouts. Robert reaches over to retrieve his knife from the Führer's body with his left hand and follows her to the back entranceway. "Take off that dreadful tunic and hat. All of a sudden you look ridiculous, Englishman!"

"Which way to the Brandenburg Gate?"

"Why, what's there, Robert?"

"Our only chance. Hana's airplane. She's waiting to take him out. Got the Luger?"

"Of course ...

"There's something I have to do first."

"What?"

He kisses her lightly on the lips. "That ...thank you, and I love you, Lisl."

Steps of the Reichstag April 30, 1945

SILVER DAGGER

"My Mom called me that. And me too, Ro … bert. Now, through there, up the stairs, turn right, then run like hell, after me!"

Camp X Tuesday 1 May 1945 1842h

It is a hectic day in the communications building; the mounds of tape spewing from the Teletypes are overflowing the waste containers with no end in sight to a flood of signals passing through Hydra, to, and from Europe. Suddenly, Hughie removes his earphones and shouts, "Yorkie, can you get Dr. Phil?"

"Colonel Truscott, this just came through … Enigma traffic, unusually informal … Bletchley passed it on; they can't make head or tail …" Hughie stated, excitedly.

Phil Truscott looked at the print out as it appeared letter by letter on the teleprinter. "That beautiful bastard Samson!" he shouted gleefully. "'Killer' just wiped the floor with Adolf! And he's on his way back with, stop the presses, a fräulein! He wants Hamish to return his Rolls. His Rolls? Get me Colonel Stedman! Damn, he's on his honeymoon with Betty in Bermuda. Major Grey's on his way to British Columbia. See if you can reach Robert Brooks, at Toronto HQ, Yorkie!"

Hamish and Jack find Rebeccah, Hugh, Sarah with another child picnicking on the bluffs. "Robert's coming home!" Jack exclaims, "with a trophy!"

"Yes, we just heard the good news! Come and join us!" I've cooked a bird and Hugh liberated a bottle or three of a better than passable Cabernet from the Officers' bar, courtesy of Andy," Rebeccah replies, holding up a wine bottle and laughing. "He forbids me to have any, the sod!" she adds, with a grimace and a 'thumbs down' gesture.

"Good for you, Hugh!" Jack calls out. "We'll drink her share!"

Taking a pair of sunglasses from his breast pocket, Hamish puts them on, and points down at the white-capped lake. "See, down there," he remarks sorrowfully.

"I don't see anything but seagulls," Jack answers.

"Try these..."

"Very nice, no glare. Made in the USA? Okay, so, what am I looking for, Hamish?"

"Sarah, Sarah, darling, not so close to the edge!" Rebeccah stands up, brushing imaginary crumbs from her prominent abdomen. "Hugh, I can barely waddle; can you please fetch her?"

"There ... my jeep," Hamish asserts.

"Son of a gun, so it is!"

"I know who did it," Hamish remarks with a sigh. "But I absolve them of all blame."

"Who?"

"Michael Heaviside and John Beck. They confessed in the bar like true gentlemen the night before they shipped out for the Citadel. It was an accident, but they were afraid I'd not believe them, so there was a conspiracy of silence going on."

"A guilty conscience is a terrible thing," Jack replies, jokingly.

"From one who should know," Hamish replies softy. "The sunglasses, please? Are you going to say anything to her before your plane leaves for San Diego?"

"Jack, Hamish, last call, you two!" Rebeccah shouts.

"Coming!" Hamish calls.

"Yeah ... thanks, best wishes to both and let me know when the baby's born," he replied, flipping a silver sixpence.

"Good show, Jack. Are you keeping that?"

"Damn right I am, Major Fox!" Jack replied, smiling. "It got the both of us out of the Fatherland and I figure there might be just enough luck left over to keep this red-dirt Georgia farm boy out of harm's way; you know: Japanese torpedoes, kamikazes, that kind of thing, while I'm on board the USS Indianapolis. Something big is going to happen out there in the Pacific."

"Keep your powder dry and smooth sailing, Major Harris! I've really enjoyed knowing you. Burton Johnson's coming with me to STS 106, in the Okanagan, British Columbia. Perhaps we'll be hearing from you, in Cherokee?"

"It's a date, buddy! Speaking of which... Hello, Sarah! Who's your young...?"

"Good day, angels ...gentle...men!"

"Well, I'll be ... Greta!" Jack exclaims, kneeling to hug them both.

"Greta Francks!" Hamish shouts with delight. "Wie geht es Ihnen, lass? "We lost track of you in England!"

"Gut, danke schön. I am speaking English now, Sir,'" she declares politely, curtseying and offering her hand. "Major Mason teaches me! She and Captain Mason are very ...freundlich ...kind ...with me," she replies, beaming. They are going to ..." she paused.

"Adopt you?" Hamish suggests. "Wunderbar!"

"Yes, adopt me, thank you, Major Fox. Now, Sarah has a message!"

"Say it, Sarah!"

"Uncle Jack and Uncle Hamish, soon the ants will eat up everything at our picnic and there won't be anything left. Mommy says you must hurry, please!" Sarah states insistently.

"Well, we can't have that, right Hamish? Okay, kids, race you there!"

Berlin 2 May 1945 0900h The Chancellery Garden

"Six children, cause of death unknown. Also, two adults: one male, one female, single bullet holes in the backs of the skulls, Colonel General Zukov, all bodies severely charred."

"Thank you, Comrade Doctor. That puts paid to the Goebbels dynasty. Such a revolting stench! Judging by the number of petrol cans lying about, the SS must have used 400 litres on Goebbels' and the leader's burial pits, yet they are still recognisable human remains!

"Let the photographer pass, Lieutenant. I wish to have this recorded on film for the SMERSH (SMYERT SHPIONAM) archives. It will have great propaganda value. Then, drench them in petrol and burn them again; and bulldoze the ashes! I want no iota of their remains for fanatics to dig up and worship!" Zukov orders.

"Doctor, I want the German leader and his woman's cadavers disinterred, photographed, then transported with us as we mop up here and then swing back east to our position at Magdeburg, where full autopsies will be performed. You, of course, are expert and know the proper procedures for their preservation?"

279

"Yes, certainly, thoroughly, Colonel - General Zukov."

"Excellent. Doctor, a word, privately."

"Yes, Colonel - General?"

"Our Directorate in Leningrad has issued a unique requirement, which I am entrusting to you and your assistants, in the strictest confidence."

"Thank you, Colonel - General. How may I help our Service?"

"Comrade Konev wants the head of the German leader Hitler dispatched to SMERSH Directorate HQ, Leningrad. Can you manage that?"

"Yes, of course, Colonel - General."

"This comes straight from Comrade Director Konev. The parcel must be packaged and readied for a direct flight in six hours. You can fulfill this?"

"Unquestionably, Colonel - General."

"Good, do it!"

"Lieutenant, Comrade Doctor Osipov will be performing some delicate forensic inquiries and must have no interruptions. Have your men hold their bonfire until he is finished. Clear the area immediately."

"The container will be delivered shortly, Osipov. Do this in such a fashion as to impress the Director, and who knows? The opposite is true, as well. Carry on."

SILVER DAGGER

"A pity, Opisov, but it all should go into the rubbish bin. The President wants no dreary reminders of the Great Patriotic War. Need I remind you we are no longer a Soviet state; we are a democratic association of free republics. He's coming next Thursday. You have to look lean and progressive, if you want to keep this dump open. You're past retirement age, aren't you, Opisov?"

"Five years. What else would I do, but be under her feet, as my Irina reminds me, daily. But surely, Minister, we should preserve some of our history of that era. Those who forget it are bound to repeat it..."

"Not a priority, Doctor. Too expensive; the upkeep is staggering, the republic's broke, who needs ancient history when we can barely make the telephone system work?' And on and on. What's that thing?"

"What thing?"

"That, the disgusting floating thing that looks like cauliflower!"

"A brain, a human brain."

"It makes me sick to look at it. What's it doing here?"

"I brought it from Germany in May '45."

"Why did you do that?"

"Orders, from SMERSH' 2IC, Colonel General Zukov."

"SMERSH? What in hell were you doing hanging around with those spooks?"

"It was a job. I was just out of school, with flat feet, eyes glasses as thick as the bottom of a vodka bottle, and no money."

"So, why this brain? Someone special?"

"No, just a ...German."

"Have you done anything with it? ... Whatever you necropolis ghouls do with brains..."

"Yes, a little, Minister. I've taken transections: sagittal, lateral...as well as X-radiation, isotopic..."

"Terribly fascinating, I'm sure, Doctor, meaning...?"

"I've taken off slices from various sections, to make microscopic slides and..."

"And what did you learn from it all in sixty-odd years, Doctor Opisov?" he interrupted.

"Fifty-seven, actually. Nothing, absolutely nothing; that's what scares me..."

"Good Christ, don't say that to the President! Lock it away somewhere immediately and remember, be upbeat, and progressive; show that the Institute's research money is relevant to today's geopolitical and social realities. There are terrorists, raving madmen of all stripes waiting to spring out from underneath every bush."

Suddenly, the fluorescent lights dim, flickering ominously, and then come back on. "Yes, I promise, I'll try, Minister," Opisov commented, looking up at the aging fixtures. "Now, if you'll excuse me, I must see to my Assistant Tupelov before she blows the circuits with her latest gadget."

"See that you do, Doctor. Make him happy and you'll be building that retirement dacha with Irina on the Black Sea!" Minister of the Interior Alexandr Nevsky calls out, "and trash these stale body parts!"

"Today Minister! You have my word on that! See you Thursday!"

"No, do it now!" he orders.

"Very well, Minister!" Opisov replies resignedly as he opens the door of the Preparation Room.

"Doctor Tupelov, turn off that damn thing and bring the waste receptacle, on a cart! I have a disposal job for you!"

'Bloody idiots!' he mutters when he is certain that Minister Nevsky is out of earshot.

"That specimen, Dina! Take it down the elevator directly to the incinerator! I'll be right there."

"Really, Doctor?" Tupelov inquires hesitantly. "It's irreplaceable!"

"I know that and so do you, goddam it. Don't drop it! Okay, good. Off you go, Dina!"

___

"It is done, vaporized, Doctor Opisov!" Dina announces primly. "May I ask why?" she inquires tentatively as Dr. Opisov slams and locks the steel door of the Incineration Room behind them.

"Perhaps Minister Nevsky is right after all, Dina. It is not the brains that matter most, but that which guides them – the character, the heart, generous qualities, progressive ideas...'"

"Dostoyevsky..." she observes softly. "My idol!"

"Old Feodor knew a thing or two about the human heart, Dina. Say, would you happen to have any of that exceptionally good Polish vodka still kicking around in your desk drawer in the Prep Room?"

"I think so, ...but your heart condition, Doctor Opisov!"

"All the more reason, my Dina! 'The cleverest of all, in my opinion, is the man who calls himself a fool at least once a month.' Make it a triple; I'm sure your friend Feodor Dostoyevsky would approve!"

___

"Hello, what's this?" Nevsky bends down to retrieve a slip of yellowed paper from the floor of his limousine. "Must be the label from one of the specimens. It's damn near illegible... Hold on, my glasses, now let's see. Hell, I can't read that!" he mutters as he throws the crumpled parchment-like scrap out the window.

'Property of: SMYERT SHPIONAM, Leningrad 2 May 1945.

Site: Reich Chancellery Garden, Berlin, Germany.

Subject: Former National Socialist German Führer, Adolf Hitler.

Sample: Whole brain, intact.

Verified: S. Opisov, Ph.D., M.D.'

SILVER DAGGER

GLOSSARY OF TERMS AND RANKS

Abwehr (Ger. 'protection')
German Military Intelligence and Counter-Intelligence service, whose Director, Wilhelm Canaris, was hanged April 1945, as an anti-Hitler conspirator.

Gestapo (Geheime Staatspolizei)
Secret State Police formed in 1933, as the Prussian secret police, 'Gestapa' by Hermann Göring; it was integrated with the RSHA (see below) in 1936 under Heinrich Himmler.

Kriegsmarine
The German Navy, 1935-1945.

KRIPO Kriminalpolizei
Criminal Police, under the control of the SD

Panzer (Ger. 'armour')
Armoured mechanized vehicles; fre quently used in reference to German tanks.

MI-5
British counter-intelligence service.

MI-6
British secret intelligence service (SIS).

OKH (Oberkommando des Heeres)
Supreme Command of the Army

OKW (Oberkommando der Wehrmacht)
Supreme Command of the Armed Forces.

Ordnungpolizei
ORPO: Order Police, regular police forces of the Third Reich.

OSS
Office of Strategic Services, USA; pre cursor to the Central Intelligence Agency; ABSIS in The Final Battle and Silver Dagger.

Réseau
Allied resistance organizations behind enemy lines.

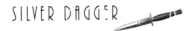
RSHA (Reichssicherheitshauptamt) — The massive and immensely complex Reich Central State Security Bureau, which included the Gestapo, KRIPO, and SD.

SAS — Special Air Service, founded in 1941 to serve as a long-range reconnaissance group; SAS is Great Britain's élite counter - intelligence and 'special means' unit. Recruits are chosen from the Army, Royal Marines, and RAF.

286

SD (Sicherheitsdienst) — Security Service (intelligence and counter-espionage) of the RSHA, formed in 1932, by Obergruppenführer Reinhard Heydrich.

SOE — Special Operations Executive formed to infiltrate and co-ordinate 'special warfare' operations in German-occupied territories.

SS (Schutzstaffel-'protection squad') — The Nazi political – police - military organization ruled by Heinrich Himmler, Reichsführer-SS, (Rf-SS). The Allgemeine-SS (General SS) was the central branch, serving political and administrative functions, and together with the Totenkopfverbände (SS Death's Head Organization of 'racial warriors') and the Waffen-SS (Armed or fighting SS), formed the core of the SS. The Totenkopfverbände provided guards to the concentration camps although at Himmler's insistence, the Totenkopfverbände Division served with other units of the Waffen-SS, and the Wehrmacht, despite opposition by Waffen and regular Army commanders. Not surprisingly, it was responsible for committing some of the worst atrocities in Eastern Europe/Soviet Russia, as were Waffen-SS Divisions Das Reich, and Liebstandarte Adolf Hitler. Waffen-SS Divisions provided some of Nazi Germany's best trained, battle-hardened, and ruthless combatants. Non - German volunteers to the Waffen-SS would include, but were not limited to Belgian, French, Hungarian, Latvian, Rumanian, Russian, and Yugoslavian nationals.

SS Ranks (commissioned)

Untersturmführer	*Junior (2nd) Lieutenant*
Obersturmführer	*Lieutenant*
Sturmbannführer	*Major*
Obersturmbannführer	*Lieutenant - Colonel*
Standartenführer	*Colonel*
Brigadeführer	*Major - General*
Gruppenführer	*Lieutenant - General*
Obergruppenführer	*General*
Oberstgruppenführer	*Colonel - General*
Reichsführer-SS	*Field Marshall*
	(approx.)

KRIPO (Kriminalpolizei)

Criminal Police branch of the SD.

SIPO (Sicherheitspolizei)

Security Police comprised of the Gestapo and KRIPO.

V-Mann

Abwehr secret agent.

Wehrmacht (armed forces)

Officially, the term for the combined forces of the Army, Navy, and Air Force that became synonymous with the German Army during WWII.

SILVER DAGGER

PHOTOGRAPHY

LYNN PHILIP HODGSON

Lynn Philip Hodgson has dedicated the past twenty-five years to bringing to light the tales of brave and courageous Canadians who fought in World War II's secret war. Their stories need to be told and he has done this in his best seller, '*Inside Camp-X*'.

A businessman for over thirty-five years, Lynn is a proud Canadian, born in Toronto, Ontario. He has dedicated himself to assuring that the next generation will be aware of Canada's contributions to the successful outcome of WW II.

As research consultant in the publication of Joseph Gelleny's book, '*Almost*' and as co-author with Alan Longfield for, '*Camp X The Final Battle*' and '*Camp X Silver Dagger*', Lynn continues to work toward this goal. With two daughters, Renee and Karen and two grandsons, Geddy and Alex, Lynn and his wife Marlene of 38 years, live comfortably on Scugog Island in Port Perry.

Lynn can be contacted at
lynniso@idirect.com

ALAN LONGFIELD

Alan Paul Longfield, B. A. (Queen's), **M. Ed.** (Toronto), has been researching and writing about Camp X with Lynn Philip Hodgson since 1977. The history of their early investigations and collaboration on the subject of Camp X is described in Lynn's best selling, *Inside-Camp X (1999, 2002 Rev.)*.

A former Toronto resident and elementary school teacher, science consultant and principal with the Toronto District School Board, Alan has lived in Whitby with his wife Judi, the MP for Whitby/Ajax, for more than twenty-seven years. Their son, Michael is pursuing graduate studies in film.

Camp X Silver Dagger is the third in a series of Camp X co-productions with Blake Books Distribution, by Alan and Lynn. Previous partnerships include *Camp X The Final Battle (2001)* and the autobiographical *Almost (1999)*, the memoirs of a Canadian secret agent authored by Alan with Joe Gelleny, and Lynn, research consultant.

Alan can be contacted at
alongfi@sympatico.ca